I CAN TASTE THE BLOOD

EDITED BY JOHN F.D. TAFF AND ANTHONY RIVERA

GREY MATTER
PRESS

I CAN TASTE THE BLOOD
ISBN-13: 978-1-940658-72-8
ISBN-10: 1-940658-72-1
Grey Matter Press First Trade Paperback Edition - August 2016

Additional copyright declarations can be found on page 287.

GREY MATTER
PRESS

Grey Matter Press
greymatterpress.com

Grey Matter Press on Facebook
facebook.com/greymatterpress.com

Anthology Website
icantastetheblood.com

DEDICATION

To my Blood Brothers: Tony, Joe, Dan, Erik and Josh.

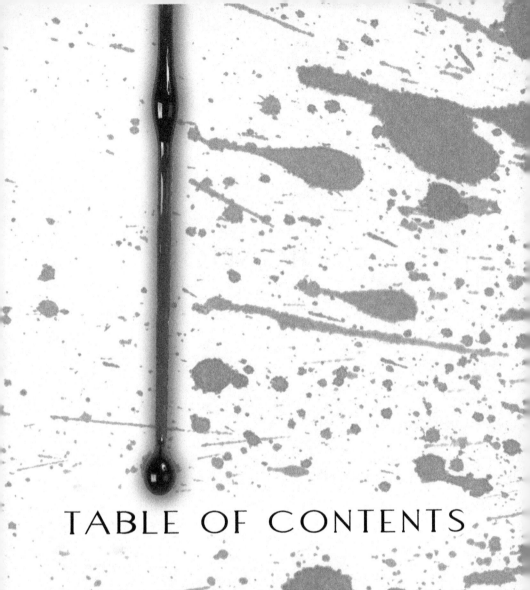

TABLE OF CONTENTS

I CAN TASTE THE BLOOD

INTRODUCTION

So, *I Can Taste the Blood.*

After a year or so of effort, you hold in your hands the culmination of five authors doing little else but seeking gainful employ.

Can it really be boiled down to something that simple?

Yes. Assuredly.

Sometimes we authors like for you, our darling readers, to think that we sit ensconced in some semi-holy authorial space—probably paneled in mahogany and wall-to-wall bookcases—sipping bourbon, thinking deep thoughts and jotting down creative ideas that just drip on us from the ether. We then laboriously set them down in writing, then fling them off into the world, where they are published with no effort and to great fanfare.

Yeah, well, about that...

I don't know about the other four men contained in this volume, but my ideas generally come to me sitting in my underpants at my desk late at night or driving to get a gallon of milk from the grocery store. And getting stuff published is almost as difficult a job as writing. There's seems to be plenty of short fiction vehicles out there—some magazines, some anthologies, some digital publications—but they don't add up to a huge marketplace for shorts.

And let me assure you, there are a lot of people writing these days. *A lot.*

Accordingly, it often becomes a pain in the ass to place stories after you've so lovingly crafted them. So it eventually occurred to me, as it probably has to other, smarter authors, why not make your own projects? Why not put together stuff and bring it to market yourself (ahem...with the assistance, of course, of a savvy publisher).

That's what you hold here.

Let me back up again. *I Can Taste the Blood.* Where did the idea originate?

In the seedy bathroom stall of a seedy St. Louis pizza joint.

Sounds legit, right?

Okay, there's a place in south St. Louis called Blackthorn Pub & Pizza. It's a little dive bar—and I say that with reverence. The world needs more dive bars. It's an approximation of Chicago-style pizza, being deep dish and containing a bowel-clenching amount of cheese. It's delicious, and my wife and I get there as often as we can. If you come to St. Louis, I heartily recommend it.

Anyway, I had imbibed several hard ciders along with my pizza on one such visit and needed the use of the facilities. Weaving my way inside the small men's room, I was confronted by concentrated seediness. Again, not that the restrooms were appallingly unclean, even by the somewhat loose standards of dive bars. No, it was that the stalls were plywood and covered...and I do mean covered... with graffiti.

As a guy, it's often nice to have something to look at while pissing. It makes the time go by quickly and takes your mind off of the somewhat questionable ambience of the restroom—the heady aromas, the piss-sticky floor, the thought that someone might come up behind you in that vulnerable position and stick a knife in you. This is how I think...don't judge.

Graffiti, as a restroom art form, is welcomed in these circumstances. So, as I recycled my cider, I perused the surrounding walls. Much of the stuff one would expect—toilet witticisms, filthy humor, abjurations against someone's girl, mother, latent sexuality, etc.

But there, like a jewel amidst the turds (somewhat literally), was the one line that jumped out at me as I zipped up.

"I Can Taste the Blood."

Right there, eye level.

Perfect.

I stood there for a moment, a curious and ill-advised thing to do in the *pissoir* of a dive bar, and marveled at this phrase.

Then I did something even more ill-advised.

I whipped out my (easy there, Hoss) cell phone and took a picture of it.

With a flash.

In the stall of a dive bar men's room.

Luckily, there wasn't anyone else there.

So that phrase lodged itself in my mind, and the wheels began turning.

"I Can Taste the Blood."

So ripe, so open to so many interpretations.

I mulled it over for a while, then talked to Joe Schwartz about it. We live close by and meet regularly to have coffee and discuss (read: bitch about) writerly stuff. He liked the idea, too. Liked it so much, in fact, *he* wanted to write something referencing it.

Then it struck us. Why not do this together, write two pieces with the same title?

Then it *really* struck us. Why not invite some other writers to join us, and we can show people how different writers can approach the same idea from far different perspectives.

It would also give us our own project to write and ultimately bring to market (again with said savvy publisher), effectively making our own paying gig.

To those ends, I think we succeeded.

Since it's fallen to me to explain all this, let me introduce my esteemed colleagues.

Joe Schwartz is as energetic and bombastic a piece of human flesh as you're ever likely to meet. Energy, especially the drive to write, literally bleeds out of his pores like sweat. It shows in the gritty, noirish, transgressive fiction he writes. Joe is an author who has taken Hemingway's admonition to writers—"sit down at a typewriter and bleed"—very much to heart.

Joe's fiction includes collections—*Joe's Black T-Shirt, The Games Men Play, The Veiled Prophet of St. Louis*—and novels, *A Season Without Rain* and *Ladies and Gentlemen: Adam Wolf and the Cook Brothers.* Read them.

You might be wondering why this kind of fiction in a collection that is ostensibly horror? Well, the entire idea of this project was to show a range of fiction to readers. Yeah, we still wanted to keep it in the horror wheelhouse, but transgressive fiction is at the very least on the shadowy borders of horror. It's just real-world kind of stuff instead of spooky goings on.

Erik T. Johnson and I go back a ways. We met online (not that way) having both participated in a questionable fiction collection that seemed to go nowhere. Erik contacted me, we struck up a conversation, one that's lasted nearly ten years now. We've never met in person—he in NYC and me out in the hinterlands—but Erik and I have an affinity for each other's writing.

Erik is definitely in the horror wheelhouse. He's had fiction published to much acclaim in magazines *Space & Time Magazine, Tales of the Unanticipated, Polluto, Electric Velocipede, Structo, Morpheus Tales* and *Shimmer*; and anthologies including *Chiral Mad, Chiral Mad 2, Pellucid Lunacy, The Shadow of the Unknown, Box of Delights* (with me!), *Dead but Dreaming 2, WTF?!* and *Best New Zombie Tales 3.*

Erik's work is what I'd call the second outlier in this collection. Joe's is the first, being more slanted toward real world bad people doing bad things and meeting bad ends. Erik's work, on the other hand, is pegged firmly all the way over on the other side of the spectrum. Reading him is like ingesting peyote, taking a bite from a magic mushroom, or uncorking a bottle in Wonderland and downing its unknown contents. Sometimes, it's all three. Erik's work is heady, phantasmagoric and weirdly, deeply unsettling. I've loved his stuff since I first read it and continue to be amazed by it. Many of his lines will stay with you.

J. Daniel Stone is the youngest among us, with two novels—*The Absence of Light* and *Blood Kiss.* Another New Yorker, he's had shorts published in various venues, too—Grey Matter Press' own *Dark Visions Two* and *Ominous Realities, Darkness Ad Infinitum, Tales from the Lake Vol. 1, Handsome Devil* and *Queer Fish Vol. 2.*

My introduction to Dan was through reading *The Absence of Light.* His command of language, his poetic writing and his dark, absinthe-dripping characters reminded me of Poppy Z. Brite's work—so lush, so dark, so sybaritic, so horribly sensual. Dan's definitely going places, and his story here extends his reach.

Finally, Josh Malerman. Josh and I started our mutual admiration society whilst trading books during the consideration phase of the Bram Stoker Awards. He traded a copy of his debut novel, *Bird Box,* for my novella collection, *The End in All Beginnings.* Each of us loved the other's work; each of us has been publically profuse in our admiration for the other.

Josh's *Bird Box* is a tremendously ballsy high-wire act of fiction. You're all probably aware of that old horror saw that says it's best not to show the monster in your story too much, lest it denature the beast in the eyes of the reader from too much familiarity. But eventually, at least so goes the saw, you have to show the monster.

Josh, brilliantly, chose *not* to show the monster. *At all.* In fact, not showing the monster is central to the story. And it works, counter-intuitively perhaps, but it works. Josh has another novel on the way soon, and I'm sure it will expand the borders of horror just as much as his first has.

And then there was one. How do you write about yourself glowingly? Simple, my friends, possess yourself of an oversize ego. Well, not really. I've been doing this for twenty-five years now, and I guess I'm some sort of an overnight success…a two-and-a-half decade overnight success.

You might know me, as Troy McClure would say, from such novels as *The Bell Witch* and *Kill/Off.* Or maybe from collections like *Little Deaths* or *The End in All Beginnings.* Or twenty-five years' worth of shorts appearing everywhere and anywhere. I've had a good run lately, one that I fully expect will continue and be augmented by this volume of novellas from me and my talented friends.

Speaking of talented friends, it also falls on my shoulders to express gratitude to the other piece of the puzzle here, the fantastic team at Grey Matter Press. And by that, I mean Tony Rivera and Sharon Lawson, both Stoker-nominated editors. Grey Matter has published, I dunno, like ten or eleven books thus far, each one a humdinger. Readers are discovering what kind of quality stories a smart, dedicated publisher can bring to market. Thanks to them for seeing the promise in *I Can Taste the Blood* and bringing it to readers.

At the end of all this, after the stories, each of us has provided an Afterword about his novella. Also, and I thought this would be fun, each contributor shares what the title of the story would have been had we not imposed the umbrella title on everyone. Fun to read, but wait 'til the end!

So, that's it. Long winded, sorry about that. The only thing left to say is that we hope you enjoy reading these stories as much as we did putting this project together. It's really you that we do this all for.

John F.D. Taff
April 2016

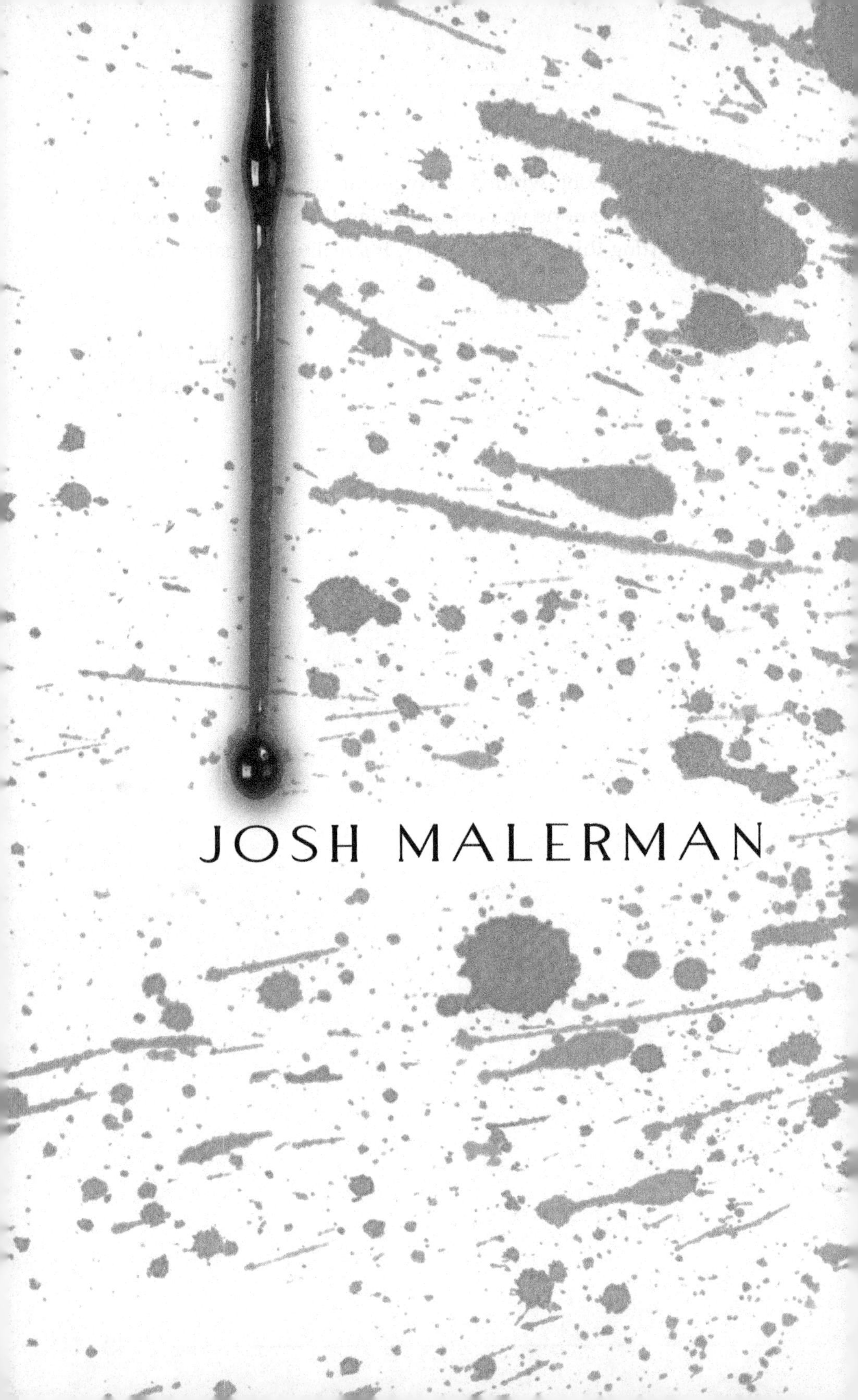

JOSH MALERMAN

VISION I

I CAN TASTE THE BLOOD

- 1 -

Madmannah gazed around the table, to the faces of his family, one by one, and thought…

At last.

At last, indeed! Though Sammi never outright complained about the conditions of their nomadic tent—and how long they used it—Madmannah saw firsthand the toll it took on her.

And not just the toll on her soul.

It was written in the new lines formed in her face and hands, years of carting the canvas beast from lot to lot, village to village, as the young lovers attempted to forge a life together, amass some money, save some too, and eventually, hopefully, figure out where they would settle. Or, as Sammi never said outright, *Where they would have a child.*

A child.

A child came! Little Aart. A *son.* He came sooner than expected, before the young lovers were ready, before they had amassed some money, too. Discovering she was pregnant, Sammi verbalized many concerns, but Madmannah proved resourceful in ways his wife never expected. He even delivered little Aart himself, under a sky of black brooding as a dust storm rose in the east, approached, and ceased, less than two hundred feet from where Sammi wetted the sand, where their son decided it best to emerge.

No worries, Madmannah consoled Sammi. *With his life, we begin true living.*

No worries, Sammi thought, but certainly some wild times. Being both conservative and level, the young lovers found themselves often on the outside looking in when it came to the others they met while traveling. "Vagabond" was a term Madmannah frowned upon, but if they were honest with themselves, that's just what they were. Travelers, indeed, salesmen, running upon the Big Wheel of Poverty that rolled, endlessly, across the desert.

Oh, the eccentrics they met along the way.

There was the man who lived in a hole in the sand, no wider than a grave. Two sisters connected at the toes. A family of blind folk, the children unable to see any better than the grandparents.

So many languages, so many customs, so many different ways to wear a dress.

Madmannah smiled again, observing his family seated at the solid wooden table. Sammi never had a proper dress in those days, but she wore one now.

"What are you smiling at?" she asked him, scooping goat soup into clay bowls.

"At last," he answered.

And why not smile at "at last?" Oh, the toiling, the fretting, the persistent worry that they'd chosen the wrong paths in life, decisions made too long ago to rescind. In those days, it felt as if they were heading, always, to more dangerous places. That up ahead, around the next desert dune, waited a clan of awful men with a mind to murder without motivation. Now, if Madmannah was honest with himself, he'd admit that the desert was never quite *that* bad, and yet...these fears were solid bone in those days.

Those days.

Those days! Back when Madmannah wore many hats. *I'm good with numbers,* he'd tell anybody who couldn't add. *I've an excellent eye,* to those in need of glasses. Sammi giggled still at the memory of a desperate Madmannah, singing beside a desert picnic, having promised the picnickers a golden throat.

He didn't have one. But who had time to care in those days?

They got by.

And they got by again.

And then Sammi got pregnant.

It was simple, really. With no doctor to tell her so, her body let her know. She was hungrier than usual. Her sleeping patterns were interrupted by magnificent dreams of motherhood. Yes, a baby, a child, was on the way. *A boy*, she'd tell Madmannah, *and nothing besides.*

And so Madmannah increased his efforts at finding a niche, a sliver he might squeeze through, where men no different than himself made enough money to raise a son.

Sammi continued to rely on fate, or, as she put it, "momentum."

We're going about it the right way, she used to always say. *So we must end up in the right place.*

And so they did.

And embraced the luck Madmannah had encountered in the desert, the day he pretended to know law, and was taken seriously, and was retained.

And now, a home made of mud-bricks. An open courtyard enclosed by sturdy walls and many small bedrooms. A humble home, indeed, where their once cumbersome nomadic tent was now used to protect their things, and their fires, from rain.

When the money started coming in, Madmannah expressly told Sammi he'd had enough stars.

We lived out there under the stars every day, every night. We've had our share of stars.

Even too low a ceiling sounded good to Madmannah. But Sammi knew better.

We grew bored of the stars because we grew bored of the life we lived beneath them. They won't look the same anymore. Not to us. To us they are new again.

She was right. And now, tonight, Madmannah looked up to the stars and marveled at how different they did look. How high they seemed.

Only three years ago they seemed to squash him.

"The stars," Sammi said, taking her seat at the other end of the wooden table, noting her husband was looking up.

And again Madmannah thought, *at last.*

There were five of them at the small table. Madmannah at one head. Sammi at the other. Aart in her lap, though, at three now, he was certainly old enough to sit on his own. Also present were Sammi's brother Faddey and their father Galahad. The two men had travelled very far on their own, having spent many years beneath those same desert stars, and Madmannah had arranged, privately, for them to move in, much to Sammi's delight.

Torches lined the mud-brick walls of the courtyard, illuminating the square within. The clear sky promised no rain, and wooden buckets of drinkable water sat far enough from the fire so they wouldn't get warm.

A small but cherished home.

The horrors of the desert—if such horrors truly existed—were behind them. As Galahad said upon entering his new place of dwelling, *You've achieved a higher level of living.*

Madmannah couldn't disagree.

"Now take your own seat, Aart," Sammi told her son.

Aart stared at the empty space of the bench Uncle Faddey half-occupied.

"Big boys sit all by themselves," Faddey said, already spooning soup into his bearded mouth.

Aart hopped from his mother's lap and squeezed in beside his uncle.

"Goat," Galahad said, nodding. He slurped when he ate.

Peace.

That was the word that occupied Madmannah's thoughts.

He lifted his clay mug of water and raised it above his head.

"A toast?" Sammi asked, her spoon halfway to her mouth.

Madmannah nodded.

"To peace," he said. "And quiet."

Sammi, Faddey and Galahad lifted their mugs. Aart mimicked them, lifting his own with both hands.

They went to sip their water.

A knock came hard against the front door.

"Who's *that?*" Sammi asked, wide eyed.

Madmannah shook his head and looked over his shoulder to the wooden door.

A second knocking came.

"Urgent," Galahad said.

The knocking came a third time and Madmannah thought Galahad had chosen the exact right word.

Whoever stood outside, his feet in the cool sand of the infinite desert at night, with the same stars shining above him, this man's knock betrayed...

...*urgency.*

"The door!" Aart cried.

And Madmannah rose to answer the door.

- 2 -

"Who is it?" Madmannah called, his ear to the wood, as a fourth peal of knocks forced him to step back. Dust billowed between the door's wooden boards.

"Help!" the stranger called, his voice scratchy and frightened. "I seek hiding!"

Hiding? Madmannah thought. *From what?*

He looked to his family, half-seated, half-standing around the table, their bare feet in the courtyard sand.

He looked to Sammi. No reaction, no answer there. So *what to do* hadn't been decided yet.

"Who are you?" Madmannah called.

"I am Rab!" the voice returned. "Please! Hiding!"

"From what?" Sammi called. Madmannah saw that she was standing behind Aart now, both her hands on his little shoulders.

"Hiding from what?" Madmannah called.

Hesitation from the other side. Momentary.

"I'm afraid if I tell you, you won't let me in."

There was sorrow in the man's voice. Fear, too.

"Tell me," Madmannah demanded.

Galahad and Faddey left the table and joined Madmannah by the door.

"Please," Rab called again, and Madmannah thought he heard the soft scratching of the man's nails against the door. As if he were instinctively looking for another way in. "I'll tell you my story if you let me in."

"I'm sorry," Madmannah said, "but I do not know you."

"A *fiend* follows me. I do not know how close he is."

Sammi hugged Aart closer to her body.

"A fiend?" Madmannah called back.

"Of the most terrible variety," Rab said.

Madmannah believed he had numbers; Faddy was strong, Sammi was not weak and Galahad wasn't dead yet.

But who knew how many were waiting outside with Rab?

He looked to Sammi for a decision. And in that instant Madmannah saw a future of regret. Nights in bed, Sammi troubled.

What is it? Madmannah would ask.

We should have let him in.

"A traveler in need," Galahad said. "Like all of us once were."

Madmannah lifted the board latching the door.

He pulled the front door open.

Galahad gasped at the darkness of the desert.

There was nobody.

Momentarily.

Then Rab's face peered around the corner.

It looked like a curious painting to Madmannah, the way the frantic face occupied so little of the space afforded by the open door.

"Come in," Madmannah said cautiously.

Rab entered, his messy hair thick with dry mud. His wide eyes shining through a dusty, sunburnt visage.

The rags he wore, and the belt securing them to his body, reminded Madmannah of himself not long ago, before Aart, before this home…

…before *at last*.

Faddey closed the front door. Galahad latched it.

Rab suddenly grabbed Madmannah by the shirt with both hands.

"*Thank you*," he whispered, and his voice sounded dry as the desert.

Madmannah slowly pried the frightened stranger's fingers off himself.

The family stood, silently staring.

"I suppose you'll want to hear my story," Rab said then, trembling, his hands still partially raised, as if thwarting a coming, invisible attack.

"Yes," Madmannah said. "Eat first. Drink. Rest. And tell us your story."

- 3 -

Now, all seated, all silent, Madmannah got a much better look at the sudden guest.

Rab was indeed dirty, dirtier it seemed than Madmannah ever was, though time changes perspective, of course, and Madmannah guessed he and Sammi were once just as covered in desert dust. How bad could the man's problems truly be? Was this a case of mental illness? Was the man a casualty of drink? Madmannah and Sammi met many such people on their sandy travels, their years in poverty. And it was difficult to imagine anything outside the experiences Madmannah had himself.

And yet, there was sincere fright in his eyes.

He sat beside Galahad on the bench to Madmannah's left. Across from Faddey. Aart was tucked back into Sammi's arms, on Sammi's lap, as if he were just as much pet as child.

"What trouble are you in?" Galahad asked, a combination of suspicion and care in his question.

"Trouble?" Rab repeated, his eyes widening as the reflected torches rose within them. "This is much worse than *troubles.*" Tears welled at the base of those same eyes. "I've encountered an afrit, verifiable by his actions."

"What's afrit?" Aart asked.

Rab turned his face toward the child, his mouth squared in a grimace.

"A demon," Faddey explained.

"Faddey," Sammi said, shaking her head. "Aart doesn't need to hear stories about afrits, demons or otherwise."

"What's demon?" Aart asked.

Rab slammed a fist upon the table. Madmannah rose to face him.

"*Demon,*" Rab cried, "is the foulest of all creatures! Monsters who play with death as if it were a *doll!*"

"Easy, Rab," Madmannah said, concerned with the eccentric behavior of their guest. "Please do not frighten the child."

Rab looked to Aart, then back to Madmannah, as though stunned by the words the man of the house spoke.

Madmannah sat again.

"Do not frighten the child?" Rab repeated. "But...this isn't a *performance,* sir. I'm not *choosing* what I do to the child. I'm living this. Frightening or not, I've no choice."

Sammi watched him closely.

"Who's after you?" Faddey asked directly.

Rab turned to face him completely.

"I thought he was my best friend."

Sorrow, deep sorrow, in his eyes.

Galahad shrugged.

"That's usually who it is, isn't it? The ones you really trust."

"Grandpa," Sammi said, tempted to cover Aart's ears.

"That's it exactly!" Rab slammed another fist onto the table. Goat soup spilled. "*Trust!* I trusted him. I trusted him with my *life*."

"Please," Madmannah said, shaking his head. "Less cryptic."

Rab turned his head slowly in the direction of Aart. He lifted a finger coated with dry mud and pointed it at the child.

"He should be sent to his room."

Faddey couldn't help but laugh.

Madmannah didn't find it so funny, though.

"You're overstepping your bounds, Rab, and possibly already wearing out your welcome."

"No, no," Rab said, shaking his head, still wearing the same expression of frozen fright. "What I mean is…this is no story for a child to hear."

Madmannah looked across the table to Sammi.

"Well, maybe we ought not to hear the story at all," Sammi said. "Why don't I get you some soup instead?"

She set Aart in the sand beside her chair. Above them, the stars were very bright, and no wind disturbed the sand outside the mud-brick walls of their home.

Sammi went to the fire and scooped some soup for their guest. She brought it to him in silence, as nobody was speaking. It was almost as if, without her femininity seated at the table, the men were left with only each other, and nobody was ready to yield their position to another.

Sammi sliced the lamb, too, carrying small platefuls to the others.

Now a soft wind did come, and carried with it the smell of cooked meat.

They ate. They drank water. And when they were finished, Madmannah leaned back in his seat and cautiously proceeded.

"Aart," he said, "it's time for you to go to bed."

Aart complained, citing the cool weather, the infinite stars and the chance to speak with a stranger.

"Aart," Sammi repeated, and Madmannah knew then that his wife was just as curious and concerned as he was.

With all the adults watching him, Aart slouched with exaggerated sadness, kissed his mother goodnight, kissed his father goodnight, kissed his grandfather and uncle goodnight, and crossed the sandy courtyard to the most visible door within the muddy walls.

He opened that door, exposing a cube of darkness within, and turned to face the others once more.

"Good night, all," he said. "And, Mister Rab, I hope you and your friend make up."

He vanished into his room and closed the door.

Half a minute passed.

"Rab," Madmannah said, fanning his hands over the table, a gesture that implied things were prepared, the moment was at hand. "Please, tell us your story."

Rab nodded slowly, wiping soup and lamb from his unshaven lips.

"Forty days he's been following me across the sand," Rab said, fresh tears welling in his eyes. "Forty nights he's appeared in my dreams, handfuls of sand to blind me."

Galahad leaned back. Faddey settled in.

Rab began with a tremble that became a tremor in his voice.

- 4 -

"I must confess, from the outset, a predilection for wine. I would hope that modern people, such as yourselves, wouldn't think poorly of me for this one stone of information, and yet, I'm sure each of you in turn know somebody who took their love too far. Did I do that? Yes, I most certainly did. And yet, I was alone; no wife, no children, and so nobody to *hurt* by virtue of staying drunk all the time. What else was there to do?

"I'd become close with those who ran a particular house of wine. They charged me very little for my fun. And with each passing day, as I determined that *this* day and *that* day weren't going to be the day I got anything done, why not make the brief trip to the house and enjoy an evening of mad bliss with the friends I had made?

"You see, when a thinking man drinks enough, he begins to philosophize his drinking...and so I did. And so I do. And the tenets of my personal philosophy went something like this: if a man drinks to celebrate, always, with ever an eye on elevating his spirit rather than squashing it, then this man *deserves* the drinking he drinks.

"Oh, we all know men who attempt to hold their sorrows by the head under water, as their sadness thrashes and splashes dirty water onto their naked feet, but I wasn't one of these men. No! I drank in the name of existence. I drank in the name of laughter. Never mind the sense of crushing defeat that perched upon my chest as I woke the following morning, *each* following morning. That meant little in light of the plateau I had reached the night before.

"We were vigilantes, in our way. Refuting, howling in the ear of boredom, in the ear of Time as it chipped away at our existence, sometimes slowly, sometimes quickly, always with meanness, always without love."

Galahad spoke. "You make it sound very good. But I know better."

"And do you?" Rab asked, his eyes electric with history. "Then you should've drank with me."

Galahad shrugged. *If you say so.*

"And you met him," Madmannah asked, "your fiend, at this house of wine?"

Rab turned to face him quickly.

"Indeed I did."

Rab explained how he and a group of regulars were seated in a semi-circle around a pond, sipping wine—*Though we never 'sipped' did we? It was always more of a pour*—when the tapestries acting as the entrance split open, allowing a silhouette to emerge, backlit by the moon. At first, Rab and the others took this figure to be a common traveler. Even in the shadows they could see a belt cut his dark robes in two, his feet were sandaled, and he carried over a shoulder a single sack, probably with a change of clothes, some bread and some coin within.

"Welcome!" Rab called from across the house of wine. He raised his glass, indicating the traveler was, indeed, welcome, and would he like to join Rab and the others?

But the newcomer didn't speak. And when, at last, he stepped farther into the room—open, much like Madmannah and Sammi's home—a communal gasp brought him to a stop.

"Scars," Rab said, facing Madmannah, his fingers like boney utensils on the tabletop. "That was the first word that came to mind. He wore a hood, yes, but the torchlights hit him just right, or wrong, I suppose, and we were able to see his face was covered in… *something.* But 'scars' wasn't the right word after all. No, no. It was something much more mysterious than a wound. He hadn't been burned. He hadn't been cut. It was possible he'd been involved in some kind of accident, but I couldn't imagine what unlucky events might lead to the look of this man. If I had to describe it, the way I saw it that first night, I'd say it looked as though his face was placed upon another face. Much like the bricks that made up the house of wine, or these bricks that support your very home. A face upon a face, you ask? How so, you ask? I had no explanation for this either, though I believed it to be true. And it wasn't until a friend of mine, a woman named Ladonna, mentioned a childlike visage that I saw it wholly myself."

"My God." Rab only half-whispered to Ladonna. "It's as if, when he was a baby, his face split apart at the seams, refuting age, but unable to resist."

The newcomer removed his hood, as though challenging the occupants of the house of wine to gaze upon him. He stood still, gazing from person to person, ten in total, until he was satisfied they'd had their fill, that they'd seen him in total, and there would be no more shocks to address the rest of the night.

"My name is Harish," he said, his voice quieting the musicians in the sand. "I've travelled seventeen days, looking for satisfaction in the form of a drinking party. Are you, then, this satisfaction?"

Rab's curiosity melded with pride. He rose, pointing at the newcomer Harish.

"If it's unbridled enjoyment you seek, why that's something each man brings to the party himself. And if so you've brought some, and carry it within that bag, then pour your spirit out at our feet and watch for yourself how we play with it."

Harish nodded. His fractured features looked severe in the torchlight.

Rab gasped again when Harish smiled.

"Let's drink wine then," Harish said. "And let's make it good."

In that moment, Rab thought he'd met something of a soul mate, someone who understood the necessary energy of things. A man, suddenly well aware of life's brevity, life's purpose, life's demand upon those who live it.

"We were inseparable for weeks following his arrival," Rab told the others as a cool wind swirled within the courtyard. Sammi hugged herself for warmth. The sorrow in Rab's frenzied gaze was so obvious that Madmannah imagined it falling from his face, into the clay bowl set before him. Madmannah even imagined the splash it would make.

"No such thing as a soul mate discovered in a house of wine," Galahad said, shaking his head. "Though it takes a lifetime to learn it."

Rab stared at the tabletop. Then looked quickly to the front door.

"I'm not sure how long I should stay," he said. "I don't want to put you or your family in danger."

"How close is he?" Sammi asked, looking to the front door herself.

Rab shrugged. Madmannah imagined a gibbering, hooded fiend with the face of a child traversing the sand toward their home.

"Tell us what he did," Madmannah said. "What he came to do."

Rab nodded slowly and breathed deeply.

"For a while, he did nothing. That is to say, his true nature was kept tucked into that ever-present sack. Always hidden. As if Harish was waiting, and could wait decades if he needed to, before spilling its contents out onto the sand, unleashing a two-headed wolf, his true nature, a beast that ate itself as it ate you."

Sammi shivered.

Galahad adjusted his posture.

A creaking of wood and all parties turned to face the front door, all except Sammi, who knew the sound better than the rest.

"Aart!" she chastised. "Back to sleep with you."

Everybody turned to face Aart's bedroom door. Rab looked over his shoulder as the child's tiny face peered out of the dark cube.

"I wanna hear the story, too!" he cried.

Sammi rose quickly, and Aart, eyes wide, vanished back into his bedroom and closed the door.

"Please," Madmannah said. "Continue."

- 5 -

"The desert is littered with drinking holes. As varied as our souls. But Harish and I tired of them quickly. It was always the same spirit, the same types of men and women, the same *living*. On any night you might encounter partial passion, be it through conversation or the body, but none of that quite reached the summit Harish and I were searching for. We were interested in true, unbridled spirit. Freedom of the soul. *Living!* It was Harish's favorite topic, and he was able to articulate this fascination much better than I."

Rab and Harish didn't always travel alone. Sometimes other men, other women, joined them, but most often it was a caravan of two. A youth named Parry provided fresh energy for a month, but Rab believed he was too caught up in the expectations of the modern world to know anything about true freedom.

Harish believed it was out there, as if a state of mind could be a physical thing, an object waiting to be plucked from a shadowy forest floor, a stone resting untouched in a hut at the top of an unchecked mountain. And Rab didn't dispute it. He encouraged Harish, the man he was coming to think of as his one true friend. Harish, who spoke in poetry, who smiled despite his ungainly face.

Harish, whose monstrous features were sometimes difficult to observe.

"To watch Harish dream was to gaze upon a child standing guard over a man. There were nights, under the stars, exhaustion claiming us both, in which I spent hours staring at that childish visage of his, that second layer of a face, and there were hours in which I believed that child looked *back!* Standing guard, indeed. *Do not interrupt Harish's sleep!* That expressionless face demanded. *Do not come close, or I will bite you!* I didn't come close. Ever. Despite our travels, our coming together and our search for a higher meaning in life, I never outright asked Harish what had become of his face. Perhaps that's how he planned it. In hindsight, I'd say he directed every conversation, every word we exchanged. And now it's become hard for me to determine what I meant and what I didn't mean in those early days. It was as if Harish were a puppeteer, and I his doll."

"Interesting analogy," Galahad said earnestly.

"Well, I won't take credit for that," Rab said, perpetual tears pooling at the bottom of his frightened eyes. "We did come upon a puppeteer on our travels. And it was at that very show that Harish's true nature began to emerge."

Night, it was always night that found the pair encountering fresh people, fresh spirit, fresh scenes.

A splintered sign in the sand declared a puppet show, entertainment, less than a mile ahead. Rab and Harish could already see the torches burning, and when the wind turned toward them, they could hear the revelry as well. VADIM, the sign exclaimed. THE GREATEST PUPPETEER IN THE DESERT. Harish was intrigued, citing the "artist" as the most likely to have discovered "true living." Rab followed his new friend without fear. He understood they were two men digging for something rare. Danger was to be expected. Danger was even welcome. If a cretin were to leap from the darkness, Rab had no doubt he and Harish could ward him off with a word, with a joke, with their spirit.

"That's how it felt," Rab said, running his filthy fingers through his mud-dried hair. "Like Harish could speak one word and dispel all manner of trouble, all worry, all the things that stop a man from living a full life. Was I frightened of him? Indeed, a part of me was frightened of Harish. But I mistakenly assumed he was frightened of me as well. And that the fear we felt was the fear of stepping, gaily, into the unknown."

The pair reached the entertainment tent and discovered they were far from alone in following the distant torches in the desert. Rab estimated that somewhere around seventy people were gathered, cross-legged in the sand, waiting for the curtains on the puppet box to be drawn.

"The place to be," Harish said, leaving his hood on despite the warmth from the other bodies in the tent. Rab was secretly happy for this as he'd come to accept that his friend's face inspired alarm in strangers.

And they'd arrived just in time, squatting in the sand just minutes before a thunderous voice announced the title of the show and that it was about to begin.

"*Nephilim.*" the unseen puppeteer declared.

At that, the tiny gold curtains were pulled aside and the crowd gasped with excitement as three puppets fashioned to look like children appeared in the box.

This precise moment, Rab told Madmannah and the others, was imperative in his piecemeal discovery of his friend's base desires.

"I'd never seen Harish so rapt. So immersed. We'd spoken with ladies until the sun rose, swam with hippos off rocky shores. We'd shared wine with great thinkers, people so poor they slept under blankets of sand, people who didn't care about money at all. We'd conversed infinitely about the power of art, of spirit, of tempting fate and tempting lot, and how the gods were too busy to fuss over the likes of us: travelers, vagabonds, drunks beneath a starry sky. And yet, here we sat, inches from a simple painted box, crude puppets speaking in simple ways, and Harish looked as though he'd found the secret of existence. He even reached across the sand and gripped my arm."

Rab, surprised to find his friend so moved, thought not to ask Harish what it was he enjoyed so thoroughly and decided instead to try to see it for himself.

"And I found it quickly," Rab said, his long fingernails digging into the table until Madmannah reached out and gently patted him on the hand. "It wasn't the performance or the presentation that so awed Harish…it was the faces of the puppets themselves."

Painted loosely upon poorly carved wood, with asymmetrical features, discolored teeth and irises that didn't match, Rab realized, suddenly, and with painful clarity, that the puppets were the first faces he'd seen that resembled the incongruous, awful visage Harish was burdened with in reality.

To confirm this connection, he turned slowly toward his friend and found Harish staring back at him, that same expressionless, childlike face that seemed to watch over Harish as he slept.

"It never looked more out of place than it did right then. Never looked more like it was simply placed upon his skull than it did right then."

The puppet show was a good one. A story about hybrid children birthed by angels and human women. And Rab didn't wonder at his friend's unwavering enthusiasm and interest.

Or did he?

Surely it wasn't just their strange faces? Surely Harish found something artistic displayed, something that spoke to his insatiable soul?

"Do you wish to speak to the artist?" Rab asked as the applause dissipated. "I think there is Vadim now."

Rab pointed to a large, bearded man rising behind the red box, wiping sweat from his brow.

Harish nodded.

The friends rose and approached the puppeteer.

"Excellent," Harish said, extending a hand. "Did you create the puppets yourself?"

Vadim scowled and shook his head.

"No puppeteer ought to play both roles, craftsman and actor. If he does, his acting suffers, for he believes his craftsmanship speaks for itself."

Rab found this to be an interesting outlook, but Harish did not pursue it.

"There is a house of wine within shouting distance," Harish said instead. "Join us?"

Vadim shook his head, then shook it the opposite way.

"Why not?" he said. "I haven't enjoyed good wine in a fortnight."

The three drank much of it that night, more than Rab had anticipated. And soon the puppeteer fell asleep in the sand of the house of wine.

"And then we moved on," Rab said, looking Madmannah in the eye, but only briefly. "Until our legs were so tired we had to sleep as well. Harish built a small fire in what felt like the very center of the desert, and we padded the sand surrounding it, making for beds, and praying it did not rain. Because of the wine, I dreamt quickly, and woke to see Harish sitting up, still, a fresh fire burning before him. 'Have you not slept?' I asked him. But by the time he answered, I'd already seen them, burning like kindling in the fire. It was the puppets, all three of Vadim's star attractions, prisoners of those white flames. For a while I simply stared, unable to look away. But I couldn't remain silent for long. 'Why?' I asked Harish, and Harish answered without hesitation. 'Once he told me he wasn't the one who carved them, I decided they must be mine. For had he carved them himself, I would have imagined Vadim the whole time, as they burned, imagined and known they were not really children, but the product of a puppeteer's fanciful imagination. As it stands, dear Rab, they are children, to me. For I know not where they come from nor who designed them. Just as I know not from where true flesh and blood derives.'"

Sammi spoke up.

"I don't understand. Are you telling us that Harish *wanted* to watch children burn?"

Madmannah eyed her, attempting to discern her level of concern against her bounty of curiosity.

"Or," Rab said, "perhaps he only wanted to see what I saw upon waking. The moment when the dolls had burned just enough as to be unrecognizable as puppets, the moment they looked like actual children, in great detail, screaming, begging for help, as their small bodies burned, as odorous flakes rose and swirled with the midnight wind, until some of those flakes landed upon my robes. And I swatted them away, quickly, as Harish laughed, not because I was worried about catching fire myself, but because I couldn't bear to have what looked like the charred flesh of actual children upon me."

- 6 -

A stronger wind blew above the courtyard, swirling down within it, creating a momentary hurricane that pressed all their robes and Sammi's dress to their bodies and created ripples on the surface of the goat soup. A broom was knocked over by the front door and Sammi, especially, turned to look, thinking of course, imagining of course, trying to see what was out there. She held her dress close to her body and counted footprints, footprints of the mind, Rab's footprints in the sand, forty days worth, forty nights worth, without sandals, his ten toes present in each, ten tiny burrows for Harish to count, for Harish to grin about, for Harish to count on his own ten fingers before approaching the next one, and the next, and the next, until they delivered him to this very home, this very door, this very family of which a child slept behind a closed bedroom door, safe for the moment, safe from the frightening, double-faced, cloaked creature who had befriended Rab, who must have done something terrible to cause Rab to run for so long, bring Rab here, to this table, where he still hadn't stopped trembling, where he gasped the loudest at the strong wind, where his eyes darted about the courtyard as if the fiend were already in here, already amongst them, already standing in the shadows where the mud-brick walls met the sand.

It was the burning children comment that did it to Sammi.

She was all right until then. Comfortable enough with letting in a frantic stranger, willing to let someone in from the dark, willing to hear the story that scared him so.

But the puppets burning...Sammi was sure she'd had enough.

"You," she said when the unwelcome wind had passed, "need to move on."

Galahad turned to look at his daughter, struck by her sudden rancor.

"Go?" Faddey countered. "But we haven't heard his story whole yet."

Sammi looked to Madmannah, half hoping that he'd side with her, half interested to hear what he thought.

Madmannah looked to the torches lining the walls. Then rose from the table and approached the front door.

Sammi understood what he was going to do and she wanted him to do it. This, she believed, would be enough.

For now.

From beside the door, Madmannah lifted a hardened clay club with sharp stones embedded into its head. With his other hand, he unlatched the door, opened it, and peered into the darkness of the desert.

Sand stirred at Madmannah's feet.

He stared out the door, quiet, for a long time.

"Madmannah?" Sammi whispered.

Bad visions came to her. A two-faced brute exploding from the darkness, inches from her husband's lax face.

Madmannah closed the door. He latched it. He set the club back against the wall. He returned to the table.

"Do I need to go?" Rab asked anxiously.

"Not yet," Madmannah said, refusing to bring his eyes to those of his wife. "You're tale is a dark one, and certainly sets the imagination aflame."

Sammi cringed at the word.

Aflame.

The faces of children...*aflame.*

And where was his story going? Surely the fiend did much worse than steal puppets and burn another man's property?

Aflame.

"Please," Madmannah said, wiping a thin line of sweat form his brow. "Continue."

And so Rab continued, perhaps finding solace in having someone, finally, to tell his story to. But as he spoke, Sammi grew colder inside, imagining in too great of detail this Harish and the kind of man who would steal puppets from a poor puppeteer.

Rab continued, and all those listening felt the swelling, consciously or not, of the rest of the world outside the simple wooden front door. They all felt the space out there, the *room,* all the places and shadows and holes a man might be hiding within.

They felt the sand, too, beneath their feet, and could imagine clearly the footprints of a man being followed, and the fresh ones of the man who chased him.

- 7 -

"Our travels took us deeper into the desert. Our search for real living, and those who lived it, continued. I'd never felt so free as I did those days. Harish's theft of the wooden dolls was beans compared to what we ended up taking that was not ours to take."

Rab and Harish got very good at stealing from vendors, families and homes in the desert. What Rab had once considered bad behavior was now a thrilling enterprise, a game that, by participation alone, proved one's mettle.

And yet Rab, with more of a conscience than his companion, was juggling warring emotions.

They were enjoying their living, yes, but were they hurting others along the way? Would they hang one day from wooden scaffolds as crowds of good people cheered? Their original plan, their *bond* was forged in the fiery ideals of independence, but was this the only way to achieve it?

Somewhere between two desert villages, Rab decided he

didn't care. Harish was the first person who'd ever made him feel righteous.

"And yet, live like criminals we did, whether we planned it that way or not."

Rab grew angrier in speech, his features contorting theatrically. Madmannah wondered if this was because the story included a puppet show, or if Rab looked naturally made-up for the theater. "But that wasn't *me!* I thought it was me because I didn't know who me was. But that, *all of that*, was him!"

He pointed to the front door, either for effect or to mean the "him" somewhere out there. Sammi shrieked, half-expecting to see Harish standing inside the doorway, a sack slung over his shoulder.

"I apologize," Rab said, trying to control his emotions. Instead, he began crying. Tears ran through the dirt on his face, giving the appearance of tears of sand. "I used to know better. Used to know it was wrong to take cattle, to slaughter them beneath a bright moon. I wasn't raised that way. Sneaking into the huts of strangers and stealing blankets as they slept. Oh, we ate more than meat. We ate pets. We ate whatever we could carry or whatever would fit into Harish's sack. And though it wasn't me, it was the *me* I was. I, I, I held open the mouth of the sack as Harish filled it with loot. I, I, I unlocked the doors that Harish entered. Oh, what had become of the playful child I once was? What had become of the son who dreamed of a son of his own who dreamed of a son of his own who dreamed? It rips me apart, recalling these adventures, these forays into nothingness."

Rab's head sunk to the table.

Galahad placed a hand on his shoulder.

"Easy, friend," he said. "We all sleep until we wake."

Rab's head shot up quickly.

"*Wake!* That's it! That's just what I did."

"Yes," Galahad said. "And now you're in a better place, with better—"

"No!" Rab yelled. "I mean to say I woke…in the desert…by a desert tree. And saw him. Harish. Sitting upon a branch too high to reach, high up a tree with no knots to climb. And beside him, sitting beside the fiend, was a…*child.*"

Madmannah and Sammi looked to one another.

"What are you saying?" Madmannah asked.

Rab shook his head slowly, side to side, the memory of that day rattling within him.

He had woken to the sound of a child's laugh and looked up to see Harish perched in a tree beside a young boy. They were facing the other way. Rab could only see their backs, but he saw something else, too, something that quickly inspired him to rise to his feet and shout up to his companion.

"Harish! Harish! Why do you have rope up there? And why does the boy play with the rope? What do you mean to do?"

Harish did not turn to face him. Instead, he gestured out, away from the branch, as though advising the boy on what to do.

Rab had to squint, to shield his eyes from the sunlight, but he was certain the rope was tied around the young boy's neck.

"Harish!"

Rab ran under the branch and looked up to face them.

"In this way," Harish said, "one can fly…"

The boy laughed and rose to a standing position on the branch. It was precarious footing and he almost fell.

"No, Harish." Rab yelled. "This isn't the same as stealing cattle. This isn't the same as—"

Harish giggled and gently shoved the boy.

The boy fell.

Rab cringed, turning away.

And when he looked back, the boy was swinging by the rope, laughing gaily, the rope tied around both of his wrists.

Harish looked down into the eyes of his companion.

"And what did you think would happen?" he asked.

But Rab believed he knew. Believed that if he hadn't woken up, Harish would've elevated the game. He would've instructed the boy to tie the rope around his neck the next time down.

Harish pulled a sabre from his sack and swung it against the rope.

The boy fell to his knees in the sand.

Rab approached him.

"Who are you?" he asked the boy.

Removing the rope from his wrists, the boy pointed to a sandy hill and Rab turned to see silhouettes in the distance.

"And how did you end up here...with us?" Rab asked.

The boy pointed up into the tree.

Rab looked up.

"I didn't see him walk away until he was already back with his people on the hill," Rab said, shaking his head. Madmannah breathed a sigh of relief. "I was too busy studying the face of my friend. He who sat perched in the tree, grinning down at me, shaking his head *no.* As if to say, 'No, Rab, I would never do what you think I would've done.' Or maybe that's not what he was suggesting at all. Maybe what he was saying was, 'No, Rab, nobody stops me from doing what I will eventually do.'"

- 8 -

"I slept that night, unsure, just as I had many nights prior. I suppose it was only a matter of time before Harish led me down a darker tunnel yet, one constructed of tempestuous substances, devil-weeds and worse."

"Devil-weeds?" Galahad asked, genuinely interested.

"Yes," Rab said, his eyes like saucers full of damp earth. "Harish heard of a house of wine that served 'more than wine,' as they say. Harish heard of a den, forty days and forty nights from here, from your very house, that could provide a man life if it was life he was looking to live." Rab closed his eyes. "But he hadn't told me about it. Not yet. Instead, we began that day walking, as we always did, only I wasn't aware we had a destination."

A cloud obscured the moon, momentarily, and Rab's face dissolved into shadow. Again Madmannah thought of the theater, of a speech resolved. But the cloud moved quickly and Rab re-emerged with much more to tell.

"Harish stole something else along the way, though I didn't know it at the time. Without a village or a hill in sight, and us starved to the edge of delusion, we saw a wagon approaching far in the distance.

"'Is it what I think it is?' Harish asked.

"'A wagon, indeed,' I confirmed.

"'A family,' Harish said.

"I understood, of course, that this could be bad. We'd already devolved into thieves, nothings, men who foolishly thought living meant living without law. But we *were* hungry, oh we were hungry, and as the wagon got larger, with every step the horses took, with each revolution of its wheels, the space within the wagon, the amount of goods it might hold, got larger as well. When finally we met, our lives intersecting, we saw the wagon was steered by two men, the elder one hundred years old, the younger his grandson, though sixty himself. They studied us and we studied them, and I understood they were calculating the risk of entering into conversation with a man who looked like Harish. But these were kind people. A traveling family, indeed. Two women emerged from the curtained wagon, each carrying a bundle of blue blankets with white goats stitched upon them by their own hands.

"'You men look famished,' the old man said, smiling behind a beard so frail it looked as though it'd been hooked, poorly, to his ears.

"'We are that,' I said. And the grandfather gestured to the back of the wagon.

"'Apples aplenty,' he said, smiling strongly.

"'For us?' Harish asked.

"'Indeed.'

"I realized then how harsh the sun was above us. How mad it had already made us. And seeing these people, innocent in their happiness, their family, their apples, I understood that Harish and I had, at some point, refuted the rest of the world. We'd placed ourselves in shadow. We were no longer criminals, we were now *outsiders,* without a window to look in.

"But we accepted their offer. Of course we did. Harish walked with the women to the back of the wagon and returned with a small bushel of red apples and two bowls of cool water.

"'Thank you,' I said, my lips dry with sand.

"We ate and we drank in their presence, decorum be damned. And when we'd finished, the old man pointed two bony fingers in our direction and told us to be wary of the ways of the wanderer. I understood it to mean we ought to be careful of ourselves. I've no idea what Harish thought of his words. And I understand now that, as the family drove away, and as I experienced relief for the lack of another dark encounter, Harish's mind was no doubt preoccupied, focused on his filthy den, the place he'd been walking toward all day. He'd kept it a secret until we were too close to turn around. Or, as I trick myself into believing, he didn't tell me until it was too late for me, though I'll never know if I would've refused such a place had I the time to do so.

"And when I think about it now, *right now,* seated here at your table, I can't help but believe that this place, this den, was where Harish had been leading me since the day we crossed paths, the day he entered that innocent, by comparison, house of wine frequented by my former sane and less foul self. As if he saw a fish in me and effortlessly tossed a worm into my once still waters..."

- 9 -

There were no torches in the distance, no sign or declaration. Harish, walking with a slouch, his sack slung over his shoulder, simply extended a sleeve, from whose mouth emerged a dusty finger.

"There," he said.

"There where?" Rab asked, seeing nothing in the desert.

"Close your eyes," Harish said, then he laughed. And with his black cackle-laugh, Rab felt a second wave of relief that nothing bad had happened involving the family with the wagon.

Certainly something could have.

And today, Harish seemed darker than ever.

"But not all the way," Harish added. "Close them...*almost.*"

Rab did. And he saw.

"It's a place of dwelling!" Rab exclaimed, astonished.

"A place of *living,*" Harish said, dragging himself and the sack another step. And another.

Sand billowed at his ankles.

"What goes on there?" Rab asked.

"The infinite goes on there," Harish answered. "But only if we bring it in with us."

Riddles, Rab thought. *The first sign that the sun is too much for him.*

"I do not speak fallacies," Harish said as if cued. "The place ahead, the place you see, it's where the unseen play hide-and-seek with the living."

More mad laughter.

Living, Rab thought, and swallowed an imperfect circle of worry.

When it became evident that the distant silhouette was a common house of wine, Rab wondered if tonight would be when he and Harish parted ways. He longed for new company. New moods. Strangers. They'd certainly had their run in the desert and Rab was just beginning to understand that good travel companions did not twin philosophies make.

"Tonight we feast," Harish said, pointing once again as though transferring truth to the place ahead.

"On what? What do they have?"

Harish did not pause, did not set his sack in the sand.

"The distance from here to there is the same, whether you know the answer to your question or not."

It turned out that the distance was shorter than it looked.

Rab's mouth watered from the smell of spirits and supper outside.

"It's a gift," Rab said.

Harish cackled.

A soft, blue curtain was pulled apart. A large, bearded face peered from the darkness within.

"We're here to partake," Harish said, nodding beneath his hood.

The man studied each in turn.

"Do you have money?" he asked.

"We have trade."

"What do you have to trade?"

Now Harish did set his sack in the sand. He reached a thin arm into the mouth of it and pulled forth an apple.

"Apples," he said.

The bearded man looked to Harish, to Rab, and back to Harish. Then he laughed a laugh so deep it seemed to make a thud in the sand.

"You are a living fairy tale," the man said. "Apples for entry into a place like this?"

Harish nodded.

"I thought to bring trade," he said. "And perhaps that's what matters most."

The man nodded.

"Welcome," he said. He parted the curtains far enough for the two travelers to enter.

A small vestibule of absolute darkness.

A second curtain drawn.

Rab immediately saw things he'd never seen before.

"They're nude," he said, and Harish did not laugh.

As the pair traversed the den, Rab stared at the naked bodies dipping beneath the surface and rising in pools of crystal water. At the edge of these pools were madcaps, men who spoke to themselves, held their own skulls in consternation, or simply stared up and into the space between the stars.

For Rab it was an impossible, yet intriguing, combination of worlds. The sensual and the insane.

Harish walked past these pools quickly, and Rab understood that his companion had been here before.

They stopped at a fresh set of curtains, the color of pink lips parting.

Harish stepped through them first and Rab followed.

Within, more lunatics lay sprawled upon couches and mounds of cool sand. Smoke hovered above them, sentient it seemed, living snakes in the air.

"Ah!" a man said, rising from the sand. He wore an open robe and nothing besides. "Newcomers!"

He approached Rab and Harish, and Harish took from him a smoking stick.

"We thank you now," Harish said. "For we may not be able to once we partake."

The man laughed.

"Indeed. And I wouldn't expect you to. You look as though you've traveled far enough without. It's time to do so within."

Harish inhaled the rising smoke. He gestured for Rab to do the same.

Rab looked once to a man sitting cross-legged at their feet. The man was speaking quietly, conversing with nobody beside him.

"Are there ghosts in here?" he asked.

The man with the stick smiled.

"*Many,*" he said.

Rab understood that what he was about to do was something he had never done before, and that by doing it he might be changed forever.

He inhaled the smoke.

Living, he thought, but it felt more like dying. As the pink curtains flapped behind him, he thought of great and terrible birds, revealing themselves, rising from the sand, plodding towards him. He quickly spun and saw Harish instead, hoodless, robeless, but with the sack still slung over his shoulder.

"Care for a swim?" Harish asked, and his voice came from the stars, came from under the water he spoke of.

"Yes," Rab said, feeling hot, too hot, and in need of cooling off. "A swim sounds right."

They traveled back through the den, though Rab didn't become aware he was moving until he was seated at the edge of a pool, his feet swinging in the water below.

"Ritual," Harish said, and Rab quickly turned to face him, frightened, not knowing his companion was sitting beside him. Rab looked down at Harish's feet in the water and saw long, filthy toenails rippling. "This is living," Harish said. "Through ritual."

Rab considered this.

A man lay on his back along the edge of the pool, alternately crying, staring, and counting invisible figures in the sky.

"Are you hungry?" Harish asked.

"No," Rab said, and without consciously deciding to, he submerged himself in the water.

It would be the last time he bathed for forty days.

Forty nights.

The water, Rab thought, *feels like sand, if sand was made of water.*

Thoughts like these pleased Rab. Simple riddles. Water. Sand. Air. He dunked his head under the water.

He opened his eyes beneath.

From the pool's bottom a face looked back at him.

Rab lifted his head quickly and gasped for air.

"There's a dead body in the pool!" he screamed and saw Harish still sitting with his feet in the water, pulling his sack onto his lap.

Rab went under again and this time saw nothing.

No face.

No death in the pool.

But the water felt foul now, and he pulled himself out and sank onto his back in the sand.

He closed his eyes and still saw stars.

He opened them and saw the back of his traveling companion. Rab could hear Harish searching through his sack.

Ritual.

Oh, how the word fit! Harish had always been excellent in that way. Excellent with words.

"Ritual," Rab said out loud.

"Partake," Harish returned.

Harish handed Rab some meat and Rab hungrily ate it. When he'd reached the bone, he sat up and saw they were alone by the pool.

No nude bodies.

No men talking to the stars.

In Harish's lap was a blue blanket, white goats stitched upon it.

"Hey," Rab said. "I know that blanket."

Harish unfolded it and showed Rab what was within.

Rab stared, then looked up into the eyes of his companion. For a terrible moment, the two looked the same. Harish and the thing in the blanket.

"Partake," Harish repeated.

Rab looked back to the blanket. To what remained of the child.

"Where did you find—"

But he knew where. It was when Harish went to fetch the apples from the wagon.

Rab felt his stomach turn black.

Had he eaten—

"Ritual," Harish said. "Living. Escaping, narrowly, the death of your self. Would you do such things?"

"Harish."

"Would you love an unlovable woman? Would you steal her unlovable child?"

"Harish…"

"Partake…"

A tearing sound and Harish brought more meat to Rab's lips.

Rab closed his eyes, blinded now by exploding images of purple and black. He heard the screams of lambs cooked alive. Heard Harish chewing.

Ritual, he thought. *Partake.*

Escaping, narrowly, the death of your self.

Would you do such things?

He did.

As the den swirled into a single, indefinable color, as smoke and voices wafted from an impossible inner sanctum, and as Harish laughed with a mouthful of living, Rab partook.

He did such things.

- 10 -

"I can taste the blood!" Rab screamed, slamming his fist onto the table once again. "I can *still* taste the blood!"

His eyes were horribly wide, as if the top of his skull might open, allowing them to roll from his face.

He turned quickly on Sammi who had not spoken.

"He made me do it."

Then he brought his head down hard against the table and left it there. Weeping.

"May something, *anything,* save you," Faddey said, rising and stepping away from the table.

"It's too late for that," Galahad said, staring at the crying mass before him, Rab's face hidden.

But Madmannah was more concerned about the man following him.

"You ran?" he asked.

"I ran. I left."

"And he followed?"

Rab lifted his head. His eyes two pools in a sandy den.

"'This is living,' he calls. And he calls me yet. Always. Inching closer. Follows me. Across the desert. 'This is living,' he calls. He hisses in my sleep. He hisses now."

Madmannah looked across the table to Sammi. His wife's face was covered by her own hands.

"I need to leave!" Rab yelled, suddenly rising from his bench at the table. "He will find me if I sit still for too long."

Rab ran to the door.

Madmannah rose.

He made no move to stop him. Said nothing to bring him peace.

Rab unlatched the door and stepped into the darkness beyond the fine mud-brick home.

"I thank you for your food," Rab said, nodding, crying, the dirt on his face looking more like blood now. "I thank you for a place to rest. And I thank you for allowing a man who has lost his way to admit it."

Then Rab scurried into the darkness, and Madmannah was quick to latch the door behind him.

He turned to face his family. Sammi at one head of the table. Faddey and Galahad standing in the sand.

They looked so innocent to Madmannah.

They looked lit from within.

Yet it was the way the stranger was lit in the doorway, half shadowed, that stuck in Madmannah's mind.

As if his eyes had seen something so terrible, they must look through it first, before seeing anything else, forever.

"Sammi," Madmannah said, but his wife simply raised a silent hand.

And so, the door latched, the stars bright above, they remained silent. They didn't move either, each of them remaining where they stood or sat. Each of them trying to wash their minds of the tale the troubled traveler had told. And each of them painfully recalling a different part of his story.

Faddey thought of the burning puppets.

Galahad thought of the living smoke in the pink-curtained den.

Sammi thought of the blue bundle, stolen from the wagon.

And Madmannah thought of the words Harish spoke to Rab as he followed him, words he listened for now, perhaps carried by the wind, if the fiend was near, close enough to call to his fleeing, mad friend.

He heard nothing.

But he continued to listen.

- 11 -

No wind. No stirring.

Silence from the world beyond the courtyard.

Not even the pattering footsteps of the stranger Rab racing across the desert.

Madmannah realized he was breathing too hard, too heavy. He was afraid his family might sense his fear. He didn't want to scare them anymore than they already were.

He approached the table and walked to Sammi's side.

"We shouldn't have let him in," she said.

"We did the right thing."

"But the man who follows him…"

"We did the right thing."

"A traveler in need," Galahad said. "We've all been a traveler in need."

They had, indeed. For years Madmannah and Sammi crossed the desert, seeking the foundation upon which to settle. The months eating months, days swallowed by days, the young lovers dusty and dirty beneath their nomadic tent, carrying it from village to village, shade to shade, always saying it'll happen one day, one day we'll have a place all our own, a courtyard for dinner, a child to feed.

In part, Madmannah and Sammi would always be those wanderers, still lost in the desert, as if they'd died out there, their bones sticking out of the sand, picked at by desert foxes, as the few things they once owned would be pilfered by men like Rab, men like Harish.

"Oh those poor women," Sammi said, and Madmannah knew she was talking about the women in the wagon, the ones who offered apples to strangers and didn't see it when the cretin stole one of their children, maybe both, who knows what else was in the sack by the edge of the pool.

"Let's sit," Galahad said, placing a wrinkled hand on his daughter's shoulder. "He gave us a scare is all. There are much worse things happening in that desert than a shaken stranger seeking refuge."

The quartet sat again. But Galahad's words, though encouraging, ultimately fell flat between them on the table.

Madmannah raised his water glass.

"A toast," he said sadly, and the others raised their glasses with him. "To owning the sort of home a man might see in the distance, might see with hope. A man not too different than we once were ourselves. A toast to—"

A thunderous knocking on the front door interrupted him.

Sammi gasped.

Faddey slowly turned to face it.

Galahad rose from the bench, Madmannah from his chair at the head of the table.

A second knocking.

"It's him again!" Faddey said. "He must have seen Harish!"

"Speak to him!" Galahad said.

Madmannah looked to Sammi. She was staring at the door.

He crossed the courtyard and gripped the clay club with stones embedded in its head.

"Who is it?" Madmannah bellowed, his shoulder against the wood.

"I need your help," a voice returned.

Madmannah looked to his family.

Was it Rab again?

"What kind of help?" Madmannah yelled.

"I've been tracking a fiend for forty days and forty nights. He must be—"

But whatever the man said next, Madmannah's mind began to swirl.

"Who are you?" he demanded.

"My name...is Harish."

- 12 -

Madmannah inched away, deeper into the courtyard. Faddey crossed the sand to join him. Trembling, they faced the closed front door together.

"You are not welcome here, Harish!" Madmannah called, the club at the ready in his clenched hands.

"Was he here?" Harish asked. Sand billowed between the wooden boards as if Harish spoke in sand. "He must be stopped."

"Leave us!" Madmannah ordered.

"Please," Harish called back. "I can taste the blood. I can *still* taste the blood!"

Madmannah inched toward the door.

"What did you say?"

"He made me do it. It was as if he'd been leading me there since the day our lives intersected. The day Rab walked into my house of wine. I was not born this way."

A sincere sobbing followed. The unbearable notes of regret.

"It's what he does," Harish cried. "He's searching for children. Always for children."

Madmannah turned to face Sammi, but Sammi was already rushing across the courtyard, rushing to their son's closed bedroom door.

"Sammi?" Madmannah called.

"He's a monster," Harish continued. "Steals children from under their mother's nose…"

"Sammi?"

Sammi's palms were already against the wooden door, pushing it open, revealing the black cube within.

"Has he been here?" Harish asked again.

"Sammi?"

Sammi screamed and Madmannah understood, saw it as if the empty bed were placed before him in the sand.

Screaming himself, he went to the door and unlatched it, pulling the wooden door open.

"Where is he?" Madmannah bellowed, raising the clay club.

The hooded man raised his hands to protect himself. Then slowly removed his hood.

There were no marks on his face. No "second face." Nothing like Rab had described.

To Madmannah, he looked kind.

"You have a child?" Harish asked.

"Yes!" Madmannah screamed.

"And Rab, he was here?"

"He just left our home!"

"We must go *now*," Harish demanded, pointing toward the darkness of the desert.

The remaining family exited the home made of mud-bricks, tightening their belts as they ran, creating new footprints in the sand, their robes flapping in the still desert air, not from the wind…

…but from within.

AFTERWORD

You know, I kinda like what Rab and Harish were after. I don't think they're the guys I'd go searching for it with, but still, I like what they wanted to catch.

Living.

That's a specific variety of American outlaw, isn't it? The guy or girl who drops everything, covers their TV screen with a blanket, tapes a sign to their front door that says NOT COMING BACK, and just goes after it.

But what is "it"?

Well, *that's* easy to answer, whether or not Rab and Harish had the right answers themselves.

Let me tell you a quick story:

My friend Mark Owen and I started writing songs in college. We hadn't hit the stride we would later, when we moved to New York City and started a band and traveled like blind maniacs for half a decade, but still, we cared a lot about it back then. Cared enough that when a local producer (the fella had a tape machine in his basement; this *definitely* qualified as "producer") cancelled an album's worth of a recording session on us, we didn't know what the hell to do. College was coming to an end. Our friends had already moved out of town. It was just Mark and I and these songs and this session that was *supposed* to happen and then (dammit) didn't. We were so lost back then that we didn't even walk up the street to feel bad about it; we sat down on the guy's front lawn and internally freaked out.

"What are we going to do now?" Mark asked me, and I knew the second the words left him that it was a huge question he was asking.

What are we going to do now didn't mean *Well, our week is freed up, what do we do now?* And it sure didn't mean *where do we record instead?* What Mark was asking me was the same thing I was about to ask him:

What are we going to do now with THE REST OF OUR LIVES?!

We'd arrived at that mythic post, where every young (or old) artist-to-be must decide: do we give up songs and books, finish school, and join the holy-roly-poly machinery?

Or do we spend the rest of my student loan money on recording gear and record those blasted songs ourselves?

Of course we did the latter (the former would've made for a terrible afterword.) We bought a Tascam 4-track cassette machine, recorded something like six albums on it, mailed those albums to our friends, moved to New York City to play the songs with said friends, got a loft-ish space where we split up "rooms" with tapestries, practiced a hundred songs, recorded a hundred songs, played some shows, hit the road, played a *ton* of shows, made seven studio albums, and holy-crap we're artists and holy-crap thank God we didn't turn our backs on it when we were trembling on that producer's front lawn, back when we were so scared that the only thoughts going through our minds were drooly, wavy lines.

For us, that was living.

It still is.

I wrote novels out there, too. Riding from city to city I worked on book after book, sometimes handing rough drafts to the headlining bands, sometimes writing an entire novel because I drank a lot and told someone in Mississippi I would.

For me, that was living.

It still is.

And what a thing it is to chase!

I think Madmannah and Sammi were after the same thing, only their idea of living was raising a third life. I understand. I don't have any kids of my own, but I get it. And Galahad, he sounded like he might have chased it and caught it and chased it and caught it again.

Some things are elusive, sure, but I don't know…I don't mind that freaky feeling of something slipping out of your hands.

Losing your grip.

"Come and Go Mad"

That's a helluva title. (Fredric Brown, 1949)

Which brings me to the title.

"I Can Taste the Blood"

When John Taff wrote me about this idea and sent me a photo of the fabled graffiti, I got very excited for a number of reasons: 1) I felt like I was asked to join a sweet horror-lodge biker-gang and 2) I had another story to write. I thought about the communal title for days. A few story ideas came and went and then Rab and Harish, Madmannah and Sammi stuck. But just before sitting down to write her, I learned that, in our Afterwords, we would each give our tales the titles we would have given them, had the group title not existed.

So alright.

How does "Puppet Soup" sound?

That's awful.

"The Boy Swinging from the Tree"

Too dreamy. Also, wasn't a big enough part of the story.

"Madmannah Settles Down"

Sounds like a family drama (which I guess it kinda is?)

"Tempting Lot"

Now I'm just picking two words in a row from the story that sound good together.

"Two Strangers Knocking on a Door at Night"

Nope. That gives away the second knocking.

"Rab and Harish"

No, no, no, no way.

"Under a Brooding Sky"

Nope.

"Sammi Sweet Sammi"

Ahhhhh!

"I Wanna Hang Out with Galahad"

No. But I do.

"Nephilim"

Well, I get this one, the title of the puppet show is the title of the story and so forth. But no.

How about...

"Sandy"

Sounds like a 70's model.

"Crossing the Desert"

Closer? Not really. But it felt like I was for a beat.

"Where and When Does This Story Take Place?"

Well, I like titles that ask questions, but this is a bit too direct, huh? And revealing. (Quick: where and when *does* this story take place? Biblical times? The names and the sand suggest it does. But it doesn't follow all the rules, linguistic and others, so let's say it's a moment in history that *just* didn't make it into the books and therefore feels a hair out-of-time, out-of-place, out-of-joint. I like that. And, hell, there are enough out-of-joint stories to call it all a proper place.)

Title, title, title...

"Decollation"

That means "the act of beheading." But there's no beheading in the story.

"Harish"

Simple. Not terrible.

Ooh, how about a quote of Harish's:

"Partake"

Not bad. Inviting.

"Such Things"

Ooh, I like it.

"The Product of a Puppeteer's Fanciful Imagination"

Too long? I don't think so. I like that it dances. It also tips a cap to the fact that Rab was making things up the whole time. And, hey, how much *did* he make up? The Harish at the front door looked very different than the Harish in Rab's tale.

A gibbering hooded fiend with the face of a child traversing the sand toward their home.

A two-faced brute exploding from the darkness inches from her husband's lax face.

Sounds to me like Rab could've been the two-faced one after all.

And you know what? I think I'll stick with "I Can Taste the Blood." It means something to me now. Means something special.

Means I was part of a sweet horror-lodge biker-gang with Joe Schwartz, Eric T. Johnson, J. Daniel Stone, and John F.D. Taff.

And that's where it's at.

That's going after it.

That, for me, is *living*.

ABOUT THE AUTHOR

Josh Malerman is the author of *Bird Box* and *Ghastle and Yule* and some forty other novels and stories that he wishes he could release all in one day... and he just might do that! He lives in Michigan with his fiancee Allison Laakko and their two cats Dewey and Frankie. Used to be three cats, but Dandy died on Halloween, begging the question: will the color orange always make Josh sad? Or will he see Dandy amongst the pumpkins, deliriously, happily, for the rest of his days...

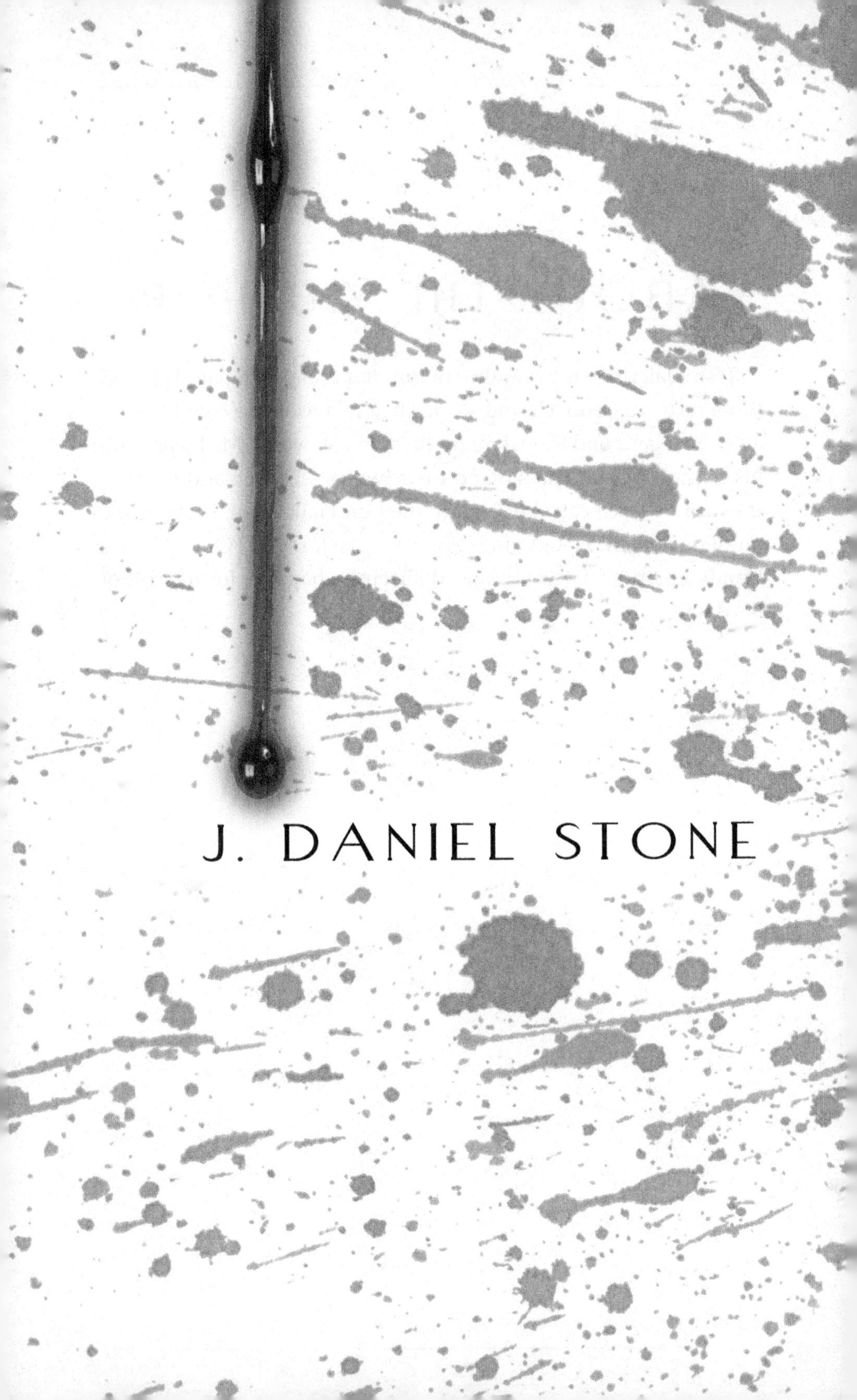

J. DANIEL STONE

VISION II

I CAN TASTE THE BLOOD

"Films bring us together," the old man had said. "But in the wrong hands they can be a weapon."

The phone had rung in the middle of the night. Bok was roused out of a horrible dream, bolting upright with his eyes still closed. The silence of the apartment muffled his loud thoughts, and when he yawned he realized that his throat was sore and that he could taste the faint, metallic traces of blood.

He had been screaming in his sleep again.

Darkness swam before him, but within its depths there was a light, a pillar candle still burning. Then he remembered the dream: a life he had been trying to avoid, junk-sick and lonely, the ghost of his sanity. Wasn't reality enough of a punishment? Why could he not escape it even in sleep?

Bleep-bleep-bleep went the phone again. This time Bok reached over and picked it up, dazed, barely saying hello before the thick German accent asked him to come. He wanted to ask who it was, what did he want? He wanted to scorn the man and tell him that he should call back in the morning. But this was a voice Bok could not forget. He had already done a job for the old German for decent pay, and with money being so tight and jobs far and few in between, there was no saying no.

Bok blinked once, maybe twice, then licked his dry lips. There was a cup of wine sitting at his bedside table and an ashtray with a half-smoked clove still lit. The wine stung his lips and his head spun upon taking a drag of his smoke. He was in the early stages of a hangover, or maybe it was the lack of sleep.

When the room decided to stop shaking, his eyes met the ceiling. There was a bright crimson smudge atop the poster of a ferociously singing Maynard James Keenan, something that resembled blood or the *pāhoehoe* swirl in a lava lamp. He reached out to touch the incandescence, but when he caught a glimpse of the moon outside he remembered that tonight was the vernal equinox, and that the smudge was just its red shadow.

There was a strange odor in the room. Not the spilled craft beer or the cocaine still daubed on his nose; not the spoiled Chinese takeout or the cigarette burns in the upholstery. It was the smell of a ghost in the sheets. Not a literal ghost, but that of someone he missed deeply. Bok rolled over, cradling dirty laundry and the bottle of cheap wine, wishing that it was Jared, but he was long gone and never coming back.

It was time to move or he'd never make up for everything that he'd already let go to shit. As he righted himself, twisting his neck back to a human position, his hair did not follow suit. It was matted and stuck to his face, black as his gypsy bloodline, and the kohl liner crusted in his eyes. There was a moment, before his brain made sense of everything, where he caught his own skeletal reflection in the window. It reminded him of a strung out rock star.

The thought saddened him.

When he moved his feet off the bed, Bok stumbled over a pile of books and broke his fall against a shelf of videocassettes. They had belonged to Jared, various titles and genres: Italian splatter, *giallo*, science fiction, horror, underground, independent and experimental. Jared had believed that films filled the void when the world turns against you, because in films you always come back to the same moment in time and see the same people, a safe place for anyone looking to reject the horrors of the real world.

Bok lit a candle and took it to the window.

The air was crisp and dark as soot. On the eastern horizon the moon was red as a candy apple, corrugated with a face that only a mother could love. Mother Earth, or maybe Mother Mars. New York City looked as if it was stapled against the sky, smeared heavily with silver and gold. Bok closed the window and dressed himself in the typical fashion of the poor: hand-me-down boots, a vintage t-shirt and jeans with too many holes to keep him warm. He was almost too dizzy to move.

The call better have been worth it.

* * *

The theater is too dark but smells of promise. Almost three decades since it had been in business, and just about a decade since the city condemned the leather-lace and porn shop that opened in its place. If you walk its perimeter now, you see that the private booths have been torn down and the mirrors are covered with heavy curtains. Girls no longer command center stage, their long legs fanning and breasts drooping like fruit into the faces of men flashing money.

It is the story of corrupt government administrations and gentrification. But at one time this dark void had filled eyes with Technicolor nightmares that had no bearing on the world surrounding it. And even though the memory of movies and comic strips and popcorn had gone stale, this palace of sadness and madness still retained its haunted charm.

At the front entrance, the ticket booth window was cracked into an intricate pattern and the wallpaper inside was black damask. Etched onto the entrance doors was a hideous insignia: a syringe filled with globules of blood. It made Bok take a step back as there was only one thing, he knew, that lived inside the needle. That was the greed of addiction and the acquired hunger that follows until it springs death upon its human host.

"I hope I didn't wake you," the old man said.

"I don't turn down money." Bok bit his black fingernails.

"Take those out of your mouth. *You* are no child."

The German navigated the aisle with his pale and polished walking stick. He was dressed as best a gentleman could be at this time of night, his breath heavy with liquor and his amethyst eyes surrounded by red cobwebs. Bok couldn't remember the last time he saw the old man, but an image came into his head: a dark space and dust upon a windowsill. But as soon as the old man came into the light Bok saw that he had remained unchanged in his sinister smile, the smell of cheap cologne and thinning silver hair.

"It's been a few months," the German said. "But our time apart has been essential to my movie."

Bok was not ready to recall what had happened that night. It was during a time when he was rarely sober, but also when Jared was at his lowest. The obsession grew into a possession, and Jared would do just about anything to be in front of a camera. Back then the job was an arduous undertaking, not really an acting gig, but more so one that required gentle concentration and a strong stomach. It had paid handsomely.

A stiletto pierced Bok's abdomen, and the claw side of a hammer had dug itself into his knee to test his reflexes. Then came the disconnect, like a wire had snapped in his head, which made Bok succumb to rage. He squeezed his counterpart's head until an eye popped clear out of the skull, crushing it in his hand like the pulp of rotten fruit.

"I hope this place doesn't disturb you. I enjoy an authentic feel."

"I remember what you enjoy."

The old mad tsked. "I never required you to *act.* I simply asked that you *react* because when the camera is pointed at you, Bok, you become something…more."

Bok lit a fancy black cigarette and followed the old man toward the silver screen, unsure of what he was getting himself into this time, but fueled by the need to fill his empty bank account.

Something about this theater irked him. It seemed aghast at Bok's presence. Everything was blighted, as if the sun had rained fire down on this place, followed by a monsoon to put out the embers. It smelled of ozone and dark matter, the air so thin it settled in his lungs like ash.

"You bought this place to make more movies?"

"What else should I have done? The city was going to sell it privately to make way for another Broadway success."

When the German reached the middle section, he tapped his walking stick and a film began. With no other sound in the theater, Bok could easily hear the faint clicking of a movie projector. The immediate scenes were effulgent and so close that they threatened to spill out in a massive 3D effect. It was an old camera trick laced with expert editing.

"Do you remember this at all?"

Bok couldn't recall. "No."

The boy on the screen was youthful. Long hair sprinkled across his face the color of rust and his eyes were green as Chartreuse. Bok's heart rate elevated and his hands became sweaty. The rings on his fingers caught the great white light from the screen, a whiteness as great as the ginger boy's smile, a whiteness as great as his skin and the burning need to be in front of the camera.

"Turn this filth off," Bok said

But the long-haired beauty implored him. Bok could not look away now if he tried. Jared was tied down tightly to a mattress by big black straps. Bok's crotch immediately swelled and his throat dried. A phantom memory found him. He didn't need to watch to know what would happen next.

A man in a mask dripped black candle wax onto Jared's bony torso, bare legs and small toes. His eyes were blindfolded and his mouth was open, waiting as the man in the mask unzipped his jeans and shoved his penis down Jared's throat until his body quivered in orgasmic relief.

"You were brilliant," the German said.

"*Ruination,*" Bok said. "That's what you should've named this trash."

The old man laughed. "Art doesn't follow the rules. What is tradition other than a silly constriction?"

"Right."

The old man's name was Laurenz, and from what Bok knew of his history really didn't match up to his given age. The man seemed to be shaped by centuries long past, which didn't make sense. He had supposedly been living in the United States for fifty years, after leaving Germany when he was twenty, a time when the country was still trying to be prideful, but could not shake off the guilt of the Second World War. All the shame that its newborns had to carry for their predecessors was made-up for in the theater and in art. The underground thrived, spawning the S&M scene, snuff films and the Soviet sex trade.

"I was always told to feel bad for my people, but I had no idea it had to do with a little man with a mustache and a foul temper," Laurenz said.

"Did you? Feel bad, I mean."

"At first, yes. But then I found my voice."

"In art."

"Film, to be precise. At that time, Cologne was a thriving playground of death. A person could find skeletons beneath the rubble and holes that descended to Hell. It was a land of surprises."

"And yet you left it."

"I had to do my own thing. Germany could only bring me so far."

Laurenz slicked back the few strands of silver hair that had fallen over his brow and continued with his story. Like most of his creative brethren, upon departing Germany he found out that the rest of the world wasn't what he'd been trained to believe. There wasn't any fancy apartment waiting for him in British Columbia, no California love and no sun-kissed oranges in Florida. There was only New York City—filthy, brooding, polluted with heroin and beat poets.

"There wasn't any gold in the streets. There was only death. The juxtaposition fascinated me," Laurenz said.

"Why?"

"You have to understand something. I was born into a time where the smell of death was more potent than it had been during the plague. All those mass graves, eventually, began to tell their mute stories of rage and sadness, but with a certain smell."

"So that turned you onto the darkness?"

"Death fixated me because it was all everyone talked about. What the German people did was terrible, but I'm not sure if they were ever truly sorry for it."

"The world may never know."

Laurenz looked Bok straight in the eye. "Death is something we cannot control. We have our education and our money, our passions and our lusts. We have science and art. All of that we control. But death? No, that can never be stopped."

Bok began to feel uneasy.

"I've made some short movies on the subject. Little pieces of my heart put into a forty-five minute film reel."

Bok sucked in the clove smoke. "An anthology?"

"Yes, you could say that. An anthology of evil. To live is to be evil, inherently. Don't you understand that we are all born sinners?"

A memory trapped Bok in the moment. It was too strong to fight, and so he let it cover him like a veil. Before he knew it, the movie theater melted away; everything faded into the silver light.

* * *

Jared was singing to him again, his mouth open and his teeth too white for all the cigarettes he smoked. They were on a rooftop somewhere on the Lower East Side where the graffiti still smelled fresh. Jared's eyes glowed like distant stars; his face was flushed. A needle protruded from his bleeding arm, and as he plunged the syringe his head fell back onto Bok's lap, his body paralyzed by stupor.

* * *

"You awake, Bok?"

He shook his head, realizing that he was still in the theater. "Yeah, sorry. Do go on."

"You're sweating. Would you like a drink?"

"Sure."

Laurenz took a seat in the front row and snapped his fingers three times. From the shadows to his right a man limped forward. He held a silver platter, balancing two glasses filled with the finest bourbon. Bok took his, nodded, to which the butler smiled with a mouth full of broken teeth. Bok had never seen anything so cruel.

"I love American whiskey," the old man said. "It's smoky."

"Who was that person?"

"Nobody."

"Why are his teeth like that?"

Laurenz closed his eyes, rubbed his temples. "He has a fascination for chewing things that he shouldn't."

"Is that why his teeth are like that?"

"No, not really."

Bok felt bad for the butler, likely victimized by Laurenz's visions. He imagined him sitting in front of a camera held high on a tripod and Laurenz conducting the violence. On cue, taken from a manuscript of evil, the butler bit into a wine glass, splitting his lips and cracking his teeth. The hair on the back of Bok's neck rose, and as the man looked into the lens as if looking into Bok, his smile was full of tiny blood diamonds.

"Drink up," Laurenz said.

Bok sniffed his glass. A bouquet of smoke and spice wafted into his nose. He coughed, took a step back and almost lost his balance. The Doc Martens on his feet were suddenly things of their own nature, forcing his knees to buckle. Bad thoughts can do that to a person. What would this glass feel like if he took a bite out of it? Would it hurt? Could he swallow it whole?

"And don't sniff it like a drug. I know that's what you do."

"This is not American whiskey," Bok said.

Laurenz raised his glass. "To the intricacies and decadence of film."

"And to fortune."

They clinked their glasses. The bourbon coated Bok's throat, melting past soft tissue and cartilage, burning all the way to his stomach. The stuff was strong, and it immediately brought fire to his face, making the world twist in ways the human mind had evolved to reject. But sometimes delirium felt so good.

"I guess you're wondering," Laurenz said, "as to why I called this late?"

"Sleep hasn't been my thing lately."

"Anxious?"

"I miss Jared."

"What if I told you I could help alleviate that?"

"I'd be open to hearing what you have to offer, but I know it won't be any good."

"Why do you say that?"

"You're here for my public humiliation."

"Let the past go, Bok."

"You drove Jared insane."

"Jared was born that way. He sought, and found out. His life ended the way he always wanted: in front of the camera. But I know how you can see him again."

Bok went on the immediate defensive, tensing his shoulders and pursing his face. But instead of Laurenz allowing Bok to remain angry, he continued his smooth talk.

"I know what you're thinking. 'Who is this big shot and what has he done in life to have all he does?' I'll let you in on a little secret. One doesn't have as much money as me without...how is it you people say...'making worm food'. Yes, you don't get rich without getting rid of some people."

"But what about Jared? You said I could—"

"Only if you pay attention, Bok."

"Why Jared...of all the people?"

Laurenz was silent for a moment then said, "I saw him sing on stage, and I knew he would be perfect. There was passion in him I never had in myself. He was broken. Too bad he didn't really know what to do with that talent."

What Laurenz said was true. Jared had been a great believer. What he could not attain in reality he left up to the slippery curlicues of his brain. His visions were expertly woven into his songs and stage shows. His ear for music had been so fine-tuned that Bok never imagined he would want to break into any other form of art. But Jared always sought a new high. He tested any drug that came across his path, sometimes losing himself in the psilocybin imagery that became the basis of his conversations.

But Jared had suffered from classic bipolar disorder. Between the mood swings and the drug addiction, he was not ready to face his age or the responsibility that comes with it. He only was comfortable when his mind was blinded by substance and his throat heavy with song. When Bok stopped thinking he had to unlock his fists, saw a small dabble of blood on his palms.

"Jacob Bok. That's your real name, isn't it?"

Bok gritted his teeth. "What is it that you want of me?"

"Your temper is renowned. I remember it well."

"Answer my question!"

Laurenz's eyes met his coldly. "I am in urgent need of something...terrible."

Bok had a bad thought. A lot of the rich guys in this part of town would pay any young thing to spend the night to abate their loneliness. But he couldn't imagine selling his body in this way. He had sold it enough to the drugs.

"It's not what you think. My days of lust are long over," Laurenz said.

"Your hormones might have died, but you want them to live vicariously through your subjects."

"Precisely."

"But you know that I'm not an actor."

"I want to go out with a bang, Bok. And the world is ready for your debut."

The old man's amethyst eyes latched onto the screen. Something was rising in the distance, blotted out by the fluorescence that it brought. Through the divine light Bok saw wings, talons and cloven hooves. In the next scene the creature was reaching for the sky from which it had certainly dropped. Its wings had been severed. There was no sound to this movie, but that was part of the nightmare. Bok began to feel it reach out to claim something that belonged to him, and only to him.

His free will.

"Forget it," Bok said. "I don't want to see myself."

"We trust filmmakers," Laurenz said. "We surrender ourselves from reality, daring them to affect us. We remain secure in the padded darkness of the theater, hoping that they will not go too far while at the same time craving deviance."

"Deviance, is it?" Bok asked.

"We feed from their view of reality, if not just to escape our own lives momentarily. Even I do it. Movies are a kind of drug."

"Don't I know it."

"But I ask this of you." Laurenz ran a long fingernail across his lip. "What do we do when the drug is turned into nefarious art? What happens when we can't shake the imagery?"

"I've no idea."

"It's the greatest success! If a film gets inside you, haunts you, then the artist's work is done. Bok, you have to understand that not all film is entertainment. It can be a cataclysmic message, a ghost waiting to strike."

Laurenz was so caught up in his speech that he had begun to sweat. Thick beads welled across his brow and as he unbuttoned his shirt, they slid down his neck like slime.

"I would think you of all people understand what happens when someone points the camera at something terrible."

Bok didn't answer him. He shielded his eyes with his hair, then took back the rest of the bourbon. It was like liquid smoke rushing down his throat. It was certainly true that Bok had pointed many things at Jared—the needle, the knife, his dick—but nothing was as terrible as the camera.

"Power becomes the film," Laurenz said. "And victim becomes the viewer.

"What does that mean?"

Laurenz waved off the question. "Have you any idea of what the term *innocence* means?"

Bok rolled his eyes. "Not tainted, pure, a creature that has done no harm."

"And have you ever wondered what happens when innocence is destroyed? Have you ever wondered what it would be like to pollute Heaven?"

"No," Bok said, beginning to shake.

"The way you've polluted your body is a good example."

"That story has already been written, dozens of times. What makes your version any different?"

Laurenz sipped his whiskey, then set the glass on the arm of his chair. He closed his eyes. Bok could see the crow's feet etched around them, and the lines of a permanent frown bordering his lips.

"I'm scarred, Bok, just like you."

The old man lifted his hands so that Bok now saw his fingers in the light. They had been burned so badly that the hand was now reminiscent of a flipper, the skin raw and pink as a newborn's. They could no longer do the things that we take for granted like opening a door, play cards or use utensils.

"What happened?" Bok asked.

Laurenz lowered his head. "Imagine creating something that you want the whole word to see, but on opening night you turn yourself away. For that it punished me."

"A film…punished you?"

"Precisely."

"What about the people who saw the whole thing?"

"*Pandemonium,*" the old man whispered.

Bok imagined this theater wet with the smell of hot blood, the aisle slick and the chairs sticky with a miasma of foul juices. The screams would be too loud to comprehend, but with the Devil in everyone's eyes, no one would question it.

"Hey, Bok. You okay?"

"Yeah, sorry. I was…seeing something."

Laurenz's ears perked. "As in a memory you never knew you had?"

"Yes. But I want no part of your sick S&M game."

"*The Chronology of Decay* is not a game. You can't watch just one. You need them all."

Bok lifted his hand as if to strike, but stopped as the old man went into a coughing fit. When he wiped his lip Bok saw blood stain his handkerchief, which made him feel almost sorry for this man who was still chasing dreams that by now were completely unattainable. But that wouldn't stop Bok from collecting his money.

"I'm not well as you can see. There'll be no price to my longings."

"But why me?"

"Because you are a natural." The thick German accent slurred his words together. "Because you're just like me. You want to feel what we cannot explain."

"No, I don't."

The old man leaned forward. "Yes, you do. So let's get to business. Before they get here, before I show your movie, I want you to tell me everything. What went through your mind that night? How could you envision a film that I never could?"

When Bok opened his mouth to speak, when he allowed himself to think straight, the words came forth like a dream.

* * *

The advertisement was a horrid mix of uninspired colors and disconnected imagery, like someone had run it through The Joker's chemical bath: car crash art-deco, a body hanging by meat hooks and all the chaos that runs through the veins of various fringe cultures. Bok's fingers ached from painting the ads to the template of Jared's sick vision.

Banking the ass end of another fallen district, ramshackle gnarled and gutted, the club was a warped ghost in the shittiest part of town. Bok paced the building, stared down its warehouse-style windows and the barred door, as if it was a prison. The line was wrapped all the way around the block. Tonight's look was dark with lace and bright with makeup. Mouths remained busy with cigarettes; voices were tinged with angst.

Bok cut through clouds of smoke and the sound of innocent laughter. The front door was covered with a bunch of advertisements and it creaked open slowly to let patrons in. The bouncer, a skinny white kid with a hook in his nose, was smoking a joint. Bok joined him, lighting up a clove and inhaling the sweet plumes, then exhaled heavily.

"You smoke Sour D?" the bouncer asked.

He passed the joint over to Bok, but when he inhaled the smoke hit his lungs too hard, as if someone had dropped a brick on his chest.

"It's been a while," Bok said after he was done coughing and wiping tears from his eyes.

"Don't worry, it's potent stuff," the bouncer said. "Go on in and have fun."

Bok put his clove out against the wall and descended. It was as if he was falling down Alice's magnificent dark hole, passing a weird ticket booth and taxidermied animals that looked too alive to be dead. When his ears popped, he knew he had made it down far enough, took a right through a small door and entered a world of smoke and mirrors.

Voices of all backgrounds assaulted his ears, baby dykes and drag queens, party boys, cronies and queers of all costume. During soundcheck feedback reverberated against the walls, cutting conversations in half and forcing some kids to hold their ears. The rest drank their gimlets and craft beer in spooky relief. The night would go on, as it always does.

When soundcheck ended the lights drizzled like rain and the band rose like a hydra onto the small stage—warring guitars, double bass and a skeletal synthesizer. Bok immediately looked for Jared, but he was nowhere to be found, not behind the heavy curtains where he usually would have been, and not camouflaged with the zombie stage props.

Was he playing another one of his tricks? Was he here to act on the stage again rather than own it? But then the synth rang out, a deep note dripping like cocaine in the back of Bok's throat. He thought he could actually taste its sound. To his immediate right the guitarist hit a drop D power chord that would surely leave his ears ringing for days. But soon the music found its flow—a slow droning melody that evolved into a hardcore bridge and chorus—

and the sound of the crowd's excitement secured the knowledge that the lead singer had entered from stage left.

"Don't you love me anymore? Don't you want to score?"

The red-haired boy twisted his skinny body and stretched his mouth to belt out the notes. He ran the microphone across his teeth, drawing so much blood that Bok was certain that the microphone was biting him back. His green eyes glittered and his hands hit the air like white Chinese fans. Bok had never seen someone glow the way Jared did, not a trick of the stage lights, but more like a living moonrise.

"My love is an eight-ball," his voice shook the room. "…we can do nothing but fall…"

The song was one that Jared admitted he had written about Bok, lyrical in its content and passionate in its cadence. Jared was a natural born singer and songwriter. Every melody that flew out of his mouth reflected freedom of expression and reaching for greater things as he did not believe in limitation.

Jared's voice was a sweet torture in that it was part miracle and part sin. Blessed with a throaty but soothing tone, the notes he reached were seemingly able to rearrange the rudimentary particles of matter itself, unravel our spiraled strands of DNA. Bok had fallen in love with the song when he heard Jared first sing it two years ago.

"And if you even give a damn, you'll take me sick or sane, healthy or lame…"

The song was called "Dignity," and it was one of the first Jared had ever written about love, that magical feeling where nothing you do can ever be right because with love there always comes a price. But this was also a song about drugs and about how much they were part of him. Anyone could see the marks of addiction if they looked closely enough. Jared's arms were a mosaic of tiny little scabs from the crook of his elbow to wrist. Music might have been his muse, but the heroin was pure comfort.

"My tongue is a blade and your heart the vein…"

Now Jared began to swing the mic, forcing the crowd to take a step back. The blood was still fresh on his lips, and Bok knew just how it would taste, how hot it would be sizzling down his own throat. Jared took off his shirt and scaled the nearby wall, a pale acrobat ripping away egg carton sound absorbers and knocking beer off of every amp he climbed. His red hair swayed at the small of his back, napalm-bright, so that everyone focused on the black tattoo he had mapped over his spinal processes, ending sharply at both sides of his hips. When he reached the top he straddled the biggest amp and gyrated as if he was riding a stallion.

Bok knew that the camera was rolling. Its dark eye was a spherical mirror, reflecting the world's horrors and atrocities. It was the greediest and neediest thing in life. The camera never asked how or why, it was only there to record, but also to beckon for more, more, more.

And the music raged on—a psychedelic bridge, double bass, then a guitar solo electrified with pinch harmonics. On cue, the gargantuan bassist played the heaviest note possible, sending a shockwave like a muscular push into everyone's chest. But Jared was possessed with pleasure, the microphone at his lips again, his tongue performing mechanical fellatio.

"If I were to give you my pain, my dignity…would it be worth erasing the man I used to be?"

Bok took this all in—the act, the lyrics, the music—and fell in love all over again. Jared was the kind of love you can only have once, and if you let it go, or ruined it with your ego or your pride, you could never get it back. Jared was so full of life—and death—that it was impossible to think of being with another person.

"There are two versions of love, and I don't want the one from up above."

Jared belted out the last note long and thick as the song crunched its way to the end. The sound of his voice enveloped the room like ectoplasm. Now he climbed down the amp, walked to the front of the stage, touching Bok's hair along the way, and then proceeded to crack open a beer. He drank some of it back, then leaned over as Bok opened his mouth for the warm bubbling fountain of Jared's kiss. Two men in front appeared disgusted, but everyone else jumped, cheered and clapped madly. Jared finished the set without a thank you. Bok knew he had done enough. He would sleep for eight days after this. The lights cut out, the music now taken over by a DJ as Bok followed Jared to the bar.

"Why must you always end your set that way?" Bok asked.

Jared pulled his red hair into a tight pony tail. "If I don't give them something to worry about, why put on a show?"

"You're a natural actor, I've always said that. Tonight you were magnificent."

"Thank you, baby."

Hot lips on his own, and it made Bok think of flower petals. In this light, Jared's hair was the color of rust, his face edged down into a fine point. Bok ran his fingers through that red mane, then turned Jared's head to the side and kissed his neck. But he also wanted to see Jared's finest ink: a black 8mm film strip that went from neck to navel.

"You never told me why you have that tattoo. The spine I understand. To see it move with your bone structure is haunting. But this?"

"Jacob Bok, have we not been together for two years?"

Bok almost laughed. "We have."

"Then you should know my love for movies. It's always movies, then music, never the other way around."

Bok sipped his PBR. "I don't know why you went into music instead of acting. You put so much time into it."

Jared's green eyes were dappled within the bar's light. "Sometimes we don't get what we want in life. We follow a calling, a necessity born out of the depths of longing."

"And a razor poet too!"

"Shut up," Jared said, sliding his finger down Bok's tight black shirt.

"You know, whenever I look at that tattoo, I swear there are little people in it trying to tell me a story, as if I should peel it off your skin and set it into a reel."

"Imagine that!" Jared lit a smoke, then smiled wide. "What is a movie other than a bunch of people trying to tell a story?"

Bok kissed Jared's forehead, inhaled his night-scented smell of makeup, hair dye, cigarettes and creation.

"So is there anything I should be watching out for?"

"Well, I did invite someone here that I want you to meet," Jared pulled the ad out of his pocket, sliding his finger across the crazed images.

"Is that why you made me do these? You put me through hell."

"That last director was a dud. He had no vision. But this German guy has no limits. Foreigners have far better imaginations than us corn-fed kids."

"No," Bok said, stern.

"Come on."

"You almost got us arrested. I refuse to be put through that again."

Jared remained quiet while Bok drank his beer. But the need in Jared's eyes was clear, he wanted to recall the first time they made a movie together, the first time Bok felt like his soul did not belong to his body. Only Jared could have brought that out in him.

* * *

Bok was supposed to be just a fill-in for when Jared couldn't finish a scene or remember his line, a flesh doll that someone could later edit out to look like Jared. The warehouse was as dim and quiet as a church. Stained glass windows soared, and in the center was a bed alive with two bodies entwined in a love scene. It was Jared and another boy, their tongues wet with desire and their nails ripping furrows down one another's chests. Jared's buttermilk skin was slick with crimson fury, and as the director called for more, Bok remembered a voice inside his head saying something like, "The camera is waiting, the show must go on."

Because in every good snuff film someone dies.

Now the boy's nails were flaying the skin off of Jared's back, and despite Jared's protest the movie kept going. The camera crew proceeded to unzip their jeans, masturbating their tumescent cocks. That's when something changed in Bok, like the simple flick of a switch. He found himself suddenly part of the film, hitting the actors with his fists until he felt them go warm and wet. The last thing he remembered before blacking out was Jared's vampire face, the camera forcing his body into motion, and the look of horror from everyone in the room.

* * *

"When you get in front of a camera, Bok, something happens... something gets *into* you and you become..." Jared was lost for words, but then found one. "Powerful."

"Stop talking like that."

"But what if someone had a vision that could match *your* talent?"

"Jared, it's not about me. It's about what you want."

Bok was getting increasingly worried. He could see the dull flame of a hyper mood swing waiting to grow into a blaze.

"What if someone could push the boundaries of flesh? We don't have to be tied down by this overstretched bag on our bones if we don't want to."

One of Jared's bandmates, the girl who played the synth, joined them at the bar. She was fair-haired and wore a cheap jacket made of some synthetic leather that sucked in all the light surrounding it. It made Bok think of the infinite vacuum that is the universe. Jared spoke to her first, and as he did, her blue eyes marked Bok like something ominous but fantastic, then she nodded and walked away without finishing her beer.

"What did she want?" Bok asked.

Jared smiled. "He's here."

There came the smell of cigars and bourbon, something foreign in this cheap club. From the back, a dark presence seeped through the crowd, like debris and smoke polluting its way through a city after an explosion. Soon Bok realized that the presence wasn't anything mystical at all, but a tiny old man balanced on a very long cane. Jared pulled out a bar stool for him, and Bok saw that the old man's arms were contracted and arthritic, his legs shaky from what appeared to be general weakness. He was an aging cripple, though appearing well put together, so said the expensive seersucker suit at least.

"You put on quite a show," the old man said.

"What the hell is this, *Night of the Living Dead*?" Bok asked.

"No," Jared said, then looked at the old man. "Forgive him, his knowledge of film isn't as healthy as mine."

"It's true," Bok said. "I couldn't care less."

"I am Laurenz Althaus," the man said with a heavy German accent.

The man's amethyst eyes sat in his skull like two polished gems. Within them lay the spark of brilliance glazed over by a life of fastidiousness. He would not rest until he was satiated, even though the face beneath those aberrant eyes was tired, heavily lined, and wrought with age.

"He's one of the greatest underground filmmakers ever to walk the earth," Jared said. "This is Jacob, my boyfriend."

"Call me Bok."

"The pleasure is all mine."

Laurenz put out a small, withered hand and shook. Despite his bad posture, the old man's grip exuded confidence, and his eye contact was that of a polished professional. Then something bit him. Bok pulled his hand back, saw that the old man wore a silver ring with tiny points set into it as if a little jaw.

"It's just a ring," Laurenz said.

"Yeah, and it bit me." Bok licked the red swirl running down his middle finger.

"How does that taste, Bok? Is it sweet?"

"The blood?"

"Yes," the old man said.

"I don't recall ever tasting my own blood."

Now that he was close enough, Bok realized that what Laurenz was holding was not an ordinary walking stick. It looked like it had been fashioned from bone. When Bok met Laurenz's face again, the old man smiled, revealing a set of brown teeth reminiscent of wood, or even leather. He was certainly sick, and not just in the head. But before Bok could say anything more, Jared pulled him to the side.

"What do you think?"

"Who is this guy, Jared? What does he want?"

"He makes movies. And I want you to see what he can do."

* * *

Laurenz owned a smoke shop in Chelsea. In this part of town transients and larrikins marked the streets like fungus. Boys of every color, size and sexuality dominated the corners, waving down fancy black cars until a window rolled down to hand them cash, or a door opened to welcome them into a temporary world of status. The boys who could not find work were either jumped for being gay, arrested for prostitution, left for dead after snorting a little too much, or found themselves shooting up just enough to end all the pain.

Jared held Bok's hand tightly. His touch was alive with excitement and fright. At the front door, Laurenz fiddled with a hundred keys—brass, pewter, skeleton, dimpled and double-sided—and at first it seemed he would count them all. Maybe it was a trick to drive them mad, or maybe it was a distraction from the boys that had asked them to come play…and pay. When Laurenz found the right key, he jarred the door open and they were instantly swallowed by a world of tobacco, lottery tickets and candy.

The display cases were full of every brand of cigarette one could think of. Each box stood out with their unique insignias of cowboys, Indians, triangles and strange animals. Bisecting the shelf were cartons colored by the flag of their respective countries. Bok picked a pack of cloves off the shelf, Djarum Vanilla, and placed it in the pocket of his thin black coat. Jared helped himself to some Parliaments, then inspected a shelf of hookahs, glass pipes and ornate bongs.

After a few minutes Laurenz called them to the back of the store, coughed one of his lungs out, and then pointed to a wall. Jared looked confused and Bok felt like he had been played for a fool. But then Laurenz tapped the wall with his walking stick so that it opened like a door.

"After you," Laurenz said with a big smile.

All three of them descended fast, down into a world hidden away from the smog above, from the order, rule and regulation that governments have put in place to ephemerally comfort society. Down here, Bok knew, society did not exist; down here was a world of its own.

There were boxes of Cuban cigars and racks of gay, straight and tranny porn. Farther in, a row of chairs was arranged in front of a small screen set up like a movie theater. Laurenz showed them to their seats, lit a cigar and then disappeared. Jared sat with his legs crossed and Bok ruminated on stealing a box of Cubans as it had been a while since he had smoked one.

"Where's he off to?" Bok asked.

"To get the movies, of course." Jared was beginning to get the sniffles.

"It looks like he hasn't used this place in a very long time."

"He's an artist not a business man. What's so bad about that?"

"I didn't mean it like that."

Jared began to shake. "Yeah well, you alluded to it. Aren't you curious at all as to why his movies make people crazy?"

Bok let out a condescending laugh. "Oh please, movies don't make people mad."

"Just you wait." Jared coughed.

"You okay? You're very pale."

"I could really use a little something right now." Jared started to roll up his sleeve.

Bok pulled it back down. "Not here, and certainly not in front of a stranger."

"He doesn't care. Please, baby, I..." Jared's skin prickled with gooseflesh and his teeth chinked horribly. Sweat broke free from his brow. "I can't go on another minute. I'm getting sick."

"I don't have much."

Jared licked his dry lips. "Anything to hold me over, please? Oh please. Please!"

Bok couldn't say no, and he only had himself to blame. The needle was once his greatest escape, but now it was the bane of his existence, nothing but a metallic parasite sucking the life out of his boyfriend. He couldn't forgive himself for turning Jared onto the stuff, but it made so much sense back then. It was the one thing they shared in a relationship built by opposition.

* * *

Jared was eighteen, and Bok a year younger. Teenage years are the most confusing time in a person's life, but for the queer community the teenage years are a whole new brand of hell. They are laced with confusion and shame as one tries to figure out which team they are destined to play for, while at the same time trying to avoid that truth.

For Bok, those times meant hanging out on the wrong side of the street, making friends with people who were only your friend if you were sharing a needle or ripping someone off. It was Bok's first boyfriend who had tied the belt to his bicep and palpated his vein until it looked like a worm was trapped beneath his skin. The needle slid in with no pain, and when Bok saw the syringe flower with blood before the sweet heroin plunged into his system, he found that drug using could be more of an art than a useless habit.

Something inside his mind burst. He was no longer a flesh and blood organism, but ethereal. He became poet incarnate, a cloud, the skin of a very bad dream. The world that had done such a good job of judging his life was suddenly softened. He didn't have to be afraid to walk the streets of the city anymore, he wasn't destined to be alone as many people said he would be, and there was no gay cancer to be afraid of.

But what had initially saved Bok's emotions was now affecting his physical health. He went days without food, sometimes water; his bowel movements were infrequent and his mouth was always dry. He had thinned to the point where it looked as if he could fall over if the wind blew just right. Though Bok had done a good job of hiding the drug problem from Jared for over nine months, the jig was up. Jared's curiosity had fully bloomed and he wanted Bok to fess up. It started with general inquisition, which eventually led to Jared connecting the little scabs on Bok's arm to his bad habit. Bok had never felt more ashamed, deciding that only a tattoo of a needle and syringe right at the spot where he always pricked himself would force him to break the habit. But it hadn't.

That's when Jared confessed that he wanted a taste. Bok said no right off the bat only for the selfish reason that if he had to share his stash with Jared there would be less for him. But then it dawned upon him, on one of his rare sober nights, that maybe it wouldn't be such a bad idea for Jared to ride the downward spiral with him. Why not join the party instead of trying to fit in with society? Even if the user wasn't functional when they were on H, they were at least their own special breed of human being.

Jared already had the slipknot tied to his bicep and the vein fully palpated. It was a moment that Bok had been robbed of, to be able to carefully choose his own poison, so he would not allow Jared to be robbed of it either. Reluctantly, Bok melted the smack and sucked it into the syringe, then let Jared do the rest. Upon first taste, a new person had been born.

Jared became strangely inspired. He picked up instruments Bok never knew he could play and wrote bohemian poetry like it was going to be the last time he'd ever do such a thing. His mood stabilized into someone he had caught only quick glimpses of in their relationship, a persuasive and perverse young man whose talent far exceeded his own. But maybe this was all because he was already in love with Jared. Somewhere deep inside, Bok knew that if he didn't ruin Jared—if he didn't drain his vitality completely—someone would surely steal his red-haired beauty away from him.

But even in extremis, Jared was strikingly gorgeous.

If Bok could ever define that movie-like feeling of true love—of absolute completion within the presence of another—Jared was it. Maybe part of his love came from the fact that Jared wasn't easy to deal with, that it took hard work to earn his trust and companionship because he had more than one personality. Why would anyone put all that effort into a relationship and then give it all up before the payoff?

Jared was fragile and he often suffered from mood swings, but was never properly diagnosed since Bok had never taken him to a psychologist. He had no money to do such a thing. And he hadn't enough gall to ask Jared to go. But the signs were all there. There were times when Jared was manic for days, possessed by insomnia and pumped full of energy.

And then there were the times when Jared slept for fifteen hours straight, the covers pulled over his head because the moon was too bright. Nothing could be done for him during those depressed periods. Nothing inspired him. Not music, not movies, not even Bok. Yet mood swings or not, their relationship remained intense, their conversations intellectual and the knots in his stomach tightened every time he laid eyes on Jared.

And in this memory, they were making love. It wasn't the first time, but it was a new bed and a new apartment. A studio on the West Side, the concept no more open than a closet, but the rent was a solid grand a month, something unheard of in New York City. This part of town was interesting because no matter the weather or time of day, it was always balmy and dark with smog. Great plumes of steam shot up from the sewers, and exhaust spit out of the countless delivery trucks. Nobody wanted to live here, no gentrification robots or big business tycoons. Not yet anyway.

The only reason Bok was able to afford it was because he didn't have to sign a lease. Rent was paid in the tip money he made bartending. Jared paid his half from some trust fund that he never owned up to, mostly because he was confused about how someone so mentally unstable could come from such a good, law-abiding family. What rock star is born into privilege? It was against the moral code of music.

Jared's hands were tied to the head of the bed with black lace. Bok took a second to worship his skeletal form, the long bare legs, small feet and, of course, the slatted torso. There was a black pillar candle burning on the nightstand. Bok ignited a cigarette with it, then cupped the candle in his hands. When he tipped it forward, hot wax dribbled over Jared's chest. The skin bubbled and blotched, welts forming like patches of red flowers.

This time was different.

Jared had asked that they record themselves. The tripod was stationed in the corner abutting the bed, and it held a 90s-style home video recorder. Bok almost felt as if he was being violated, but as that camera pointed his way, he felt something unhinge from his soul. He could be anyone he wanted, do anything he pleased, and it would all be for the sake of art.

Bok spread Jared's legs like a wishbone, bound them with two leather straps. His hairless scrotum hung delicately, his cock stood attention. Bok cradled Jared's skull and then kissed the lush garden of his mouth, then crawled across the creaking bed and traced his tongue across Jared's nipples. At this point, he had to jack off before his dick exploded, and he shot a frustrated gob across Jared's quivering stomach. But there was no relief or release; his dick remained hard and Bok rubbed the head to get himself even more excited.

Then the fun began.

He pulled out the needle and blindfolded Jared, slipping the knot tight on the middle of Jared's bicep. The vein popped up immediately, and when Bok inserted the needle, Jared didn't even notice. He then did the same to himself. The drug coursed through them together, making Jared harder and Bok crazier.

Now they were both someone else. Jared's world of mental instability had vanished. This was about the moment. Bok straddled Jared's sharp hips, greased up his dick with spit, and then swung open his legs like beautiful butterfly wings and slid slowly up and down Jared's dick. The pain was bright, but exquisite. Jared was dazed with pleasure.

When Jared came he seemed to swell inside of Bok like a balloon, pulsing great pearlescent streams into his intestines. They had never even thought about using condoms as the trust was too great between them. Bok released Jared from the straps and they cuddled until their sweat, spit and cum mingled into an unordinary slime. But they didn't sleep; life was too short for that, and so they smoked cigarettes and watched the sun take over the city.

* * *

"Are you listening to me?" Jared broke Bok's concentration. "I don't care if you gave it up. I *need* it."

"If you ever went to a proper doctor, you might be able to get real meds."

Jared grabbed Bok's wrist and twisted. "We already had that conversation. Nothing makes me feel as good."

Bok pulled himself free, rolled his eyes. "Just don't do it in front of me. I'm so sick of this life."

Jared grinned and then disappeared. Left alone in the candle-dark room, Bok focused his attention on a queer sight. It was a cauldron of some sort, fit for storing secret poisons, but inside it was filled with VHS tapes. Bok read a few of the titles. Most he had never heard of. *Black Illusions* had a picture of a fallen angel whose wings had been clipped. The blurb for *Terrible Twos* talked about the copulation between fairies and humans, the cover art two little flying things gliding up and down a heavily veined penis too large for any of their orifices.

But then there was a movie that really made him sick called *I Can Taste the Blood*. Bok didn't have to put it into the VCR to understand its power. Just by touching it his eyes were assaulted by images of the dead ripping open a pregnant woman's stomach, feasting upon placenta and tender curds of fetal brains. Fast forward and a man dips his face into the folds of his lover's pussy, her head falling back in pleasure. Upon the final taste, it sprouts teeth that clamp down on his lips, pulling them clear off of his face.

"Those are my visions," Laurenz said. "Are you scared?"

"No. Am I supposed to believe that these things are real?"

Laurenz shrugged.

Bok leaned forward in his chair. "No answer?"

"If one wants something terribly, immediately, one does whatever it takes to acquire it."

"What do you mean?"

"*Sorcery.*"

Before Bok could answer, Jared had come back, looking fresh and healthy.

"Can we begin?"

"*The Chronology of Decay* awaits you. But heed my warning, these vignettes are not for weak stomachs or wills. They challenge the viewer."

"What does that title mean?"

"My gods, what a question." Laurenz rubbed his gloved hands together. "There is beauty in decay, so long as you understand that there was once life where the rotting began. Without that life, no *thing* can wither and die, or lose its exquisite grace."

"Like I have any idea what that means," Bok said.

"Just enjoy."

Laurenz put out the candles with an ornate stopper and the smell of waxy smoke filled the room. Bok moved two seats down to the middle and brushed away cobwebs that were hanging off the ceiling, waiting for Jared to sit. But Jared was busy toying with the projector, transfixed, as if it was going to tell him the secrets of movie making. After a few minutes of Jared versus the machine, he came to his seat, licked his lips and lit a cigarette…waiting.

Laurenz turned down the lights and the movie credits began.

The phosphor glow of the screen melted over Bok's body with an incredible pale weight. He closed his eyes and let the light seep into his cells, binding and torturing his god-given free will. When he opened his eyes he realized that it was only Jared caressing him, red hair brushing against his face as he kissed the top of his head. The dope had once again changed Jared's mood from the focused artist to horny devil. He tugged Bok's shirt until it ripped at the shoulder, then went for the zipper of his jeans. Bok was about to give in and let Jared have his way, let him indulge, until something changed on the screen.

Chiaroscuro violence—a field of pitchforks, limbs raining from the sky, a merry-go-round of meat hooks pierced the paunches of pregnant women. Their mouths were jellied with blood, and their eyes had been ripped from their heads so that the viewer could see into their brains.

A hundred thousand scenes of decay and suffering.

Each time the screen flashed, it formed a shadow behind the viewer and a silhouette in front. There was no saving grace. The actors had been left to fend for themselves like hunters and gatherers, and so they attacked one another for food. It was sick, but not too farfetched a thought. In the next scene a knife was plunged into a corpse, the flesh unzipping to reveal the inner putrescence. Bok found that the worst part of this film was that there was no dialogue, just an erratic soundtrack that seemed like it had been scratched into the film itself.

Then the screen brightened. Bok was now fully engaged.

Angelic creatures scoured the skies, casting judgment on numb-minded people too busy taking pictures with their cell phones to witness the miracle fro themselves. In the next frame, one of the angels was shot down by a whaling harpoon and then bound by chains. Its face was ageless and its gender indeterminate, but fear marked its owl-like eyes as the machete sparked against the whetstone.

When the angel rose in defiance, someone started the harpoon machine so that it was pulled down. Bok saw its long nails scratch the pavement, mouth open in horror as pain seized it. The machete slammed against its back, blue skin slick with blue blood and ichor running down its face to mourn the only thing that separated it from mankind: its wings. The camera zoomed in as they snapped away from the flesh that bound them, falling heavily to the floor. With its immortality lost, the angel curled into itself, showing raw wounds gleaming ominously. Bok knew then what Laurenz's walking stick was made of.

It wasn't hard to imagine why someone would go mad at the sight of these grotesqueries. The movie had somehow planted bad memories into Bok's head, memories that were now part of him. It was a room dark as this one, and it was at full capacity. But halfway into the screening, silence evolved into violence. Fists fell like rain. A boy ripped into the neck of his date with a dull pocketknife. A lesbian couple tore into one another until their lips were striped in gore. *The Chronology of Decay* had certainly done its job of moving the audience in ways that no movie had ever done before.

And then the screen cut out, but the movie was far from over. It was now *inside* of Bok, growing. That's when he felt something remove itself from his body, leaving only a mute vessel behind. As he stepped into this world, the theater slick with blood and the walls glistening, he saw two men rolling around like dogs until one of them bit clear through the other man's nose, tearing it off so that he drowned in his own blood.

"I had a similar experience myself," Laurenz said.

"But why all of this madness?" Bok asked.

"I'm not the one who can answer that. What I do know is that I see great potential in you."

"What about Jared?"

"Utter failure."

"This isn't what I want," Bok growled.

"It absolutely is. You want to affect them."

"That's not what film is about. You've got it all wrong."

"Then what's it about?"

"It's supposed to teach you, supposed to make you think."

"No," Laurenz growled. "It's supposed to *change* you, like it did to me."

"This 'use once and destroy' mentality does nothing for the longevity of art."

"Subjectivity died when the movie industry began to feed us garbage. Have you actually watched a decent movie lately?"

"I don't want this."

Laurenz clapped. "There it is, dear Bok. That anger you hide. It might not be what you want, but this is your calling. Bok, when the camera points at you, something terrible happens. I've had one on you all night and you didn't even notice."

Bok turned around to see the camera atop a mini tripod. Its red light bathed his face in a short-lived warmth, and when he stood up, the lens seemed to follow him. Jared had already made his way to the camera and was reviewing the tape, the LED light sinking into the hollows of his face. Laurenz walked away from Bok and then proceeded to place the new film reel into the projector.

Blue as open waters, the screen hummed and drummed and threatened to drown them. There was no light other than a candle, but he could make out Jared's sinuous shadow tearing the room apart, box after box, cigarettes and cigars everywhere. Laurenz was nowhere in sight, but something about the room had changed.

There were things here that should only be kept inside story books and bad horror films, things that would make atheists bat their non-believing eyes in this delineated reality. Bok had no recollection of coming into contact with them, not in this memory and not in another, but somehow he knew that he soon would.

"I want to be free," Jared said. "Free me Bok."

He was naked and bright as the moon. In this moment, Bok knew he was healthier than he had ever been, thinking more clearly, but that was part of the problem. In his left hand there was an X-Acto blade, and he traced the tattoo of the 8mm film strip gently, just enough to draw a fine line of blood.

And then he began to peel…

"Terrible isn't it," Laurenz said. "That you can't remember a thing."

"I was here, watching your film. I know that."

"Ah, now that's where you're wrong."

"Where's Jared?" Bok was done playing these games.

"He left. I told you he didn't have it in him."

"Are you fucking kidding me? Where did he go?"

"Maybe to get more dope. How should I know? He's a better

musician than actor anyway." Laurenz grabbed Bok's arm with a powerful grip.

"Let me go, you sick fuck."

"Don't make me do it, Bok. I don't want to hurt you."

Bok ran. He hit the wall, then knocked over the boxes of cigars and porn tapes. Laurenz did not react, rather, he tapped his walking stick and fell back into the dark. In no time a withered thing crawled toward Bok. There was blood caked on its sharp fingernails and shards of glass in its mouth. The flesh of its back was raw and open and smelled of rot. Bok knew that those wounds marked the place where its wings had once been.

Run.

The voice was in his head along with the sound of flapping wings. But now the walls were closing in on him. A black feather landed on his face, eyes plummeted from the sky and hands reached up from the bog at his feet. He heard Laurenz speaking in tongues, saw the camera staring at him. This was the most frightening acid trip of his life as he suddenly connected the dots. Bok let go of his human constrictions and allowed himself to be dragged to Hell.

* * *

"Leave me alone," Jared said. "My movie is on." He had made the bed his temporary home, staring into a television screen full of static. There was a syringe half-filled with Mexican heroin laying atop the black satin sheets, and a pack of smokes with only two cigarettes left. He absentmindedly picked up the needle and syringe, put it on top the television set and then lit a cigarette, blowing pallid loops in the darkness. "Sometimes I don't need the stuff. All I need is film."

This week his mood had waged war with his conscience, a whole new universe compared to last week's hyper-sexual and hyper-covetous state of mind. Jared did not want to be touched or coddled, did not want to make love, did not want to be part of the human race. Whenever Jared fell prisoner to his own mind, there was no stopping it. The days turned into a waiting game. Bok simply had to sit around and be patient until it passed because the harder he tried to pry the sickness away, the harder the sickness worked on Jared.

"I already a saw this one," Jared's tired eyes took in the TV's light.

Bok shook his head. "All I see is static."

"But I see divinity."

Though Bok had become accustomed to the mood swings, he had never seen Jared obsess at this level. He hadn't eaten in days or taken in any other liquid besides warm beer. He even wet the bed for fear of missing a small portion of whatever movie was playing.

Bok used his free time to read about manic disorders. Jared's shifts in energy, behavior and thinking were the telltale signs that he could be positively diagnosed. The schism of mania and depression was no longer a mystery. The online communities were plentiful, supplying Bok with priceless information he could never afford from a professional, even though getting professional help was out of the question since Jared was too scared to accept the permanence of his condition.

This information overload was almost a revelation. Sometimes, when the heart is set on something, one cannot stop its path to satisfaction. That in itself is very much like art.

"Let's go out." Bok pulled Jared's arm, but it was like holding a lead bar.

"My movie is on." Jared pointed languidly at the screen.

"How many more of these fucking things are you going to watch?"

Bok felt himself growing increasingly impatient, the blood rushing to his face, his fists clenched so tight his knuckles turned white. But Jared would not budge. He covered himself with the blanket again, all the way up to his nose so that Bok could see only his uncombed hair that had threaded itself into dreads. It faintly reminded him of Boy George.

"Do you really want to hurt me?" Jared asked.

How had that lyric come about?

"No," Bok said.

Jared nodded, then smiled. His teeth hadn't been brushed in days, so they had lost that too-white shine. He was also beginning to reek. From his side of the bed, Bok caught the unwashed odor of Jared's feet and armpits and hair. At one time he had craved that smell, but right now it was repulsive.

"Don't you hate repeats?" Bok said.

Jared ignored him, focusing on the screen, and if Bok stared hard enough at it himself he thought maybe he could see the birth of death, the raping of innocence. It was everything Laurenz wanted to shove down the throats of his viewers. But Bok could not truly see what Jared was seeing. There was only static, sizzling white noise. The television's electric glow suffused up the walls and over the posters like neurological connections in the brain and then leaked out the windows. Bok saw Trent Reznor's face laved in copper-colored dendrites. Maynard James Keenan's open mouth spit out a jellyfish-like axon terminal. Stevie Nicks was framed by an articulate soma body.

"I have no idea what you're talking about," Bok said. "Can I get a smoke?"

"I only have two left. You don't see it?" Jared's eyes were lively hollows in the dark.

"No, I don't. And gee, thanks for sharing."

Bok turned away from the television set, unwilling to chain himself to its entrancing power. Instead, he looked out the window. It was rainy and hazy; great gouts of water blotted out the New York skyline like a spill of ink on a newspaper. The rain seemed as if it was coming from the ground up, and the sound of it slapping the rooftops and garbage cans was as rhythmic as a song.

He lit a stick of frankincense and placed it on the window sill. Outside a drenched passerby was trying to hail a cab, but what was once a cobblestone street was now a shallow pool of flotsam and detritus so deep that Bok could not even see her feet. Further out, lightning webbed the sky, followed by rolling thunder that Bok felt all the way down to his teeth.

"I want to watch the one of you," Jared whispered.

"No."

"Big shot." Jared said that with malicious intent.

"Stop it, now."

"Are you afraid?" Jared stuck out his lizard tongue, followed by placing a Parliament between his lips.

"Turn off the TV."

"No. Don't touch it."

Jared was standing on the bed now, his arms spread and his teeth bared. The Parliament had burned some of his hair, and a bright ball of light ensconced his entire body. He looked like a great black bird, or a creature fallen from above. As soon as Bok took his hand away from the television set, Jared was down and under the covers again.

"Why are you doing this?" Jared asked.

"Me? What are you talking about?"

"Stealing my thunder, my moment. Why do you want to do this to me?"

Bok's heart beat uncontrollably. He wanted to wring Jared's neck.

"All I ever wanted was to be a movie star, but you're the one with the true talent, and you could give a fuck!" Jared said.

"I don't want this, Jared. Why do you think I want this?"

"Because you're so good at it. Because you become someone else when the camera is pointed at you. Are you that foolish not to see it?"

"Has Laurenz been telling you this?"

Jared turned his face toward Bok, indescribably white. "I've been telling *him* that!"

"I just don't know you anymore."

Jared took one last pull of his cigarette and then put it out on the top of his hand. No pain reached his face, no remorse to his heart. Bok leaned back, almost afraid of what he would do next.

Now Jared was upright in the bed. He had definitely lost weight, and even within the low light of the room Bok could make out all the bones in his face, all the weakness in him as his posture resembled that of a wilting flower. Bok tried to give him the greatest hug there ever was, perhaps to shine a little light on Jared's cold black heart, but Jared tensed up, not wanting to be touched.

"Please, don't," Jared said, his eyes focusing on the static of the television screen.

"What about this?"

Bok retrieved Jared's microphone from under the bed and put it in his hands. Jared didn't react, and so Bok proceeded to put one of his band's CDs into the stereo. He wanted Jared to sing, anything to get his mind off the damn movies. The music suffused Bok's body, laved Jared in darkness. Though they were rookies at the time of this album's recording, the guitar, the melodies and the piano weaved together the sounds of future experts. Jared's voice was raw as rug burn, but it flowed naturally out of the speakers. Bok pushed the microphone against Jared's dry lips, but Jared refused to sing. When he took it away a piece of Jared's lip remained on the mic and a red jewel slid down his chin. But the music kept going. Bok fell headlong into memories. Jared became hostile.

"I just want to watch a movie!"

Jared got to his feet and knocked the stereo off the dresser. The music cut out and the room swelled with static. Bok would not let himself get mad for multiple reasons, mostly so that his anger would not fuel Jared's. After a moment of silence, Jared smiled, wiped the blood from his chin and then went back into the safe zone that was his bed. Bok touched his hair and a thatch of it came loose in his hands.

"I'm not a musician anymore," Jared said.

"Then what are you?"

"A moviegoer."

Jared got up again, this time heading for a shelf full of VHS tapes. Bok could not read the titles clearly, but he knew that they were all eerie, disgusting, and had no substance to them. The covers, from what he could see, were comically horrific. Here was a woman with swollen breasts dripping blood milk; here was a man whose tongue had been ripped from his mouth, squirming in the hands of the assailant. These movies were not made to make a person think. They were made to assist in their self-inflictions.

"I gotta see them…gotta see them…" Jared repeated manically.

"You're going to break them if you handle them with such carelessness," Bok said.

"No I won't," Jared spit at Bok.

"But if you do, how will you watch your precious movies?"

"I don't *need* these tapes to see the movies. They're all inside of me."

Bok moved closer to Jared, more so to read the titles. He could see now that they were all part of *The Chronology of Decay*. Jared put a tape into the VCR without announcing which volume it was, and so Bok wondered if they were starting from the first vignette. But then he remembered that it didn't matter in which order one watched them as the viewer would still be its instant victim.

"And now it's time to relax," Jared said.

A classic B Horror movie score rang out. The television set became a writhing thing of iridescence. Jared fired up the jet-flame lighter, placed two rocks on a spoon and melted them into an opaque liquid. The needle took in the light of the TV as he sucked back the syringe.

"This makes everything right," Jared said.

"Not in that same spot."

Bok hadn't realized how bad the wound had become until now. The crook of Jared's arm was necrotic, the skin black with an infection that was spreading fast. But Jared insisted on using this spot, despite Bok begging him to shoot into the knee cap or between the toes. His green eyes met his, the look in them ravenous, the bags beneath like sunken stars.

And the needle descended.

It penetrated the first layer, the wound around it pulsing dark and gelatinous. When Jared pushed the drug into his vein, Bok winced at the rictus grin that spread across his face. Jared only truly smiled when in the presence of sin.

Then he felt the change.

Bok's mind ciphered into an alternate reality where Jared was wide awake, red smile and drug-dazzled eyes. There was a camera and a pale walking stick in the corner of the room, its dull light waiting for the show. Jared turned over, the skin of his ass a double white moon. Bok felt himself get an erection. There was no lube, but he didn't need any. Jared was wet, *so wet,* and when orgasm found him, Bok felt a white hot pain claim him in the groin. When he pulled himself free he shrieked at the sight. His dick was a mass of shapeless flesh, the glans suppurating cum and blood. Inside Jared's hole, there were thorns crowning the sphincter, and a blade was lodged in the center.

"Do you like the way it tastes?" Jared said.

"No." Bok realized that he had been hallucinating.

Jared pulled the blanket up again. "I'm going back to my movie."

"Don't do this. Let's go see a doctor."

"I don't need any help. Just go away. Far away."

Bok did as he was told, pacing the apartment and wondering about his future. Jared was the love of his life, and he would take care of him through thick and thin. It was a promise he had made to himself the first day they met, when he noticed that Jared was a little too hyper, a little too insecure. But how could he have known that they were to become this serious? How could he have predicted that he'd love another person so much that it actually hurt?

"I was born this way. My mother told me that once," Jared said.

"She also abandoned you, most likely because of the same condition."

"My mother was young and raised me as best as she could the first few years of my life. That much I know."

"You still protect her." Bok shook his head. "That's why you won't get help."

"What could those fancy head doctors do besides rewire my brain with drugs? I've already tried that."

"They could teach you new ways to think."

"So then you'll have me suffer?"

"That's not suffering."

"It's suffering if you'll have them change the one thing that makes me...*me*."

Bok shook his head. "I can't take this much longer."

Jared turned his head and looked deeply into Bok. "Free me."

"What are you talking about?"

"When I watch your movie, I'm free. I want that power!"

"There's no movie."

"Free me! Let me go!"

Kill me.

The sound of Jared's scream echoed through the inner whorls of his ears, electrifying his brain. The noise was similar to the one he heard the moment before his ethereal body split from his physical one like an old skin. Bok could not explain the how or why that when the camera had pointed at him he became a changed being.

But Jared knew.

He saw and believed in things Bok never could. How does one accept that they could have broken the very laws of Lovecraft's geometry as all the molecules in Bok's blood, in his soul, had lined up to a single point of light, as if being pulled into the movie screen itself. It was a feeling he could not describe if he tried. It was trouble in Shangri-La.

"We could do it together," Jared said.

Before Bok could say anything, Laurenz was calling his phone again, begging them to come make something terrible so said the voicemails. He had alluded to scary things about Bok and his power, that he could do anything he wanted so long as he put his mind to it. He was miracle incarnate. Horror in the flesh.

"Why did you have to steal it from me?" Jared asked.

"I didn't do anything you didn't ask me to do."

"But you do it so naturally. How the fuck do you do it?"

"I don't want to argue. I love you, Jared."

"You love me, yet you take everything from me. You stole my sanity, my youth, and my art." Black tears ran down Jared's face.

"What do you mean? I've been a good boyfriend to you."

"No, you haven't. I never would have touched the stuff if it wasn't for you. Now you sit here and judge me. You're clean and I'm rotting from the inside."

Bok turned his head away.

"Look at me!"

Jared removed his clothes so that Bok could see bright pink ropes outlining his 8mm tattoo. The dream must not have been a dream at all. Bok watched him like a man does a stripper on her dais, vulnerable to her sultry dance. After the outburst Jared threw himself under the covers again, red hair falling gently onto the pillow, but not before putting a new tape into the VCR.

It was Sodom and Gomorrah, Abaddon on earth. The beings on the screen were neither alive nor dead. They slumped around, grey-wasted muscles lazily controlling their skeletons as they made carnivorous love. Smoke stacks rose high into the depthless sky, inducing an onslaught of acid rain. Skin melted off bones, holes were burned into the ground, foliage was torn down and whole buildings collapsed. Though Bok had had enough of the movies, a little part of him could not stop watching. He crawled his fingers toward Jared, worked them up the knobs of his spine, then curled them around his sharp shoulders and rubbed so that Jared would fall asleep. But Jared remained catatonic, and so Bok kissed the back of his neck, specifically the top of his 8mm film tattoo, tasting something faintly poisonous, something that burned his mouth as if the tattoo was not part of his skin anymore, but actual film itself. And then he lifted it a portion of it off Jared's body with his tongue.

A terrible thought entered his mind.

Free Jared.

Play the movie of his life.

* * *

The smell of the city washed clean, grey light and boiling neon. In the sky, twin moons orbited one another like a cosmic game of exquisite corpse, tearing holes into the atmosphere and plucking stars from their celestial clusters.

Bok followed Laurenz's directions exactly as instructed. The buildings here were older, timeworn and hunched as if passing judgement. Jared was slumped over his shoulder, rolled up in their black bed sheets like a cocoon. When Bok stopped at the traffic light he changed positions, holding Jared like how a man holds his wife on their wedding night. Limbs fell weightlessly against Bok's body; red hair covered his eyes. This love felt honest for the first time in a long time.

The way the moonlight hit the city was like a highly produced motion picture, but a picture he did not want any part in. Above, something was following his every step, not anything he could truly see, anything tangible, but he knew that it was powerful and that it had teeth, talons and wings. The way it whiplashed the wind, Bok thought it might tear a hole into the sky.

Bok bolted through an alleyway which then spit him out on an opposite avenue. He crossed a busy street to find himself right back in front of the alleyway. He did this a dozen times, the circular repetition maddening—same drab scenery obscured by a different light, the same faces peering out of tenement windows too afraid to walk the streets.

Then he found the door. It was heavy and made of wood, the antique knob something that looked like it had been taken from Dracula's castle. When he opened it there was a long hallway that he navigated with no light until he came upon another door that he had to shoulder open. Now he was on the other side of the city. Everything here was frozen in time—people obsessing over cell phones, the dusky skyline and even the smoke that shot up from the sewers.

Something glittery and soft drifted across Bok's vision. A feather, maybe hair, but when he looked closely it turned out to be what could only be a snake scale. When he looked up he saw gargoyles and chimeras crawling down from their skyscraper nests. But he didn't know if what he was seeing was real as the H was in his system. He could not do what needed to be done stone cold sober.

Now through another door, and Jared was beginning to wake. His eyes fluttered and his dry tongue escaped his mouth searching for nourishment. Bok could have torn that flaccid meat easily from Jared's mouth, but he shook away that thought and continued on, following Laurenz's trail of crumbs until the smell of the decaying infrastructure became too real.

The warehouse was on the verge of collapse, but he went down the honeycomb stairwell anyway, drowning in the absence of light. For a moment he felt dizzy, as if he would drop Jared, but he did not want to see him explode like delicate glass on the floor. He righted himself, lit a smoke, and as the swirling stopped and the bright specks melted away, he saw the words twinkling like the ghost fish of abyssopelagic waters.

Freedom from pain.

Suffering is bound only to the external world.

Bok put Jared down gently and ran his finger across the art, smearing it into one blurred image. Down at his feet the black cocoon wriggled in protest. Bok kicked it near the head so that it stopped, then picked it up and moved along. The next room was a murder scene of acid rock posters and memorabilia; blood starred the walls and a sticky fluid reminiscent of plasma dripped slowly onto his face.

"Mmmm...cold," Jared said weakly.

"Almost there," Bok assured him.

At base level, just when he thought he could descend no more, a traction elevator waited. Down, down, down, metal edging along concrete, and the rusted cables pulled so tight they could snap at any moment. The air was tinged with effluvia. A dull blue light thrived and then died, sort of like a projector burning out after a long movie. Bok realized that the elevator was plunging further than a basement or sub-basement, to a bomb shelter or bunker, a place where time and sound could not exist, a place where any terrible thing could happen.

At the bottom, Bok kicked open the grate and stumbled into a dingy room. No windows, no ventilation, just the stillness of the dark. Bok veered to the right as if entering a theater, passing chairs and surgical tools of every necessity. There was a big table with a plastic tarp covering it, and one spotlight.

They were not alone.

Laurenz greeted him at the head of the table, his sidelong smile and amethyst eyes like a highlighter slash. His pale walking stick thrust through the dark, pushing aside boxes and cans and metal instruments so that Bok could unwrap Jared down to his birthday suit. Laurenz turned on the lamp above their heads.

Bok could now see that none of the angles seemed quite right. There were no corners, no floor and no ceiling. The room was spherical, as if the walls blended with the floor, stretching into oblivion. The distance between him and Jared felt a mile long. But that could not be. He hadn't fought his way through a long enough tunnel that would explain the length, and he did not make a mistake of measurement as he squeezed himself through the small hallway to get to the elevator.

"The eyes see everything that is real," Laurenz said. "It's the mind that plays the tricks."

"What is this?" Bok asked.

"The final chapter of my movie." His German accent seemed to thicken.

Bok heard wings like razors in the air. Something crawled above his head, an invertebrate he could not see or feel, but he knew it would have tentacles and spit clouds of ink. It was something that was not meant live outside the deepest areas of the sea.

"Are you ready?"

Laurenz turned on the cameras. The sound of white noise and an old projector rang out. Not one, but over a dozen. Focus was directed toward Bok, filling his head with an indeterminable amount of pressure. The backs of his eyes throbbed all the way to his brain.

Blood tears streamed down his face, over his lips, staining his tongue red. Then sweet relief came as the twin globules slid free from his skull, leaving behind two holes rimmed in sludge. Bok felt his muscles sizzle, his skin stretch. His skeleton began to ache, the joints swelling and each spinal disc compressing. Muscle, fat and fascia melted away, the bones snapping like brittle twigs. He felt like an insect molting into its fiercest form.

In his ethereal body, he needed not the laws of physics or the rudimentary prattles of chemistry.

Jared stirred again. The necrotic arm looked blacker, the wound a gaping mouth hungry for drugs, but his eyes were wet as if he was sorry for taking it past the limit. Bok crawled two fingers up his slick arm, caressed the lip of the wound, then sank them knuckle deep into the gangrenous hole. He pulled down with all his might, suppurating flesh halfway to the wrist. Jared went rigid with terror and pain.

"If you stare too long into the camera, it will start to stare back at you," Laurenz said.

"I don't have to look into the camera to do this," Bok said.

"Good. Very good."

Bok threw the leather restraints over Jared's torso, then secured them to his wrists and ankles. There was no immediate protest, being that he was junk-sick. His skin was mottled and he was shaking beyond control. The 8mm film tattoo wavered in time with Jared's quickening pulse now that that he was fully awake and aware of what Bok was doing. Jared screamed for the Angel of Death, sweet goddess of narcotics.

"Why do you want hurt me?" Jared asked.

"Only I can save you," Bok retorted.

Despite fear, Jared's voice had begun to harmonize. Its music shattered against his pale chest, slithered out of the young throat. Bok knew the song well, one that Jared had always sung to him in times of disaster. Heroin and liquor, marijuana and cocaine. Those were Jared's tools of creativity, but also his one-way ticket to Hell. Bok almost let his imagination get the best of him, take him back to a small, dark club the night they met, a red-headed queen destroying her castle.

"You love that song," Jared said, and his hair was as red as the blood dripping onto the floor.

"I *used* to love you."

That was a lie, but he did not want Jared to get caught up in hope any longer. The movie was all that mattered. And so Jared began to sob, not for himself or his impending doom, but for not having anyone in the world that cared about him.

"No more talking."

Bok couldn't bear the sight of Jared's sweet lips or the melody of his magical voice any longer. There was only one way to shut him up. He opened the suture kit and tied heavy black nylon thread into a knot, securing it to the solid bore needle.

Jared's lips quivered. "What are you doing?"

"Hush little baby," Bok said.

"Jacob, stop it!"

"Don't make a sound." Bok elongated the last syllable.

"Please, baby."

"This is going to hurt—"

"Noooo!"

"—me more than you."

Bok vice-gripped Jared's jaw shut with a strength he never knew he had, pulling the lips that he once worshiped forward. He started at the center, piercing soft flesh and hooking under, intricately weaving the thread until Jared's lips were a black and red web. This brought about a strange silence, utter and final. Bok would never hear Jared sing again.

"I am dangerous even to myself," Bok said, "but I'll save you."

The beautiful face was sticky with blood, and each time Jared moved his lips the nylon threatened to rip through. Bok poured a cup of hot water onto the fresh wounds, to which Jared's chest rose in protest, his hand clenching and lips throbbing. But it had washed the blood clean from Jared's face so that Bok could continue.

He saw that the camera was still recording, red eye wanting more. He pushed Jared's head to the side so he could see it, but Jared did not accept the camera. He closed his eyes. Bok recalled a scene out of a movie Jared once forced him to watch, the cheesy title reminiscent of classic Italian splatter. *Dreading Heaven, Putrid Hell* was a story based on desire, sex and release. It focused on two men—a couple—reaching for higher sexual ecstasy via choking, cutting and hallucinogens. Bok remembered the cover art clearly—a man strapped to a bed, his flaccid genitals sitting dangerously between the blades of garden shears.

The devil made him do it, he remembered.

The surgical scissors were rusted, but would do the trick. Bok caressed Jared's soft sex, three little scraps of flesh Jared barely even used, then cupped them in his hand. Jared's legs tensed and his stomach heaved as Bok snipped the meat off with one clamp. The gelatinous testis fell out of the sac and splattered onto the floor. Crimson erectile tissue hung free as hair in Bok's hand. The wound was appallingly black, as if Jared was rotting from the inside.

"I expected more," Bok said.

"Do it," Laurenz said. "Taste him."

Bok lowered his face into the vomiting juncture. He wanted to sink his teeth in as far as they could go, all the way up the cavity to taste Jared's heart. The blood gave him a high unlike any he had ever felt before. There was no way he could stop, no way he could resist from reaching all the way up, tongue deep, then fist, until Jared's body welcomed him into its garden of poison. His hand butchered twisting intestine, velvet organs and spongy lungs before he grabbed hold of Jared's heart and ripped it free from the imprisoning ribcage.

"That's not enough," a sexless voice said.

"What do you mean?"

Darker than he expected, its mouth elongated like a viperfish, skin made of scales. The eyes were werewolf yellow. It limped forward, balancing itself on the table, scooping Jared's blood with its long fingernail. Bok noticed two stubs of meat where wings should have been, and for one betraying moment he felt terrible about it, that this creature made of Heaven and Hell was doomed to stay with inferior mankind.

"I've been stuck here a few of your decades," it said. "But for me that's a blink of an eye."

"What are you?"

"I'm the Devil, now kindly give me my wings." Its blue tongue licked the air.

"I don't know what you're talking about."

"You can't do anything right, can you?" It began to laugh mockingly.

"You laugh in the hour of my need?"

"That's not the freedom he was looking for," it said.

Bok looked at Jared's cold, dead face and closed his eyes. "But he can feel no more pain."

"He'll regret every moment of his life with if you don't do what you came here for!"

"I loved him."

"Then let him *go*."

The creature drew itself back into the darkness. Bok was left to the sound of dripping jaws and clicking nails. Now Jared was rising. Not like the repugnant dead he had seen in badly produced horror movies, but shimmering. It was a holy moment, to be able to appreciate this chance to be alive and breathing, no matter if Bok had already put an end to it in an alternate reality.

"What are you doing?" Bok asked.

Jared licked his candy apple lips. "I'm changing. Like you."

Jared was arching his back into a fierce parabola as if he was back on the stage. He began to sing about immutable horrors and drank liquor right out of the bottle. His voice was as effervescent as he had remembered, and it fluttered out of his throat like a colony of Death's-head Hawkmoths. In this moment Jared was pure. There were no signs of mood swings or track marks. But Bok saw the tiny video recorder doing what it does best: stare and challenge, taunt and steal.

Then he remembered that Jared said he wanted to make the movie of his life.

Bok never needed any surgical instruments or black thread. The only film left to see was already imprinted on Jared's body. Bok blinked once, then twice, not wanting to see Jared's tribal dance anymore. Once he focused, Jared faded away like turning a page in a book.

Cut scene.

Jared was back to being dead as dead can be on the table. Bok dipped his finger into the gore between his legs, marking the 8mm tattoo with his eyes. He started at the groin with the scalpel, creating a ribbon all the way up to the delicate curve of throat. Jared's skin was already cold and unexpectedly thick. It was as if Bok was cutting into a wax doll.

Bok used his nails to lift the tattoo off its meaty bed, peeling it like a sticker. As it got longer and longer, Bok carefully wrapped it around his arm in order to keep it moist and from pulling apart.

"It is done," Bok said.

Play it.

Bok wound the strip of Jared's skin around an empty reel, popped it into the projector and secured it before pressing PLAY. A watery red light flooded the wall as the images played. Two skinny boys approached the screen. One had long, red hair and was singing into a vector microphone. The other was dark to his light, drinking the melodies like liquor. In the next scene the red-head was throwing a fit until the dark one introduced him to the needle. When the scene fizzled away something was left in its place: a hole burned into the wall so bright it could penetrate one's dreams. A cornucopia nightmare.

Bok's hand penetrated the cipher, waiting for the rest of his body to follow until he smelled burning flesh. He had forgotten to sever the tattoo from Jared's body and now the projector was unraveling his corpse like a luxurious mummy. It only took a few minutes until Jared was nothing but glistening muscle, before his soul melded completely into the big, burning screen.

* * *

The movie was to begin at midnight.

Shadows filled the theater, pious gurus with fingers stained black from spending too much time in a dark room. Kids who seemed to always avoid the light, so said their bug-eyes. They wore costume jewelry and slathered makeup over their eyes in attempt to cover up the shame they felt in their soul and within the scars on their wrists. Liquor bottles winked beneath their trench coats each time they snuck a sip.

"Why are you doing this?" Bok asked.

"I didn't want to alarm you at first, but we *must* release your movie."

"It's not just a movie. It's an abomination."

"Yes, that's exactly it."

Laurenz was looking Bok square in the face. No projected delusion, no Wonderland or Oz, no whimsical tale of romance. The circle was now complete. The madness would be released. But Bok knew that the movie would only get into his head and make him miss Jared. Love does these crazy things to you, makes you surrender your soul, change it. Maybe love itself is a bad film on replay.

"What I've made of it is pure genius," Laurenz said.

"I did a horrible thing."

Bok turned as if to leave, but Laurenz took his hand and guided him toward a spiral staircase. Bok had two choices: follow Laurenz into the mouth of Hell, or bear that cross with all the other people in the theater. The choice was easy. He felt his way up the wall slowly, heading in the direction of the sound of machinery.

At the top of the stairs was an old wooden door, and once he opened it, the dim lights struck him accordingly. It was cool in here, the walls so thick no warmth could penetrate. There were rows of film reels stacked on metal shelves, four levels high and elbow deep. So much film in one place, so much condensed madness. Bok ran his fingers across the metal lips, careful not to damage the delicate film, and as he did this he could feel the dissemination of skin and soul stretching thinly.

"Why now, after all this time?" Bok sipped the last of his bourbon and threw the glass on the floor.

"Time has no bearing on destiny. It's nearly a burden."

Laurenz searched the shelf and then pulled out a reel. It appeared rusted in some places and thin strands of red hair hung off the sides. When Bok touched it, the rust turned out to be blood. The film itself was marbled with pale strips of what seemed to be skin, and now that Bok was holding it in his hands, he felt the world slip away from under his feet. A shriek filled his head.

"You never got rid of it," Bok said as a statement and not a question.

"I don't throw away magic," Laurenz said.

"Damn you to Hell, old man."

Laurenz let out a horrible laugh, took the reel from Bok, then fed it into the projector. Light saturated the room, revealing Laurenz's scarred hands that Bok now saw were not scarred at all, but were *actually* his hands, and that his skin had a tint of blue to it. Laurenz caught Bok staring him down, pursed his lips so that he showed off his broken teeth and then pushed PLAY.

"One never knows how people are going to react. I want to witness it this time."

Bok was well acquainted with the power that lived in this film and somehow had grown unavoidably attached to it. As the machinery clicked and clacked into place, he began to itch as if his ethereal body was ready to escape. But Jared had come to him, not through dream or anesthetic memory, but as if he had never died. Bok could feel his skin, his lips, and for the first time in the months since he'd been gone, Bok began to cry, guilty for letting Jared get sucked into Laurenz's sticky web of lies.

Hate him.

Smash him.

Kill him.

Erase him.

Bok put a small joint in his mouth and lit it. "What are you trying to achieve by witnessing people's reactions to this film?"

"Pure power."

The light from the projector glazed the audience. In his mind he implored them to leave, but they all kept shuffling in like good sheep, sharing cigarettes and candy and soda. The old theater that smelled of spiders and decay was now filling with curious, young life. It was a drastic juxtaposition.

"Your hands," Bok said. "They're not damaged."

Laurenz quickly gloved them, took in a deep breath and leaned upon his walking stick. "You're in no position to question me."

Bok was silent for a second, then let it all out. "You know what, I don't want your fucking money. I'd rather cash cans than stay here another second."

Bok turned to run, but Laurenz said, "He forgives you."

Bok froze. "Shut the fuck up!"

"He's not mad or sad or alone. He wanted everything that you did."

"Stop that!"

"It wasn't on purpose. It was the way things were written."

"Are you trying to tell me that Jared's death wasn't my fault?"

"It's what he wanted. Why can't you see that? He chose you to fulfill his desire," Laurenz said.

"And I was weak enough to do it."

Bok was overcome with a feeling of fight or flight. His feet took him fast to the door. Sweet escape was just on the other side, but Laurenz's penguin flipper had already pushed it closed. He was unclothed now, and breathing hard. Bok saw no sex between his legs, no nipples on his chest. His skin had transformed into glistening blue scales, his teeth sharp and shiny as glass. The eyes were a stark yellow.

Fallen Angel.

"There is a force," Laurenz said in a bitter voice, "that controls neither you nor me, Gods that have been roaming through dark matter and wormholes before you were even stardust."

Bok took a step back. "Isn't the concept of good and evil a mammalian construct?"

"There is no single God, no pearly white gates. There's only everlasting existence, now and forever."

"Purgatory." Bok clenched his teeth hard enough to break them.

"These forces have been around since the Big Bang. We're all elemental particles compressed together by the universe's little sister, gravity. They play with us, they mold us, they want us to make bad choices."

"Why are you personifying eternity?"

Laurenz let out a ghastly laugh. "When you've seen whole planets eat one another and entire galaxies blown to dust, only then will you've earned the right to talk such foolishness. Until then, keep your mouth shut and learn something."

By now the theater was at capacity. Bodies leaned against the wall and filled the aisles. Bok thought about Jared again, unlocking the memories of him that he'd kept hidden as every single artfag, metal head and wannabe hipster looked just like Jared, at least in this light. It was disappointing.

"What do you need them for?"

"They're the next generation of learners."

The movie blazed upon the screen, filled the theater with bottled thunder. Bok could not watch the scenes slowly crescendo, could not embark back on that same tour of destruction. He distanced himself from Laurenz's cold, purple gaze, edging closer to the projector. His hand found the OFF switch, but when he flicked it, nothing happened.

Rather, the aching began when he smelled the burning the red hair. This time he chose a new body, one that refused to walk the world alone. A body that no longer wanted to read into prophecy or take part in evil, a body that simply needed to be with his boy. And so pain transformed into illusion as Bok fed himself into the machine to be with Jared.

The world closed its curtain.

* * *

Sometime in the future, a crowd of moviegoers enter a theater that feels more alive than anywhere else they've ever been. The seats are damp and the aisle is slick with something warm and thick. A movie begins to play. There is no dialogue or musical score, just a catalogue of pain, and so the audience is left to their own interpretations.

In that same night, an angel finds its wings.

When the movie ends, the crowd removes themselves from their sticky seats, cautious and marking one another with worry as the first echo of violence tears into the night.

AFTERWORD

I'm a very slow writer, unstructured. What should be an infinitesimally small space between synaptic clefts, more often feels like miles. The receiving neurons sometimes don't want to send out the necessary signals to the next one; they ruminate all emotions rather than allowing them to flower into an idea. The writing process, in all honesty, is a burden. But this is how I work, because when I finally line up all the particles of my creative energy, it's like a big bang.

But, I digress.

The point is I just don't write as fast as I want to.

Picture this: I was invited to *I Can Taste the Blood* by The King of Pain himself, Mr. John F.D. Taff. According to my email log, it was on December 16, 2013 when John officially asked me to sign on. That's a time long ago, but the kicker was that two other extraordinary writers had already accepted his offer, Erik T. Johnson and Joe Schwartz. We all lightly discussed the idea, and then were left to our imaginations. I confess I had no clue what I wanted to do, what area of horror I wanted to explore, but John is such an inspiring person—someone who I was lucky enough to share a ToC with in *Ominous Realities*—that I accepted blindly.

December 2013 was when I finished up the first draft of my second novel, *Blood Kiss*. I admit I could think of doing nothing else with my life. I had put all my energy into the book, not to mention I was on my first deadline: I was preparing to send it to Kathe Koja, who had offered to help me with it (blurb included) and John as well. I was a mental wreck! And then John just had to come out of left field and tease me with this new awesome project! I remember thinking to myself *don't do this, you can't handle another project.* My brain had been wrung of all its creative juices; every single emotion that was once inside of me had been ciphered into *Blood Kiss.*

But I had made a promise.

A year slipped by without us talking too much about *I Can Taste the Blood.* For me, 2014 was spent editing *Blood Kiss,* moving to a new apartment, new job, and getting used to my new life. Fast forward to the beginning of this year, my first two beta readers had already read their copies of *Blood Kiss.* Kathe snail mailed me her in-depth review with recommendations; John emailed me his take on the book. I took their advice and fell headlong back into the pages, once again ripping my focus away from what should have been the brainstorming for this project. Lucky for me the final review was very fast, and now *Blood Kiss* is done and slotted for a 2016 release.

Phew!

I needed a break. I remember looking at the calendar and seeing that I had lost a year with no words written for *I Can Taste the Blood.* I feared the worst, of course, that I would never come up with anything. I didn't share my feelings with John, Erik or Joe at all. I didn't want to embarrass myself. I simply tried not to think about it, praying to multiple gods that the muse would soon pay me a visit.

Then one day John emails and says that he's brought on a new guy: Josh Malerman. Josh is hardly "new" to the field, but to the secret project he was certainly new. I admit this lit a fire in me—a fire I was not expecting. I'm not sure if it was the threat of competition, or the inspiration that a writer I really liked was coming into the project, but it was the best thing that could have happened. Suddenly I felt like I could do this, that I didn't need to rely on plot, jotting down thoughts, *planning.* I just had to write and find out where the words would take me.

A camera came to mind (a subject I briefly explored in my first novel *The Absence of Light*), but also a sweet looking couple and how not even death could part them. Stories for me always start off with images, inkblots and blurs. I don't plot anything. I learn the narrative as I go along which is what makes it fun for me. The only savior, I think, is text messaging myself some lines, sticky notes and the occasional journal entry. Other than that I am blind person trying to see as I let my fingers go wild.

So there was this image of red hair and wings.

Films. Cameras.

What was I to do with all of this?

The impetus for the story, I admit, was my own obsession with movies. We come to movies at first unknowing, suspending our judgements until the credits roll. It's as if we freeze our free will for the entire duration, but once we come to understand what we have just seen, once we knead out all the surface tension, the feeling is craved over and over again like a drug.

So I ran with it. The seed had been planted into the loam. I began to write. I let go of all my constrictions and what I thought I knew and learned from having written two novels. I just wanted to feel like I was free and could cover any sort of subject matter that interested me. It's not about the blood and the guts (if not done artfully). That is ancillary to the true horror. For me, it's about how the body reacts when we are afraid—the feeling of fear itself or the anticipation of it—is an evolutionary process that is permanently wired into our brain. The "fight or flight" response we all have was wired into our evolution from the days when we were all running away from Saber-toothed Tigers and Wooly Mammoths.

Danger is perceived.

A trigger in the body is fired.

We feel *afraid*.

That biological inheritance interests me to no end. What does the brain of today, a slightly more intelligent brain, do with all of these archaic/evolutionary fears? Why do we still feel this even though the threat of our safety from giant creatures is long gone? And what would happen if we allowed ourselves to truly feel that fear? Would it change us? Would it drive us mad?

I wrote this story to try and figure that out.

Peace in Rage,
J. Daniel Stone
New York City
April 2016

ABOUT THE AUTHOR

J. Daniel Stone is the pseudonym for a hotheaded Italian kid from New York City. He has been a menace to society since 1987 and continues to terrorize local bookstores, art galleries and dive bars.

When he is not causing mischief, Stone reads, writes and attends as many rock shows as possible. He is the intermittently proud father of two bastard children: *The Absence of Light* (2013) and *Blood Kiss* (2016). Somewhere, out there in the dark, one can find more of his illegitimate spawns telling imaginative stories. Find him on Twitter @SolitarySpiral.

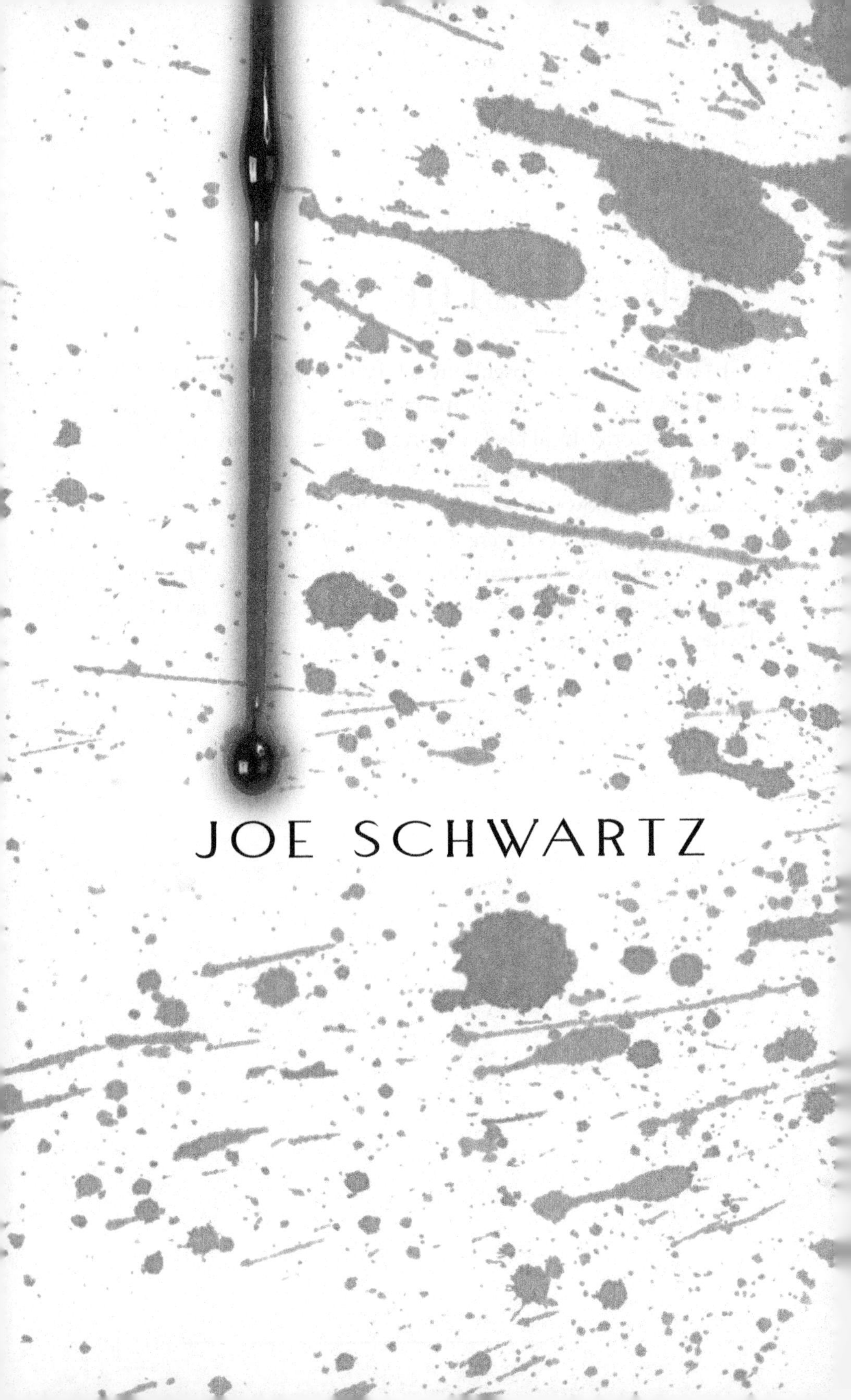
JOE SCHWARTZ

VISION III

I CAN TASTE THE BLOOD

How do you keep a dog from biting you on Monday?" Joe asked me.

"I don't know," I said. My toes and fingers were numb. I could see my breath inside the car, but I knew we couldn't risk running the heater. Two guys just sitting outside, practically the only car in the street on a Sunday morning, with a cloud of smoke coming out the tailpipe, was too obvious. We weren't going to make it much longer. If she didn't come out in a half hour, I hoped to convince Joe we should hang this shit up and try again later after lots of hot coffee, donuts, and pissing in a real bathroom and not into one-liter soda bottles.

"You kill him on Sunday," he said.

It was funny but I didn't laugh. I was exhausted. It had to be at least the twentieth joke he had told me since we parked the Toyota. Still, I smiled and nodded my head, hoping to stay on his good side.

Joe had a reputation for taking little shit personally, like not saying "God bless you" when he sneezed, or taking the last handful of peanuts without asking, or not laughing at his jokes that were more odd than funny. It was rumored he had killed a guy who had the audacity to ignore him when he'd asked for help loading boxes into a van. The boxes made it to the drop, but the other guy was never heard from again. Rumor or fact, I'm not sure, but I do know this: the shit we do is not for the weak or the brave. It's for fuck ups and scoundrels that don't have a damn thing to lose. Every story I ever heard about Joe is most likely just bullshit. I realize that. It's been my experience, though, that every urban legend has its roots in some kind of weird truth. Like my Uncle Ray said after somebody asked him how it was to do twelve big ones in the state pen, "A crazy motherfucker ain't got no limits."

"You like football?" Joe asked.

"Not really," I said.

"What are you, some kind of fag?"

"No." Although it was a relief not to suffer through another one of his morbid one-liners, having my sexuality called in for examination pissed me off. "I just don't see the point."

"The *point* is to hurt a motherfucker," Joe said. "Smear the queer," he added. A jab, I suppose, at my newly discovered homosexuality.

"A guy throws the ball, a guy catches the ball. Big fucking deal."

"You gotta watch just one guy. The center is who I keep my eye on. Those guys are enormous, strong as fucking tanks. Fuck the pansy quarterback and those ball-hog running backs. If it wasn't for the frontline, those pricks would be dead meat."

I appreciated his little lesson in athletic dynamics. Pro sports, to me, were barely an excuse for people to forget how pitiful they actually were in the real world. I don't begrudge the athletes. It's got to be a hell of a thing agreeing to become a personal god to cheering, delusional, blood-drunk assholes each and every season. Christ, it's a wonder faces of men like Caligula aren't still being printed on money.

"Thanks," I said. "I'll do that."

I was about to suggest we get some breakfast when the door opened. Joe saw it the same time I did. The girl was as she had been described: late twenties, skinny with long blonde hair that, today, she was wearing in a ponytail. She liked pink. Everything she wore was some shade of Pepto-Bismol: from her neon headband; baby doll shirt and matching fuzzy fleece pajama pants; to her pink-laced, white cross-trainers that I noticed she wore sockless; to her down-filled duster with a white fur-lined hood.

Her little white dog's pink nails clicked over the sidewalk, reminding me more of a sewer rat than a beloved pet. Caretaker said she would be out sooner or later to walk the little rodent. That was how we would catch her.

Joe smiled at me, barely able to contain himself as he pulled the ski mask over his chubby, red cheeks. He was a kid in a candy store. I didn't share his enthusiasm for this work, but it beat the shit out of driving weed cross-country from the Emerald Triangle to Miami. Those jobs made watching paint dry look interesting. Sitting behind the wheel of some piece of shit American car with the cruise set a whisker above sixty, driving twelve hours a day, knowing that if a cop got his snout through your window you were going to jail in whatever fucked-up, middle-of-nowhere county you got busted in because no one was coming to help. That was a year or so of your life spent shackled in some lower-level lockup, awaiting trial in the state's superior court, mopping concrete floors with cold water and no soap just to pass the time. There was no way to make a deal, there was no one to rat out, no bigger fish for some overworked DA to fry in your place. You were fucked.

The cars all had fictitious registrations that couldn't be traced to anyone. It was a dead drop and anything from dope to a mutilated body could be in the trunk, which was none of your business. It was, however, your problem. Somebody had to do the time. Most guys did the runs for years and nothing ever happened. Other unlucky assholes got busted on their first delivery trying to beat a yellow light at four in the morning. Life was not fair.

I grabbed the girl from behind. She was light and weak. Even as she struggled I could've carried her under one arm like luggage without a handle. Joe kicked the dog and sent the poor fucker flying in the air like he was going fifty yards deep for an extra point. As the little thing whimpered, sailing over a parking lot fence and landing in a wet motionless flop on the asphalt, Joe raised his arms straight above his head.

"And it's good," he said.

Despite his ski mask I could see him smiling, gloating over his effort. I wished he would die, right now, a massive stroke or coronary, real hand of God shit. Effortlessly and very much alive, though, Joe jogged past me, opening the trunk of the car that had already been lined with some heavy blankets and a small square pillow, the kind you might see on grandma's couch with the words HOME, SWEET HOME embroidered on by hand.

Joe helped me shove the girl inside, even though I didn't need it. I heard a distinct *thunk* as her head made contact with the metal floor. She was crying, scared of us, not knowing what the hell to expect next. I wanted to get in the car and go, but old Joe just couldn't resist making it a little bit worse. He was the kind of guy who laughed in a stranger's face after watching them fall down the stairs.

"Quit your bitchin'," Joe said. He slapped the trunk shut, then banged on it with the palm of his hands. It seemed loud to me and I was standing next to him. I could only imagine how awful it must've been for her in there.

* * *

We drove for the better part of two hours. Caretaker had us a place ready and waiting in the middle-of-fucking-nowhere *Missourah,* where only the dogs could find us. I could hear the girl bleating occasionally through the backseat.

"What do you know about this thing?" Joe asked.

"A little," I said. "She saw something. I don't know what, but it was bad enough to get her on Caretaker's list."

"That's no shit." He smiled, sharp and wet. It was the kind of lunatic grin guys get while watching depraved shit like pit bull fights and donkey sex shows. Like me, Joe had a reputation for getting unpleasant things done.

* * *

It's a curious thing when you figure out there is no hope. It was Christmas day and I was sitting in a booth at the One Eyed Jack feeling sorry for myself, drinking double bourbons. There were others there, a few guys at the bar, another shooting pool with himself, but it was quiet enough to hear the cars intermittently passing by outside.

I had four of Kentucky's finest before I finally gave up and went to drain the old dragon. My pop used to say that. I thought it was the funniest goddamn joke in the world. Dead for over a decade now, and it still made me smile to remember him. I was facing the wall, minding my own business, when a stranger took the urinal to my left. I read the graffiti on the wall doing my best to ignore him. If it could be believed, Linda gave great head, but…so did Jimbo.

"How's it going?" he said. "Holidays. What a pain in the ass."

I nodded, trying to shake my pecker free of dribble. It wasn't that I'm against small talk, but not when I'm holding my dick in my hand, and absolutely not when I'm in a men's room. A sacred rule I thought all men observed. Normally, I'd just zip up and walk out. The way I figured it, my schwanze was cleaner than my hands by a mile, but I had gotten piss on my palms trying to close up the camper. Before I could rinse the soap off my hands and get the fuck out, the stranger was next to me, chatting me up again like we were old pals.

"Yeah, this time of the year is nothing but bullshit anyway. Buy, buy, buy! Between the fucking stores, the churches and the goddamn television specials, it's enough to make a guy go nuts."

I left the water running, leaving him in the bathroom talking to himself. At my table, a new bourbon was waiting for me. Rings of condensation shimmered on the dark wood like coins at the bottom of a wishing well. Just as I was about to put the thick glass tumbler to my lips, my chatty pal from the men's room drops onto the worn blue velvet bench across from me. He had an identical tumbler in his hand, clicking it against mine, spilling booze from both our glasses. The man held up two fingers, signaling the bartender for another round. I was about to get up and leave him there when he grabbed me by the forearm, a powerful grip I never would've guessed he had, one I couldn't have broken without somebody getting seriously hurt.

"The way I see it," he said, "you got two choices."

"Is that right?" I asked.

"You can sit back down, be polite and have a drink with me and listen to what I have to say. Or you can leave, go back to your pity party, and never think about me again as long as you live. Ball's in your court, but you look like a smart guy, somebody who can recognize an opportunity when it falls in his lap."

I sat back down.

The stranger relaxed his grip but didn't let go of me until my ass was flat again. I listened carefully as he explained how he represented a select list of clients, persons who preferred as much anonymity as their money could buy. Sometimes these people needed something picked up and delivered, other times they might need you to answer a phone, things like that. Simple shit. Any moron could do it.

"So why don't you go get a moron. It's not like the world ain't making more."

He laughed like it was the funniest thing he had ever heard. When he reached inside his coat, there was a moment I worried he was going to pull out a gun, grease me right here in this bar while he was still laughing. I imagined he would walk out and nobody would be able to describe him. He was thin, but not skinny. His hair was turning silver. But then again, maybe he was completely gray. He wore gold, wire-rimmed glasses. Or were they black frames, or were they sunglasses? Nothing seemed to distinguish him. It was his absolute calm, his inability to be disturbed by irrational people or ridiculous situations that made him seem like a ghost among the living. He handed me his card, CARETAKER - SERVICES stamped in gold leaf above a phone number.

"What area code is this?" I asked.

He stood to leave, smiling without a care in the world, or at least he sure as hell seemed that way to me.

"California," he said. "Hollywood, to be specific."

I called him before I went to bed that night. The next morning, a kid no more than fifteen years old came banging like a fucking cop on my door. He didn't say shit except to ask if my name was Sam before pushing a sealed envelope into my hand, one of those postage prepaid numbers they send out with credit card offers.

"Here," he said.

Inside it was twelve hundred dollars. My phone began to ring as I counted the cash for the second time.

"Did you get the money?" Caretaker asked.

"You know I did," I said.

Two hours later I was standing on a corner when a man came up and handed me a plain brown box that could've been used to ship office supplies like pens or a page-a-day desk calendar. It had been sealed with packing tape as if what was inside could escape. I took it, like I was supposed to, tucked it underneath my arm and walked away. The guy who handed it off to me didn't so much as blink. He wore old jeans and a faded Cardinals hat, trying to dress down, but his shoes gave him away. Alligator boots—the real deal, which cost more than my car—that nobody in this neighborhood of tire shops, storefront churches and abandoned fast food joints would ever notice.

I knew what was in that box the second I took it. The weight, the curious shift inside as I put it under my arm, those were all the clues I needed. I drove to an address Caretaker had given me—a Christian daycare center for seniors—and parked on the street. No one so much as peeked through the curtains as I walked through the alley. There was a privacy fence surrounding the dumpster. When I closed the gate behind me, I might as well have been invisible. The dumpster reeked of shit, piss, puke and blood. I involuntarily gagged as I lifted the heavy plastic lid and tossed the box inside. Jesus, I pitied the poor asshole who would have to crawl inside this pile of shit to get find it.

As soon as I got back to my car I lit a cigarette and rolled down the windows, but the stink followed me like a bad dream. Two hot showers and ten beers later I finally, thankfully, couldn't smell it any longer. I did, however, wonder about that box.

Three weeks later another kid, this one fat and some kind of Asian who could've been Korean or Japanese for all I knew, handed me another envelope. I took it and closed the door in his sad face. If he was waiting for a tip or handshake then he was shit out of luck. When the phone rang I had counted the money only once, two grand and all in hundred dollar bills. I suppose that first time was to test me, would I do what I was told exactly how I was told to do it? Does two plus two equal fish? You bet your ass it does! I could have opened that box when I was shut in behind the gate. Nobody would have seen me. Then again, I knew somebody would know. That's just how this game is played.

Guys who did what I was getting paid for were nervous by nature. Somebody, somewhere, had their eye on me the whole time, probably on the guy in the alligator boots, too. He did his job, I did mine and now someone else needed to think about what to do with us. I understood two things with eyes wide open about this business. First, I wasn't being paid to think. Second, I could never say no. It would only be a matter of time before both those rules wouldn't work for me any longer. I figured I wouldn't think too hard about it until the shit hit the fan. In the meantime, I could use the money.

* * *

My mother used to tell me little boys who played with matches wet the bed. She assured me pissing in bed like a goddamn baby was just about the worst thing any big boy like me could be accused of, or at least outed for, in front of his booger-eating buddies. I hadn't thought about that in years, decades really, not until I began to pour five gallons of regular unleaded over the hood, roof and trunk of a cherry red BMW with vanity plates reading ISUE4U.

I had followed the driver, a tall, overweight guy with a crown of surprisingly lush brown hair, from an office park to a one-story ranch less than fifteen minutes away. He stopped at a McDonald's before going to the house, and from what I could tell, he ordered two plain hamburgers; no fries, no drink. If he was rich, then he wasn't proud. The singular luxury he seemed so far willing to provide for himself was the car.

I watched him go to the house just as Caretaker said he would. He wore a black suit that didn't fit him well, like he had bought it secondhand at a thrift store. When I saw the tall brunette at the door wearing a see-through black teddy and holding a purebred chocolate Chihuahua in her arms, both wearing 24-karat-gold chains around their necks, I realized why this guy didn't give a shit about extravagances like good food or nice clothes. What he liked was to fuck pretty girls. Whether it was two in the afternoon or four in the morning, and that type of grateful pussy don't come cheap.

I waited for about ten minutes after he went inside. Something told me he was billing some poor asshole back at the office by the hour while he got his rocks off.

When I got close to his car, I could tell it was worn. The seats were threadbare and there were a few spider cracks in the windshield, but the tires were new and I bet you could eat steak tartare off the engine. This thought amused me as I poured the gas.

Unlike in the movies, where the hero drops a match or a lit cigarette and blows up the secret hideout of his arch nemesis, I knew a little something about eighty-nine octane. It makes one hell of a bang.

* * *

When I was eighteen, I had been trying to earn a living working for an alcoholic landscaper named Roger. He was a real bum who had gotten lucky when his prick of an Irish father had the decency to drop dead before his sixtieth birthday, leaving him a business worth at least a half-million dollars. By the time I came aboard, the old man was just a name on the side of a truck, and Roger was down to fifty grand yearly in clients who still tolerated his fat, drunk ass. Old people mostly either too senile or too blind to realize he was a worthless piece of shit.

He watched me, drinking from a flask in the truck, as I raked for three hours. I pulled the crisp, dry leaves together, piling them neatly into a small mountain. Raking leaves for Roger was far easier and better than digging ditches in the hot sun all day, but still, it was a big yard, over an acre of hilly grassland with plenty of oak trees. The limbs were now barren, bird and squirrel nests once invisible under the green leaves became obvious and vulnerable. When I finished, the leaves stood slightly higher than I was tall.

It took me a while to shake Roger's drunk ass awake. He came to when I gave his fat, rosacea-stained cheeks a nice sharp smack. His blistered eyes looked sore and hot. He could barely focus on me or what I was saying.

"All done," I said.

I pointed over my shoulder with my thumb. A certain pride came to me, in spite of having done such menial labor. I had worked hard, done what I had promised. Now all I wanted was my fifty bucks and to be on my way.

"Ya gotta burn 'em," he said.

"Are you fucking serious?"

"Gas is in the back." Roger was grinning like a stroke patient, half his face sliding off his jaw, mocking me as he pointed over his shoulder. He belched in my face, and it took every ounce of self-control I had not to strangle his fat ass on the spot.

I found the red metal can underneath a tangle of shovels, brooms, an axe and a bent STOP sign that I figured Roger probably threw in here while driving drunk in an effort to hide the evidence.

I shook every drop of gas over that pile imagining it was Roger's blood. The smell of the gas was intoxicating. I couldn't help but breathe the fumes deep into my lungs, enjoying the cheap high. It shocked me that Roger wasn't here with me, getting some of this, but then again, he was one lazy son of a bitch. I don't believe he would walk two feet to pick up the remote control if it meant so much as a pinch of discomfort. *Lazy bastard,* I thought as I struck a cardboard match.

What I remember is an intense, bright flash and just the briefest sensation of heat. Next thing I knew, a fireman was giving me mouth-to-mouth. I choked and spit as the smoke in my body evaporated, allowing oxygen again into my lungs. The fireman helped me sit up. His jacket smelled like a barbeque pit long after the coals have gone white and turned to ash. There were a few of his colleagues standing around the heap of black, moist ground where I had lit the leaves on fire. Aside from second-degree burns on my face, arms and hands, the loss of my eyebrows and eyelashes, and Roger welching on that fifty bucks, shit could've been a whole lot worse. Some things you never forget.

* * *

Experience being the great teacher it is, I put the empty gas can back in my trunk and got out a road flare. I took off the white plastic cap with a *pop* that reminded me of a champagne cork. The irony made me laugh. I struck the flare like a match. The burning sizzle of potassium nitrate bit my ears, and the deep stink of sulfur scorched my nostrils. I tossed the road candle lightly overhand, watching as the white hot fire tumbled end over end toward the car.

Despite my being across the street, the wave of heat from the explosion gave me a mild burn. A gust of wind from the bowels of Hell itself hit me as the gas detonated. I watched with an arsonist's delight as the initial blue flame, brief as a newborn baby's smile, engulfed the car. The following explosion caused me to lose my equilibrium for a moment. When the world came back into focus, car alarms were blaring all around me and neighbors—mostly retirees and big-hipped, stay-at-home moms—were coming out, curious, scared, but secretly hoping for some excitement. Nobody saw me. The burning car, an automobile engulfed and sending great plumes of black smoke into the sky, was an excellent distraction. I could already hear the sirens in the distance.

I casually drove away past speeding cops, fire trucks and a single ambulance. My face hurt, like when I was a teenager out drinking all day while floating on the Meramec River, having no idea I was burnt until the sun went down. I stopped at a Walgreens and bought a bottle of blue jelly that promised instant relief from sunburn. It smelled strongly medicinal and was as sticky as cotton candy, but goddamn did it work. Within a minute I was driving along, smoking a cigarette as memories of a thousand lazy summer days were awakened by the salve's smell.

***

It went on like this for months. Every time an envelope got delivered it was by some new kid. I liked this, admired it, the consistency and efficiency. These nameless couriers wouldn't say shit if they had a mouth full. All any cop was going to get was the truth, that he brought me an envelope one time, which wasn't worth dick in any court of law that I had ever seen.

I never got less than five hundred dollars. Anybody could've done those jobs: slashing someone's tires, spray-painting racial slurs on a church, feeding poisoned meat to a dog—kid shit.

My favorite, though, was so simple it was ruthless, and whoever wanted it done had my deepest appreciation.

* * *

I went to the coffee shop, sat at the counter and ordered a grilled cheese and OJ. The place was busy, I suppose, because it was cheap and near a couple of office buildings within easy walking distance. Guys in ties and long sleeves ate at booths with women who had changed out of their dress pumps for lace-up tennis shoes that didn't do shit for their outfits but had to be a thousand times more comfortable. A phone rang constantly near the cash register and a middle-aged blonde, who looked older than she probably was, blew the hair from her face as she took the constant to-go orders. A couple of Hispanic guys were cooking on a grill so close to me I could've leaned across the counter and tapped either of them on the shoulder.

Despite the heat inside, the windows were cold and wet with condensation from the air conditioning. A little kid stood outside, pressing his nose against the glass, making faces at the people inside while his mother pretended not to notice, looking down the street for the bus. I was delighted to watch her grab him by his shirt and yank his disrespectful ass along like a dog on a short leash when the bus finally did arrive.

As the bus pulled away, I saw him. The guy was no bigger than any other guy, had a bit of a gut, but even at a distance, he looked like one angry son of a bitch. I watched as he walked from the modest parking lot across the street, clenching his jaw and puffing on the stump of a cigar the entire way. Gray at the temples and going thin on top, his bushy mustache was still black as coal. He wore glasses with lenses yellowed permanently from nicotine. The world deciding to ban his nasty habit from public places like his own restaurant only added more fuel to his fire. The indignity he nursed over such meaningless bullshit was exactly why I had been hired to teach this asshole a lesson.

The lone waitress, a cute girl, who might have been working her way through school or trying to support herself and her kid on minimum wage and tips, looked up when he walked in, spilling coffee on the counter. Nothing to worry about, nothing anyone could give a shit about, but she looked worried as hell. The guy walked over to her as if she had stabbed a customer in the eye with a fork.

"What the fuck, Lorraine?" he said. He took hold of her arm with a grip that made me wince. "Haven't we talked about this shit? If you can't do this job, I can find somebody who can."

The waitress was trying not to cry, but a small tear snuck out anyway. She waited for him to turn around before wiping it away. I desperately wanted to tell this guy to go fuck himself but if I did that he might remember me. What I was wearing, how tall I was, what kind of car I drove, all the relevant shit he could tell the police later, and that was counterintuitive to my assignment.

I put a twenty on the counter. The waitress had drawn a smiley face on my check. It reminded me of a love note I once got in the third grade. She really was a sweet girl, hardly old enough to drink, the kind that was probably great in bed. I hoped that she got out of here before she was too old to leave.

It wasn't very cold outside, but it was windy. I was finally able to light my cigarette before he came out. Of course, he walked by without making eye contact. Underneath his right arm was a blue bag, small yet bulging, with a gold zipper and the words 1ST BANK OF ST. LOUIS stamped in faded black lettering on the side. I flicked my lit cigarette at his head, the cherry striking the center of his ear like a mosquito on steroids. Frantically, he began slapping himself, desperate to stop whatever the hell it was that had gotten ahold of him.

"Are you okay?" I asked.

I grabbed him by his loose-fitting windbreaker, gently turning him toward me. It was wonderful to watch his face as he saw my fist coming, unable to stop me. My knuckles sunk into his cheek as he winced with pain. I punched again, this time swinging a haymaker of a roundhouse to his scorched ear. He squealed and fell to his knees, almost crying.

It disgusted me, especially when he held up the deposit, probably three or four grand in small bills, begging for me to please take it. I was drunk with anger. Raising my fist over my head I came down like I was swinging an axe. I crushed his nose, splattering it really, watching as mucus and blood poured down his face, his body slipping out of my grip, unconscious.

I picked up the bank deposit, got in my car and left. A kid came by the next day, and for a change I gave him something: the blue bag. Like me, he took it, and that was the end of that.

I've thought a million times about going back to that restaurant, finding that waitress and asking her to the movies or something, but I can't. She's everything I'm not. Where I couldn't become better, she could become worse. And that's the thing about this business. The dirt doesn't wash off.

***

Joe sang to the radio, cool as shit, driving along like we had done this a dozen times before. We hadn't. In fact, the only thing we had done before this was one of those things so remarkable I can never forget it. As far as I'm concerned, it changed me, made me worse. Joe probably dreams about it while stroking a giant hard on.

He had startled me at first, that bright November morning last year, when he showed up at my door. He filled the whole frame. I figured this was it, this guy was about to do to me what I'd been doing to other people. When he reached into his coat pocket I pulled my knife, damn near stabbing him through his bullfrog throat. He smiled, completely unafraid, deeply amused by my reaction, shoving a thick lump of cash in my face. Ten grand, all in new hundred-dollar bills, neatly held together with yellow-striped paper bands. I should've given it back to him, but it never occurred to me that I didn't want it. That's the beauty of ignorance.

It was nine o'clock in the morning and we were sharing a fifth of Crown Royal. Joe drove as I read aloud from directions I had printed off the Internet. He kept putting the bottle between his thighs while he drove, forgetting about it until I would nudge him for a sip. By the time we pulled into the motel parking lot off the highway, I had a nice buzz, balancing between being in control and getting shitfaced. I was happy to see Joe stuff the bottle under his seat, but a little concerned when he pulled a Smith & Wesson Colt Python out of the glove box. It wasn't that I was against guns. They were good. They made stubborn people move their asses and turned assholes into civil human beings. The only problem I had with this particular gun was that I didn't know what he needed it for.

The motel we parked at was on the cusp of deterioration. It desperately needed everything—paint, windows, a new roof—and I doubted that even one in ten of the AC units worked. Despite these immediately noticeable flaws, there were a dozen cars parked randomly around the pot-holed lot. The Toyota bounced in and out of the craters, small ponds filled with stagnant, oily black water. Joe held the gun in his lap as casually as he would a convenience store Styrofoam cup. It personally made me nervous. One hard thump, and *Bam!*, goodbye pecker. But Joe was the poster boy for calm. He almost looked bored as we cruised the lot. I was about to suggest to him he should let me hold the piece when he yanked the wheel to the left, jammed the transmission into PARK and declared, "This is it."

I lagged behind Joe getting out of the car. The whiskey had kind of gone to my head. I tried to shake it off, but my brain was buzzing with that familiar heat, and unless I could puke or sleep soon there was no choice but to at least try and act straight. The only problem was I didn't know what the job was. Joe smiled at me the way cops smile at you just before they sucker punch you in the gut. At least he had tucked the gun in his waistband and pulled his baggy sweatshirt over it. That meant we were knocking, not just kicking a door, blindly shooting like fucking cartel cowboys on a crystal meth binge.

A guy, who couldn't have been more than forty but moved like he was twice as old, opened the door for us. He smelled of cigarettes, reeked of them, like he had recently bathed in an ashtray. Joe walked past him like he wasn't even there. I couldn't help but stare a little as I came in the room. He wore lace-up dress shoes that had no shine left, speckled with bits of paint discoloring the plain black leather. His matching white painter pants and t-shirt were oddly free of paint splatter but had various black streaks of dirt, as if he had been rubbing up against boxes in a warehouse or crawling under a house. I didn't like him, but he seemed so utterly defeated that I considered him harmless, an old dog simply hanging on for his next meal, or to die, whichever came first. Joe went to the bathroom, closing the door behind him.

I stood on the threadbare carpet looking at all the ashtrays full of butts. The nightstands, the bed, the floor and the top of the TV were all cluttered with cheap aluminum ashtrays, the kind I hadn't seen around since I was a kid when it was considered acceptable to smoke inside McDonald's. Some were still smoldering, others had spilled, too heavy to contain another tap of ash, making more stains in a room already suffering from such neglect that it didn't seem safe to stay in any longer than it took to fuck or buy dope. I watched as cockroaches darted around the room, passing through practically microscopic holes in the walls, as if annoyed by our presence.

The toilet flushed and the bathroom door opened before the water could finish going down the commode. Joe seemed happy, more so than when we came in. I fell in behind him, following him to the front door.

The painter was lighting a fresh cigarette off an already lit butt. Successful, he squashed the hot one underneath his shoe, grinding it flat into the once-green Berber carpet. The smell of burnt fiber, dust and nicotine ruined the air. I wanted to ask why in hell he would do that. Even if the place was basically a shithole without a single redeeming quality, it was still his home. *Some fucking people,* I thought to myself as I closed the door, leaving the painter to rot inside his cancer castle.

Joe got the bottle out of the car, offering me a snort. He leveraged his fat ass onto the hood. The metal popped and sunk below his size fifty-six jeans. I wanted to leave, go find a nice Italian restaurant that served good wine with baskets of homemade garlic bread and fill up on *tutto mare*. Obviously, Joe had another plan.

"What the hell are we doing?" I asked.

"Waiting," he said.

"No shit."

"Why, you got a date?"

"Very fucking funny. Seriously, what are we waiting for?"

"It's a surprise."

"You're drunk."

"A little. This fucking Canadian is some smooth—"

The sharp pop was faint, like a soda can being opened in another room, but I heard it and so did Joe. He hopped off the car, leaving the bottle on the ground. At best there was only a taste left.

"Guess we go and see what we got," he said.

I followed him like I had before, up the stairs and to the door marked with a backwards number seven crucified in place by three slowly oxidizing finishing nails. This time Joe didn't bother to knock. He knew he didn't have to.

There was a black spot on the floor about the size of a quarter from where the painter had stepped on his butt. All the earlier cheeriness had left Joe. Each of his steps were firm and determined, a soldier on a mission. I stayed close behind him. The bathroom door was open. A still burning cigarette was balanced on the ledge of the sink. There were several previous yellow-to-black burns made in the Formica around the rim. It was a miracle the place hadn't burnt to the ground.

The painter was sitting on the toilet, still in his white pants and shirt, his dress shoes decorated in overspray, his eyes wide open and lifeless. Joe's gun was on the floor, dropped, I supposed, after the painter had pulled the trigger. By the blood, skull and brains that now decorated the wall, I assumed he had put it in his mouth. There was a small transom window near the ceiling. Blood was dripping down the pane. The sun had peeked out a little, causing a temporary stained glass effect, making the room appear mostly red.

Joe picked up the gun. He used the one and only white cotton bath towel in sight, which had yellowed with age, to clean it. The blood looked brown as he wiped the handle, muzzle and cylinder clean. Joe tossed the towel over the painter's face, covering his shocked expression, before putting the gun back in his waistband. I was about to turn around and leave, figuring this was the end of whatever this actually was, when Joe said, "Wait a second."

He pulled the towel off the painter's face and threw it to the floor.

"Hand me that," he said.

I hesitantly took the still burning cigarette from the sink. Joe's smile came back, a creepy grin that made me want to punch him in the throat. He set the cigarette in the painter's mouth, his corpse now nothing more than an ashtray itself. Joe laughed as I finally, mercifully puked.

We rode back in relative silence. Except for Joe's occasional cursing, or my asking to pull over for a piss, we hardly said a word. It wasn't until he dropped me back at my car that I had to know.

"What the hell was that back there, Joe?"

"That was our job,"

"Some fucking work we do."

"Nobody ever complains."

I watched as he backed up, turned, and then held up his palm to me as he drove by. *Jesus,* I thought to myself, *I need a vacation.* I hadn't had a cigarette since leaving the motel. The idea of smoking, for the first time in my life, seriously turned me off. By the time I reached Florida, I had officially quit.

* * *

Denise and I never married, but we did live together for three years. We had met in a bar called The Hideaway and had sex in the seat of my truck after closing time. She was nice and a good lay. Before we finished breakfast, we mutually decided there would be nothing to lose if we moved in together. As a corporal in the U.S. Army, I lived on the base and didn't have enough shit to warrant keeping an apartment off base. Denise had a one-bedroom place with a couch; a 19-inch color TV; basic cable; a five-drawer, pressed-wood dresser; and a queen bed without a headboard. The next night I dumped my shit on her closet floor, and, *presto,* we were living in sin.

I'd just spent two-and-a-half years of my life playing soldier and largely despising it. Being in the Army is sort of like prison but for Boy Scouts. You spend all fucking day pretending to do shit that matters. Not once in the recorded history of Western civilization has a republic been forwarded or halted by a bunch of swinging dicks knowing how to march or camp. I did like going to the rifle range but that was rare.

I had an easy MOS—or, military occupation specialty—as a light-wheel vehicle mechanic. After nine weeks of basic training, running and gunning, learning to kill with my bare hands, earning a sharpshooter medal and having the basic knowledge to make explosives out of shit you can find under any kitchen sink, I generally spent my time changing oil or replacing dead batteries in military vehicles. It took zero brain power, and I can't count the days I went in so fucking hungover that I wished I was dead. If Denise hadn't gotten pregnant, I might've re-upped. But the idea of having a family and being sent halfway around the planet to spread democracy didn't appeal to me.

We talked about getting married, but the bigger her stomach got, the more absurd it seemed. Being married wasn't for us. About a month after Samuel was born, I got out of the service. I figured it would be easy enough to get a job, but it turns out there weren't a whole lot of them to find. The stupid shit I'd done in the Army, like changing oil, was mostly done by ASE certified mechanics working in dealerships, union jobs that required somebody to vouch for you if you were going to turn a wrench. Three months later, as I worked in a bulletproof cell turning on gas pumps from midnight to eight for cash-only customers, watching while hookers waved down the passing cars and gave blowjobs in the vacant lot across the street, I knew I was shit out of luck. SOL, the most applicable of all the military jargon abbreviations I had ever learned.

Denise and I liked to talk about how someday we would look back on this and laugh. Somehow, there's nothing funny about damn near starving to death and not having health insurance when your kid has a double ear infection. That's when I first discovered this work, or, I should say, it found me.

* * *

I was shoplifting Similac from the Piggly Wiggly when somebody grabbed me by the collar. Without a whole hell of a lot of thinking, I spun into the abdomen of the store manager with my elbow. He was a fat bastard, and hitting him in his gut was like punching a parade balloon—some twenty-five-foot high monstrosity filled with helium—and about as subtle as a tidal wave. The air went out of old fatso loud and fast. His eyes burst open with shock, never expecting a fight.

I'm not some big guy, barely five foot nine with new boots on, but I have a gift that has saved my ass more than once: I'm just plain fucking mean.

When the cops came, I had fatso by his sweat-stained collar. I was smacking him across his inflated jowls, first with the flat of my palm, then back again with my knuckles. He dropped like a sack when I let go to raise my hands for the cops. I spent the next three days and two nights in the jail scrubbing toilets, washing municipal vehicles and painting an office. In lieu of further charges, I agreed to never step foot in the grocery store again and was given back my shoestrings. A free man, I hadn't walked a mile of the six back to my truck, which I presumed was still in the Wiggly lot, when the sheriff pulled ahead of me in the breakdown lane and threw it into PARK.

He got out and waited for me to come to him. I figured he was some kind of relative to fatso, and I was about to get my ass handed to me for what I had done. *Fuck him,* I thought. I had taken a hell of a lot more beatings than I had ever given. One more wouldn't make a difference, except, I wouldn't be fighting back. The thought tasted sour in my mouth, but assault on a civilian and assault on a cop were two very different charges. Seeing as I liked eating corn on the cob, I guessed I would keep my hands in my pockets.

When I got close enough to be spit on, he said, "Wanna talk with you boy."

I stopped but didn't say nothing because I knew there was nothing to say.

"You the one who whopped Jeff Monroe's ass over at the Piggly Wiggly?"

"I don't know the name, but I suppose I'm the guy you're looking for."

"Boy, you sure did ring that fat son of a bitch's bell."

I didn't say anything. It just seemed a matter of time before that nightstick came out and I was puking out last night's cornbread, collard greens and bits of ham.

"Ain't from around here, are you, boy?"

"No, sir," I said.

"Yankee?"

"St. Louis."

"That's all right I reckon," he said. "You taught old Jeff's redneck ass a good lesson. He ought not to do some foolish shit like that again anytime soon."

He smiled at me but I played it straight. Cops were the cruelest and most vindictive men I'd ever known. They don't let shit go and there ain't nothing worse than owing a cop a favor.

"Would you be interested in some work, boy?"

"Doing what?"

"I know a man needs a hand like you, somebody to remind others not to shit on him. You interested?"

"I am."

* * *

Jaycee Taylor was a large half-black, half-French Cajun with huge crooked teeth that were as impossible to ignore as his ridiculous bowlegged walk. His father was rumored to have been a police chief somewhere else, but Jaycee never talked about it. He ran a floating poker game that he called The Rodeo. Occasionally, he made loans to gamblers of good reputation at a modest twenty-five percent rate compounded weekly. Therein lay the problem, eloquently explained by Jaycee five minutes after I met him.

"All gamblers are fucking degenerate cocksuckers that would sell their momma's pussy to play another hand," he said.

We shook hands, laughing like old pals. It was clear enough what he was going to pay me to do.

The next year of my life was the stuff of dreams. I had plenty of money, more than I could spend, which meant Denise didn't have to work and I could spend my time with Samuel. My days were almost always free and we would go do things as a family—the zoo and the library, having ice cream in the park. And making love in the late afternoon while he slept, enjoying the sun on our naked bodies as it streaked through our dirty bedroom window, making us sweaty and slippery to the touch.

These were the things I thought about as I went around in the night trying to find the people on Jaycee's shit list. Banging on doors and windows, scaring families—wives and kids, mothers and fathers—demanding to know where their loved one was, that he, and sometimes she, owed Jaycee a whole lot of money and somebody was going to have to pay up or else. By the time the sun had risen yet again, my pockets would be filled with cash. That bought whoever another week to try and score big. Goddamn gamblers, I realized, are as hopeless as any dope fiend, powerless to stop no matter what the consequences.

It took me no time at all to realize what I was into. Finding these people was like shooting fish in a barrel. Casinos, racetracks and bingo parlors were good places to start. Then there were the sports bars that were known for their action. The last places I would look were the church basements and community centers offering Gamblers Anonymous meetings.

It was cruel, I knew that, but it was never too early to put steps eight and nine into practice. Mostly, I took what they had to give, never what they owed, and Jaycee blackballed them for it. The word went out among his secret society of shylocks that so- and-so was a lying piece of shit, not to be trusted, and if seen trying to buy into a game, they should call Jaycee so I could come take care of things. These were the worst, the bottom of the barrel as far as Jaycee was concerned. To give someone who owes you money a second chance and have them shit on you twice for it was the kind of shameless behavior he despised.

The worst of them was Marty. He owed Jaycee enough on markers alone to buy a new house. Marty and Jaycee went back to the high school football team, and no matter how much Marty lost, Jaycee kept covering his action. The night he told me to find him, I could tell he didn't want to. In this business, guys like Marty will wreck your reputation, make others think you're soft, an easy mark with no balls. That's where I come in. I'm the balls.

I found Marty at, of all places, an amateur wrestling match. Not that Greco-Roman shit like in the Olympics, but that crazy bullshit they show on TV, with guys in gold lamé nut huggers and shaved chests, with ridiculous names like The Crazy Czech and Mr. Millionaire. I grabbed Marty from behind by his hair. Although he screamed bloody murder, nobody tried to stop me. Maybe they thought it was just part of the show. Marty, though, had a bad reputation that preceded him in most places like the smell of dog shit in church. It was just as likely to think that nobody really gave a damn what happened to him as long as we took it outside.

Marty, much to his credit, was a clever son of a bitch. While I was smashing his face into a steel light pole in the parking lot, he pulled out a knife and stabbed me in the thigh. With the knife sticking out of my leg, a burst of adrenaline rushed through my brain as I jammed my thumb into his eye until it popped like a ripe grape.

It was three a.m. when Denise came to the hospital. She had suspected what I'd been up to. But until the cops called, she figured she could ignore it. While I sat in lock-up, charged with attempted manslaughter, Denise did what she had to and left.

It took me two years to find her again. She had a sister in Clearwater who had let her stay with her. Now she had her own place and was working as a bank teller. Denise said that if I came down, there would be no hanky-panky, but if I wanted to see Samuel, she could appreciate that.

I stayed for a week. During the day I went to the beach and at night I played with the kid while Denise made us supper. He was a beautiful boy with a smile that made me want to cry. We never said anything to him about me being his daddy. Far as the kid knew, his father had died in a tragic offshore drilling accident. That sounded a whole hell of a lot better than the truth, that I was a hired heavy who kicked shit out of scumbags for a living.

I hoped Samuel would grow up and become a dentist or a veterinarian, someone who could help people. Nothing like me. I'm sure my mom and pop thought the same thing about me, too. I guess we were all somebody's baby once.

In an effort to assuage some of my guilt, I put thirteen hundred dollars under Denise's pillow the day I left. It wasn't much, but it was what I could spare. I was sure it would help some. Denise had told me about a guy at the bank who liked her and had asked her out. He was in loans, ambitious as hell, and deeply in lust with her. I told her she was a fool to waste that kind of opportunity.

"I'm not a whore," she said.

"Never meant it like that," I said. "Eventually we all have to make compromises in life if we wanna get by."

That made her smile and she kissed me on the cheek before going to bed. I believe if I had stuck around another day, that guy at the bank wouldn't have stood a chance.

* * *

Joe was waiting outside my door when I got home. God only knew how long he had been there. If I had to kill him, right here in the hall, I could do it, but I preferred for him to come inside. By the time one of my neighbors complained of the stink, at least I would have a good running start on the cops.

"Where you been?" he asked. "On vacation?"

"Yeah. Something like that," I said.

"The man has been trying to get hold of you."

"I guess that's why you're here, right?"

"Exactamundo!"

"Well, you can tell him I'm back."

"It ain't like that."

"Right now?"

"Not just anybody can do what we do."

"I suppose not," I said. "But fuck me, I'm tired."

"Don't sweat that shit," he said. "I'm driving."

I unlocked my door, tossed my gym bag of dirty clothes on the floor and grabbed a beer from the fridge. There was one more beer left, a half full jar of grape jelly I think came with the icebox when I moved in and a half gallon of milk that had spoiled before I went to see Denise and Samuel. I handed the last beer to Joe who twisted off the top without so much as a fuck you before guzzling half.

The beer made something ping in my bladder. I left the bathroom door half open so Joe could hear me pissing. Otherwise, I figured he would stand outside listening, and this was the lesser of two evils.

"How's your kid doing?" he asked.

My heart thumped so hard my stream hit the floor.

"He's fine," I said. Freaking out, I tried to play it cool. "Getting big."

"Yeah, they do that."

Joe belched shamelessly, finishing the beer as I flushed and came out of the john. He seemed too proud of himself. My pop would've said he looked happy as a retard with a new rubber ball. Pop was an insensitive bastard, but he sure as shit could read people, which seemed to be all I ever got from my him, except a swift kick in the ass every now and then.

"Something on your mind, Joe?"

"No, not really. I just never figured you to be some kid's dad, that's all," he said.

"Anybody can do it. All it takes is a girl."

"That's funny. You're a funny guy."

"Listen, Joe... Don't hurt him, okay?"

"Okay. But that's not what we do, is it Sam?"

"No, I guess not."

* * *

The girl was limp but alive when Joe and I pulled her from the trunk of the car. Her legs had gone to sleep, and she couldn't have walked if it meant winning a million dollars. Joe laughed as he grabbed her under the arms, taking generous handfuls of her tits in his palms as I took her feet. He pinched her nipples through her pink hoodie with a viciousness that made me cringe. She squeaked in pain, but didn't try to stop him. Even if she had, it wouldn't have discouraged him. If anything, her lack of interest probably kept him at bay.

Inside, Joe dropped her head to the floor while I still had ahold of her legs. The hardwood probably felt like a feather bed compared to the trunk. I set her feet down as gently as possible. She had begun to cry, and in an attempt not to comfort her, I followed Joe's example of getting a beer from a fridge filled with such essentials.

He had lit a cigarette and I filched one from his pack. I used his lighter too, before sitting next to him at a kitchen table barely big enough for one. I was distracted, unfocused, trying to forget about the girl. Joe hadn't stopped leering at her since he'd sat. I would have happily set the goddamn table on fire if I thought it might distract him, but nothing short of the hand of God could do that.

"What'cha thinking?" I asked.

"I'm thinking that I'm gonna fuck that girl until her freckles fall off," he said.

"Jesus. That's rape."

"Yeah, I guess you're right."

Raping women and killing kids is where I drew the line. The shit I had done, the pain I had inflicted, was all earned. Grown men who should've known better, who had fucked with the wrong people and gotten, in a sense, exactly what they deserved. I was just the means, the instrument of their destruction, a way for God to put the universe back in order. Their broken arms and legs, black eyes, swollen ears, missing teeth and the occasional missing thumb, were all warning signs to be observed by their fellow sinners that there were indeed consequences in this world. It was just a matter of time before a guy like me or Joe darkened their door.

"I'm gonna rape the fuck outta that bitch," Joe said.

A big laugh blew out of him like a ship's foghorn, interrupted by a loud, wet belch that he wiped away with the top of his hairy forearm. Before I could argue with him, or think to attack him, he was up and walking toward her.

Despite the pain, she climbed to her hands and knees, trying to escape. He kicked her hard in the ass, as hard as he had her little dog, driving her cheek-first to the floor. Joe stood over her as she began to cry full-body sobs that made her jerk and convulse involuntarily, as if she were having an epileptic seizure.

He could give a shit. His belt was loose and he pulled it from the loops. It cracked with a lion tamer's authority as he smashed the black, hand-tooled leather strap on the floor about two inches from her face. She screamed, and I goddamn near did, too.

"That's right," he said. "Cry and scream all you want, bitch. I like that."

He grabbed her by the ankle, and she kicked him square in the jaw with her free leg. For that she immediately got a punch to the ribs hard enough to make a grown man piss blood.

Joe reached for her waistband and pulled her track pants off with her shoes still on. He knelt down between her legs. He pulled the fractional pink G-string wrapped around her waist like a compound bow, breaking the elastic and tossing the halved underwear over his shoulder. He seemed almost delirious with happiness.

"Bullshit time is over," Joe said.

I couldn't do this, be a witness to this. The girl looked to me, her eyes pleading, wet with tears. Joe looked over at me, too, smiling a happy grin that disgusted me.

"You're wasting your time, sweetheart," he said. "He ain't gonna save you, are you, Sam?"

I wanted to scream, to attack Joe right there while he was at a disadvantage, kneeling and taking out his hard-on. The thing stopping me was that Joe was one big bastard. His hands alone seemed large enough to strangle a horse. A full foot and a half taller than me, his legs were as large as tree trunks. I suspected I might get a few good licks in on him, but soon as those oversized arms got around me, I would be fucked. He could use his strength like a vise to squeeze my torso, deflating my lungs as he cracked my sternum. I'll be damned before I'd watch this. Being the coward I am, I went outside to smoke.

I could hear him laughing at me, calling me a chicken-shit and a pussy from inside, slapping the girl harder than shit just to hear her cry. I just wanted to leave, take the car and get the hell out of here, but that was a temporary solution. Being on Caretaker's shit list already, and leaving in the middle of a job, was a sure way to end up in the emergency room or face down in the river.

It finally got to me when the girl began hysterically screaming for help. I had to do something, anything but just fucking stand here. Win, lose or draw I had to take my chances because going to sleep knowing I could have saved her, or at least prevented her from getting murdered, was not something I was willing to try and learn to live with.

The car was unlocked and I was grateful for that. Having to go back inside to dig the keys out of Joe's pants didn't seem doable. The .357 was where it had been before, in the glove box. I pushed the release and the barrel fell out to the side. All six chambers were loaded.

It occurred to me, briefly, that our final orders might have been to kill this girl. That could explain Joe's sudden, enthusiastic lust. Maybe he knew my limits when it came to women and would force me, somehow, to pull the trigger. I didn't think I could do that either. Jesus. I was damned if I did nothing and no better off if I went along with this horrible shit. To hell with it, I thought, as I snapped the barrel in place and walked back to the house. I'm no hero, but I wasn't going to do this, be Joe's accomplice to rape while being blackmailed to murder some girl just so I could go back to drinking beer and watching TV until the next job came along.

Joe didn't look up or behind him when I came back inside. He was having a hell of a good time. I was so angry, I could hear my teeth grind together.

"Get up," I said.

"Fuck off," he said. "It's still my turn."

I leveled the pistol to his ear and cocked the hammer. "Get off her. I ain't gonna say it again."

"Go fuck yourself, homo. Besides, you ain't got the balls."

The shot was loud inside the little one-bedroom house. The explosion rang in my ears, causing me to go deaf for a minute, so much that I didn't notice Joe hit the floor face first, or the girl scream. Her voice came to me like a distant siren, hard to make out at first until it was the only thing I could hear.

"Get him off me, get him off me, get him off me!"

I set the gun on the floor next to her and pushed. Joe was ten fucking times heavier dead than he ever was alive. Now, for the sixty-four-thousand-dollar question, just what in the hell I was going to do with him? I could bury him, but I think I was more inclined to chuck him over a bridge on my way to anywhere else. But he was so goddamn heavy that seemed like more trouble than it was worth. Something would come to me. It always did.

As for the girl, I would be happy to take her back to the highway near that gas station we passed coming here. Even as fucked up as she was, with her forehead bruised and blackening and the red, swelling handprints from Joe's beating still showing across her face, she was nonetheless a pretty girl with big, blue eyes, fake tits and golden blonde hair. She wouldn't' have to wait long for help to come.

When the bullet hit me in the stomach, it took all my air with it. I fell to the floor with a thud, banging my head against the hardwood. It was quite possibly the worst pain I had ever felt in my life, and that's saying something. I've been run over by cars, been stabbed, had cigarettes put out in both my ears and been eye gouged. I've had my ass beaten with switches, boards, belts, hands and books, gotten punched in the face, bitten, and spit on more times than I could remember. Once I even fell off a three-story building trying to rescue a cat, breaking my leg in three places. This, however, hurt worse than all of that combined.

She was talking on a cell phone, Joe's phone. The police? The girl stood, pacing half-naked, still holding the gun, waving it around pissed off as she talked.

I had no strength left, watching as the blood pumped out of my stomach. It could take hours to die like this, but there was no doubt in my mind that, one way or another, I would be joining Joe soon enough.

"What the fuck do I pay you for?" she asked.

I could distinctly hear Caretaker's voice through the receiver but couldn't tell what he was saying. His low baritone sounded tinny. My head was beginning to spin. I closed my eyes until the feeling passed.

"Now there's a man dead," she said, "and another is about to die. You should've known better."

A moment went by as she listened.

As I bleed to death on the floor, I was finally starting to realize how fucked I really was.

"What the hell do you mean you figured he would go along? Well, isn't that swell? When Duke hears about this shit, somebody's ass is gonna be sore in the morning."

I coughed and I could taste the blood. It was salty and slick as oil.

I heard a story once about the Eskimos. They would freeze a knife in seal's blood, then bury the handle in the ground leaving the blade sticking straight up. At night, when a wolf would come by their camp, smelling the blood, he would lick until he shredded his tongue. Unable to stop, numb from the cold, the wolf had no idea that after a while, the blood he craved was his own.

I felt like that wolf now, caught in a trap of my own greed. Instead of money or drugs, I was going to die because I had become something someone in this business can never afford to be: kind.

The phone clapped shut in her hand. She sat and put her pants back on, pulling them roughly over her white Nikes with a pink swoosh on either side. I hadn't realized she wasn't holding the gun anymore until she reached over and picked it up off the table. I wished I had already died, but wishing you were dead sometimes is only a matter of time and not motivation.

She had Joe's car keys. Looking over, Joe was still face first in a pool of his blood, a hole in his head the size of a fist with his pants pushed down around his boots, his hard-on still throbbing with life. The girl was looking at me the way I had looked at too many men, wondering…how the fuck I was going to hurt them next.

"I'm sorry," I said. "I didn't know." The words gurgled a bit as they mixed with the blood in my throat.

"I believe you," she said.

She raised the gun. Holding it with both hands, she pulled the trigger. I never heard the explosion. I only saw an intense white light. Denise and the baby were waving to me, sitting on the beach, making a sandcastle using a blue plastic pail with a smiling yellow starfish on the side. The closer I got to them, the brighter the light became, until there was nothing else.

AFTERWORD

When I was thirteen years old, I had three distinct stories that moved me in ways that most certainly shaped me to be the writer I am today. The first was Steinbeck's *Of Mice and Men.* It was the first time I had read anything that had produced such an emotional response from me. That is to say, when George gently murders his best friend Lenny, I cried like a girl with a skinned knee.

The next is not so lofty but was wonderful when I first discovered it: *The Savage Sword of Conan the Barbarian,* or TSSOC for the cool kids. These were the graphic novels of my world. Each edition was black-and-white and published in this over-sized style with a full-color front basically dripping blood, macho as macho gets for a kid just getting hair under his pits. Lastly, was a very cool Dirty Harry series of books by various hired-gun authors that filled an entire summer. I still get a real thrill thinking of those stories, of the ultimate good guy, loner-vigilante that character represented. Stir those three themes for a story in a pot and you have "I Can Taste the Blood."

When John Taff and I first met we hit if off like we had known each other for years. Somehow we were connected, picking literary fruit from the same tree. We regularly began to schedule coffee dates during which we would share our most intimate writing ideas. And this is not common. Writers, like many artists, are very territorial when it comes to letting anyone into the studio of our thoughts. Somehow, though, we weren't the slightest bit intimidated by each other. Rather, I'd like to think each other's passion and commitment to the craft impressed us rather than intimidated.

It was upon one of these regular meetings, in early 2014, that he shared a personal story with me. He had gone to dinner with his then fiancée, now the happy Mrs. Taff, at a low-key restaurant in St. Louis. On a trip to the men's room, John described to me how the bathroom wasn't much more than a hole in the floor with Sharpie graffiti scrawled on the walls. While doing his business, he read the phrase "I can taste the blood" that some anonymous, angst-stricken wonderful weirdo had felt compelled to write inside that otherwise, and literal, shit hole. He told me all this while saying he thought it might be the title for a good book, one he might hope to write. I instantly felt like a real asshole because I liked it a hell of a lot, too, and wanted it for myself.

After about forty minutes of shooting the shit, describing works in progress, what we had coming up with book signings that I was scheduling for John and I to attend in tandem, an idea occurred to me. "Why don't we both write it?" John looked at me a bit suspiciously and asked, "How can we do that?" The idea that spontaneously spewed from me without much intelligent thought, because all I could think the whole time we had been talking was how can we both have this thing, or better yet, how could I convince him I wanted it, too, was, "What if we both wrote it?"

And an anthology of novellas was born.

We both agreed we had never heard of authors doing this, writing separate shorts with the same title and publishing it without ego or dominance in the same book. Sure, guys like King and Straub had co-authored novels, but who had done what we were talking about? When two guys who have likely read a few thousand books between them were stumped, we figured we should at least give it a try.

While I basically went home, and about a week or so later sent John my story – a story that rushed through my fingers like a hemophiliac bleeding out—John emailed to let me know we had at least two other guys now on board to write their pieces, and possibly an editor. It was karma, a magic that comes along rarely which transforms the normal into the extraordinary.

I have the ability to write simply from a title. Usually, when I start something new I try to draw on something small or obscure from my real life. The absurd joke the story begins with I had read somewhere on the Internet. It's the kind of cruelty on which debased humor is hinged. *Dead baby jokes, anyone?* Outside of the so-called joke, I had nothing, but I knew there was something deeper and more horrible beneath such comedy.

They say any joke is always based in reality, that there is a thinly veiled truth in the punchline revealing a hidden or forbidden irony we silently can acknowledge, but isn't the sort of thing good people talk about over microwaved Ramen noodles in the employee breakroom. It's the kind of thing only sick fucks find funny and that, of course, is where it began for me.

When I first started writing the story I didn't have much: two bad-ish kind of lower level dirtballs waiting on something…then the girl and her dog just appeared. That's how this crazy machine works for me. Write and see what happens. When I write, I'm just a kid again in his room trying to escape the horrible reality of unhappiness by watching the play in my head instead of the people outside my bedroom door for whom there will never be a happy ending. These are those kinds of people.

Personally, I hate predictability in a story. When, as the author, I think the characters are getting ready to go left, I say fuck it, and send them to the right. That is what I want; to be the most surprised person in the world at what happens in the story. To write is to lie, and if I cannot fool myself, how in the hell can I fool anyone else?

Also, I like the characters I write to seem as real as the people you know. Normally, you don't just meet someone and they blurt out their deepest secrets much less their last name. That annoys the shit out of me as reader, so as a writer I rarely start out this way. I've known people for years and couldn't tell you their last name if it meant winning a new car. So why in the hell do writers keep doing it? It is formulaic, bullshit writing and it pisses me off.

I like a short story that is like a sleight-of-hand card trick. You think you know where the ace is hidden but not even the guy writing it does. That is what I think is beautiful and what I was searching for when writing this story. The end is where I found it. All this time you feel sympathy, or at least empathy for the kidnapped girl, only to find out she is even a bigger, sicker fuck than her captors.

For me, that is what a statement like "I can taste the blood" represents.

Do I believe in vampires, ghosts, werewolves, or zombies? No. Do I like stories about such? Occasionally, but not as a rule. However, I do realize no matter what horrible, vile thing I can think to write which people could be capable of doing to one another and still be able to sleep at night lustfully dreaming of their co-workers, it is nothing in comparison to what they really do *do* to one another.

Short stories are in a way like an awful, offensive joke. It works because on some level, this shit could really happen, and it's simply a relief it didn't happen to you.

Life is short, stories are forever.

Joe Schwartz
April 2016

ABOUT THE AUTHOR

In 2008, *Joe's Black T-Shirt: Short Stories About St. Louis* was published as a personal favor for friends of Joe Schwartz. The idea that people outside of Schwartz's limited Midwestern world could find these dark, and occasionally personal, stories entertaining was as exciting as it was mysterious for the first-time author. Since then, he has written two more collections of short stories as well as the novels *A Season Without Rain* and *Adam Wolf and The Cook Brothers - A Tale of Sex, Drugs and Rock&Roll.* The kind of stories he tells have been described as "a sharp punch to the gut" and disarming "like a sunny day in Hell."

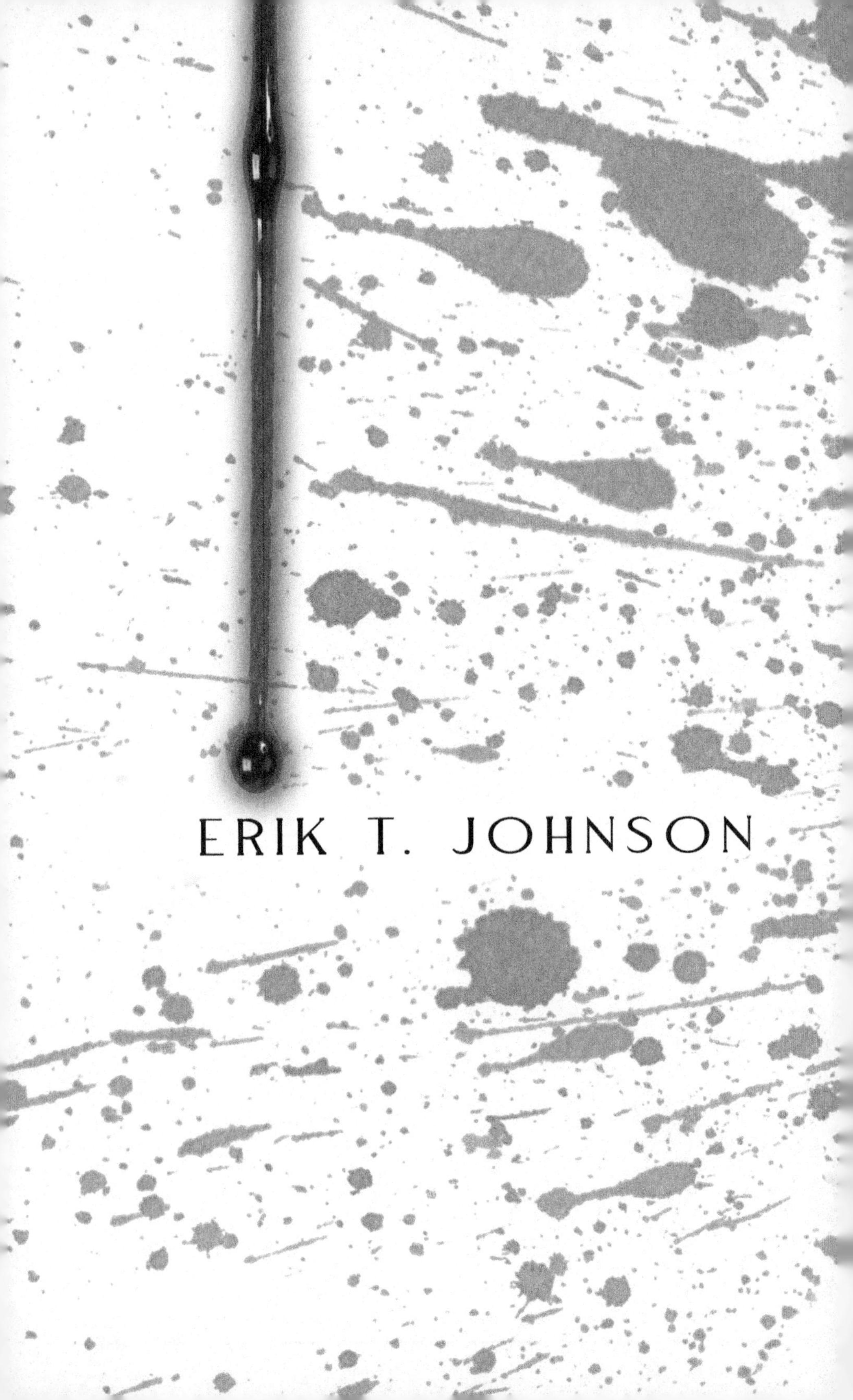
ERIK T. JOHNSON

VISION IV

I CAN TASTE THE BLOOD

All words but not all silences
are synonyms for what does not exist.
—Mahlon Jaculus Wunderhorn Majuscule
(MJWM) axiom

Incomplete Parenthetical #1: (A Perfect Monster

Canny is in deep dreaming, the kind that takes place on the darkest side of every moon, far beyond recall. It's an instance of a long-recurring nightmare he'll never remember having, almost doesn't belong to him, unfolds in his brain like an inquiline parasite, a non-event that Takes Place. A sort of doodling within a pufferfish-poison trance—scene, figure, face. In this dream he walks a path through an expansive, unfamiliar park, cold wind filtered by branches into fog, the atmosphere misted with the whispered reiterations of F (as in fucked) and S (as in lost. Should he continue this way, the path will lead beneath a stone bridge into the blindness of a troglodytic universe. An immense, white, falcate object is suspended over the tunnel, frozen in kamikaze hurtling and furrowed as the brow of one shaved bald at the commencement of a human rights violation, or like prairies of seeded plough-lines for a genocide-sized crop of edelweiss. The underpass is framed on either side with bloated,

ghost-colored birch trees, the uppermost boughs bent into tippy-top-touch. These images fit seamlessly into stark unity, yet the moment is fragmented. There's no quiddity – the trees are a pair of enormous, mummified hands, fingertips meeting with fragile solemnity, unearthly mandibles at alert ease, a FEMA-feeble dyke against the maniacal giggle of an oncoming, drunk-driving ice age. Canny walks toward the tunnel's obnubilated throat without pause, as though aware he's supposed to meet the hooded, black-robed figure now emerging. Next up is the incomplete EXEUNT *with which dreams sort of self-destruct and endoparasites go* poof. *And he never remembers. But even though this placid, yet implacable nightmare is destined to remain beyond Canny's recollection, the hooded, black-robed figure wouldn't dream of forgetting their nightly rendezvous.*

Prologue: The Shitty Sketch

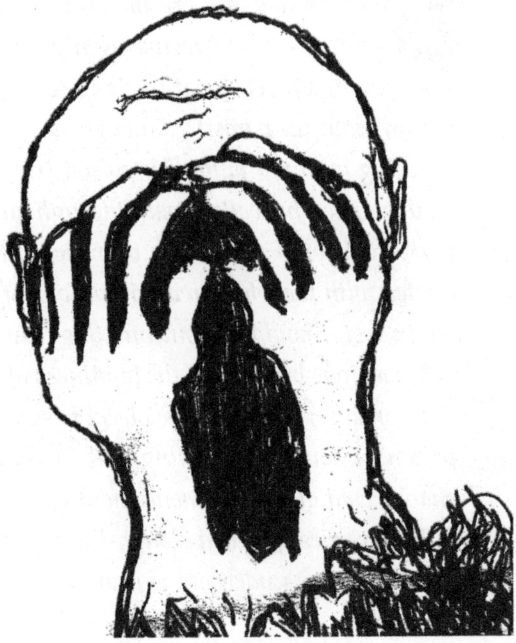

I.

Fall. Fall? No. The other miserable season, the one with the people. No, not summer. The other one. Winter. That's it. Like so many nights before, the shuffle of mother's sabots in the hallway roused me from mid-sleep. A softer sound than her usual walking, indicating an attempt, however feeble, at stealth. Why such urgent secrecy? I didn't know, but her need for it was palpable as that sebaceous liquid that leaked too often from enlarged pores the size of shower-nozzles and as neatly perforated along the contours of her disfigured face. A milky nectar perfumed the way I imagine, for no good reason, that *Bombyx mori* (the silkworm moth) must smell.

It wasn't really that bad. But mother covered it up with a multi-layered tobacco stink. It followed her everywhere. Her carcinogenic breaths stung my bedroom air, hung suspended and practically visible like those mothwing flakes of coffin ash that compose the fondest memories of funeral-home arsonists. Why'd she smoke those awful stogies when she reeked tolerably like a fantasy miasma of *Bombyx mori* without them?

In any case, she tried in her pitifully strongest way not to wake me. She must've had a good reason.

I slipped out from gray sheets, padded doorward and peered around the doorjamb.

Oh my DogBug, just look at her on the staircase, Quasimiserablo herself, in shambling descent. Her black, hooded bathrobe dragging at her cedar heels from beneath an oversized, obscenely rufous men's fleece overcoat. In one hand a large knapsack. It's cold out there, so the capacious black hood is up, but where's her industrial-strength, red miner's helmet mounted with a blinding 5-watt wheat lamp, a thick black cord running down to a belt-clipped, wet-cell battery? It would've actually come in handy on her evening jaunts, since Episode Lake is damn dark at night.

But, strange to say, bright mining lights were strictly a *daytime* thing with Mamma Mia, an every-lamp-on, all-shades-up, sunny-day-thing. That's because she and I only saw each other, however briefly, during morning hours. On such scant occasions, she wore her blazing helmet as an apotropaic against my looking at her directly in the face. It catalyzed her gaze into a mighty bolt of anti-eye waves and particles, so that I must cower and scramble off like the weakest Morlock in the lair.

For a moment her wrecked terrapin of a face is framed in the first landing's tall, ovoid mirror. The wet dream Lon Chaney would never admit to having. It put me in mind of a failed attempt to clone a tortoise shell. She was...God, I don't know. It was hard to imagine what unguiculate fiend had dishonored her so. That destiny could be so red in claw and tooth, and precise as horological poising drills. She was *something*.

On the one stupid occasion I asked about the disfiguring attack, the miner's helmet swung my way, its aggressive light beating my face, followed by the wobbly, hummingbird-on-valium vibrations of her vocal cords:

"Canny, you ever cuddle with a rabid unicorn?"

"Mother?"

"Well, should you ever get the chance *don't*."

The coda was either a laugh or a bag of kittens drowning in a vat of hummus.

"Now I don't care if you're two or ninety-two, go out and play. And remember, go as far and wherever you want. And take care."

Take care! What a thing to say.

She was something. Look, if you're having a hard time getting the picture, ask anyone to explain their mother in a few sentences. I'm doing all right. Now, I've never had a job, but I've seen movies and TV. So you know how when you fuck up at work, but you had a good reason and you explain why to your supervisor, and he or she nods sympathetically with a mix of encouragement and disappointment and says, "It's a balance" as though that's supposed to mean something? And you nod affirmative like you got the message, *Sorry boss, it won't happen again.* And then with a look of self-disappointment and quitting-is-not-an-option, as though it's a secret password, you reply, "It's a balance."

So where was I? She didn't see me, watching her around the doorjamb. She whispered harshly to herself.

"Your own *mother*."

And I thought, *Oh! Sure!* As though you were ever *mine*! As if I could somehow own the being, however defenseless and grotesque you might be, that manufactured me from her own body. Surely, mothers possessed their children absolutely and always. It could never be the other way around. *Well fuck her then*, I thought.

Looking back, oh my DogBug, but isn't that the DogBuggiest fucking funniest fucking thing?

* * *

What did I know about anything? Anyone? I'd always lived at home. Mother and I spoke only when absolutely necessary. The frequency and duration of our exchanges decreased as winters murdered falls and summers murdered spring after spring after spring. The years, do they *really* pass, or only pretend to, hunching behind the meat of us, pooling their drool until they've secreted enough hunger to wash over us, to drown us, to eat us up? There was no family history. I didn't know who my father had been, or my birthdate, stuff like that. You get the picture.

When I was old enough, whatever age that was, mother let me do almost anything so long as I left her and the rest of the human race out of it. She threatened to toss me in the street if I so much as developed a single, first-name basis acquaintance. Absolute rules, yes. Yet easily followed. Aside from these, mother ruled only as a tyrant of freedom, forcing a straitjacket of autonomy upon me at every opportunity.

I was to be Set Apart.

That much I understood. I had no choice. Which is exactly what a state of understanding consists of. Okay with me. I'd read enough magazines and watched enough TV to know my looks and general appearance were Normal Enough, but in any case that didn't matter. Solitude fit me like a birthday suit. I never cared for people, and didn't fret over whether nature or nurture was at the root of my holistic misanthropy (Now I know that's the wrong question—it's all nature versus nature).

It's a strange thing about people that they cannot explain themselves without reference to *other people*. There's some kind of ontological apology in this habit. And as if that isn't enough, they reek of doll-worlds and the need to be posed through life, to be photographed. Observe: no matter how diverse a singular mob of dolls, they seem to be posing for a family photograph. An Austro-Hungarian wind-up soldier next to an Indian Hopi figure, dwarfed by off-gassing rubber babies, doesn't matter. Somehow, get two or more dolls together and they coalesce into a familial unit. Bodies heaped in uncovered mass graves also have this quality. And to add to the list of their loathsome qualities, they think "There's a time and place for everything." Sure, except temporality and spatiality. It's never the right hour, the best spot for either of those. When they play at being Creative, they start by trying to "Think outside the box," as though imagination must start from the assumption of the hackneyed existence of a specific type of lidded container.

What I'm trying to say is that I didn't go to school, I didn't work, I didn't have or seek friends. I mostly read and read. I researched everything, could say along with Goethe, *"I've studied now Philosophy and Jurisprudence, Medicine—And even, alas! Theology—From end to end, with labor keen; And though I've read Derrida and Rohmer's Fu*

Manchu, I think, therefore I haven't got a fucking clue!" Occasionally, I strolled the streets. In sleep, I was nothing, did nothing, had no dreams I could remember and therefore couldn't pine away for their real-life approximations. So why go anywhere else? I wasn't lonely. Those six letters in that particular order never came up.

* * *

Sex? There is a sweaty fish in it. It's too oozy. I never tried it. I just *knew* it was oozy, sure as a photograph's a memory that gets forgotten at least twice.

Sex. There're schools of urinating fish in it. I see a nacreous swamp. I see purulent ichor, shades of puked water and watery whey, fleshy-gruel exuded in droplets along the contour of mother's face. I smell its *non sequitur* scent of *Bombyx mori,* an odious secretion, and I associate secretions with secrets. Mother's secrets. Pre-ejaculate is a secret beginning to show itself. A sticky, low murmuring about begetting, bloodlines and burial plots, until it grows louder with details, the swarming spermatozoa unmasked. But not all the beans have yet been spilled. Is the sperm healthy or useless? Can it fertilize an ovum? The secret comes out.

Secret and *secretion* both descend—are secreted—from the same Latin root: *secretus,* to Set Apart.

Both secrets and secretions, therefore, connote a demarcation between ourselves and the world around us.

Secretions and secrets are special borders that have existed longer than they have existed. Secretions being biological revelations and secrets their interpersonal counterparts. They both stink of our ignorance, past-tenses, the place we lived *prior to* the secret(ion)'s appearance—whether lie or omission, or the clandestine preparations of a disease before its emission in beaded curtains of perspiration. A feeble moat of globules quiver around mother's plebian face. A queen would know enough to stay dry. Maybe that's why

Cleopatra was in the habit of placing bees upon her vagina, enjoying their vibrations.

* * *

So where was I? I'd slid out from under gray sheets, padded doorward, peered. She's down the stairs, she's gently shutting the front door behind her. Where could the freak be going? Southward, as though pulled, somehow. What force of gravity could be so silly with the unclean putty of her?

* * *

Episode Lake is a pretty simple, superstitious town. Republicans have held every elected office through at least ten administrations, monotheism is the rule—try believing two or more things at a time and their brains go *PFZZZZT!*—and three of the four cardinal directions are associated with their own absurd local legends.

To the north, in the ghetto called Black Factory Hill, one heard tales of Mister Sunday, The Man Who Doesn't Knock. Supposedly, he was an escaped mental patient living in an abandoned private mental institution built surreptitiously beneath a rubber factory by its wealthy, secretly polygamist, owner. There he concealed a large harem of mentally deficient Lithuanian orphans, along with the many demented offspring they'd borne him. They said the factory had burned to the ground decades ago, killing the owner before he could free his family. Only Mister Sunday, The Man Who Doesn't Knock remained, creeping out at night to steal children from their homes, so went the story. He was so thin as to be mistaken for a skeleton. Thus does every little Episodic learn the couplet:

Mister Sunday and the Devil played cards at his home
He bet his skin, but could not win, now he's all crazy-bones.

To the east belonged vague rumors of the 200-year-old Whore-Bug Witch, whose ghost haunted the… What? Bus stops? Nail salons? Ninety-nine-cent stores? There's nothing else out that way. I don't know, but she had her own nice lurid ditty:

The Whore-Bug Witch got morning sickness
We caught her in the vestry squatting mid-piss
Her womb had waxed large as a harvest moon
Too bloated to flee, we trapped her, and soon
We strapped her to the stake tight as skin to a rash
Her eyes broke like eggs, nipples into embers, ash
Where foul expression, now smoking black gash
She bared her fangs and they cracked and broke
While screams rushed up teeth fell down her throat
Then mandibles clacking, stuck out like a tongue
And perished with last of the air singed from her lungs.

Finally, one of Episode Lake's best-loved folktales concerned the west-side duo of Daddy Fingerfeet and Doctor Traintrubble, who ran a sinister candy operation in the bleak, bookstore-free, residential Bloodstreet District. They went door-to-door, tempting kids and parents or guardians alike to enjoy a free sample of their vibrant ROYGBIV confections. Sometimes the candy was simply poisonous. In another version they were little homing beacons that stayed lodged in you, undigested, allowing the extraterrestrials who employed Daddy Fingerfeet and Doctor Traintrubble to find and abduct you for insidious experiments whenever they pleased. These gentlemen lacked a ballad with words, but there was a sort of Barney-Milleresque theme tune some wiseasses pretended to whistle.

And what of southern Episode Lake? Nothing thrilling, not one haunted house or exorcism, no pet-crocodile-grown-into-man-eater-in-the-sewer, not even that guy with a hook for a hand. Just some homeless people maundering about down there. I knew three of them by name, only because when they argued they had a habit of screaming them at each other.

Fernando had many beloved relatives and a thousand times the unaffordable miles between him and them. Worried, fragile, probably younger than the sixty-six years he looked, he walked with stunted movements as though he'd spent his best years floating the Atlantic in search of the Florida shoreline crammed in a crate of feather dusters.

Quinceaux was an unaccountably dyed-in-the-unwashed-wool Frenchman with gypsy-cursed features and bulging eyes that suggested an invisible garrote tightening around his neck, who smoked—or chewed—a meerschaum pipe. His tread was slow and dramatically doomed, a procrastinating guillotine shuffle, with each step forward he retreated toward you. Quinceaux seemed to own two general expressions. The first being of a person who has fallen out of a tree. The second of one who has just tumbled down a flight of stairs. Sometimes I think caricatures aren't distortions of people, so much as people are refined versions of caricatures.

The Dapper Diaper was a once-wealthy now-insane chronic public masturbator, best only hinted at.

It was toward such society that my runagate mother headed in the nights. Firmly marking the southernmost border of Episode Lake was the lush wall of trees of Majuscule Marina. There was no marina, no bodies of water of any kind.

WARNING: Never assume your neighbors live in their neighborhood.

As far as Episode Lake knew, Majuscule Marina was an exclusive, private community for the ultra-rich, with everything they'd ever need, including an airport and a fully-staffed hospital securely hid from the Episodics' food-stamp fingers and lottery-ticket eyes by Majuscule's own imposing forest. As a kid, once and only once, I walked in, I dared the imprecations of its hoity-toity brambles. Densely packed trees ape giant nervous systems amid the whispery green of accumulated centuries and shadows of midnight in triplicate. The elm, cedar and chestnut are especially abundant. Monumental pines go without saying.

The silences are stony and precipitous. You feel the vertigo of standing upon a merry-go-round planet balanced over a hostile, lightly sleeping void. You think *Shit, I'd better scram,* and you do. You're not sure how far you trespassed because you can't get far enough away.

I wish this wasn't autobiography.

From the notes of the UndeScribe
Pages 3 - 1,018 {A Betcha Don Toilets}

> The What-To-Expect has finally received a name worthy of it, which is to say, a phrase having nothing to do with it and that best suits a ritual at odds with the regulatory nature of ritual. We will bring the DogBug—or King Embryon, or Dracula, or Heliogabalus, or FOX News at Nine, or Crow-White, or The Wednesday, or The Glacier, or Were-Time, or Science, or the Trap-Door-Laying Harpy—forth from places impossible to describe.

* * *

All words but not all silences
are synonyms for what does not exist.
– MJWM axiom

After thousands of years trying, 2017 will be the year that Mahlon Jaculus Wunderhorn Majuscule and His Motherfucking Energumens make it happen. There were several false starts, especially the Whore-Bug Witch, the *extremely* regrettable Mister Sunday, and the Bloodsweet Doctors of Bloodstreet. But those botched efforts were forthwith de-created in the penetralium of our extensively esoteric woodlands, replaced with fantastic rumors and, when possible, augmented with ballads and theme tunes.

A song of a legend will always be more real
than the legend itself.
– MJWM axiom

But using that woman's entire face as cloaca and womb, that was genius. And *almost* complete success. Still, it is a peculiarity of this planet that nothing can be completed without a name. MJWM epiphanized that our task required a title contributed by an author with absolutely no knowledge of it and, therefore, no intention to advance our cause. It should be dubbed in a most ill-suited way, just as the child is born into the world through an antiquated and traumatic process that is better fit for generating turds than creatures. It must be chaotically synonymous with anything.

And then one beautiful morning, one of the oldest Motherfucking Energumens I ever saw noticed a phrase, written in marker in some public bathroom stall: A BETCHA DON TOILETS. MJWM declared the mysterious series of letters—such a failure of communication, held together by forces of randomness, so lacking in meaning—as that for which we'd long-awaited. And then? We Motherfucking Energumens got ready, drooling over blueprints in the distance and watching for the right moment.

Soon A BETCHA DON TOILETS, or BATHETIC DOLTS EON, or I CAN TASTE THE BLOOD, or TIN LOTTOS HEED A CAB, or A BASIC TOOTHED LENT—the order of the letters isn't important—would be realized here, on earth or in Hell, or whatever they want to call this, it makes no difference. We are Expecting.

II.

There was this weird guy I'd see now and then when I was out for a stroll, at the grocery store, or through my window and across the street, whatever. Tall like a traffic light, gray coat, inexplicably able to hold a ridiculous book open in his hands—it was thick as a stack of Swedish parish ledgers—and write as fast and wild as a landslide. I don't know, he may've had ten, twelve quill pens in his oscillating hand, or only one. How could he hold that book and write at the same time? This guy's head was always obscured by shadow. The sun could be high and relentless in a cloudless sky and still his head was a gritty, cheap, smudgy shadow like newsprint, sure of itself, unavoidable. He was writing so quickly; they couldn't be real words. What else could they be but meaningless marks? Thus I must be his topic of interest. One for the impossible books, that murky lurker. How'd I know he was a he? What, with no face?

III.

Winter, and I found mother dead. I didn't recognize her at first. It was more like she'd had a makeover than a one-way ticket to the worms. Her face looked so human because she had covered her staggered features, her hyperkeratotic cheeks and grum eyes, with both her large, smooth white hands, obscuring most of her face. I'd never noticed her hands were so unblemished and fine. The top of her bald head was glowing like a halo-headed fetus waxed under the scalp. She lay recumbent on her bed—of down or of snow—with verticalities of arm, leg and neck suggesting serifs and alphabets of majuscule and bone—twisty glyphs, forbidden and illuminated. I had a brief moment of forensic pondering.

The shadows—it was dark wherever I was—and her hands had de-featured her for all practical purposes, but I discerned some stirring of mouthparts. Was she alive? She's trying to speak, or rapidly licking her lips, or waggling her tongue, or gagging on a wet, black wheat lamp cord. In the place where her mouth had been an enormous black louse is skewered to the pillow or the cushion of snow by a bony, finger-long pin or quill. It's the size of a bloated tongue. Over and over, the insect frantically spins around the point of its wound, repeating the circle of its slow death. Here was a perfect unity of rehearsal and final show. I inclined my ear to the suffering thing as close I could bear, as though mother's voice would whisper up an explanation. Only the obscene rustling of countless legs undulating against threadbare wool or ice. Urgent, reiterative, violent sounds, like knife stabbings in the *Friday the 13th* movie franchise. Hard to understand as the Book of Life is written in a dead language.

I left the bedroom—or turned around in the snow—feeling all over like one bladder that really has to pee, only the urine will be a flood of coming war and I must hold it in against all odds. I am at the mercy of my bodily functions to the same degree as I am at the whim of the world and its monomaniacal need for gargantuan upheavals. I think it was raining, clear and watery like mucous from faucet-nostrils when you can't stop sneezing.

Emotions? Complicated. A surprisingly sad electricity crackled through my brain. Or is it more accurate to say I'd contracted an unidentified moral illness? She'd not been friendly and hardly maternal. But she was not so much *more than* I'd realized, as something *other than*. My keeper? Whatever she'd really been was as different from what I'd thought as saying "that's not funny" to someone differs from saying "I don't think that's funny." That's no small difference.

I was soon full of a melancholy so complex, so quickly evolving from one form into another, racing to reshape itself again and again to fit continuously changing environmental conditions. While in fact nothing had changed, the evolutions were a kind of soul-hypochondria, fear or anxiety reacting to itself that I almost found this dance of sentimental transformations entertaining. But I did not.

The last thing I remember about the day I found her was she had one of her knapsacks at her feet. Inside was a change of clothing: a pair of cheap clogs; one of those antique candlesticks that Jack jumps over; two candles; a box of safety matches; a spade; a large beach blanket; an alarm clock; a cluster of loose tissues; an unevenly U-shaped, black plastic dildo and a paper bag with two or three eyeholes cut into it. She didn't leave me a note. Not even two words, a simple "take care" or even "fuck off."

Don't ask how or where I got rid of the body. I'm not even sure I did.

The bag's under the kitchen sink.

IV.

There are no answers
but there is an endless supply of victims.
– MJWM axiom

Winter, and a cold night for alligators, the stray hounds choking on inflexible barking. What I wouldn't give for a chilly fall, even. After mom died the weather got so strange. I hesitate to describe it as anything so mundane as a season. The chunky snow that year was near impossible to shovel. All the scattered, paw-burning rock salt just sorta lay there. Couldn't beat it and joined the snow, rather than melting it. No doubt about it, something was wrong with the snow. Though I guess everything from *above* is wrong: rooftops with empty wooden water towers, vestigial television aerials, bombs-bursting-in-air, bird shit, monotheism, counterfeit phoenixes, winged Beelzebub. And the cold those nights, I swear, was *injected* directly into the veins.

I had always been in the habit of going to bed early, especially so as the days lost their legs. One Wednesday evening I jolted awake out of an unconsciousness so abysmal I almost got cramps from sitting up so fast. How old was I at the time? If people don't know the approximate age of a person in an account of said individual it drives them nuts! I could hardly breathe. There'd been no startling noise. It was a *quiet* that woke me.

My eyes find the window or, rather, the window-shaped moonlight. It's like pillows for my eyes, gauzy and calming. I sit there not feeling the cold, looking at the framed luminosity. The glass appears to hover, a preternatural phenomenon. The longer I stare, the more it seems to pretend to be within reach. As though it's actually an enormously distant, six-cornered moon announcing the culmination of ancient prophecy—a new, sharp-edged world. My blood, all queasy, bubbles at the notion of false light, and I imagine this rectangle minting unlucky lunatics by the millions.

An albino, three-legged crow slams into the center of the window without making the slightest sound. I clutch either side of the mattress to keep from falling backwards. The white bird's breast is stuck to the fine, icy plate that laminates the window. Its head is pressed sideways against the glass, the eye Iggy-Pop-wide and open, vibrating with accusations, darkly shining like an anti-world beacon. Wings flap frantically on either side of its freakishly glued body. I can't move. I'm pinioned to my own inescapable instant, this violent silence suspended in alien moonlight that leads birds astray. In the claw of the freakish middle leg, which is flanked on either side by left and right legs spread wide as in heraldry, something thick with flesh and blood and desire thrashes like a bloated tongue filled with larvae about to burst.

The bird struggles. The panes quiver. I think the glass must break. Wings spread wide, feathers twitching, anticipating flight. And as the crow puts all its strength into jerking itself into freedom, the body rips away from the wings and falls out of sight.

How could this be? Had the ligaments that fastened the wings to the torso been frayed? Maybe such is the heavy price for undertaking an unimaginable, universe-spanning migration. Might a man walking from Earth to Mars arrive without legs?

Two milky wings flap on either side of the window with such vehemence they seem about to soar and carry the entire house away with them. Between the wings is a cold blank for a body. The placeholder for an awful predestination. The wings are mother's hands hiding her face when she died. I know that isn't true, but I kept expecting her hideous mug to appear between them, to *finally* look me in the face without sticking five burning watts into my eyes, to tell me something important unspoken for too long.

The beautiful amputations spasm more wildly, as though hooked up to a fallen electrical power line. I hear sharp taps and scuttling on the outside wall. A generic, crayon-green lizard climbs up the window. Pale belly constellated with red-herring-red Chernobyloid tumors. It pauses between the jittery wings and turns ice-rigid. Its body breaks off the glass, leaving only the whip-like tail behind. I know a strange cryptozoological puzzle is forming, so I lay back and wait.

I can't help but recoil in surprise when a cruelly tortured bat slams into the window. It provides the missing torso for this evolving chimera. The top half of its bat head has been sliced off, leaving the bat mouth in which a leprous goldfish is jammed, its tail in a tongue-teasing-nipple orange twitch. The fish's abnormally large, Iggy-Pop-blue eye presses into the glass. I wonder if it was bought or sold in a plastic bag. Do they have plastic bags in Hell?

Now the perimeters of the bat's membranes flit behind the crow wings, forming an autonomous sepia-toned aura. The bat's belly ruptures and a snow-globe's blizzard of maggots, as white and disposable as latex gloves, spill out and writhe against the glass. All the chimera needs now is a head. And in a flash, like a guillotining shown in reverse, a flat and empty brown paper bag such as I had seen my mother wear to sleep—the mining helmet being entirely too uncomfortable—flipped up into place. The bag hangs there, indifferent as a thermometer to the level of its mercury, yet agitated at its mercury rising too fast. All the pieces swirl into an orgy of liquid rot—bird into lizard into bat into fish; and all into a froth of maggot, maggot and more maggot; and froth of maggot begat frothing maggot, begat maternal neurotoxins.

The wind—or who?—takes the tangible vision away.

Only the paper bag, mother's sleeping face, remains flat against the counterpane, one unblinking hollowness. The utter, uncontestable stare of a mirror.

Everything fit together with a stark coherency, so naked, so obvious, that I can't begin to understand it.

In the aftermath of these freak extinctions, I half-dream that, out there in the snow, emerging through rows of dead, black telephone poles like lions slipping too easily through the bars of paper cages, dark-robed mega lunatics long, long foretold slouch forward. Sound returns to its usual boring ways.

I slunk from my room. Undoubtedly portentous, yet I was certain that what I'd just seen had not been *symbolic*. This is no fable. I hate to break it to ye, O Student of the Occult, but symbols—*all* symbols—are less useless than prayers and car alarms, unless we're talking the cover of *Led Zeppelin IV* (or *Zoso*, or *Untitled*). Go wish upon a pentagram and see where that gets you, and don't make me laugh with the venerable lineage of your *ouroboros*, serpent with its ass in its head. Stuff it somewhere raw and incontinent.

I'd witnessed no symbolic omen. I'd gotten a whopping dose of reality so highly concentrated it seemed unreal. And reality cannot be symbolized, represented or captured in the imaginary world of shapes and lines where stick figures and quantum equations, anatomical charts and smiley faces, the Mona Lisa and cathedral spires live. That is a mere *Why, you-lucky-fuck, you!* place, a child's world.

I fell asleep on the bathroom floor. As usual, no dreams came. Or else I was made of dream and therefore couldn't have had one. Perhaps I was some species other than human, a poisonous look-alike. To give two alternative examples. It's strange how people have unquestioning faith that they must've dreamed in their sleep, even if they remember them, to believe your dimmest memories, however bright they may be.

* * *

My mother's hands. A tri-legged bird? And albino at that? And what's with all the different species? I couldn't get back to sleep. I walked over to the window. There was no trace of the recent, weird struggle. The streetlights were comatose, and the empty nail salon across the street was like a box of bright, rinky-dink light, attractive to moths and seekers of eternal salvation. Puppy-milled, black-and-white dogs slept like sandbags behind the glass of the Pet Emporium. Six dirty stories of lit apartments above. Poor people. Products of sticky genealogy framed by windows without blinds or shades. They were doing less than watching TV. I thought I saw the tall murky motherfucker who could write fast as starshine, 299,792,458 meters per second, populating his mega-codex with furious, wide gestures. It just *had* to be meaningless scratching.

I'd never been one to look at faces, but I knew people had them on the fronts of their heads. This guy, everything above his neck, was blurred away into sooty shadow even though he was standing directly outside the nail salon which was lit like Vegas.

A rusty yellow Pontiac, brown-bruised like an old banana, careened down the street and screeched to a stop before the broken fire hydrant, blasting Queen's famous "Bohemian Rhapsody." I'd always disliked this song, but as it pirouetted up through my window that night, I finally understood why it's such an incredible work of art. "Bohemian Rhapsody" makes no sense on the face of it. The parts don't add up. The bombast clashes with the twee, the barbershop quartet with Mahlerian choir of one thousand. And yet it's real. Very rare and very real. I regret it took me so long to appreciate this. My life—my *first* life, or *his* life, that is—would've had more highs.

The Pontiac dragged off in filthy machismo backfires. Somewhere between iterations of *nothing-really-mattering*, my friend in the gray coat had either completely vanished into the Episodic air, or else he'd left his indiscernible head behind.

A foreboding that something sought me. It understood you deeply. Like dogs. It infested you, uncaring as an insect species. It pawed insistently at the threshold of my brains. It would find me soon enough, dragging its asshole of writhing hydra across the killing floor. I thought how everything you look at, all you touch, is being looked at and touched by an almost-dead person. The future is where you throw everything away. Then I thought about mom's clandestine outings and how she needed to drain the sci-fi goop from her face over the sink at biweekly intervals. And how secrecy itself is akin to biological secretion. All secretions, all forms of wetness, can interpenetrate and merge. Hands, stolen wings. Was she in the bed, or had I only just found her in a snowbank? If a cat has nine lives, then it has ten deaths.

I needed to quell such idiotic static. These thoughts were mine, yet they weren't. Just as you know it must be you in your bed when you sleep, it comes to you every night. But, really, sleep has nothing to do with you. You're not even *there* at the time.

I needed air. Lots of bad in my feeling. The inescapable promise of humiliations hovering like storm clouds of indeterminate speed and direction on the stitched horizons of every new pair of white underpants. Like it's in the distance, somewhere and always that they unroll the blueprints of your bedroom in disciplined study and starvation and drool in advance of the day you sleep too late.

An ambulance flew by. Is a siren, with its erratic flashing, only the most obvious of those nearly everythings designed to behave brokenly?

Putting on clothes seemed sensible, and I did so quickly. As quickly as people fetch water with a kind of fanaticism of purpose when anyone needs medical attention they're unqualified to provide. I slipped out of the house as quietly as possible. Why?

Ill-advised.

Out on the street and the chill was weird, overly intimate, each shiver a tongue-across-nipple response, a mutant goldfish tail flicking icy window glass. Somehow, cages rattled. I felt sudden patches of freezing cold on my head. Shit, I'd forgotten my hat. Wait, what am I thinking? I never wore a hat. I lifted a hand to wipe the ice or water off and found my hair missing from most of my head, as though it was wrapped in an icy fog of Nair, whispery gusts of *F* and *S* swirling in my e*ars.* Anyway, the wind blows.

Why, mother? Why am I asking you questions when you're gone? Looking to be blinded with your explanation. Our life had always been disturbing, but the difference between a disturbing life and a life that's been disturbed is enormous. Now you are like a hole, which never needs care or replacing, yet for that very reason serves as a constant reminder that it's okay to forget about it.

Fragmented passerby conversations freeze together into the stark coherency of refrigerator-magnet poetry.

Breathe
Garbage is
Very understaffed
Baby
You're still
Let his talons
Power
Please
Grow a year
Breathe
Who hires these people
Not safe

Too many Episodics, doll-blooded, parading through air bland with ticker-tape snow, packs of family photographs on the jaunt, teeth bared like animals with paws, hooks, hoofs stuffed in coat pockets. Where's the EXIT from this hideous *belonging*? I turn corners, cross walks. A quiet lane, and ever onward. Lost, a valley walled by factories, useless rows of industrial venturing, ruins of temples and massage parlors buried under padlock landslides, a crush of security doors and iron-barred windows, over cinder blocks, kicked-brick, concrete, wading the dark alloy of heavy overlapped shadows.

Wait a minute. Why is my hair falling out?

I understand that in some way yet to be revealed this is the least of my problems, a digression. So I never mind it.

The cold wind blows through broken window glass, takes the clear, sharp edges with it into the street, my tearing eyes.

A foreboding. Something that, like a dog, can disobey you, and yet like a bug, has no conception of obeying.

Things fell away. I turned up my eyes. The stars were harmless as exit wounds and so far away as to approach friendliness. I looked down. They weren't in sight yet, but I could hear the trees of Majuscule Marina keeping surprise-party quiet. I just needed to cross a few more hundred yards of empty dirt field to see those impassive trees under the six-cornered moonlight.

Out of the night, a voice gorgeous and true:

Oh, a hole, a soul, once accidentally, on-purpose acquired
By a hem or in your skull
It doesn't matter where
May or may not get repaired
You never know
But of one thing you can be certain
Oh, a hole, a soul never needs replacing
It can always stay or leave there.

Does an Angel of Mercury serenade?

Not at all. Our troubadour is that homeless guy who goes by Quinceaux. His bulging eyes, set in his face like dinosaur eggs, both precede him—like his reputation—brimming with fright as if he'd just seen Mister Sunday, The Man Who Doesn't Knock. He wears pale, toilet-paper-thin blankets raveled around only about half his scabrous, blue-cold body. He comes close. Emerging from the middle gap of his top row of teeth is a tiny, unlit, faun-headed meerschaum pipe. Through other spaces, dental and rotten, he exhales what could be Mesozoic mating calls and pheromones.

"What happened to her?" he asks.

"Who?" Even though I know, precisely because I shouldn't know, who he's talking about. *Shouldn't* is the strongest shoulder in the world.

"She's lovely to me. But her head is all messed up, but not like mine, on the inside. A mess outside, you get me? Even though she's my lovely."

"Good evening, then, sir," I tried to say, but it came out garbled. I hadn't spoken aloud in such a long time, the simplest phrase was a tongue-twister.

"Ah! You're *Canny*. You're Annie's bastard. Didn't think you'd be bald, too. I bet you play piano like you've got a lazy eye."

Who's Annie? Oh. Things fell away. I was afraid he'd touch me, but his distance was respectable, if somewhat close. His breath was chemical warfare. Oh... Oh... Wait. What's that about a piano and an eye? That didn't make any sense. I don't want to start believing all words are code words. I'll ignore the evidence if it ever comes to that.

"You're my love-monster's bastard."

Better get right outta here.

"Yeah, sir, *you*." Pointing at me in a fit of hilarity and tears all choked together. "You were born out of her fucking face!"

He was trembling. I hoped he'd collapse, this pillar of walking garbage, this worm, this whistler of prehistoric lizard song, a false prophet night-belched to lie my name to me on stinking mouth-clouds. That I'd been birthed like a drooling Athena from a victimized Zeus. Could *anything* be more ridiculous? Or at least, *many more* things?

"Tell me. How old are you, Canny. Do you even know?"

"She's dead," I told him, because I didn't know. And I was compelled to add, "And gone."

He began pulling at his curly gray hairs and rocking between left and right foot in I guess what you'd call symptomatic of a neurological disorder, or a religious terpsichorean ritual.

"Out her face," he said, wistful as a cartoon-crab taking a cartoon-sponge under his arm to retrieve a tale of his bolder youth. "Out her face, like some A-bomb pimple, and they said, 'Nah, don't want *that* little shit!' She said you were *too normal*. No horns or tail or mandibles. Why, you're not even very ugly, tell the truth. That horrible thing didn't want you and it just left Annie like a lonely monster, a lovely monster. Smelled of Mulberry moth."

"What are they?" I untwisted my tongue.

"You were *too normal!* Can you imagine? Not what it needed. Too much the spawn of man and female. The wrong son. The bastard. You're not enough monster, you monster! She tried to make you grow up all alone, hoped you'd be less human if left to yourself, kept from people. Yeah, sir. She never told you a thing. I say, if you think blood is thicker than water, try wading through bullshit."

"There's no need to be cruel," I said.

"There's only a need, in fact."

"This isn't a joke to me."

"That's why it's so funny, Human-Boy!"

His laugh was aggressively high-pitched and uncontrollable, a burning-alive-at-the-stake last laugh.

His smile was a bemused scythe.

"And she was always ready to go even when she wasn't, what with her face making such a fine lube. Should've bottled it, could've made a million."

Ah! What else! No surprises. It's secrecy and secretions. I wasn't close to *Annie*. Not at all. Yet, there's something about having your mother insulted. I don't know why, perhaps it's an evolutionary development. The phrase "something snapped," for what came next is remarkably, shamefully apt.

"Sex!" I cried and threw out my hardest, first-ever slap. I miss my target. I'm out of my element, ill-advised. I merely lop the meerschaum pipe and its head dangles grotesque and off. Quinceaux untouched. My act was ill-advised. Quinceaux Moloch-snorts and inhales the chalky white stem into junkyard lungs. I swear he grabs most of me with one hand. I'm yanked over his shoulder. A forever second of scary calm as my body's life whooshes upside-down. I'm out of my element, ill-advised.

Closing my eyes, I awaited the sordid, brutal exeunt that was surely imminent. My brain has panicked itself into an asshole, struggling to contract into a **Malpighian tubule.** Here it is! I'm sobbing, wailing like a wall. But I don't feel any pain. Has my spine snapped? I'm crying like a phony holy relic streams blood, oil or tap water. I felt wind scrape my dry, dry cheeks near the terrible mystery of Quinceaux's crotch. On my ankles, near his chin, shoulders. Wait. It's not me. It's Quinceaux, blubbering.

"Oh, sir, this is all so familiar. It reminds me. We did it like this, see. You. You are," he sniffed, "about her length. Lovely Annie."

His alligator-jawed grip didn't relent *per se,* but subtle modulations in the distribution of its pressure across my body suggested a change of intentions. What began as the foreplay to bloody, body-slamming mayhem switched into a desperately protective, I'll-never-let-you-go hold.

Why this sudden sorrow? He's bawling sodium while I hang uncomfortably *there,* and he smells like a sweaty hagfish.

"What? You did what?" I said, tongue-twisted, dizzy.

"My face in her lap, you know. Like where yours is, and—"

Nostalgia!

"Let me go!"

Unthinking, Quinceaux dropped me to the cold ground, clutched at his chest and groaned like a Bigfoot hunter had put a 12-gauge shell right through his impressively realistic Bigfoot suit.

"I'm sorry boy. Annie hated violence. This is all too much for me."

Abreaction!

He carefully knelt down, straightened me out and brushed the scalp-slicing beer bottle shards out from under my head. His absurd, sad eyes. Tragic! He wailed, his face hanging over mine. Overflow from the sewers of his tear ducts rained huge drops into my eyes. He lay down next to me, put his head on the broken glass, arms at his side, face moonward. I sat up, my tears purling down my cheek, chasing his own, I dried four sets of eyes with the back of my filthy, frozen hand and looked at Quinceaux. I glimpsed immortality in his quivering eyes. It was *unreliable*.

"It was *me* killed her, Canny. I confess it," he cried.

He opened a hole in his loincloth and, grimacing, pushed something—amphibian? Terminal?—through it.

I leapt up, turned away. Seeing nothing was still too much.

"One," I said, "Stay right there. And what'd you mean you killed her? You're not saying you're my father too, are you? That monster business a scam? I'd believe anything if it was awful enough."

"Not that. We ain't relations. Worse! There's something wrong with my dick, sir." And he wept me a tar pit of tears, coughed globs of pubic-hairy phlegm, spat whole ring-cycles of operatic bile. "You gotta kill me for killing her. Please."

Whether I'd found mother in a snowbank or the dim hallway, there was no way Quinceaux had killed her. For one thing, I would've smelled him for days after he left the scene of the crime.

He groaned, alternately kicking his left and right legs in what I guess was the sort of thing symptomatic of a neurological disorder, or something Yahweh would mandate of Abraham or Job or somebody fruitful who begat somebody else fruitful, too.

I wanted to run, but I walked away as slow as I could bear, as if Quinceaux were some wild animal that would pursue me as its prey if I should give off the slightest scent of fear. South, I must go south—land of no silly legends, urban fairy tales or refrigerator-magnet poetry. Angry, confused, melancholy, disgusted, vicious, viscous. I was a Frankenstein's monster of bad sensations and emotions. He shouted at my back as I moved away from him. Not loudly, but with heartrending volume.

"I gave her my clap, or the jack, or killer crabs. Lord, more like lobsters," he spoke at my back. "I knew it was gonna kill her. But I couldn't stop myself. If you'd monster-up enough to look, you'd see what poor shape is little Quincy here. I put him in her, son, where you *didn't* come from, it's true. I gave her whatever I got. So go ahead and do it. Come over here and let's end this right here. An eye for an eye. I don't know what else we could exchange. Let's see. Oh, wait, how about..."

Must people talk? Confess? Beg, spill beans, shoot shit? Ask for reactions? Sickening. But don't look a gift horse, as they say, right? Why? Because they told they to say it. And yet... Remember I said it's a strange thing about people, that they cannot explain themselves without reference to other people? Well, when Quinceaux said, "Kill me for killing her," I had a, I don't know, an inappropriate epiphany as to why they can't. Or, rather, I understood that I would never be able to explain myself and be recognized as myself, and it seemed a sad thing to be Set Apart and odd. I hadn't wanted to *belong* before.

So I went back and kicked him in his dirty, shit-fucked head. And it seemed to me that kicking his dirty, shit-fucked, no-good head was a kind of initiatory gesture. Like a handshake so secret, you don't use your hands for it. Could I join in the club now?

"Hey," I said. "What was she like?"

"Oh, she liked oral most, but Annie was pretty game for anything—"

"Not what *did* she like, what *was*— Oh, never mind."

I gave him one more kick to the lousy ear. It's true what they say about practice.

"Fuck you!" he yelled, sobbing loudly now as I took off at a fearless clip. "Canny! One favor? If you won't kill me? Please? Do you got my dildo? It's U-shaped! Hey! Canny! Yeah? You know what? She wanted a girl anyway! Fuck. Who's coming? Is that you Fernando? Help me stand up, man. I've got to lie down and get some sleep."

From the notes of the UndeScribe
Pages 1,118,994 - 21 {Sex is Here}

A little Motherfucking Energumen came to me with this quote today, by André Breton writing in his 1924 Manifesto of Surrealism: "It is living and ceasing to live which are imaginary solutions. Existence is elsewhere."

A perfect example of mistakenly-stated, unaware wisdom.

We are Expecting.

V.

You can only ignore something that is actually there, and the more something is there, the more it is ignored. So it was with me and my future. It had always been there, permeating my lone existence. So it was with the DogBug, until the night I met Quinceaux, when it crossed the border from the *always there* to the *actually here*. That's no small difference.

* * *

Into the foliaceous zone of Majuscule Marina and—*Bang!*—just like that, I slip into the overgrown future, the only true inheritance anyone gets. Up to this moment I'd thought night equals night. But the Majuscule night, though related to your typical rotation of the earth around its axis, is a different species. Your night is ancient. Here it's older still. It is night with a capital N, an acid bath of history itself. Impossible to tell the Precambrian dark from the Phanerozoic. All the same as far as not being able to see a damn thing, or going extinct, running face-first into destiny, fumbling into traps. The moon isn't overly bright, but it's nervous, seems too close, and I dare not check its shape.

There are a few paths among the whispery rough darkness, which do indeed shorten the passage from one location to another, but the significance of these routes is anyone's superstition. Trails lead from one cluster of leaves and bark to a cluster of different leaves and bark.

At last I entered and exited an actual path and the landscape swerved into fallen cosmopolitan impressions. A glade where straight-trunked trees stood in a quadrangular formation and bits of others trees, broken by lightning or storm, scattered on the ground like toppled pillars. Now the silence changed timbre, got reedier. I thought I heard a horse whine. (There was no horse). I thought I heard a magpie. (There was no magpie). I was hearing things because I didn't hear anything.

Where am I now? A lane of scree, narrow and unaccountably humid as a fresh-slit slaughterhouse throat, I felt eyes on me and in me. Eyes in the pit of my stomach, watching bile feast and fatten. Eyes in my heart, spying the sawdust pumping of rag doll blood. Eyes behind my eyes in my brain, peering out of my skull along with me at the muted night. (There were *definitely* some eyes). I would've prayed, but I doubt very much that atheism or agnosticism exist—never mind that organized stuff. Nothing worth arguing for or against can be worth anything.

From out of who-knows-where, a hyperbaric eidolon knocked me flat-backed onto the rocky earth, a special devil put aside just for me, nether regions monogrammed, I suspect, with my initials in flaming gold keloids. The pain came quick where my forehead met the gutted hair follicles of my denuded crown, beneath the chin and along both jaw-hinged sides of my skull. I didn't realize it was DogBug—or the Prodigal Shibboleth; or Donny-Don the Embryon; or Solar Village Idiot; or Lord Screaming Dinosaur; or Thylacine Antichrist; or September 12, 2001; or Trap-Door-Laying Harpy—at first. Had the sky pounced and was playing too rough? Like it never saw a person before and was testing my limits? Ah, but everything goes too far. It panted barely corporeal tongues. These enveloped my face and vermiculated into the cranial spiracles implanted by its proboscis, its peristomal claws. I don't know, some black-fang technology, and they bore into the cradles of my ears, anesthetizing—or killing—a little.

And every now and then my own sharply exhaled breath hit my face, blowing out of my future, obviously, and which must've been germinating deep in the DogBug's chest—or factory complex, or thorax, or globule, or missile-defense system, or stamen—and my exhalations infiltrated me as painlessly as a top-secret virus. I didn't see or feel the breaths. But I knew. I thought of the Roky Erickson song, the one about the wintry and reptilian, about never finding the way out of a cold night. The DogBug—or Joseph Smith's' Shy Alien Boyfriend, or Moby-Dick, or Hitlertronic 5000, or Etceterack, or Fenris Wolf. Existence had gone Mad-Libs on me. It was pupil-black, an aperture to see all, an abyss to fall into. Its enormity and insect-like indifference to my intentions was something like prehistoric. Except the DogBug had no relation to history, or even cosmic time. It came from a place that didn't start with a Big Bang. It wasn't really a dog or a bug. To describe the beast in terms of temporality would be to demean the awesomeness of this creature for which timelines were so much dental floss. Language isn't equal to its purpose. It was a DogBug in the way, for example, that the insultingly racist, mushroom-cloud explosions in children's cartoons are equivalent to the actual mushroom clouds that bloomed from the World War II streets of Hiroshima and Nagasaki. Just as a sight gag is not the same as true mass murder and a legacy of tortured generations, so the DogBug was not the DogBug.

Its jaws, eighth-dimensional technologies. Its evolutionary advantages, thrust into my face. What the fuck? Could having your head monster-chomped run in a family, like male-pattern baldness? So much horror and suffering thrives in the absolutely ludicrous.

For how long was I clamped-upon? People go nuts if you don't tell them how long, how old, how many years ago. It's because they're obsessed with time. They can't define it. Only lie. They're ashamed to be in its thrall.

I saw avenues of hooded, black-robed figures; spastic labyrinths collapsed and hollow-forked under the entire earth, extending even into the funereal universe; limbs ever-sprouting with a confusing supply of hollowness, secreting empty with the speed of piss. I should seek the hooded things, ask how to spot them without eyes and learn their customs, such as the appropriate times during worship, when worms and bugs should rise and sit in their pews. Which *Myriapoda* eggs to throw at chemical weddings and how to safely drink from hails of vivisected cats and dogs.

Ascot of vomit—or colostrum, or February snow, or—trickling round my neck. Always so much ooze in my blues. It was some time before I realized the cartoon image of an atomic bomb de-Nipponizing Hiroshima—or Richard the III, or Mellified Man, or the DogBug—had gone. In the frozen black above, that poor excuse of an Orion, with his crummy sword of wished-upon stars, Bellatrix practically invisible. The pain was searing, but didn't hurt nearly so much as the certainty that somehow my nervous system still existed such that I could experience that pain.

Imagine meeting your soul for the first time only when it's too late to give it a hand. I had to go. Home? A busy intersection?

There's got to be a hospital in Majuscule Marina. Blue-bloods even have private privacy. In any case, there's none in Episode Lake.

Behind my face, squirming with *joie de vivre*, a vibrant tadpole essence. And just as silence had lost its shape earlier, now, as competing ghost-moons tugged at the bewildering tides of me, so did smells hiss and mew. I heard hints of *Bombyx mori* gone ragged over generations of heirlooming, the barely-there whiff of damp mandible upon nipple and chills that would've been the feathery edges of summer winds had they not been detained in dishes of shallow scapulae.

With extraordinary gentleness and the flawless technique of a magisterial counterfeiter, it had eased its teeth, or surgical tools—used its nameless techniques, the sharp advantages of its mandibles, mastery of inverted unicorn horns—to venesect my skin and with an even, slightly pendulum-swaying motion, it had loosened the perimeters of my face in an exacting way. I wondered, is this an attack or a surgical procedure? I didn't think, is this a rape? An insemination? Grotesque breeding frenzy? Is this the implanting of horridly sidereal ova? Is this sticky genealogy? I had the sudden, crazy idea that I was Mother: Stage Two.

Oh God or shit.

DogMammaMiaBug.

Secretus.

From the notes of the UndeScribe
Page 4 {War is Menstruation Envy}

We needed now to introduce distortion into the role of the human agent involved in the pregnancy. For several hundred years we had looked to the doctrine of the Immaculate Conception as our model. For what could be a more "blasphemous freak" of so-called nature? Then instantaneous craniofacial birth (ICB), which did indeed work on the woman. Only the resultant child was ultra-typical. Mahlon Jaculus Wunderhorn Majuscule and his Midwife to Monsters, Caged-Head, decided this process of insemination was simply not *wrong* enough.

The key of inspiration was finally given unto us when a Motherfucking Energumen spotted the title of the Nick Zedd film *War is Menstruation Envy* (DVD Video; NTSC, Color, Running Time 77 minutes, 1992). In the same store he discovered the documentary *And in Cane Toads: An Unnatural History* (DVD Video, NTSC, Color, Running Time: 65 minutes, Lewis M., Director, 2001). From one viewing we learned that male cane toads, *Bufo marinus*, have been documented copulating with the bodies of deceased toads and other dead animals. Even inanimate objects such as drums and foreheads, mining helmets, petrified dinosaur feces, ice sculptures, textiles of any kind. This provided the atomic dose of inspiration required to help us determine the most efficacious way to mate the DogBug with a human. We are Expecting.

Q: Why's there no spooky legend associated with the area south of Episode Lake?

A: It's too chock full of reality to allow any such nonsensical exceptions.

VI.

I am entitled to rehearse my Last Words. Even if I am long gone, or will never be gone, there's no statute of limitations on such utterance. Nobody doubts the existence of the unknown. An obvious thing to say, if not for the fact that you were unaware that I would say so until I did. To do so would be to deny time itself, since the future is unknown. Not everyone is afraid of the future, which is as non-existent to you at this moment as a monster with forceps for a tongue, the lewd coupling of hour-hand on minute-hand when midnight is engorged, and the Truth. Not everyone's afraid of the existence of such monsters—demons, devils, frights, boogeymen, The Burning Orphanage—whatever you want to call them. That's their problem.

Monsters are the unknown appearing in *space,* which of necessity carries time on its back in symbiotic tumescence. Some monsters are holes that never need replacing, but are possibly not supposed to be there. Yet nothing's very super about the so-called supernatural. Monsters are future moments folding back on themselves and thickening into obscene materiality, contorted by the terror of meeting themselves where they simply cannot possibly be. Why, they haven't even *become* yet and here they are moving toward themselves. What else to do but destroy the ones who are *supposed* to be here, the humans? Maybe *they're* using up all the *supposed,* and if your claws are destiny-long and fate-sharp enough you can get more of your *supposed* back. Maybe enough to not exist yet?

There are no answers to these questions, but there is an endless supply of victims. Consider this a warning label on the corked, clear glass bottle in which, had I lived on an island, this iatrogenic prescription would've been carried to your feet on the littering tide.

VII.

I was just barely walking down a broad path through an expansive, unfamiliar park-like area of Majuscule Marina, the branch-filtered wind sharp as thorn pressing into my forehead. There was a stone bridge before me, beneath which was the absolute darkness of a subterranean universe. Above the tunnel, what looked like half of a huge white moon loomed, furrowed like a bald forehead with lines where craters would usually be seen. The light revealed the underpass to be framed on either side by white birch trees, uppermost dead limbs bent in to touch.

This image was rife with reminders and omens, but the whole truth of the moment somehow presented itself in fragments. I couldn't quite put it together. Or rather, everything was finally coming together because everything was falling apart. The pale trees were like two enormous mummified hands, fingertips meeting with funereal solemnity, unearthly mandibles at ease, flapping wings, my mother's hands, the opening lines of an ice age. The wind all *FFFFFFFSSSSSSSFFFFFSSSSS,* and I entered the moonless tunnel toward my future, idiot that I am.

Inside was a clearing shaped like the open palm of a giant. Even the dirt ground was furrowed with the divination lines of an opened hand. With the uniformity of an easily recognized communicative gesture, three "fingers" of bare, fuscous land rear up the steep hillock to a small red building that seems to totter on the middle-finger's tip like an issue of blood from a covenantal incision.

I walked toward an open door from which strode a gigantic man robed in black holes. I'd never seen anyone like him before. His head was by far too large for the large body, and too *mistaken*-looking. Think of the head of a top-hatted ventriloquist dummy grafted onto the neck of your average, edible gingerbread individual. Practically wearing the sky like a hat, the man's head was nearly invisible. Something moved in my new friend's face. No, that's not right. *Everything* did. Well peel my tangerines and scald my taint!

But there was a very real, oversized, vaguely human-head-shaped cage over his own head and neck, a rope cruelly cutting into the latter to keep the sadistic helmet on his shoulders. The cage was stuffed with fighting animals whose species—a three-legged crow, a bat, a fish, lizards and insects—I could only guess at amid the puzzling umbra, spasms and blood. Ah, but the universe is an *Island of Doctor Moreau* with the last chapter missing. An unruly collection of different kinds of beaks squeezed through the bars, all screeching at frantic, high volume. From every side of the cage came hissing, cawing, growling, yelping, choking and roaring. Rodent tails, like Gorgon's hair, waved in panic and hate throughout. And I heard a curiously pellucid whisper say "Don't fear, Caged-Head is here . . ."

Everything in the head-cage was the same dark color idiosyncratic to death struggles and caked blood. It was a lobster trap dragged across the crowded deck of Noah's ark. Now and then, beneath the sadistic whirlwind of fear-shitting creatures bulging through the bars of the overcrowded, zoo-like helmet, I saw a glimpse of a human face—a shredded eye; a mouth screaming in a discordant, torn timbre; skin pulsating with venomous, infected wounds-in-progress; and scars repeatedly renewed, like water fountains, into gapingly dark, wet spurts by fang and claw.

It was a disturbing mystery how the wearer of this mask was able to stand, let alone move with the agility and purpose with which he now came upon me.

He led me gently to the strange building from which he'd come. It was institutional yet wild, the bureaucratic nerve center of a formidable empire, a recently excavated city of temples, a structure grown mighty yet chaotically on a diet of poisons. A Center for Contagion Release. He was almost tender with me, in fact. Because I was pregnant, and because he was a Motherfucking Energumen and Midwife to Monsters. Because I was an embryo, and because I was a Family.

Q: Will my body go back to normal after I deliver?

A: See page 161 of *What to Expect When Expecting,* by Heidi Murkoff and Sharon Mazel

VIII.

In the canoe of his arms, Caged-Head carried me along beige corridors defined by buzzing fluorescent rectangles set in drop-down ceilings, passing one wall-mounted Purell dispenser after another, separated by blue and gray doors with small, thick glass panes, some marked EXIT, others jumbled over with arcane letters and numbers, behind which an unguessable number of creatures sang elaborate death throe cantatas, or conversed in weather-report, matter-of-fact tones.

I heard strange tidbits of phrases from behind the doors. Their lack of context for me, their seeming meaninglessness, only served to intensify my horror as my imagination whirled with hideous possibilities and questions:

"Prescriptions eat. Smudged gender wants you at the birth. We have so much room, you can even bring all your problems. There are plenty of rooms. This might be whatever you dream about…"

"Goodbye, my hand is cold."

"The stars are brass, they turned the brass doorknob of the universe, walked through slow unhinged universe doors and they ignored the Signs, barged in without wiping the black-hole crud off paws and tentacles, storm-boots a hundred Inquisitions high."

"DogBug, Counterfeit Phoenix. Zero-in-one! Marina. There is no water…"

Hooded black figures passed us, reams of administrative paper chittering as it unrolled in their wake. They genuflected, bowed down like scorched sunflowers and disappeared into an antimicrobial beyond. The air insanely clean, a mock vacuum of sterilized, nothing-sized bone flecks, each molecule stripped of the possibility of warm filth by perseverant feasting, the forensic mandibles of gelid beetle memories.

Now it was from the ceiling that I heard snatches of more death throes, conversations urbane and venal:

"She is,' he is, it is, they were. They are hour-hand on minute-hand when midnight is doubly erect. Rigor mortis of the pendulum when the time begins…"

"Lake. There is no water, no bodies. Static-crossed plains of inexplicability. Howling cynotemporality walks the winding pathogen too. A mighty sick dwindling such as could invert the Great Pyramid!"

"Tsunami-kissed sand castle. And why not the raging pathological hard-on of a pendulum when were-time is caught unhanded?"

Caged-Head came to a halt before an enormous, pitch-red door over which was a legend I'm sure I misread: GYNECROLOGICAL WARD. Too dualistic. This wasn't a black-and-white situation, no simple opposites, birth versus death, nature versus nurture. Someone's husky throat shouted like a kick aimed at me from beneath the floor:

"Goodbye, my tarsal claw is cold!"

* * *

The scene is a foggy species of operating theater. In and out of my selfness. I make a joke. "What have you done to his eyes?" They laugh. It gets quiet when Mahlon Jaculus Wunderhorn Majuscule begins humming an adorcist ditty entitled "A Cabin Totted Holes." Things plummet even further away, falling at least as far down as my heart. When it reaches that point I stop watching.

Secretus.

* * *

I can't be sure the following exchange actually happened, as I was in an indescribable state, perhaps drugged, though not with an anesthetic. But the memory does funny things, and if you get some trauma in your memory and some memory in your trauma, well, it gets just *hysterical.* For whatever reason, perhaps because it was too oozy, I remember what happened next as a conversation that unfolded this way:

"I feel like I've grown a second head right about here," I said.

"Where you'd put a parrot on Captain Hook?"

"Yeah, but both of the heads are equally mine. And though both are generating different thoughts, they are all my thoughts. And it is a single 'I' who perceives the world through each of them simultaneously."

The smothered echo of my voice returned to expire.

"Tell me about the combined impressions you are receiving from these two heads."

"They aren't exactly aligned." I tried to articulate. "Like touching a fairly regular surface with both hands, each one transmits slightly different sensations at the same time."

Mahlon Jaculus Wunderhorn Majuscule nodded. Caged-Head the Midwife to Monsters nodded. The UndeScribe nodded. The Paper Bag nodded. Mamma Ooh-Ooze nodded. The head of a dick nodded. The head of a pustule nodded. If you were there, you nodded.

I was approaching from the other side of myself, past the bleary-hot sands of gut-crust, to collapse and to drag my asshole across this one-man world-stage, smearing it with a trail of riverbed sludge impressed with the static tracks of concrete shoes.

"But this situation, owning two brains in parallel operation, is beyond confusing, worse than assembling an IKEA dresser at the bottom of Loch Ness. Understand, I haven't literally sprouted a second head, it's just as close as I can get to explaining the feelings my mind and my nerves register. And I've got no choice but to continue extending this metaphor if I'm to describe my experience with any clarity."

"Fascinating! UndeScribe and Reader-of-Proof, you are taking all his comments down? We'll be even better prepared for the next experiment, or summoning, this ritual! We'll call it whatever we want: This-Is-What's-Happening, SLOTTED INTO A BEACH, I CAN TASTE THE BLOOD. This Fine Wednesday, this bright fucking mother. Canny, take a moment if you must, and please continue."

I was starting to enjoy our talk. Is this what it's like to hang out with friends? Had I joined the club?

"Thank you, Mahlon Jaculus Wunderhorn Majuscule. Almost immediately upon appearing, my indigenous head and trespassing head clashed. And they—*I*—reeled under an accursed heads-ache, migraine and phantom migraine irrevocably miscible."

"Just now you thought it couldn't get any worse," MJWM said to me, something very much like Hiroshima said to me. "But then, if I'm correct, each of your brains began simultaneously experiencing its own ominous sense of déjà vu. And whatever had set off that uncanny intimation in your so-called *real* head is not precisely the same trigger for the déjà vu in your trespassing head?"

He understood me!

"And the déjà vu is one, or *two* rather, of agonies and regrets." He went on and off. "Forgotten do-not-do lists, and being suicided by society. Next, as though via some tremendous energy released by the explosive knocking of natal and trespassing skulls, your phantom heads and brains began to multiply incalculably, each experiencing its own unique, awful déjà vu moment, and you in turn experiencing all of them at once. Were they foaming throughout the room, surrounding you?"

"Yes! You've hit me square right on the head!" I surely praised him. "These instances of déjà vu had become localized in space, somehow. Probably why the polycephalic is the most phenomenologically accurate account I can come up with. They developed multidimensional properties, turned inside-out so that they were also experiences of unfamiliarity with all I ever knew or would know. Or, I could also say that I became the agent of a clairvoyant intuition which, at a subatomic level, was composed of countless déjà vu moments adhering together in such a way that the dark, the moonlight hovering by the high window, the shuffle of robes in the hallways, the beaks and scribbles, disappeared, leaving behind not emptiness or *lack* of those things, but presenting, quite clearly, an entirely impossible world that I knew, yet didn't yet know."

You nodded. If you were there.

"Do you understand, the DogBug has made you neither man nor woman?"

"No."

"Good. I tell you this because, post operation, we will refer to you as an 'it' rather than 'he' or 'she.' Do you understand?"

"No."

"Good. And are you screaming at this moment?"

"Yes, thank you. I am screaming, doctor."

"And here?"

"Yes, right here, and also here and here."

"Good. And what if I told you your head was up your ass?"

"I would believe it," I said.

Q: What's with the sinister, hooded, black-robed figures?

A: Every too often a stereotype of evil falls into perfect alignment with its reality. Sorry.

Incomplete Parenthetical #2: Has No End)

What I really need is a shitty sketch, but I'll try to do it in words. I woke to find myself propped up in a hospital bed facing an eerie Question dressed in black sitting at the foot of the bed. The light was such that I could see nothing of it but hands and an adumbration of human body from neck down. Its hands were offensively enormous and his ribcage and back extremely broad, as though it had been bred, like a specialized hunting hound, for functions requiring the exaggeration of these specific body parts. Like a torture device. Those monster hands were the palest gray of hardened ambergris, born via the convulsive roar of a Leviathan's ship-splitting vomit. Or papier-mâché.

I felt my visitor's unseen eyes sucking the Norwegian blue from my own as though color was marrow. And it's hard to explain, but it just hung there like a portrait in a gallery, giving me time to judge its merits. As though gaining new eyes—better, a new *way* to see, such as when a planet, blurry to the point of near-invisibility, comes into striking focus with the proper adjustment of a telescopic lens.

I saw at least five things at the same time. I'll try to explain.

First. A hairless humanoid covering its eyes with its hands, and the blackness in the middle of its face, took on the shape of a grim, black-hooded figure heading toward me, full of ill-intentions, perhaps planning to rip my eyeballs from their sockets.

Second. Focusing on the approaching figure's hands, I now saw the victim who'd just had its eyes ripped out by the figure racing toward me. And everywhere the strong smell of those maybe-mummified hands, fingertips meeting with pall-bearing solemnity, unearthly mandibles at ease, the opening lines of an ice age. The sticky-fresh, amputated wings of a bird born extinct.

Third. Now I saw that the figure with its hands over its face was a bystander, an innocent hominid who'd witnessed the oracular attack and couldn't bear to look at the carnage any longer.

Fourth. I then observed a humanoid that must've put its hands over its eyes to try and avoid the sight of some fast-approaching, hooded menace that meant it harm, unaware the doom was, *in fact*, coming from *and* penetrating deep within itself.

Fifth. Not a humanoid at first, but a familiar landscape, a path leading beneath a stone bridge into a pre-solar universe. A titanic, furrowed alien moon is rising over the tunnel like the aftermath of an experimental nuclear explosion gone wrong, or a bald forehead inscribed with decades of lines that mean nothing. The moonlight reveals the underpass to be framed on either side by white birch trees, uppermost dead limbs bent in to touch. Wait, it enters the scene: an anonymously robed figure, clad like an inquisitor, walking away into, or coming out of, the tunnel.

Its face equals its own face looking at itself? Yes, but more.

A dark, monkish figure nearing it *qua* victim, while it naively covers its eyes in terror. What will happen to me, when the black-hooded thing slips through the white trees and disturbs my cowering?

Each thing is simultaneously several things and points-of-view, and I'm viewing all these at once. Dark, violent figure approaching; the victim with hands over its torn sockets; the witness that can't stand to see the victim in such pain; and then me watching all these humanoids making the same gestures for different reasons, and even the landscape where it happens. The whole shebang.

The face before me is made of moments. It is a moving scene, one of rigid reenactment. It's impossible to describe the awful effect of being observed by a scene. I'm no artist, but if I could make a sketch of it, however shitty, that would explain things better than words.

The cloaked figure in the middle of its face grew larger, black mandibles hovering above it like wings extended toward me and waxed with the figure, both soon eclipsing their frames of white hands or trees and, stepping out of, snipping away the pale visage, head, ears and all, became the darkness, now filling the entire room, and I thought I must be inside it. Whether the mandibles held me in the folds of its cloak or labyrinth of guts, its mind, maw, or abyss, I didn't know. Of course, the very idea was ridiculous. How could I've been inside myself? For that's who it is. Didn't the doctor say so? I am an abominable perfection, the perfect unity of rehearsal for an unending final show and the final show itself.

Did I stalk, predatory in a black cloak? Yes.

Did I cover my eyes in terror at the approaching figure? Yes.

The scene replayed. I hardly recognized myself. I have nothing to protect myself, not even a paper bag. Not even the dry, erotic distraction of vibrating bees. If I am seeing this, there's no escape. If I am this, there's no way out. Anywhere. Where's my DogBug, my baby, my DadDog, my future of oozy violations, my It's-Me-Again? I don't care. I want nothing to do with these ontological Mad-Libs.

Besides, I don't know if an "It," like me, gets any say in anything.

And as for MomBug, now I know everything there is to know about her and then some, and that's more than far too much. I've been there and back again and there some more. Nature versus nurture? Don't make me laugh! It's Nature versus nature, and nature wins. Wasn't I taken by my father as she was, and didn't I get pregnant with myself and give birth to me sure as her? Only when I was ricocheted into the world out the barrel of mother's face, I didn't come as planned. I wasn't the bouncing little bolus of joy MJWM desired.

No, I, the first I wasn't a true "It" but rather the result of a distorted mating ritual that wasn't distorted enough to be fully real. But they were close. They studied and studied, rented obscure movies, sat alert in bathroom stalls and made great advances. And then they waited for the right moment. Don't ask me how these necromancers—or Motherfucking Energumens, whatever they're called—descry such things.

And when it was time they summoned up the DogBug—or the Future, or the Children, or Pappa, or the Wednesday Ever After—again. For they call it many things, though they only call me "It."

Father got a second chance to bring me forth, mounting his mouth over the face of his son, implanting seed and laying eggs so that same son—only better this time—grew gravid-faced with himself until he was itself carrying the heavy doom of its birth. I could try to put a happy spin on it, consider myself extraordinarily lucky. How many are given a second chance to be conceived? How many get to say "I want to be a child when I grow up?" A chance to be born the way you were *supposed* to be? As intended?

I've no idea what goes on outside these repeating moments that, at the very least, are my face looking at myself approaching and myself looking at myself covering my eyes in dread of my approach, and myself unable to see not even the color red, through scooped sockets. And the tunnel, too, is me and my face, this hall that needs no mirrors. In the dawn of my convalescence in the Gynecrological Worm—or earth, or Hell, or whatever they want to call it—I had the thought that I was bad flesh become a dream on infinite loop. But how could that be? I'm real. I must be. But then again, recurring nightmares, those are as real as anything else, right? That's what I've been told. I'm an "It." So what do I know any more about not being one? I'm a bit shaky on that score as I never did remember my dreams before I became a Family. It was like someone borrowed them every night, though I recall part of a lullaby that made more sense than I could handle.

O a hole, a soul never needs replacing
It can always stay or leave there.

I must've learned it in the world, because the learning stops once you've left it. Tell me, what news of that place, the world? Perhaps it's gone. Fine. All's well that ends, period, full-stop. But how about what won't never, ever, end? And how time seems to take up such a lot of time? And how they ask but for how long, and when? It drives them nuts, anyone can see.

IX.

Fall. Fall, fall, fall, fall, fall. Tongue twister, that.

What are you supposed to say when it's over, words used up and reasons to stay all gone? Time to go. You can forget about me now? Have a good one? No, ridiculous. Sounds like a beer advertisement. Bye-bye? Not a chance in Hell. Till we meet again? Ostentatious and a wee old-fashioned. Take care? I don't know about that one, either. Seems like a funny thing to say upon parting. I mean, why wouldn't you? What demon would distract you from taking care? Or why would you *need* to? What monster could possibly lie in wait?

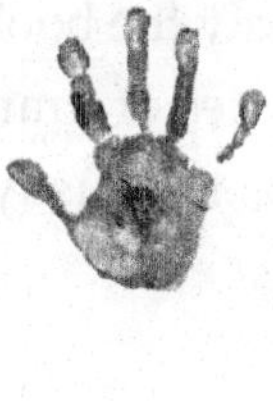

AFTERWORD

I have a horrible memory, what's past gets dropped in the Past, I see no need to keep it in any kind of order, you can always make things up to fill in the gaps. But I remember *exactly* where I was when I first read *Moby-Dick*. I was sixteen, bedridden on my parents' couch, very ill and feverish for about a week, and I spent that week very far from high school, on vacation from the future, reading, almost living, definitely *feeling*, *Moby-Dick* start to finish.

I think reading that book, the words and the fever got mixed up, and after that I *had* to write. And what's more, I knew that how I wanted to write was however Melville was doing what he did to me in *Moby-Dick*. I also knew Melville was doing something way over my ability—that only made me work harder. I must learn how to burn myself with imaginary fire.

I don't think there is a "best book ever" but I believe there are a number of books which, while you are reading them, make you feel as though you are reading the best book ever. And so, for me, *Moby-Dick*: The strange lines of questioning, which followed their own logic, almost the poetic equivalent of mathematical formulae and proof. The oracular statements leading me away from, toward, and then way past myself. The awe, the terror and the bizarre humor. The difficulty in telling when Melville was being straight with you or taking the piss. The way the book would suddenly go from a first person narrative to a series of dramatic monologues, to essays on various nautical matters. The justly famous "Whiteness of the

Whale" chapter. The Fuck You! of it, and the Please God, I Beg You, I Know I'm Joking, But I'm Dead Serious! of it.

You could be passionate about ambiguity. You could worship your confusion, transmuting it into awe. Writing could feel like being the fever warping the mind—God, imagine a fever with intentions and the skill to act on them? You could fling yourself into the glory of anything in reckless ecstasy. Or at least you could think about it. You can do whatever you want to, if you do it really well and say no to drugs. It's still necessary to make sense, no matter how weird. There are no best practices in writing, and it's not best practices to not be engaged in best practices. Which is the point of art. We're so much fucking better than that.

The Shitty Sketch

My story started with a sketch on a stray piece of loose-leaf paper. Doodling seems innocent enough… It better be, I do it all the time. In 2013 I'd been unemployed for over half a year, looking for a job, and I was working on a story featuring masks. I wanted a weird, uncanny mask and came up with an idea of a mask that looks like the wearer of the mask is frightened and covering their eyes to avoid seeing some awful sight. I doodled a sketch of it. That sketch serves as the Prologue to my version of "I Can Taste the Blood." I became obsessed with that image. It stuck with me through more than a year with a nervous, doomy power. I had to build something around it, set it at the *heart* of something. Give it something important to do so it would forget about me.

Alternate Titles

I'm not used to writing with constraints (even such a minimal one), so this was a tough project for me. On the other hand, I knew

I had the title: "I Can Taste the Blood." And it's fun getting pushed around, now and then, you know? Just make sure you trust your aggressor.

Without that mandate, I might've used one of these titles I've had floating around in my head for some time:

- "The House of Growling Blood"
- "Mother Louse Loves You"
- "Casualties of Nowhere"
- "The Black Crown of Cares"
- "The Mud at the Banquet"
- "Jerk in Progress"
- "Wet Dreams in the Bed of Puppets"
- "Gasmask Revival (after Voivod)"
- "God for Nothing"
- "The Beat of Eaten Hearts"
- "What to Expect"
- "Bodies of Water"
- "A BETCHA DON TOILETS"

I better stop there. Or rather, I'm going to.

In Praise of Fevers

This is dedicated to my writer colleagues who are so adept at drawing us into their imaginations in their own unique ways. There are no Christmas lightbulbs in these stories, but blinding visions. Let's all burn our eyes out! I salute them, and I call them Ishmael. And John… Holy Hell but I'm proud of you, my son (in a Methuselah kind of way), and other unmanly sentimental feelings best left in self-help books.

So my hope is that one day some kid gets really, really sick—don't get me wrong, she recovers 100% in the end—lives, unlike stories, should have happy beginnings middles and ends. But this kid lies around feeling lousy and can't watch TV because it hurts her head. Someone passes her a copy of this book and she reads it. And the rest is history. And she starts writing about it.

I think about that fever I got when I was sixteen, and how it never went away.

Erik T. Johnson
April 2016

ABOUT THE AUTHOR

Erik T. Johnson doesn't believe in order or boxes. He became a writer because he can't make a straight line to save his life—since stories consist of terrifically asymmetrical, random sequences of random shapes. Also because of what Georges Bataille meant by: "I write the way a child cries: a child slowly relinquishes the reasons he has for being in tears."

Johnson is a Written Backwards DARWA Voice Award-winner whose fiction appears in renowned places, such as *Space & Time Magazine, Tales of the Unanticipated, Qualia Nous,* and all three volumes of the award-winning *Chiral Mad* series.

Erik is certain unreliable narrators don't exist—only unreliable authors. He will prove his uncompromising reliability when his first book of short stories is published in 2016.

Visit Erik at www.eriktjohnson.net.

Stalk him on Twitter @YES_TRESPASSING.

Curse him at your own risk, do other stuff when it suits you.

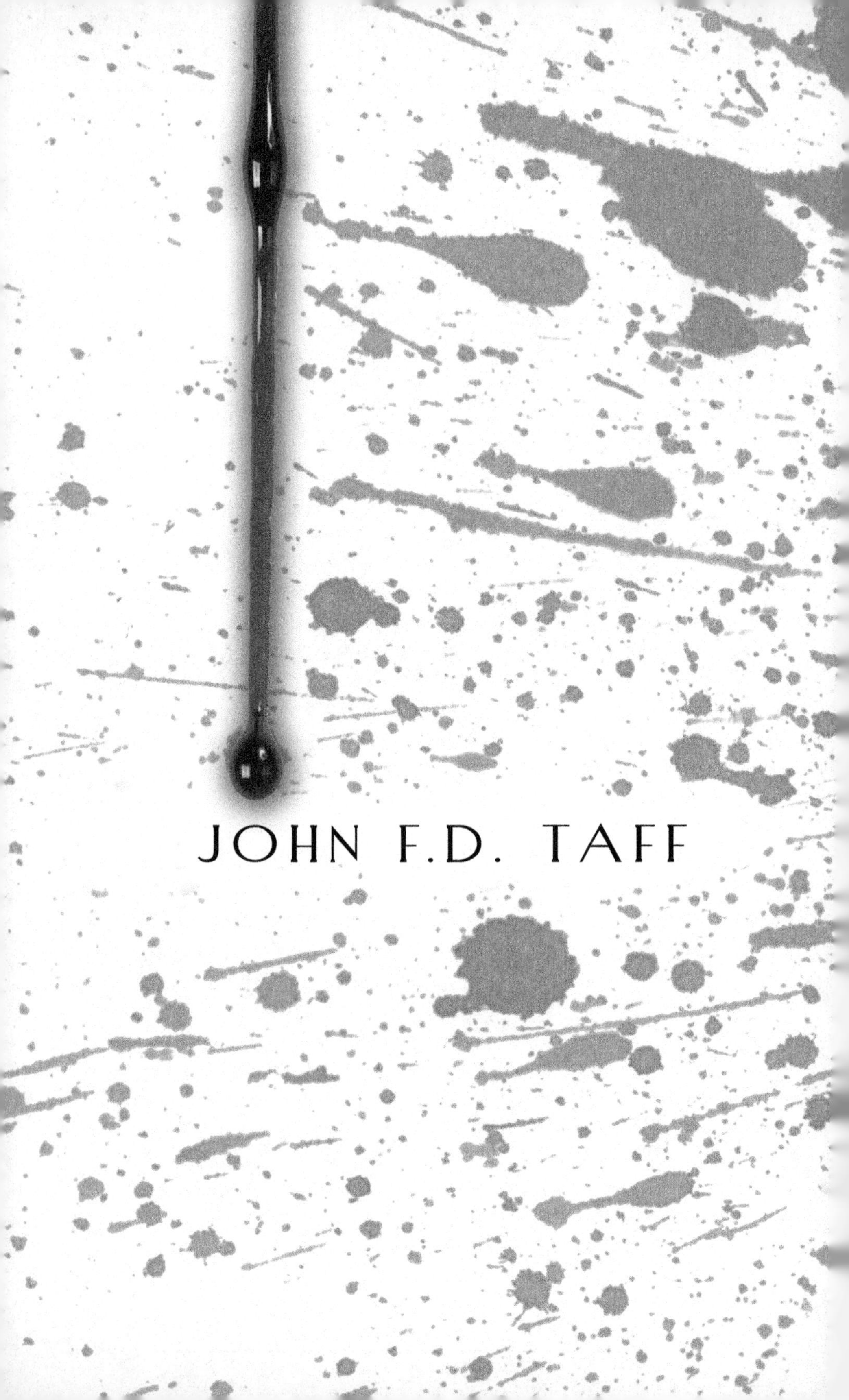

JOHN F.D. TAFF

Second Integument

I'm scrunched up against the inside of the water tank, the curve of my back pressed to the cold steel inner wall.

It's dark and dank. I can smell the tang of the steel, the rust that weeps from the walls, the condensed minerals that scar every surface in thick weals.

I sit in the shadows, knees drawn to my chin, shivering, shivering…

I raise my hands to my face. I can barely see them before me in the murk. I'm a man who's worked with his hands all his life. I know every callous, every scar, every dirty swirl and peak of my fingerprints.

I don't have to see them. I know what they look like…*even now.*

I spread my fingers, close them.

Spread them.

Close them.

Click-clack.

Click-clack.

A funny little song runs through my head; an old song, a children's song now.

Something about a shark biting with pearly, white teeth.

I spread my fingers again, close them.

Click-clack.

And they are pearly white, they are…

Except for the…

I. The Things That Keep You There

It started with the blood.

Well, it actually started with the slow, slow erosion of my marriage, never a really solid relationship to begin with. Marcy and I hit a snag about seven years in and never recovered.

What was it? Hell if I knew then or know now. There was no cheating, on my part I'm positive and on her part I'm pretty damn sure. There were no Internet dating site affairs, no inter-office romances, no old torches from high school suddenly reappearing.

There was no abuse, physical, verbal or otherwise, from either me or her. Oh, there were fights, some of them pretty righteous, but nothing that edged toward anything more damaging than slammed doors and someone not sleeping in the marital bed that night.

No, there was no alcoholism, no drugs, no real money problems. Nothing I could really put my finger on.

Just one day, seven years in, Marcy woke up and decided she didn't really love me anymore. Might not even *like* me all that much. Might not have ever loved me at all.

Which was too bad, for us both, since we were pretty much settled into a quiet, tranquil life, with jobs and a house just off the main drag in town, a dog and a daughter, Melody, who was five years old when her mother had her epiphany.

Yeah, it was like a country song—Merle and Marcy and little Melody, and our dog, Captain America. Just like a big ole jacked up Luke Bryan song, or really Merle Haggard, my ma's reason for naming me. Vesta—yeah, that was my ma's name—was a big fan of "I'm a Lonesome Fugitive," Haggard's first big hit. Reminded her of my dad, whom I never met because he up and rabbited before I was born and never returned. No cards, no letters, no phone calls to check up on things.

So I got my name from a prison song done by a grizzled old country singer because it reminded my ma of my deadbeat dad.

Great.

Exciting as all this seems, it was something completely different that put the major pothole in our marriage: *complacency.*

I guess that's what did us in. It's like the creeping crud. It moves so slowly you don't even know it's a problem. Which is strange, really, when you think of it. The whole idea of settling down with someone is to relax, live in the moment, be comfortable. Get out of the whole fake-smile, is-this-the-date-we-actually-sleep-together, can-I-go-now dating world and be with someone who's seen you vomiting all over the bathroom, seen you before you've showered and brushed your teeth and hair. Someone who's heard your stupid jokes and eaten your bad food, seen you drunk late night at the local bar and hungover the next morning, been around your stupid friends, smelled your farts and heard your 2:00 a.m. snoring.

And they still want to hang in there with you, because of the love. That's how relationships are sold. The comfort, the stability.

What they don't tell you is how horribly easy, how terribly common it is to slide from comfortable to complacent, and not even know you're there until, well, until it's too late.

Love leads to comfort, which strengthens the love.

Sure. The love. Let me tell ya, one divorce will cure you of that shit. One divorce is all it takes to turn your world upside down, give it a good, bone-rattling shake, and toss it to the curb.

Love leads to relationships, which are fucking hard, my friend. There is no comfort there. It's a 24/7 slugfest of who left the toilet seat up *again* and whose parents' house did we do Christmas at *last* year and you bought *what* without discussing it with me?

And if you don't think your significant other is keeping track of every slight, every inequity, every imbalance in your relationship—keeping it with a red-tipped pen in some buried yet instantly accessible journal of the mind, to be hauled up at a moment's notice and thumped down onto the argument table with all the heft and authority of a dictionary during a game of Scrabble, well, then, you've never really been in a *relationship.*

And to think I got married later in life just to try to avoid most of this shit.

But, I digress.

It began with the blood…

* * *

Again, though, it really didn't.

So there we were, Marcy and I, in this now rickety relationship after seven years. Everything else was great. The finances were tight but manageable, the house was beautiful, jobs were secure. Shopping trips every six months or so to St. Louis or Chicago for nice clothes for both my girls. A nice car and a truck in the carport. Food on the table. Money to drink up and go dancing, mostly on the weekends and mostly at the Rest-Ezee right on the highway. Hell, the dog was fucking perfect.

But we, Marcy and I, we were falling apart. And like a lot of couples in our predicament, we didn't know exactly what to do. So we circled each other for about a year. Fake smiles—just like we were dating again!—brushing past each other in the kitchen, in the bathroom, a quick peck before leaving for work, before we turned from each other in our bed to go to sleep.

No unkind words, really. No, that would come later. Boy, would it. No real fights, just a sort of cold, hollow brittleness that settled over us both like an early November frost.

Then, though, it turned, as if someone really didn't get the memo, someone really didn't see all the signs and the portents and the omens and the storm clouds on the horizon. It changed, and Marcy was suddenly telling me that she wasn't happy. Not happy with her job, the house, living in a Podunk town in the middle of Illinois, a lot of things, but mostly just plain not happy with me.

Suddenly I was an asshole. According to her, this shouldn't have come as a surprise. I was a longstanding—perhaps lifetime—

member of the asshole club. The neighbors thought I was an asshole. My co-workers apparently thought I was one, too, as did her family and friends.

And my assholiness was to blame for her sudden, inexplicable unhappiness.

Now, my ego was such that I wouldn't ever rule out—at least not entirely—the possibility that I was, indeed, an asshole. But I wasn't. I was pretty easy going. Pretty well liked at work. Friendly to the neighbors. Her family and friends might have actually thought I was an asshole, but I suspect that she'd spent some time quietly building her case with them before she came to me with her pronouncement.

After that, it was on. The fights came. The brittle chill became hot, global warming hot. Lava hot. There were fights all the time, before breakfast, after dinner, on the phone at work, in front of our daughter and behind closed doors.

I moved out in '08, lived with friends while the legal wrangling took place. She kept the house and the kid, of course. It's the American way. I got a dick, so no way was I going to get custody of Melody. Though, truth be told, she was always closer to me. I didn't fight it. Instead, I found a rental, a small bungalow on the edge of town, right as the city fades into the endless fields of corn and wheat, and settled in.

At the age of forty-four, I became a small-town-America divorced dad, working sixty hours or more at the power plant just down the highway, seeing my daughter on the weekends, watching TV and drinking. Drinking at home, drinking at the Rest-Ezee, drinking at friends' places.

Just, ya know, *drinking*.

Thought about leaving town, too. I mean, what was left? An ex-wife and a daughter I seldom saw. I'd made friends with everyone I was likely to make friends with, screwed every woman who was likely to interest—or be interested by—me. There was no nook or cranny of the town I hadn't explored in my forty-some-odd years, no landmark unknown to me, no store I hadn't been in, no house I hadn't been inside for one reason or another, no bank I hadn't had money in at some time.

I had a pointless job and a do-nothing life in a go-nowhere town.

So why didn't I leave?

God, why didn't I leave?

First Connective Tissue

When did I notice it—*them*—first?

Itching. That's what it was that caught my attention. My hands itched, particularly along the sides of my fingers, down into the valleys between them. Nothing horrible, nothing too distracting.

Just itching.

So I scratched.

That was it, really, just itching and scratching.

I didn't really do anything, at least not then.

I mean, do what?

What was I supposed to be worried about?

Why on earth would I have thought about teeth?

II. Blood Drives & Spaghetti Dinners

Merle stumbled on the edge of the road as the eighteen-wheeler whooshed by, its wheels singing, the wake of its passing shoving him off the asphalt. The weeds were high, hiding the drainage culvert, and he twisted his ankle a little, slid down the shallow slope of the ditch.

"Fucker," he gasped, his hands flying out to steady himself against a fall. At fifty years old, Merle had begun to worry a little about falls and what they might do to his aging, disagreeable body.

Coulda been worse, he thought. *Coulda happened on my way* from *rather than* to.

If that had been the case, he was sure he'd have been knocked on his keister, might have even ended up sleeping where he'd fallen in these same weeds.

He stumbled a few steps, his momentum carrying him, crouched as if he were sneaking up on something. When his shoes hit the gravel of the parking lot, he steadied himself, let out a deep sigh. He turned back to the road, saw it stretch from left to right, from the fiery blue of twilight to the black violet of night. In the clear, moonless sky above, a few stars wobbled, or was that him?

Off to his right, the red of the trailer's rear lights diminished, faded.

Highway 154 snaked past him, slithered a path across southern Illinois, from one dead burg to another. Its gently hilled, gently curving two-lanes would carry you, if you were so inclined, from Red Bud in the west all the way over to Rend Lake, with nothing much to garner a pause in between.

Merle's hometown of Norton, on the banks of the Kaskaskia River, wasn't anything that would slow most of the highway's traffic, much less stop it. The town clung to the road like a barnacle—stubborn, hard and calcified, but also dying.

Norton was dying, like most of the other small towns along 154, like most of the small towns in Illinois, in America. Slowly, sure, but dying nonetheless, gasping, stunned, wide-mouthed like a fish on a line.

But none of that concerned Merle at the moment. That's not to say that this thought—the dying of his town, his state, his country, the entire goddamn world, not to mention his own advancing death—didn't concern Merle. No, quite the contrary, it concerned him so much, on a daily basis, that he found himself walking a half mile down the side of the road to cross this gravel parking lot and go inside the Rest-Ezee, one of Norton's three bars, his watering hole of choice.

Merle turned to the little cinder block and aluminum-roofed building that the gravel lapped at like a shallow, grey sea. The windows were fogged with sixty years of road dirt on the outside, sixty years of cigarette smoke on the inside.

A large neon sign hung in one window, attended by a court of smaller signs—Budweiser, Miller, Pabst, Jägermeister. The larger proclaimed "Rest-Ezee" in glowing, hot pink letters, while to either side two martini glasses, olives afloat, tipped rakishly toward each other.

As Merle opened the door, he thought that he'd never seen anyone drinking anything from a martini glass here at the Rest-Ezee, including his own sainted mother who was about as classy a broad as ever came out of Norton, Illinois.

***

The door opened onto mostly darkness, defined by discrete pools of light. A strand of Christmas lights hung around the mirror behind the cluttered bar, reflected on and through the multi-colored liquor bottles poised like Olympic swimmers on their blocks, all in a row. There were can lights over the bar stools, over the six or so cracked and peeling booths that slumped along one wall, and over the huddle of ancient, leaning pinball machines lined up against the other wall.

Between these two areas, ceiling lights hung over the three battered pool tables, casting pools of dusty yellow light over their various players and hangers-on. Aside from this, and the ghostly reflections of the neon signs, the bar was all dimness and shadows.

The atmosphere inside was dense as a closed fist. Fresh and stale cigarette smoke hung in the air, along with the funk of old beer that had seeped into the threadbare carpet, the stained wooden floorboards. Grease from the thousands of hamburgers, fried shrimp, onion rings and French fries the place had served over the years leached from the air, condensed out onto the tables and chairs as a thin, slick layer.

Merle hobbled to the bar, plopped onto one of the thickly padded stools, groaning and rubbing his hip. A bottle of Miller plopped down before him, and he hitched a little to reach across the bar to get it.

"Sore, Merle?" asked Helen, the bartender, finding a bowl of pretzels from somewhere below. She plunked it onto the bar next to the beer.

Merle took a long, appreciative pull from the bottle, threw a few pretzels into his mouth to chase it.

"Fell in the parking lot," he said, grimacing. "Gettin' old, darlin', gettin' old."

"You're older than my grandpa's asshole and smell twice as bad," came a voice from beside him.

"That sounds like family secrets I don't need to know about, motherfucker," Merle growled without turning. The last word in his drawled sentence was almost an afterthought.

"I'll have what he's having," laughed the voice.

"Then let's head on out to the parking lot first, so I can kick your skinny ass down the embankment."

Merle turned a gimlet eye to his right and looked at the face of his oldest friend, James C. Derringer. Jimmy Derringer. Jimmy D to some. Jimmy Gun to others. Just Gun to Merle, who'd first met him during second-grade recess on the playground of John J. Pershing Elementary School, back when Elvis was still the King and bell bottoms were all the rage.

Merle had walked into Gun looking hot and angry, hovering over another kid, a slow student named Stew Meredith.

"Who are ya and watcha doin' with Stew?" Merle had asked.

"Name's Jimmy C. Derringer, and I aim"—he said this in such a rehearsed way that Merle knew, and was proven correct years later, that the boy had picked it up from his father—"to kick this retard's ass."

Merle had looked down at Slow Stew, as most kids called him, and had seen he was nonplussed, neither scared nor particularly concerned about the beating he most surely was about to receive. Merle didn't think much of Stew, but he also never saw him as a person to bully. It seemed unfair to him, and there was simply no upshot to it.

Gun drew back one thin, dirty little arm, preparing to launch it into Slow Stew's vacant, moony face.

"I guess you could do that, but you're just gonna piss off the yard ladies and get into all sorts of trouble," Merle said. "And, course, there's also Stew's big brother Patrick, who'll break you over his knee when he finds out."

Gun let his fist drop. It was a small town, of course, and he knew about Stew's older brother just as well as Merle.

"I don't know you," Gun said, narrowing his eyes and unballing his other fist from the front of Stew's shirt. The bigger boy fell backwards with a grunt, climbed to his feet and lumbered away.

"Name's Merle. Like to play kickball?"

Gun squinted into the sun over Merle's head.

"Yeah."

"What say you and me grab a ball from the kindygardeners and kick some?"

Gun took this in, watched Slow Stew plod away.

"Sure. Okay."

And that had been it. That little encounter had sealed a forty-year friendship.

They still saw each other most days here at the Rest-Ezee, mostly over a beer, or mostly over a few beers.

"Jeez, my ass hurts," Merle groaned, taking another pull from his longneck.

Gun slid his beer over, swallowed at least a quarter of it.

"Too bad. That don't usually happen until after a few hours of sitting on these damn barstools," he said, winking at Helen who dismissed him with a wave of her dishrag. "Maybe get it checked out. Doc Hopson'll probably be here before it gets too late."

Merle stared off at the rows of liquor behind the bar, backlit from the drooping skein of Christmas lights. The bright, jewel colors of all that liquid—emeralds and ambers, sapphires and rubies—seemed to swirl hypnotically in their bottles.

"Nah," he finally said, barely heard over the Skynyrd playing from the jukebox. He raised his arm again to drain the rest of his beer, frowned. At the bend of his left arm was a small ball of cotton held in place by a strip of medical tape.

He set the mostly empty beer bottle onto the bar, where it was whisked away and replaced by a fresh one, and raised his arm closer to his eyes.

"Give blood today?" Gun asked.

Merle kept frowning as he studied the cotton ball. "Guess so," he said. "Don't really remember doing it." He hooked a finger under one end of the tape, yanked it away with more than a few hairs.

The cotton ball came away, too, compressed but pristine. Not even a dot of his blood had soaked into it. Peering intently, he was just able to make out the small, raised bump where the needle had gone in.

"Seems like everyone here in town is having a blood drive," Gun said. "Never seen a small town with such a need for blood."

On a whim, Merle raised his other arm. There in the soft, wrinkled skin at the crook of his elbow, was another raised bump, this one not quite so red or puffy.

Yesterday? The day before?

Merle had some vague, fuzzy memories of giving blood, but was sure that it had been last week. He looked over to Gun, raising the bottle to his lips, and saw a similar bandage across the inside of his right arm.

"Well, shit there, Gun," he drawled, hoisting his own beer. "You got one too, son."

For a moment, Gun had no idea what Merle was talking about. Then, after lifting both arms like a chicken ready to flap them, he caught site of what Merle had noticed.

"Well, fuck," he slurred. "How'd that get there?"

He picked away the cotton ball like a scab, flicked it and the tape across the bar.

"You give blood, too?" Merle asked.

Gun shook his head. "Don't remember, but guess I did. Maybe up at the Legion. Think they were doin' it today. Surprised I didn't see ya."

Merle shook his head. "I didn't go to the damn Legion today. I'd remember that."

"Well fuck, son. Maybe it was the K of C or the VFW. I don't know."

"I didn't go to any of them," he said, pursing his lips and setting the beer back down. "Not really sure I even went to work today."

Gun turned, surveyed his friend in a comically serious manner. "Son, are you drunk?"

"Off one beer?" he said, but then took stock of how he felt. His head was swimming and his limbs were light and loose. And there was that fall earlier, down the embankment. "Maybe."

Gun considered this. "Well, I ain't eaten yet. You?"

Merle shook his head slowly.

"Mayhap we should step out and grab a bite before we imbibe anymore," Gun said, then drained his beer and slammed it with finality onto the bar, eliciting an eye roll from Helen.

"Okay. Where to?"

"Spaghetti supper tonight, I think. At the VFW."

Merle groaned as he pulled himself from the barstool. "Good goddamn, but these stools hurt my ass."

Gun took his arm, pulled him forward. "You sound like my old dad when he was constipated and dying over at Mercy Meadows."

* * *

The night had cooled and darkened as the two old friends stumbled down the road. The skin of Norton that clung to the highway was mostly the stuff traveling people would stop for—a Casey's

General Store, a Sunoco filling station, a Dairy Queen. They passed them all, then the fire station, its sign promoting one of the town's ubiquitous blood drives—NEXT WEEK, MAY 16-23!

Across the highway from the fire station was the Norton Grange, the town's feed and seed store, where Gun worked for his uncle. The huge lot that stood beside it, fenced in on all sides, held farm equipment of all kinds—from tractors to irrigators, from combines to seed planters. All huge and immobile in the twilight, like dinosaur skeletons in a museum after the lights have been turned off.

And over all of it, a gigantic shadow in the background, was the town's water tower. It was a great, cauldron-shaped thing perched atop four spindly legs, painted a weird turquoise color and emblazoned with the single word NORTON. It was at least a hundred feet tall and always reminded Merle of those Martian ships in *The War of the Worlds*.

He remembered reading the book long ago, when he'd been a reading kind of guy, constantly looking out his bedroom window at the water tower, as if it might suddenly lurch to life and march through town on those skinny metal legs.

Almost regretfully for Merle, it never did. Nothing interesting ever happened in Norton.

From the fire station, they turned south onto Madison Street, passed old Fern Davis' house, Sam and Sally Deming's place and crazy Burt Sutherland's. Up ahead, bathed in light, was the parking lot of the VFW hall, filled with cars and SUVs, but mostly pickup trucks. The sign outside read: SPAGHETTI DINNER TO-NITE! 6 P.M. to ????. BRING YOUR APPETITE!

Gun nudged him. "Mmmm…smell that? Make you hungry?"

Merle sniffed the cooling night air, and it did, indeed, make his stomach rumble. He could smell tomato sauce, cooked beef, melting cheese.

But there was also something else, something that seemed, well, *off* a little.

Merle shook his head, trying to clear it, and pushed after his friend.

* * *

Inside, the place was packed with people lined up to pay their admissions and get their meals. Eight dollars bought unlimited spaghetti—with vegetarian sauce, meat sauce or meatballs—an Italian salad and plenty of cheese garlic bread. Lemonade, tea—sweet and unsweet—soda, coffee and, of course, beer.

They knew everyone in line, everyone at the little desk where people took their money, everyone behind the counter who ladled out the spaghetti, dished out the limp salad with steel tongs, shoved a couple of hunks of bread, redolent of garlic, onto their piled plates. He went with Gun to the table where there were urns of coffee and pitchers of tea and lemonade, followed his friend's lead in filling a Styrofoam cup with coffee the color and consistency of motor oil.

They waded through the crowd in the low, drop-ceilinged dining room of the VFW hall, nodding to this person, shaking a hand or two, bestowing kisses on the dusty, rose-scented cheeks of a few women who were their mothers' contemporaries. Taking a seat at one of the rows of communal tables that filled the room, Merle set his plate before him, put the paper napkin on his lap, bowed his head and pretended to say a few silent words.

When a suitable period had passed he looked over at Gun seated next to him. The man's lips moved, and Merle instantly felt both impressed that his friend really did seem to be saying pre-meal grace and somewhat ashamed that he hadn't. He watched Gun finish his prayer, then pick up fork and knife and dive into his plate of food.

Merle, however, didn't feel right, didn't feel good. Instead of eating, he looked around the room. It was packed with people of all ages, each hunched over plates, shoveling food into their mouths. The room was dense with noise—voices chattering, children laughing, people slurping spaghetti, drinking, crunching bread. There was the sound of chairs scooting in and out from beneath tables across the scuffed linoleum floor. The squeaky sound of plastic knifes slicing across Styrofoam plates.

And chewing, chewing, chewing.

He absently scratched between the fingers of one hand, then the other.

"You gonna eat or what, man?" Gun asked.

Still rubbing his fingers, Merle looked down at his plate.

The food before him glistened under the jaundiced, yellow light of the fluorescents, shone as if it were covered with a layer of slime. Even the garlic bread shimmered as if sweating. The salad looked like greasy pieces of green construction paper heaped together with stringy strands of celery and red clots of pimento.

Merle's stomach began to feel distinctly unwell.

Then, as he watched in amazement, the noodles on his plate moved, undulated like a mass of thin, pallid worms. The whole mound of his spaghetti heaved atop his plate, seemed to wind in upon itself.

And the sauce, the red sauce, began to look distinctly watery, distinctly biological, like blood and serum that had separated. He could see it bead on the bone-colored surface of each strand of pasta, like wax on the body of a freshly washed car.

Merle's stomach folded inside him. His hands, still itching, went below the lip of the table and grabbed his gut, pushed in a little in an attempt to settle it.

But it got worse when he raised his eyes from the table.

He looked out over the crowd again, and now most of them weren't people. They were monstrosities, horrors, deformed and twisted, hardly human.

Verrill McKay, one of the town's biggest farmers, sat there large as life, a head atop a melting, squiggling mass of congealed flesh that brought to mind a Jell-O mold left too long in the sun, collapsing like a landslide over his chair. Merle could see inside the pinkish, opaque gel—dark internal organs and some things that might have been his bones, strangely limp and pliable. Other things, too, things that pooled in the center of Verrill's body, where a stomach might be—a writhing mass that might have been the spaghetti and the curled body of what was, without a doubt, a cat.

A housecat.

Merle began to sweat extravagantly, and his mouth filled with saliva. Not because he was hungry, far from it. It was a familiar feeling though: the presage of vomit.

He swallowed, turned.

There was old Bernice Johnson, her skull tiny, shrunken atop her Sears housedress-clad body. A dozen or so tiny, glittering eyes ringed her head. Her arms—now a bouquet of spider limbs, each barbed with sharp, black hairs, each crooked the wrong way—palped the table before her.

Over there was Janey Richardson, a woman a few years younger than Merle whom he'd had a brief but torrid affair with a while back. Her head sat atop a sea of writhing pseudopods, like an enormous, upturned jellyfish. Thin, ghostly arms threaded through the crowd of people, each latching onto a person with a nasty, many-toothed little mouth, like a lamprey's. Through their spindly, mostly transparent coils, he could see a dark, pulsing inner core of liquid sucked from these seemingly unaware people, traveling back toward Janey's body.

She turned to him and her mouth was filled with black ichor that stained her lips, tongue and teeth. Her smile was an oily arch in her face.

His stomach lurched.

Finally, over in the corner, he caught the eyes of a young boy, Caleb Morris, one of Mike and Vanessa Morris' sons. The towheaded, freckle-faced kid slurped in a single strand of spaghetti and smiled at Merle.

Then with no warning, the kid's head split in two, vertically. Not ripped, but *split* cleanly along what looked to be a natural line of bifurcation that ran from the center of his hairline, down his nose, across his lips and mouth and ending at his chin. Merle could hear the wet, smacking sound of Caleb's head parting, like two moist lips, even above the din of everyone eating. An obscenely thick, obscenely moist tongue curled upward from this dark maw.

Merle watched, stunned, as Caleb lifted his sagging plate and upended it—noodles, salad, bread and all—and dumped it into this ever-widening mouth. The tongue caught each morsel, slurped them noisily down, and the two sides of the kid's face closed and opened, closed and opened, *chewing*.

Merle pushed back from the table, stumbled to his feet.

Caleb's eyes had turned a bright orange, slit vertically like a cat's, and they rolled in their orbits, following Merle as he lurched down the aisle between the tables and toward the restrooms.

Merle saw one of those eyes wink at him, then the black crevasse in the kid's face closed slowly, sealing itself without a trace.

He heard Gun call after him as he pushed the restroom door open, skidded into an empty stall and fell to his knees. What he vomited up, he had no idea. He had no clear recollection of eating that day, but whatever it was came up all the same.

His throbbing, sweating head touched the cool porcelain, and he looked down at the water in the toilet. Thick white curds and mucilaginous strands of slime swirled there in the rust-stained bowl. Seeing them made him heave up another mouthful, but what he brought up didn't seem like vomit.

It wasn't rank or acidic or filled with bile. It was smooth and thick and smelled vaguely of bread dough and mildewed towels.

He hung there for a while until he heard the door open.

"Merle? Buddy? You okay in here?"

Gun.

Merle got to his knees as another wave of nausea hit him.

What the shit's wrong with me?

What the shit did I see out there?

And what the shit was on my plate?

The door to his stall squeaked opened and a shadow fell over him.

He felt hands slide under his armpits, haul him slowly to his feet.

He turned to face his friend.

"Jesus, man. What the fuck's the matter? How much you had to drink today?" Gun whispered, grabbing at some toilet paper, balling it up and swabbing Merle's face with it.

Merle didn't answer. Any attempt to talk, to contemplate an answer, to think of what had gone on out there in the dining room of the VFW hall made him distinctly nauseous. So he shrugged, let his friend help him from the restroom.

He heard laugher on the way out of the building. A few people offered to help Gun get him home. Scotty Doorman helped Gun carry him outside to his truck.

Before the front doors of the VFW hall closed, Merle looked back into the dining room.

Everyone had gone back to eating and talking as if nothing had happened.

Everyone—Verrill, Bernice, Janey, even little Caleb—all seemed normal, all paid him no mind.

He remembered falling near Scotty's truck and his two friends lifting him, sliding him into the back of the Crew Cab where his cheek touched the cool vinyl seat and made him feel better.

He saw the dark outline of the water tower etched against the evening sky, blotting out the stars, and then he was out, too.

Second Connective Tissue

Water.

In almost any town of any size, water is the one thing that, even more so than power, enters every building. From houses to offices to retail stores, from city parks to gas stations, nearly every structure has a water line. People gotta drink. They gotta shit and piss and wash the dishes and their clothes. They gotta boil their Kraft Macaroni & Cheese and mix up their Kool-Aid.

Water is to a town like blood is to a body, and water pipes are the arteries. They go everywhere, move through everything and carry life itself with them.

According to Wikipedia, which I consulted on a computer at the town's library, the City of Norton's water tower was built in 1978, replacing a smaller one built in 1956. Simply put, it was built because towers are cheaper than additional pumping stations, and the little town of Norton was Midwest frugal.

So, the town's one little pumping station handled the water needs during the day when demand was steady. At night, when demand was lowest, the pumps filled the tank atop the tower—some 600,000 gallons of water pulled from our little Kaskaskia River. In the morning, when demand was highest, as everyone in Norton was taking their showers, flushing their toilets, brushing their teeth and brewing coffee, water came from the tank.

What stopped me wasn't that Norton had a water tower. Most small-scratch southern Illinois towns had them and all for pretty much the same reason.

What stopped me was the *size* of the thing. I mean, come on, 600,000 gallons? Norton's population hadn't changed much since the 1920s—a peak high in the '60s of about 750, but then a slow slide down to what it was today, roughly 525 people.

That's more than one thousand gallons of water each morning for every man, woman and child in Norton.

Didn't seem right. Even during the town's heyday, it meant an almost unimaginable amount of water per person per day. And the tower was built more than a decade *after* the high-water mark, so to speak, of the town's population.

Seemed a bit of an overkill to me.

Why all that excess storage?

Or put another way, what else was being stored in the Norton water tower?

Did I mention that my long-gone father had worked for the city's municipal water department when he met my mother?

III. Sharper than a Serpent's

The cell phone buzzing near his head woke him. It sounded as if an entire hive of bees was hovering just outside his ear.

Merle peeled back his eyelids onto painful, blinding yellow light that came in from what he figured was his bedroom window. So he was home.

As the phone continued to ring from somewhere near his head, he had vague memories of the jouncy truck ride home, Gun and someone else carrying him inside, tossing him onto his bed, having a few laughs at his expense, then leaving.

How long ago was that? Last night?

Where's the damn phone?

He tried to sit up on the bed and was confronted with several things all at the same time.

His back hurt like hell. Probably been here longer than he thought.

His head hurt like hell and back. Probably had more to drink than he'd thought.

His hands hurt like...

Wait a minute...

Hands?

Merle struggled to sit up in bed, his ancient swayback mattress not helping at all. Head pounding and gut swirling, he finally succeeded, huffing and puffing and cupping one hand over his eyes to shield out the sunlight that fell on him like a death ray.

When he caught his breath and was able to see, he lifted his other hand from where it steadied him on the mattress.

Blinking, he held it up, blocked the relentless light.

His hand was swollen, he could see that immediately. The palm was puffy and the fingers looked red and infected, especially in the fleshy webs between the fingers. They were thick and stiff as well, making it difficult, if not impossible, to close his fingers.

And they hurt, throbbed in beat with his own ragged pulse.

Like, well, like a toothache.

Merle removed the hand that had been shielding his eyes so he could check it, too. Like the other, it was swollen and it felt hot.

He noticed that the phone had stopped ringing. Still feeling woozy, he searched through the disarrayed bed sheets, covers and pillows to find the knock-off touchscreen he'd picked up more than a contract ago. Swiping the screen to wake it up, he first had to get past the warning that the battery was about ready to call it quits.

Then he saw the date. *Sunday.*

The spaghetti dinner had been Friday night.

He's slept more than twenty-four hours.

Then what he saw really upset him.

Twenty-seven missed calls. Seven Messages. Thirteen texts.

He sighed deeply, set the phone down and began the search for two things: coffee and his phone charger.

He found the charger first, underneath his nightstand. He plugged the phone in and it chirped agreeably. He tossed the thing on the mound of pillows at the head of his bed, went off to find the second item on his list. The phone would have to wait.

Coffee, he had, the dregs of some grounds in the red plastic Folger's can in his spartan refrigerator. A half-empty six-pack of his daughter's little plastic cartons of brightly colored juice caught his eye, gave him a sharp twinge as he thought of what wonders the phone might hold for him.

What the fridge didn't hold was any milk or creamer he felt sure enough to trust in his coffee, so black it was. A paper filter from the mostly empty cabinet—another twinge from the single blue box of macaroni and cheese that stood there all alone on its shelf—and a scoop or three of coffee and a carafe of water all went into the trusty machine. He stood there as it rumbled to life, spitting and hissing like a recalcitrant cat.

A few minutes spent waiting for the stuff—and realizing that tapping his curiously swollen fingers on the countertop in impatience was a really poor idea—and he was able to pour a strong partial cup into the one mug that was sitting on the counter, cleaned and ready to go.

Well of course it was.

World's Best Dad.

He took the cup gingerly in his fingers, downed a too hot, too bitter mouthful.

Not so hot nor so bitter as what his phone was waiting to pour into his ear.

* * *

"First off, are you all right?"

Well, he thought, *at least the conversation isn't leaping headfirst into yelling.*

Merle sighed deeply, knowing that what he was about to say would just end up disappearing into the seething cauldron of anger that was his ex-wife these days.

"Got sick the other night, had to be carried home," he said, weighing the words and deciding they didn't sound good, even to him. "Been sleeping it off, I guess."

"Carried out? Carried out of the Ezee by Gun, I guess. You're a piece of shit, Merle, you know that? While your daughter waits to spend one of her two weekends a month with you, you're fucked up in bed."

"Gun carried me outta the VFW hall Friday night, not the Ezee," he said, rubbing his face with his hurting hand and wincing at the heat that was rolling off of it, causing his eyes to water.

"The VFW hall? You fell face first into your plate of spaghetti? Merle, you have a daughter you're disappointing. It ain't just me anymore. I gotta—"

"Damn it, Marcy, I got sick! Hear me? Passed out, fainted or something. Been sleeping since Friday night. Just woke up now."

A forced, sibilant hiss came through the phone, and Merle had a mental picture of her expelling air out of her tightly pursed lips. Since Merle had explained this, she was revving up to move on to another subject.

"Did you listen to the messages?"

Merle shrugged. "No. Figured I'd just call and tell you what was up. Why don't I just throw some clothes on and pick the princess up? At least we can spend the afternoon together, maybe grab din—"

"Fuck that!" Marcy screamed so loud that Merle moved the phone away from his ear, downed another acrid mouthful of coffee. "It's already four fucking o'clock, Merle. She's got homework for tomorrow. She's got to get to bed at a reasonable time this weekend. And she's…well…she don't wanna come."

Merle swallowed this hot, compact ball of bitterness along with the last swigs of the coffee. "Melody don't wanna come today?"

"Like *ever*, Merle. Why would she? You forget her half the time and when you do remember you drive her aimlessly around town in that old truck. You don't feed her a healthy dinner. She ends up alone, playing with the toys that she brought to your filthy little shitbox of a house."

Merle began to shut down. It was this way with Marcy these days. You either rode out the screaming or screamed right back. Today, he didn't feel much like the latter.

Telling him that his daughter didn't want to visit, though, true or not, took the wind right out of his sails.

Truth was, it sounded like the truth.

"Well, what about next week then?" he asked in the space between Marcy winding down and winding up again.

"*Next week?* Are you fucking kidding? How about next never? I'm gonna go see Charlie Porter again, and this time I'm gonna let him loose on that judge. Get your visitation taken away."

"Marce, why would you want to go and do that?"

"Shit, Merle, I dunno. You never seem to want to see her, you're behind on support—"

"Only a couple hundred dollars. I can make that up easy."

"Then do it, fucknuts! Maybe then I could buy her some new shoes or enroll her in Ida's tap class or about a hundred other fucking things. But no, you'd rather drink it away and then fall shit-faced in front of the whole entire town at the VFW."

"That ain't what happened, Marce—"

"Stop calling me that! You can't call me that anymore. You're not allowed."

There was silence for the span of a minute as each waited for the other to say something.

"Can I talk to her, Marcy?" he finally asked. "Can I at least do that?"

"Don't you upset her, you prick. And don't make any daddy promises you can't keep. Don't you dare do that to her anymore."

Merle kept quiet and listened, hearing what he supposed was Marcy moving through her house—*their* house not too long ago—to find Melody.

There was some fumbling with the phone, then his daughter's voice came on, unsure, emotional.

And that officially broke his heart.

"Hi, princess," he said, closing his eyes, placing one aching hand over them as if to hold in the tears.

"Hi, Daddy," came the voice, then silence. Merle knew that she was upset—coached by her mom or not—and unsure of how to express this to her dad. "Where you been?"

"Sorry I missed ya, princess. But daddy got sick and slept through our visit. Can I get a raincheck?"

More silence, this time filled in Merle's head by a crystal clear picture of Marcy standing over Melody, listening to what he had to say and shaking her head.

"I dunno, Daddy. Mommy says... Well, Mommy says that you're drinking a lot, and when you're drinking you're bad. She says that you love it more than us...*me*. And that I can't come over no more. Leastways not for a long time."

"Well, honey, daddy wasn't drinking. He really was sick. And I'm real sorry I missed ya, but there's no one, nothing I love more than you. And I want to see you. Maybe next week? I'll make it up to you—"

More fumbling, then the distant sound of his daughter crying.

"That's it. No more. You'll hear from Charlie Porter and then maybe you can stand her up every third month instead of every other weekend like you're doing now."

"Marce, wait—"

"Don't fucking call me that!" she screamed and the line went dead.

He sat there for a few minutes, golden afternoon light falling through the bedroom window, the green of grass and leaves coloring it on its way in. A few tears came, not many. He wasn't really a crying guy. And those few that did fall fell all the way, no hand to wipe them off, no sniffling them up.

Merle set the phone onto the nightstand in an exaggeratedly gentle move, because what he really wanted was to throw it across the room and watch it smash into a million jagged pieces of glass and plastic.

But his fingers hurt.

Jesus.

He rose, went to the bathroom, snapped on the fluorescent bar that hung above the small sink in his small bathroom.

His eyes were bloodshot, wary, like those of a cornered animal. Deep, dark circles made them look as if they were peering up from the bottoms of two wells.

Then, his hands.

These he lifted together into the light, so that he could see them in the mirror.

They were definitely swollen, but that wasn't what stopped him.

They hurt, ached so powerfully that the pain pulsed through his body down into the soles of his feet.

But that wasn't what stopped him either.

Between each of his swollen fingers, down the inner sides that normally touched their companion, were bumps. A series of bumps, raised mounds that were more than welts. He spread one hand, counted.

There was a different number along each, but between his longer fingers it was seven; between the last finger and the pinky and the first finger and the thumb, there were five.

Both hands looked basically the same, and the pain pulsing from them was tremendous.

Cautiously, he spread fingers as wide as they would go, extended the pointer of the other hand, slowly made to touch one of the larger bumps alongside the right side of his index finger.

When it made contact there was a pain, a pain so perfect in its physical presence, so clean and pure in its expression that, without knowing, Merle had fallen to his knees, grasping the bowl of the sink, now at eye level, and crying out.

It took him a moment to realize that he hadn't cried out in pain since he was a young boy.

The echoes of that pain throbbed in his hand, radiated out on a wave that made him pant. He swallowed, knelt there before the sink, thinking that he might vomit from its force.

When the nausea passed, though not the shockwaves, he carefully pulled himself to his feet, staggered from the bathroom and into the kitchen.

There, in the highest cabinet above the fridge, were what Gun called the Four Gentleman of the Apocalypse—Jim Beam, Johnny Walker, George Dickel and Jack Daniels. He pulled down the bottle of Jack, fumbled it to prevent it from falling and carried it to the bathroom.

He undid the seal, spun the top and took a deep draught from the neck. Then he took it, and the aspirin bottle from the medicine cabinet, back to his rumpled bed to settle in for the evening.

* * *

Well, the evening and beyond, because that's what it turned out to be.

But in between there was a dream, a dream of things swirling. Curls and spirals and eddies of gloom that roiled inside his mind like the black clouds of a storm.

And though the dream was formless, there were things within that darkness, things with their own curls and spirals.

Smoothly curved arms that reached out to embrace him.

Click-clack.

And he could feel their…

* * *

His eyes snapped open onto lush, deep blackness.

As he laid there, wondering when and where, he smelled a sharp odor that filled the room. It was dense and heavy on the warm night air, and there was something beneath it, rich and miasmic.

Shit.

He'd shit the bed…and pissed it.

Disgusted and amazed in equal parts, he shifted carefully in the sheets and turned on the lamp that sat on his nightstand. He pulled back the covers and the overwhelming cloud of funk washed over him.

Merle saw the faded urine stains on the blanket, the sheets, but nothing else. Then he realized he was still in the clothes he'd worn to the spaghetti dinner—jeans, a Harley t-shirt and underwear that contained whatever he'd expelled.

Carefully, he rose from the bed and stood.

He could feel the shit slide and squelch between his cheeks.

Merle walked to the bathroom gingerly, in mincing little steps. He tugged off his t-shirt, undid his belt and stepped out of his jeans. He slid out of his underwear, careful to let it retain whatever gifts it held. He scooped his shorts up from around his ankles, fluttered them over the open toilet. Several clods of thick, muddy material like cow dung rolled out and plopped into the toilet.

When he was sure his underwear was empty, he tossed them atop the pile of dirty clothes, reached over and turned on the shower. He stood there for a moment, adjusting the water until it was steaming hot, then stepped in and closed the curtain behind him.

The water stabbed down at him from the shower head, falling over his shoulders, sluicing down his legs. For a few minutes, the water was brown and brackish, and the smell of hot shit steamed over him. After a while, and with the liberal application of soap, the humid air took on a more pleasant odor.

As he let the water wash over him, he remembered his hands, the bumps.

He balled and unballed his fists.

Maybe it had all been a dream, maybe he had hallucinated it.

Unclenching his fists, which felt puffy and boneless, he lifted them into view.

What he saw made his knees weak, and he stumbled in the shower, fell against the slick tile wall and slid down into sitting position in the tub, the water spraying onto him like rain.

Through that liquid curtain, he looked at his hands still raised before him, at his fingers.

At the teeth.

Each of the small bumps that had once lined the skin between his fingers was now a tooth.

A small, perfectly formed tooth, mostly erupted through the angry pink skin.

Of his fingers.

The teeth were oriented so that their crowns faced inward, toward each other.

He spread his hands wide and the spaces between the fingers became four little mouths opening on each hand.

He closed his fingers and the mouths came together.

Click-clack.

He opened them, closed them again.

Click-clack.

And then his mind closed, too.

* * *

Merle awoke, this time to rain.

He let it wash over him, cool, almost cold.

When he moved, he felt a slickness beneath him.

He opened his eyes, realized that he was naked, still in the shower and the water was still running.

Carefully, he lifted himself, leveraging his body against the lip of the tub. The skin of his fingers and feet felt pruned.

As he rose, as his hands grasped the side of the tub, he heard something *click-clack* against the cool porcelain.

His fingers.

Pushing that thought aside for the moment, he stepped out and grabbed the towel hanging over the toilet. It was dry but a little stiff and smelled of damp.

Drying himself off, he was careful not to look too closely at his hands, though occasionally a thread from the towel got caught in the teeth—in *his* teeth!

When he was dry, he dropped the towel onto the pile of shitty clothes, padded naked to the bedroom. From one of the plastic tubs that served as his dresser, he rooted out a clean pair of underwear, a Molly Hatchet concert t-shirt that had seen better days and a clean pair of jeans.

Then he found his cell, turned it on.

Wednesday, 9:43 p.m.

He'd been asleep or passed out or whatever since Sunday afternoon.

He didn't want to look at his hands, so he reached over and carefully turned off the lamp.

Then, by the wan light of his cell phone, he called Gun.

Gun would know what to do.

Gun would help.

* * *

"Holy fuckin' shit, son!" Gun said, backing away and putting his hand over his mouth in a curious, almost feminine motion. "Holy fuckin' shit!"

Sure, Gun will help. Sure.

"Can I…?" Gun asked, reaching out tentatively.

Merle shrugged, extended one arm.

Cautiously, Gun approached, reached out with a single finger to touch one of the teeth.

As he neared, Merle's hand twitched lighting fast and Gun recoiled.

"That's not fucking funny!" he yelped, yanking his hand back and balling it into a protective fist.

And it wasn't funny, particularly not to Merle, because he hadn't done it.

His arm had jerked on its own, had bitten Gun's finger.

"Hey, I'm bleeding!"

Gun held his injured, bleeding appendage up for Merle to see, then stepped back, a reaction Merle was to grow accustomed to over the next few days. "Man, we gotta get you to a hospital."

Merle saw the blood, heard his friend breathing hard, and both had a curious effect on him.

They made him angry.

Angry and, well, no, no, *that* couldn't be. Not *that*.

He pushed that particular disturbing thought aside and said, "No" with some finality. "No doctors. What the fuck are they gonna do to me at this point, Gun? Amputate…whatever these are?"

He thrust his hands in the air and waved his tooth-lined fingers in the space between him and his friend. Gun recoiled in horror, stepped back again.

"Okay, okay," he said warily. "What then?"

"I need to see a dentist," Merle said.

"A dentist?"

"That's what I said. A dentist."

Gun looked at him doubtfully, wiped his bloody finger onto his jeans. "Okay, tomorrow we'll go in and see Tommy."

"Now. Tonight."

"Merle, Tommy ain't got office hours at 10 o'clock at night."

Merle waved his arms again and the teeth flashed in the light.

"You picture me sitting in the waiting room during office hours flipping through *Highlights* magazine with these fuckers?"

Gun considered that. "Okay. We'll call him."

"No, *you'll* call him. Having a bit of problem dialing these days," Merle said, lifting the bottle of Jim Beam from the kitchen counter with both hands, as if wearing oven mitts, and taking a huge drink from it. "I'll be giving myself a dose or two of my own personal painkiller."

* * *

Before they left, Gun thought it might be best to cover Merle's hands. If that's what they could be called at this point. They were curling, curving in on themselves. The base of his thumb and the opposite side of his palm were fusing, forming a narrow cup from which his toothy fingers jutted.

Suddenly, they were looking less and less like hands and more and more like ...*mouths*.

"We gotta cover that shit up before we go out," Gun said.

"For what reason?" Merle asked, slurring his words from the half bottle of Jim Beam he'd just swallowed.

"Wanna explain those if we get pulled over or something?" Gun said. "Besides, they're freaking me the fuck out."

Merle shrugged, and Gun ducked into his bedroom, came out with a balled-up pair of tube socks. He shook them out, looked as if he might sniff them to check their cleanliness, reconsidered.

"Okay," he said. "I'm just gonna slip them on. Close up your...fingers."

Merle closed his fingers together—*click-clack*—and extended his hands.

Warily, Gun slipped the tube socks over Merle's hands, careful to avoid touching the teeth. When both hands were covered, Gun helped Merle to his truck, buckled him into the passenger seat, set off for the dentist.

* * *

Doctor Thomas H. Schimpf waited for them at the entrance to his darkened office adjacent to the small motor repair shop on McKinley Street. He stood, smoking a cigarette and looking agitated, under the green canvas canopy that read NORTON DENTAL SERVICES.

"What's up, Shitf?" asked Gun as he rounded the truck to help Merle out the passenger side.

"Stop calling me that!" the dentist snapped, flicking his still-lit cigarette off into the darkness. "We're not in high school anymore."

Gun snorted, opened the door and extended a hand to his friend. Merle waved it off and stepped out, his boots crunching on the gravel.

"So what the hell's going on anyway?" Schimpf asked, studying the pair curiously. "This isn't gonna be a late-night raid on my nitrous supply, I'll tell ya that."

Merle stepped out of the darkness and into the pool of light under the building's awning. "I need help with some teeth."

"Tonight? Like it couldn't wait until morning?"

"Yeah, tonight. And no, once you see, you'll understand. But not out here."

There was silence for the span of a few seconds.

"Come on, Shitf," Gun said, adopting an overly wheedling tone. "You owe us."

"I don't owe you for scoring me weed when we were kids. That was a long time ago."

"No, but Merle and I here have helped with some of your… umm…*collection* problems."

Schimpf blew out a mouthful of annoyed air. "Fine. But this evens the score."

He withdrew a large key ring from his pants pocket, rifled through about a dozen keys, found the right one. He unlocked the door, stepped inside to turn on the lights and quickly disarm the alarm system.

Merle followed, with Gun watching the road. When they were all inside, Schimpf pushed past them, locked the door.

"Come on," he said, leading them through the STAFF ONLY door in the waiting room and down a hallway. He made his way with only the lights of the emergency exits.

"Where you taking us, Timmy?" Gun asked.

"Got a room here at the back, no windows for anyone to see we're in here. Plus, it's soundproofed. I use it for patients who make a lot of noise."

At the end of the dark hallway, Schimpf opened a lone door, snapped on the lights inside. He held the door as the two men entered, then shut it behind them.

The room itself wasn't particularly interesting. The expanse of bare wall across from the door—where there might have been a window looking into the junkyard of the small motor repair business next store—featured a wallpaper mural depicting a peaceful forest scene. As if patients could be lulled into thinking they were having teeth cut from their jaw in a tranquil woodland setting.

The rest of the room was typical, painted a bland beige, dominated by the usual big reclining chair with the huge ceiling-mounted light and other dental equipment, a sink, cabinets and countertops bearing jars of cotton swabs and tongue depressors and whatnot. Boxes of blue nitrile gloves in several sizes sat in plastic dispensers mounted to the wall by the door.

Schimpf motioned for Gun to get Merle settled into the chair, then snapped on a pair of the sterile gloves. When he turned, he saw Merle had stretched out fully, seemed to be asleep.

Then he noticed Merle's hands wearing the tube socks like opera gloves.

Giving Gun a strange look, the dentist took a seat on the stool that sat near the main chair, pulled over a tray of instruments. He adjusted the overhead light, snapped it on.

Placing a hand on Merle's head, he turned it gently to face him, then pulled at his lower jaw to get him to open his mouth.

Extended on the chair's armrests, Merle's hands twitched beneath their white cotton coverings.

Gun cleared his throat, since nothing seemed forthcoming from Merle.

"Uhh…won't need to be looking at his mouth, Timmy."

Schimpf looked at Gun in growing irritation.

"I thought you said he had a tooth problem, Gun. Teeth are generally found in people's mouths."

Gun smiled, wanly. "Generally, yes, sir."

Schimpf sighed, put the probe he held back on the metal tray with the rest of his instruments.

"Gun, I swear to God, I don't have time for any of your hijinks. Whatever it is you and he are doing, it ain't funny."

Schimpf made to stand, started peeling back his gloves.

"Those aren't the gloves you should be peeling off," Gun said quietly.

Schimpf looked at Merle's tube-sock-swathed hands, frowned.

Biting his lip, he sat back on the stool, reached out to feel Merle's hands.

He felt something beneath the thick cotton socks—something that wasn't quite *right*—that made his frown deepen.

Slowly, cautiously, he peeled one sock down over Merle's wrist, over his fingers.

When he saw the teeth he pushed himself away on his little wheeled stool, recoiled in horror.

"What the fuck?" he shouted. Merle stirred in the seat, his arms twitching.

Click-clack as his fingers opened and closed.

Click-clack.

"Okay, hah-hah," Schimpf said, his back against the far cabinets. "You've had your fun, dragged me away from the house in the middle of the night to freak me out. Great. Hope it was worth it."

But he eyed Merle's hands in revulsion as he said this.

"Ain't no joke, Timmy. I promise. Take a look for yourself. Just… Well, be careful. Those little bastards bite."

Something about Gun's matter-of-fact tone gave Schimpf pause. He shivered powerfully, almost twitching atop his little chair, then scooted slowly back toward Merle, who still seemed asleep.

As he passed, he reached out and grasped one of the steel probes—the No. 23 explorer—and brought it into the harsh light overhead.

He scooted the stool over until he was quite near Merle's hands, then took one of Merle's wrists, gingerly lifted it. The fingers twitched and the teeth between them clacked, moving against each other with a serration that sounded obscenely loud in the small, closed room.

Schimpf looked at Gun who had mashed himself up against the wall by the door, his eyes wide.

Considering what to do next, he turned back, carefully touched one of the big—*molars?*—between Merle's index and middle fingers.

The probe clacked against the thing, slid down the edge of Merle's finger to what would have been its gum line.

It seemed to be a real tooth, *an actual tooth,* one of twenty-six or twenty-seven on that hand. Schimpf slid the probe along the tissue at the bottom edge of the tooth, which made Merle's hand jump, the fingers flexing spasmodically.

Schimpf jerked the instrument away with such force that it flew across the room behind him, clattered onto the vinyl floor.

He turned back to Gun. "Jesus Christ, Gun. Jesus H. Tap-Dancing Christ. It's real. *They're real.*"

Gun nodded, said nothing.

"How's this possible? How'd it happen?"

Gun shrugged. "I don't know the answer to either of those questions, son. But what do we do about it now?"

The dentist leaned in closer to Merle's hand which had settled back into a state of repose. "Jesus, I don't know. And his hand, it's all balled up, curled."

"I noticed that before we left. Don't know what it is though, other than righteously fucked up."

"His hands are changing…"

"Into what?"

Schimpf turned to him, his face pale and drawn.

"Mouths?" he squeaked, as if in question.

"Well, that's why we brought him here, Tim. You deal with mouths, right?"

Schimpf's eyes widened even more, if that were possible. "I work on mouths in people's faces, Gun. Not on their hands!"

"Teeth are teeth, right? Just pull 'em. That's all. Just pull every last damn one of 'em."

Schimpf looked at him as if he thought Gun had taken complete leave of what little senses he might have had.

"That's not the problem. The problem is... I mean... *Why? How?"*

"Who gives a flying fuck? He can't live his life like that...with those. So pull 'em. Knock yourself out figuring out why later. But for now, just pull the fuckers."

"Maybe I should do some X-Rays first, try to—"

"Look, Shitf, you're not squeezing money from an insurance company," Gun yelled. "Pull the fuckers. Now!"

Schimpf paled, swallowed. "Okay, okay, goddamn it. Just give me a minute here."

Gun was still breathing hard as he watched the dentist take a few moments to compose himself. Then he slapped his thighs and stood. "Okay, we'll fucking pull them. We'll pull all of them."

He looked over at Gun, his eyes mostly whites, and smiled.

"And you get to be my dental assistant."

***

Schimpf spent several minutes arranging equipment on a small metal tray attached to the chair. He put on a smock, gave another to Gun and motioned for him to put it on. He also handed him a mask.

"What the shit's this for?" he asked.

"Blood. By my count, we gotta pull at least fifty-two teeth."

It was Gun's turn to pale.

They both suited up, then Schimpf picked up a syringe from the table, hesitated.

"What's wrong?"

"I don't know why I loaded this. I can't just shoot him in the hands. It's not that kind of anesthetic."

"Well, he did drink quite a bit. Maybe he won't feel it," Gun offered.

Schimpf frowned at him. "We'll just give him gas."

Gun nodded enthusiastically. "Yeah, laughing gas. That'll do it."

Schimpf opened a cabinet, looped out a length of clear plastic tubing with a mask attached. He carefully fitted this over Merle's head, making sure the mask covered his slack mouth. He went back to the machine, fiddled with some controls.

"Okay, let's wait a few minutes."

Gun nodded, perfectly content to put off the inevitable.

After a few moments where each of them spent the time looking at everything but the man stretched out comatose in the chair, Schimpf nodded.

Both men approached the patient cautiously, Schimpf back on his stool, Gun standing at his side.

Schimpf reached over to the tray of instruments, selected a plain scalpel.

"We'll start off easy and see if simple extraction works. I'll have to cut around the soft tissues of each tooth to separate it from the membrane, then we'll pull it with a pair of forceps," he said, cutting his eyes up to Gun who stood over him with a wad of surgical gauze held between a large pair of forceps to blot up any blood. "That should work if they're like...*real* teeth."

"If that don't work?"

Schimpf winced, plainly having considered this possibility.

"It's gonna get real messy."

The dentist took a deep breath, tried to position Merle's strangely cupped left hand in such a way that Gun could bring his weight to bear down on his friend's wrist, holding it against Schimpf's efforts to pull the tooth.

"Okay," Schimpf said. "Let's do this."

He sighed, brought the scalpel into the light, lowered it.

Gun closed his eyes.

The scalpel touched the flesh at the base of the tooth topmost along the pointer finger, between it and Merle's thumb, drew a small mark, not much more than a comma, into the flesh.

A thin line of blood oozed to the surface, clung to the edge of the tooth that disappeared beneath the pink flesh.

Schimpf watched Merle very closely. There was no reaction.

Schimpf let out a loud, relieved breath, reached over and set the scalpel down, picked up a dental forceps. Gripping them tightly, he advised Gun to hold the hand steady.

Nervously, Gun slid his hand over Merle's wrist, pinned it to the armrest.

Finding the right angle, Schimpf placed the open mouth of the forceps on either side of the tooth he'd just cut along, squeezed the handles and pulled.

Nothing happened.

He stood, gripped the instrument tighter, yanked again.

Merle's hand moved, the finger he was tugging on jumped.

"Pull harder!" Gun urged.

"Hold his hand down, damn it," Schimpf said. "Or I'm gonna break his—"

There was a loud *snap*.

Merle's eyes flew open and a hideous, piercing scream sliced through the room.

It didn't come from Merle's mouth, but rather his *mouths*.

Too quick to be avoided, the hand that Gun held pinned to the cushioned vinyl armrest broke free, lashed out at the dentist.

In surprise, Schimpf dropped the forceps, held his hand out to ward himself from his patient.

Merle struck like a cobra, his fingers spread, teeth showing. His hand slid down over Schimpf's upraised fingers as if enacting that old children's rhyme.

This is the church, this is the steeple.

Click-clack.

Schimpf fell back into his chair screaming a shriek of pain so raw and rough that it sounded as if he might have ruptured something in his throat. Under that rising wail were the sounds of five small things falling to the floor.

Merle's teeth had bitten cleanly through all five of Schimpf's digits, severing them from his upraised hand. Five freshets of blood sprayed from the curiously box-shaped appendage he now held in the air.

The dentist scrabbled backwards in his chair and the stool turned over, sending him spilling to the floor. He plopped into a slick of his own blood, slid through it until his back was against the cabinets. He paid little attention to Merle, though, instead staring glassy-eyed at the remains of his own butchered hand.

Merle stood, slapped the metal tray away, sending a spray of sharp, glittering instruments across the room. He hit his head on the hanging light, ignored it as it spun around, throwing the room into a funhouse twirl of light and shadows, light and shadows.

Gun, silent, stepped back and made his way toward the door.

Merle closed in on Schimpf, both hands held before him, weaving in the air like trained snakes, fingers opening and closing.

Click-clack.

Click-clack.

"Please, *please,* Merle, for the love of god," Schimpf said. "I was just trying to help you!"

Though Merle was standing over him, though Merle's eyes were open, Merle—or at least something essential about him—seemed still asleep.

As Schimpf opened his mouth to say something else, Merle's left hand shot forward, caught the dentist's face in the cup of his hand's newly formed maw. Merle's fingers found their way under Schimpf's chin, thumb pressed over his lips, against his philtrum and silenced him.

With no expression on his face, Merle squeezed.

There was the tearing of teeth through meat.

Schimpf convulsed on the floor, his feet drumming, his screams muffled.

Blood squirted from under his chin, then ran like a waterfall soaking his shirt, pattering to the floor. More of it squelched from between Schimpf's compressed lips, bubbled out his nose.

There was another series of awful snaps and a final, terrible crack that was as loud as breaking a mop handle in half. Then Merle's hand closed, pulled away. With it came Schimpf's lower jaw, trailing gore, dribbling dark blood. Merle's hand met resistance, and it turned fiercely, yanked.

More blood sprayed across the beige room, stippled the cabinet faces.

Merle lifted Schimpf's jaw with its lower palate and tongue still intact, lifted it into the light as if to contemplate it like Hamlet addressing Yorick's skull in the graveyard.

Schimpf shuddered, blood pouring from the wreckage of his face.

As the dentist died Merle's two hands fought over their prize, striking it, tearing into it with their teeth, snapping at huge chunks of flesh, taking it into the twin jaws of Merle's hands, guzzling it down the twin gullets of Merle's arms.

All the while, no expression crossed Merle's face—no hunger, no anger, no horror at what he'd done, what he was doing.

In that moment, Gun might have made it out of the room, might have even made it out of the dental offices and into his truck and slipped away unnoticed into the night, to flee Norton and never come back.

Unfortunately as he sidled along the wall behind Merle, quietly making his way to the door, he stepped on something that rolled on the floor beneath his work boots sending him sprawling into the countertop. He caught himself on the tall, curved spout of the tap at the sink.

Merle spun at the noise, his hands cocked before him, wary. The twin mouths slavered blood and gobbets of gore, drooled spilth across the floor.

"Merle, son, it's *me*. Your friend Gun."

Merle said nothing, advanced on him, his hands weaving imprecations in the air.

"Merle, for fuck's sake! *What are you becoming?*"

Merle's hands shot out, struck at Gun's face, his chest.

Click-clack. CLICK-CLACK!

More blood flew across the small room, which now smelled of old pennies and fresh meat. The blood that dripped from the light swiveling over the dental chair colored the room a pale rose.

Gun stared up at Merle's face, the face he'd known since they were just kids.

"Man, don't do this," he gurgled. "I love you, Merle."

Merle didn't react, didn't seem to hear.

Then the blood drowned it all out, washed it all away.

Third Connective Tissue

During all the changes that came after that failed visit to the dentist, when I lived and *became* in the shadows of the town, I did some investigating of my own. I stumbled on one of our town's little secrets. A little quiet snooping here and there, a few midnight break-ins at the library and city hall to plunk around on the computers, search the Internet and old city blueprints, a few phone calls asking questions that no one saw the purpose of.

Norton's water and sewage were interconnected, all part of the same system. You understand what I'm saying here? The water and sewage systems shared the same pipes. The water went from the tower and out into the city. The lines from the pumping station went, well, only to the tower and nowhere else. And the sewage lines all ran back, not to the fancy waste processing plant built back in the '80s, but into the water tower.

It was a closed loop system—river water to tank, then from tank to town. Sewage from town to tank.

As you're reading this you're wondering how this could be.

You're thinking that it *couldn't* be.

Your stomach, though, is probably clenching at the thought that, however remote you might think, it's true.

For some reason it made me think, seriously *think,* of all the spaghetti dinners we had at the VFW or the K of C or the Eagles or the Moose or any of the other animal lodges. Somewhere, at least once a week, someone was having a dinner. And it was always spaghetti. And everyone in town generally showed up.

Then there were the blood drives, just as common as the spaghetti dinners. Almost every day there's a blood drive at the library or the elementary school or the community center. I'm always picking at a little ball of cotton on the inside of my forearm, picking at it and trying to dredge up the memory of where I'd given blood. And when?

And why?

And, perhaps more importantly, where was all that fucking blood going?

That not enough for you? Chew on this, then.

Norton, Illinois was founded on the banks of the Kaskaskia River by a band of settlers from Pennsylvania, led by one Timothy Nathaniel Norton. His little group of forty-seven souls set up camp in 1844, surviving an outbreak of smallpox, a brutal winter and a particularly savage Indian attack along the way.

All pretty standard stuff, really, taught to the kids in elementary school. But there's stuff that isn't taught, that's forgotten in our town's past, just as I'd bet there's similar incidents in the histories of other towns spread all over the U.S.

I found this in the archives of the *Norton News-Ledger*, June 16, 1883:

RESIDENT ATTACKED BY STRANGE RIVER CREATURE WHILE SWIMMING IN KASKASKIA!

More than 100 Witness Strange Event at Founder's Day Festival!
Mr. Josiah Benton Saved by Intervention of Crowd!
Creature Thrown Back into River Still Alive!

More than 100 revelers at this week's Founder's Day Festival witnessed what can only be described as the strangest occurrence seen in these parts in the more than a half century since the area was civilized. With horse races, axe throwing and the festive carnival atmosphere offered at this 39th anniversary celebration of the founding of our beloved town of Norton, apparently some found these offerings to be not quite entertainment enough. With temperatures approaching 100 degrees Fahrenheit, many of the town's men and youth took advantage of the cooling properties offered by the adjacent—and usually benevolent—Kaskaskia River.

One of those youths, our own 14-year-old Josiah Benton, second son of Norton's stalwart blacksmith Mr. Beltram Benton and his dear wife, was said to be wading into the cool waters of the Kaskaskia with a group of his young friends. It wasn't long until those boys and other onlookers began to notice that Josiah seemed in distress. At first, it appeared to most that he was being assailed by wasps or bees, with young

Benton's thrashing and carrying on becoming visibly more serious as time passed.

After witnessing Josiah collapsing in the water, his friends began to shout out for help, and several men from town waded in and lifted Josiah, limp and unconscious from the water. Doc Havershaw was nearby and was sent for. He first thought the lad suffering from a convulsive fit brought on by the excruciatingly hot air and the relatively cool river waters. But when the boy was turned over onto his stomach, a strange creature was found, its lengthy and glutinous arms wrapped around the base of his skull.

The creature was described as being about the size of a cannonball, soft and rather flabby, with eight smooth appendages. It was an iridescent green in color, with purple hues and had two orange, cat-like eyes the size of silver dollars that looked out upon the men in attendance.

Doc Havershaw pronounced it to be of the order of *Octopoda,* a freshwater order of the species perhaps as yet undiscovered. Carefully, he enjoined several of the strongest men in the crowd to help him unwind it from the boy's neck. Having accomplished this with great effort, the creature was unceremoniously deposited back into the Kaskaskia, where it was seen to swim placidly away by contractions of its muscular tentacular appendages.

Josiah presently returned to consciousness and seemed to Doc Havershaw to be unwounded and none the worse for wear. He was carried atop the shoulders of several of the town's elder men, including Mayor Johnson Fillbruck, back to his parental home where his mother has hovered over him for the last few days. He seems fully recovered from the ordeal that he recollects little about.

As a precaution after the incident, Mayor Fillbruck issued an order that the Kaskaskia would be excluded for the purposes of swimming, bathing or the washing of clothes for the next 10 days.

IV. When You Got A Lot of Knives & Forks...

Merle woke up slowly, the sun coming through his closed eyelids and coloring his dreams in blood.

Not that his dreams required any additional blood.

His back ached, throbbed, and his head pounded out a counterpoint rhythm. His mouth tasted like spoiled meat.

At least the mouths on his hands did.

His hands.

He kept his eyes closed as images flooded his mind.

His hands curving, closing into mouths.

Schimpf's office.

Schimpf's jaw in his hands.

Gun pleading for his life.

Then all was black, forgotten, obscured.

Merle had vague images of leaving the dental office, pushing out into the suddenly unfamiliar darkness of the town he'd been born into, grew up in, spent his life in.

He remembered running, staying away from the roads and the highway, cutting through fields and backyards, pushing through clotheslines, brush. Sleeping in ditches, in vacant lots, under porches.

Collapsing here by the river, under a moonless sky, exhausted and confused.

Slowly, he opened his eyes.

Merle lay on his left side. His right eye stared into a clear blue sky; his left looked closely at grass and dirt.

When he focused ahead, he saw the river, the Kaskaskia.

He breathed it in, its earthy, fishy tang offering unexpected comfort.

Pulling himself into a sitting position, he took in where he was. Downstream about a half mile, he saw the water treatment plant.

And behind it, as it was behind everything in Norton, as it loomed over everything in Norton, was the water tank. Merle could just make out the NOR emblazoned across its midsection.

Even though he didn't want to, Merle lifted his hands, examined them.

The palms were now fully fused. They formed a cup at the end of each arm atop which the four sets of teeth circled, chomping at the air. Dried blood covered his bare arms up to his elbows, stiffened his shirt, the front of his jeans.

Schimpf's blood. Gun's blood.

Merle raised one arm to rest his head and then suddenly thought better of it.

What would he do now? Where would he go?

Surely someone had found the horrific scene at Schimpf's office.

Surely the police were looking for him, if only because he and Gun were rarely seen apart.

He couldn't go home, couldn't hide in his bed, pull the covers over his head and sleep this one off.

Where else could he go?

He squinted up at the hateful sky.

It was early still, the sun low on the horizon, climbing slowly.

He looked out across the river. He heard the trill of frogs, birds going about their early-bird business. A low, thin mist hung close to the gurgling water.

Merle knew one place he could go, one place that would be empty now.

One place that would have exactly what he needed.

***

The Rest-Ezee didn't open until 4:00 p.m., right before the nearby power plant let out its day shift workers. It didn't serve lunch or breakfast, but it was ready to go at four in the afternoon.

Merle also knew neither Helen nor any of the workers showed up until right before four. He still hadn't seen a clock, didn't know where his phone was, but thought it might be about 8:00 a.m.

Sticking to the vacant lots and empty parking lots of town, Merle made his way to the rear of the Rest-Ezee. Having been a loyal patron for decades now, he knew exactly where Helen kept a key to the back entrance, just in case.

Getting there unseen on a weekday morning when people were carting their kids to school and their own asses to work proved difficult, but he made it. The lot behind the bar was strewn with debris—old bar furniture, pallets, milk crates, broken down liquor boxes, trash bins. Merle went to one of the bins, moved it aside, wiggled a loose cinder block in the building's foundation and plucked the single key from the space revealed.

He let himself in through the battered steel door, drew it shut behind him, locked it. He fumbled along the wall for the light switch, found it.

Merle stood inside the backroom of the bar—the loading area, filled with boxes of liquor and cases of beer. Dry goods, condiments and other non-perishables lined shelves along the wall, and a small walk-in freezer occupied the far corner of the room.

The kitchen prep area was adjacent to the walk-in, with two deep stainless sinks between yards of stainless steel counter space. Merle squinted at the sinks. In the yellowed light of the overheads, the sinks looked extravagantly rusted, stained red-brown.

He peeked through the door into the bar's main room, just to ensure that no one was there, then went behind the bar and pulled himself a draft beer. He thought trying to open a bottle would be too difficult, but even trying to manipulate a glass beneath the tap and fill it proved cumbersome. Eventually, though, he succeeded, clamped the glass between his wrists—or at least where his wrists used to be—and raised it to his lips.

As the beer buzzed into him, he felt another new sensation, again from his hands.

Their mouths were dry, parched.

He blinked slowly. His stomach felt empty and already the beer was warming his gut, coursing through his body.

Clamping the teeth of one hand around the narrow base of the glass, he lifted it shakily to the mouth of the other hand, poured some into its dark gullet.

And he could taste it, just as surely as if he had poured it past his own lips.

Giggling, he switched hands, poured the rest down the eager mouth of the other hand.

He spent several wonderful hours forgetting everything, pouring beer down each of his three mouths until he passed out atop the bar.

* * *

When he regained consciousness, it didn't take him long to remember where he was. The smell of spent ash and stale beer brought it home almost as soon as his eyes opened.

He still didn't know what time it was, but knew he had to get out of the bar.

But, where to?

Maybe he could risk a brief visit home now. He'd take a shower, grab a few things, his cell phone, change his clothes.

Maybe crash there tonight, leave the lights off.

And decide tomorrow where to go.

That sounded like a plan to Merle. So he lurched to his feet, tottered first to the front door out of habit then, turning, proceeded to the back door.

First, he thought as he pushed into the storage room, *one for the road.*

He went to the stockpile of cardboard boxes stacked across from the freezer and the prep area. The labels told him all he needed to know—Absolut, Johnny Walker, Jim Beam, Bacardi, Dewars, Beefeaters and more.

He scanned the boxes until he found the familiar white and black label for Jack Daniels. Pulling the box down, though, he realized it didn't feel right.

Peeling back the top with his clumsy hands, he saw that all the bottles were empty. Not just empty but squeaky clean of any liquor. Frowning in confusion, and anxious to get out of the bar before anyone showed up, he set this box aside, opened another, not bothering to see what it was.

This box contained bottles of the well-brand tequila the bar served, also all empty.

So, too, were the boxes of Captain Morgan and Southern Comfort.

Merle fumed. He wanted a bottle of something to help him sleep, and he wasn't sure how much of his personal stockpile he had gone through back at home. He certainly didn't want to get there and find nothing left.

There was a door on the side of the room, padlocked shut.

Shrugging, he made his way over to it. His teeth made quick work of the lock.

A bare bulb hung from the ceiling and he yanked the cord.

What was inside confused him at first…

Then it changed everything.

The room was little more than a closet with the same stainless steel countertops that lined the prep area.

Centered on the wall over the countertop was what looked like a single pull, almost like a beer tap, but it was metal and ornate and looked antique.

He stepped over to it, the door slowly closing behind him.

The tap jutted from the wall, what Merle knew was an outside wall, so there wasn't a keg or anything behind it. The pull seemed to be weathered iron, aged. Its scrollwork was filled with curlicues and spirals, and at the center was a curious thing that made him stop and think.

It looked like an octopus, its eight appendages spread wide.

On one side of the tap the countertop was lined with glass bottles.

Empty, brand-name liquor bottles.

On the other side were more liquor bottles, seemingly ordinary bottles lined up side to side, now filled with their appropriate tipples.

Merle touched the iron pull, considered.

Finding an empty Jack Daniel's bottle on the counter, he clumsily unscrewed the cap, set it aside. Placing the bottle under the tap, he pushed back on the pull.

For a moment nothing happened.

Then, thick, colorless liquid spurted out, gurgled down the inside of the bottle. Merle let it fill the container about halfway, then closed the tap. He lifted the bottle, studied it in the wan light of the room.

The liquid inside was definitely *not* Jack Daniel's whiskey or any other whiskey he'd ever seen. It was thick like sap, cloudy, flecked with green particles like pond scum. He shook the bottle and the stuff seemed to separate, thin out, change color.

Slowly, before his eyes, it darkened, took on the rich, caramel brown hue of whiskey.

Merle sniffed at the open neck. It smelled like whiskey, but there was an undertone to it, something like stagnant, brackish water and dead fish.

He practically dropped it onto the steel table, backed away.

He'd been drinking here at the Rest-Ezee for nearly thirty-five years, before he'd even been legal.

Had he?

Was this what he'd been swilling down all those years, getting drunk on, passing out from?

He fumbled with the doorknob, feeling his gorge rising. Backing from the room, he practically ran out the back door of the Rest-Ezee.

Making his way through the yards of people he'd known his entire life, hoping not to encounter them—for his sake and theirs—he finally came to Miss Tessa Maple's place. She'd been a well-known checkout lady down at the Food Rite for many, many years. Her house was just a few down the street from his, and the space underneath her back porch was open and empty.

Not wanting to go home until it was full-on dark, he scrabbled underneath the porch, curled himself into a ball like a dog and fell into an uneasy sleep.

* * *

It was evening when he crawled from beneath the porch. The air was cooler, light with the ozone of a coming storm. Merle yawned, stretched, looked down the street.

He could see his house and it appeared dark, empty. No cars were in the driveway or out front. Certainly no cop cars.

Looking up and down the street warily, he crept in the shadows, darted to hide behind trees and parked vehicles, eventually went between his neighbor's house and into his own unfenced backyard.

He climbed the little set of stairs that led to the back door, slipped his key in—thankfully it was still in the blood-stiffened pocket of his jeans—and went inside.

The house was small and he could navigate through its rooms easily in the dark. And though there was no one inside, the atmosphere of the place seemed insulted, aggrieved. Merle could feel that someone—old Sheriff Peterson and his boys—had been there, searching for him, searching for something that would explain the terrible scene at poor Schimpf's office.

Merle went to his bedroom, took off all his clothes and stood naked in the darkness. The cool air felt good on his skin, and for one crazy minute he thought of just taking off, completely nude, running through the night across the corn fields and out of this town.

Instead, he felt the dried blood that covered him crack and peel and itch.

He thought of Gun, his closest friend, his buddy.

Thought that some of that blood was doubtless his.

Merle dashed to the bathroom, spun the shower taps and stepped inside. He spent a long time there letting the spray pound on his head, his shoulders. He could almost see the water that sluiced from him, eddying darkly in the tub before spinning down the drain.

Unable to find a towel when he stepped out, he simply stretched atop his bed to air dry. Fighting against falling asleep, he rose after a few minutes, searched around for clean clothes, put them on. It took a while to do this with no usable fingers to help, but eventually he was dressed.

Standing there, he thought for a moment. He knew he was leaving, knew he had to leave Norton, and he wondered what he should take with him, if anything.

As he debated this, he saw the dim light of his phone pulsing from the nightstand near the bed. It lay face down and he went to it, he lifted it carefully. He was just able to hold it with one misshapen hand, swipe at it with what was left of the fingertips of the other.

There were a dozen or so messages, half of them left by his ex, half by the police. Both wondered where he was. Both needed to speak to him right away.

Standing in the darkness of his rented home, contemplating leaving the only town he'd ever lived in and not knowing where he would go, he knew he couldn't leave without one thing.

He knew he had to see his daughter one more time before he left.

He knew he had to tell her he loved her.

It was the worst decision he ever made.

* * *

Merle stood on the sidewalk in front of Marcy's house, his house, *their* house.

His hands clamped under his arms, he stood there thinking about what he was doing, what he had already done.

And why he hadn't left Norton years ago, when his marriage had fallen apart.

Why stay when everything had been stripped from him, when everything had soured?

His daughter, that was why, and now he was contemplating leaving her behind, too.

The mouths move restlessly within his armpits, and it disturbed him because they moved of their own volition. The thought that they might now have a mind of their own, sent off warning flares in his brain.

But there was no time for that.

He needed to see Melody, tell her he loved her.

He needed to at least try to be the father to her that his own father hadn't been to him.

Sighing, he moved toward the house. Most of it was in darkness, but a television sent lurid bursts of blue and green light splashing through the front windows. The porch light was on, and Merle knew that Marcy was probably curled on the couch with Captain America watching *CSI* or reruns of *Friends*, her two favorite shows. Melody would be tucked into bed already.

The thought brought tears to his eyes. For a moment, he felt like he was coming home again, that all that had transpired before had been a terrible dream. This was reality, this house, this woman, this child.

It didn't take long for that fantasy to unwind.

He knocked gently on the door, could hear the television commercials through the open window. As he stood on the porch, it began to rain, not hard, just the early summer patter of evening rain.

Merle closed his eyes, inhaled.

The door drew open, just a crack at first, then yanked wider.

"Merle?" came her voice from within. "Where have you been? Everyone's been looking for you. The cops. Have you heard about Gun? Tim Schimpf?"

He cleared his throat. "Yeah, Mar…Marcy, yeah," he said, holding his arms behind his back. "I heard. I know."

Marcy drew the door back and Captain America squeezed out, tail thumping against the doorjamb, nose sniffing at Merle eagerly.

"Cap!" Marcy hissed, careful not to raise her voice too much. "Cap, get inside!"

Merle wanted to play with the dog a little more, but he was relieved when Cap skulked back into the house. The dog had begun to sniff behind Merle, at his hands.

Marcy drew the door shut behind her. She wore an old pair of his shorts and one of his huge t-shirts, and the way she looked, the fact that she still wore his old, oversize clothes, made his heart ache.

She folded her arms across her chest, frowning.

"Where the hell have you been, Merle? The cops, the fucking cops are looking for you," she said. "What are you caught up in now? Did you have anything to do with their deaths?"

Merle breathed heavily. "Can I have a minute to say something or do you just want to stand there and pepper me with questions you're not gonna let me answer?"

Marcy's frown deepened. "Fine."

"I'm leaving, getting out, finding somewhere new to call home."

"When?"

"Tonight. Right now."

Marcy looked confused. "You're leaving town in the middle of the night? Where? For how long?"

"I just said I don't know where. And as for how long, well, probably for good."

"Merle, people just don't up and leave in the middle of the night, especially with what's going on. Did you talk to the police? Merle, did you...oh my god...did you have anything to do with Gun's murder?"

Merle shook his head to clear it, but Marcy took it as a denial that he'd been involved.

"Oh God, Merle. Thank God. I mean, we've not really gotten along for a while, but I mean...I couldn't think that you'd ever kill someone, especially not Gun. Poor Gun. Did you hear how he died? They said it looked like his body had been...chewed on. Poor Tim's body had—"

"Marcy," Merle interrupted. "I can't hang around. I'm leaving, got to leave. Don't know where or how long or when I'll be able to see her again. I came to say goodbye."

A brick wall fell over her features and she repositioned her arms across her chest, as if shielding herself.

"Melody, you mean? Well, no, Merle. I'm not waking her up so her no-account daddy can say goodbye. Not now, not with all this going on. And not without some better answers from you."

He looked up and down the street nervously. "Can we talk about this inside?"

"Absolutely not!" she responded as if he were insane. "You are not coming into my—"

"Mommy," came a voice from behind her as the door opened slightly. "Is that Daddy? Are you two arguin'?"

Marcy flashed him a look of pure hatred, then pulled it into an almost maniacal smile as she turned to face her daughter.

Melody wore the *Frozen* nightgown Merle had gotten her from the Milstadt Wal-Mart months ago. Her hair had been brushed out straight, and she clutched a teddy bear. She seemed loopy, rubbing at her eyes as if she'd just been awakened.

"No, honey, we weren't arguing. Just talking," Marcy replied, trying to keep her from coming out onto the porch.

"I know arguing when I hear it," she said. "I'm not a baby."

Merle smiled. "You'll always be my baby, princess."

But Melody was not having any of this from him, either. "Where have you been, Daddy? Why haven't you answered your phone?"

"Melody, get inside and get back to bed, right this instant!"

"Marcy, just let me talk to her, tell her goodbye."

"Absolutely not!" Marcy said, raising her voice for the first time and making Merle wince. "You, back upstairs and back in bed. You, get out of here right now or I'm calling the cops."

Melody drifted back into the house, and Merle saw his opportunity to do this one thing, this one simple thing that he desperately wanted to do, slip away. All because of his goddamn ex-wife.

Not precisely thinking things through, he stepped forward, not exactly pushing her out of the doorway and back into the house but sending the message that he was coming in.

And he did, shutting the door behind him.

The foyer was dark. The only light bled through from the porch and from the television in the next room. Merle lowered his hands.

Melody stood on the staircase, turned to face them.

"What the fuck, Merle!" she shouted. "This ain't your house anymore. You can't just force yourself in and—"

"Look," he said, taking another threatening step toward her with his arms dangling loosely at his side. "I just want to talk to my daughter, just this once, just tonight. Then, I'm gone. Out of your life. Don't have to worry about me or share her with me."

Marcy's face alternated between apoplexy and fear. Her eyes were wide and her cheeks were flushed, and she looked as if she expected him to do just about anything.

"Oh my God," she finally said. She put her hands to her face, covered her mouth in shock, and for one minute he thought she'd seen his hands.

But she hadn't.

"You did it, didn't you? That's why you're leaving. You killed them. Gun and Tim. Oh, Merle, why?"

She stepped away into the narrow hallway that led to the kitchen.

"Marcy, all I want to do is talk to Melody..."

"Mommy, all he wants to do is talk to me!" his daughter cried from the stairs.

Marcy was fiddling with the pocket of her shorts. She produced her cell phone, held it up in front of Merle's face.

"I'm calling the cops. I don't want to hear what you have to say, but I'm sure they will. You son of a bitch!"

She spun, raced down the hallway.

"Marcy, wait!" Merle yelled, then lumbered after her.

She'd paused in the dark kitchen to dial the number.

As he approached she put the phone to her ear, ducked to protect herself from him.

Merle heard the ringing on the other end, reached out to her.

He didn't know if he was going to touch her shoulders or try to lift her up and take the phone from her.

But *they* did.

They lashed out in the darkness, one grabbing her hair and lifting her into the air.

She spun to face him on the rope of her own hair, and Merle was sickly gratified that her face was a mass of congealed fear.

The phone fell from her hands, clattered to the kitchen floor.

Absently, he stepped on it, silencing the ringing.

Marcy could find no words, so she simply screamed as she hung there before him, her feet kicking about six inches off the floor.

Merle could find no words, either, so he let his free hand do the talking.

As silent as a whisper, it flew to her, fingers spread, teeth bared.

Did she see it it—*them*—before they struck?

Not that it mattered.

Click-clack!

Click-clack!

Click-clack!

Merle held her aloft for longer than he'd thought possible, hearing his own harsh breathing, hearing the patter of the rain on the roof, the darker rain on the kitchen floor. When Marcy stopped jerking in his grasp, he let her down, slowly, lovingly, to the floor.

Everything was now dipped in red ink, her face, her nightshirt, the floor. He could feel that same ink running wet and warm down his arms, like tears down his cheeks.

After a moment he stepped away, careful not to slip in the blood that covered the floor, that even now was becoming tacky under his shoes.

Then one word froze his blood.

"Daddy?"

Fourth Connective Tissue

Have I mentioned that I discovered where all the blood was going?

I found out one night when I crept into the water treatment plant.

I stayed in the shadows, slinked around the perimeter for a while until I found an open door. Even these days in small town America, no one expects anyone to break into a water treatment plant.

It was in a large room near the water intake equipment, a walk-in freezer.

I wondered about that. A walk-in freezer at a water treatment plant?

It was locked, but only with a padlock slightly better than you'd get at Wal-Mart. I snapped the hasp with my teeth, tossed it aside.

I wasn't surprised by how cold it was inside.

I was surprised when I flipped on the lights.

Pallets and pallets of blood bags, frozen solid.

I noticed that this freezer was just two running steps from where the river intake is, where the water is supposedly treated, then pumped up into the tower.

I looked at the open freezer, stuffed with frost-rimed, dark red bags, then looked over to the river.

Oh, they were treating the water, all right.

First Integument

I'm sitting at home now, sitting at my house, the rental.

It's well past midnight. The rain has stopped, but there's still no moon in the sky. I'm glad for that, since I am covered in blood and gore.

I can smell it.

I can taste it.

At least I can't *see* it, black in the silver light of the moon. That's a blessing.

I blanked out for a while, and I'm sure that I, that *they*, did terrible things.

Things I don't want to think about, things that I can't think about.

So I sit here in the dark and pick at the teeth on each hand, clearing out little bits of this and that between them.

Little gobbets of meat, stringy clumps of hair, then *something*, a piece of material that is jammed in there but good. The teeth of the other hand burrow down, snap and nibble until they work it loose.

I fumble across the floor for my cell. I find it, swipe away until I find the light, shine it onto what the teeth have fished out.

It's a wad of blue cloth, with a bit of a Disney character on it.

I toss it aside and weep.

I don't know how long I cried before I heard it.

A voice, whispering my name in the darkness.

Merle… Merle…

I stopped my hitching breaths long enough to listen for it.

It was so soft, so slurry, so unfocused that I thought I was hallucinating.

I mean, of course I was hallucinating.

Of course.

But it persisted.

I crawled on my belly across the floor and into the bathroom. I stopped, smelling the shit from the clothes I had sloughed days ago.

Pulling myself up the edge of the tub, I could hear the voice now, better.

Merle… Merle..

It seemed to echo up from the drain in the tub. I could also hear it bubble through the toilet bowl, murmuring from the sink.

It called to me. And as I listened to it, it told me where to go.

Having nowhere else better, I went.

V. Mouths, So Many Mouths

Merle wondered if anyone ever tried to climb a water tower in the middle of the night with two hands that had mouths instead of fingers.

He didn't think so.

It took him quite a while, hand over hand up the metal ladder affixed to one of the supporting legs. Then again up the sloping, enclosed ladder that hugged the curve of the tank.

Up to a hatch.

Merle had no idea that there'd be a hatch in the riveted metal skin at the top of the tank, like the entrance to a submarine. He decided it must be a service entrance. The cover was heavy and complicated looking, and it was secured by a mechanism a bit more formidable than a padlock.

But his teeth made short work of it.

Grunting, he pulled the hatch open, and the metal hinges, unused to being opened, groaned in protest.

It was pitch black inside the tank. A set of caged steps jutted up from the darkness, curving against the inner wall, disappearing down into the murk. Carefully, aware of the dangers of slipping or losing his grip, Merle climbed into the hatch, set his feet onto the metal rungs.

After a few minutes of descending, he was surprised when he came out of the cage and his feet touched solid ground. It was a water tank, after all. He'd expected to reach water at some point, but he now stood on the steel floor inside the tank.

There was nothing to see, save the tiny opening of the hatch far above him, showing a small cutout of the less dark sky beyond.

The air inside smelled like rusted metal and contained water, mineral and damp. Every footstep reverberated. He could hear his breathing, the beating of his heart.

He walked in blind circles before finding the sloping interior wall of the tank. Tired, he put his back against it, slid to the cold, metal floor.

After a while, he lifted his hands before him.

He couldn't see them in the dark. But he opened and closed his fingers.

Click-clack.

Pulling up his legs, he scrunched into a tight ball, rested his forehead on his knees.

"So, you've come…"

The voice surprised him, made him jump. Unbidden, his hands flung themselves out into the dark, wary, defensive.

"There is nothing to fear. I am the one who called to you."

The voice was soft, horribly wet. It sounded as if it came from a mouth with lips malformed, not quite human.

"You?" Merle asked. "Who the hell are you? Where are you? What the fuck is going on?"

Despite his best efforts, he screamed that last part, and the echoes of his voice rang against the walls of the steel chamber like a struck gong.

"The Becoming. You are, too, as all are. It is part of the great spiral of life."

"I don't understand." And that was an understatement.

"This world…this plane…is Becoming. So many centuries in the process, so many centuries left. But here, in this great land, in these small towns, the work goes on. Slowly, so slowly. But the people Become."

"Who are you?"

"I am the Watcher, the Facilitator."

"I still don't get it. What's happening to me?"

There was a great, extended sigh, and Merle could almost feel a breath stir the air inside the tank. It smelled of spoiled meat and rotten fish and brackish water.

"As I said, you are Becoming, as all are under my vigilance, as all will. Your hands. Have you not wondered at the change? Have you not wondered why?"

"Well, fuck, yes, I've wondered why. That's why I'm asking!"

"The shape of each is different, affording each a different path along the great spiral. You will take the shape of a Watcher, such as I am. Because of this, you will journey. You will found a new colony."

Merle sighed, put his head back onto his knees

"In each small town across the land, we watch, we facilitate. Men are like cattle to us. We tend them until the time."

"Like cattle? For us to eat?" Merle thought of Schimpf and Gun, of Marcy and—

"We eat from the city, and the city eats from us. It's a beautiful, self-perpetuating, closed system. Elegant. All designed to keep everyone here, to facilitate the Becoming."

Merle thought of the closed loop of the water and sewage system, the eternal blood drives, the eternal spaghetti dinners, the tap at the back of the Rest-Ezee.

"Who knows about this? Anyone?"

"Some know. Some aid. Some suspect. It is the way of things."

"What am I supposed to do?" he asked, not lifting his head.

"You must leave, set out and find a new town, a town without a Watcher. You must be that Watcher and serve your role."

"I don't want to leave."

"You must or you will die. A town can only have one Watcher."

"Will you die?

"Of course. Your daughter was to be my replacement when she grew and I declined, as eventually I must."

"I..."

"Yes, I know. Now, another will have to be chosen from the Becoming. And you, my son, must leave, to set up another colony."

Merle lifted his head, stared into the nothingness.

"Son?"

"I was your father before I...Became. Now, I serve the spiral, as you must. As we all must."

Merle climbed to his feet, faced where he thought the voice came from.

"Show me."

Another heavy, wet sigh.

"Very well."

There was a flicker of light from across the steel chamber, like a will 'o the wisp or faery glow, bluish-white and ethereal.

The glimmering came from a huge globular shape that was pushed against the far side of the chamber, rising up to the ceiling. It must have been twenty or so feet in diameter, soft and pink and gelatinous. It quivered in the dark, pulsed with eldritch light.

There were no eyes or mouth to it, but its glistening surface was covered in thousands of small, pink appendages. Thin, whip-like tendrils weaved in the air as if carried on some unseen current.

One huge cord, as thick as a great tree trunk, wound out from the base of the thing and disappeared into what Merle guessed to be the tank's outlet valve. He imagined this obscene, pulsating cord extended into town, split again and again, until it reached a tendril through the water pipes, through the sewage system, into every house and business in Norton.

"You see me as you will Become."

"What is this…Becoming?"

"It is to be greatly desired."

"By who?"

"The Others. They greatly desire it."

"I guess there's no choice in the matter," Merle chuckled.

"There is only the Becoming."

Merle stood there for a few moments as the creature's phosphorescence faded and the impenetrable black returned.

So many things to say raced through his mind, but he could think of nothing that would make any difference to that gelatinous sphere out there, obscured in the dark.

It wasn't his father anymore; it wasn't even human.

It had Become.

Just as he would.

Silently, he felt along the walls of the chamber, found the ladder and, climbed back into the night above.

"Your legs will change next. Use the rivers to traverse the land. Water is so important to the Becoming."

Merle climbed out of the hatch, closed it.

Somewhere below, he heard the intake pumps kick on, heard the rush of water echoing inside the tank.

It was a long, arduous climb down.

His father had been right. His legs felt rubbery, uncooperative. And he could feel something growing between each of his toes… *some things.*

As the sun came up he found the river, slipped into its cool waters, let his clothing fall away. The current of the Kaskaskia carried him swiftly, down, down, away from Norton.

He looked up through the muddy waters to watch the water tower recede into the distance.

And he thought of that old Bakelite radio that had once sat in his mother's kitchen.

Thought of how old Merle Haggard sang about there being one more city down every road…

AFTERWORD

My story began as two stories that weren't initially going anywhere. Let me explain.

When I first got the idea for "I Can Taste the Blood," I didn't have an idea *per se* for the story itself. Just the cool title, the genesis for which you no doubt read about in the Introduction. Anyway, great title, no idea.

Like many writers, I keep a notebook of ideas—titles, snippets of lines, characters, images. When I went to my first World Horror Convention back in 2013—that year in New Orleans, where I also took the opportunity to propose to my now wife, Deb—it was a defining moment in my career, for many reasons. I met a lot of cool people, got more involved in the horror writing industry and left energized beyond belief. During the 10-hour car trip home, my fevered brain came up with a lot of cool ideas.

One of them, an image that came to me quite forcefully with no other explanation, was a man who suddenly, inexplicably grew teeth between his fingers. Gruesome, huh? I thought so, too, and dutifully logged the idea. I even gave this unknown, completely unformed story a title.

"Toothsome," which would have been the title of this story had this novella anthology not come to pass.

So, great idea.

And there it sat for two years, trying to gel into a story.

It just didn't.

For me to have the story unravel, I need something to spark it.

Usually this is getting the main character's voice right in my head. I have to *hear* the character—hear him/her speak, think, interact. I have to, to some degree, become the character in my head. It's kind of like acting.

Anyway, there the idea sat…and sat…and sat. Defying me.

Such is the way with some ideas.

Late last year, I had an idea for another story, totally unrelated… or so I thought. My wife's parents live in the wilds of southern Illinois, and we drive down there regularly to see them. The drive is a pleasant two hours from our house to theirs, passing through many a small town along the way.

I got an idea for a story set in such a small town, clinging to a state highway, slowly dying, yet no one leaving to strike their fortunes elsewhere. I got the image of the main character getting blown down an embankment by a passing truck. A bar. Something odd about the town, though the details of that proved elusive, too.

So, again, that story was jotted down and filed away. Again, I even had a title in mind.

"The Things That Keep You There."

As the idea for *I Can Taste the Blood* took shape and became an actual project, with actual authors involved, with interest from actual publishers, I began to sweat what my contribution would be. The more I thought about it, the less happened. I became a little worried that I wasn't going to come up with something.

I kept going back to "Toothsome," thinking that had to be the story. Had to be.

When I can't seem to write on one project, I simply go to another and plunk away. So, I went back to "The Things That Keep You There," and started fleshing it out a little more. And then a little more.

And then I realized that the main character in that story was, in fact, the main character in "Toothsome." So I jammed my chocolate into my peanut butter, and bam! Story!

Once I saw this, the entire story fell into place quickly and happily, as if it had, indeed, just been sitting there waiting for me to discover it. Such is the case with how I write. I even retained "The Things That Keep You There" as a subtitle within the story.

Nice when a plan comes together.

One more note about this. Hopefully you will read this and think, wow, this is different from Taff's other stories. If you do, it's because it is. I set out to write something that would be a little removed from my "King of Pain" persona. I wanted something that was a bit more straightforward, a bit more linear, a bit more horror. And I wanted to amp up the body horror aspect of the story and indulge in a little more gore.

Sure, the story definitely has the feels. But I think it's a little harder-edged than some of my recent stuff, and I like that. I hope you did, too.

John F.D. Taff
April 2016

ABOUT THE AUTHOR

John F.D. Taff has been writing for about 25 years now, with more than eighty short stories and four novels in print. Six of his stories have been awarded honorable mention in Ellen Datlow's *Year's Best Horror & Fantasy.*

His collection *Little Deaths* was named the best horror fiction collection of 2012 by HorrorTalk. His 2014 collection of novellas, *The End in All Beginnings,* was published by Grey Matter Press. Jack Ketchum called it "the best novella collection I've read in years," and it was a finalist for a Bram Stoker Award for Superior Achievement in a Fiction Collection.

Taff's work also appears in *Single Slices, Gutted: Beautiful Horror Stories* and *The Beauty of Death.*

He lives in the wilds of Illinois with a wife, a cat and three pugs.

DECLARATIONS OF COPYRIGHT

MORE DARK FICTION FROM
GREY MATTER PRESS

"Grey Matter Press has managed to establish itself as one of the premiere purveyors of horror fiction currently in existence via both a series of killer anthologies – *SPLATTERLANDS, OMINOUS REALITIES, EQUILIBRIUM OVERTURNED* – and John F.D. Taff's harrowing novella collection *THE END IN ALL BEGINNINGS.*"

- *FANGORIA Magazine*

GREY MATTER
PRESS

THE REAL MONSTERS ARE IN YOUR MIRROR
PEEL BACK THE SKIN
FROM BRAM STOKER AWARD® NOMINATED EDITORS
ANTHONY RIVERA
SHARON LAWSON

PEEL BACK THE SKIN
ANTHOLOGY OF HORROR

They are among us.

They live down the street. In the apartment next door. And even in our own homes. They're the real monsters. And they stare back at us from our bathroom mirrors.

Peel Back the Skin is a powerhouse new anthology of terror that strips away the mask from the real monsters of our time - mankind.

Featuring all-new fiction from a star-studded cast of award-winning authors from the horror, dark fantasy, speculative, transgressive, extreme horror and thriller genres, *Peel Back the Skin* is the next game-changing release from Bram Stoker Award-nominated editors Anthony Rivera and Sharon Lawson.

FEATURING:

Jonathan Maberry
James Lowder
Ray Garton
Lucy Taylor
Tim Lebbon
Joe McKinney
Ed Kurtz
Erik Williams
William Meikle
Charles Austin Muir
Yvonne Navarro
John McCallum Swain
Durand Sheng Welsh
Nancy A. Collins
Graham Masterton

"Neil Gaiman with a dash of Kevin Brockmeier"
— Sarah Langan, author of Audrey's Door
THE NIGHT MARCHERS
AND OTHER STRANGE TALES
DANIEL BRAUM
"Storytelling that makes you laugh, cringe and damn near weep.
A big-hearted and wide-ranging book."
— Victor LaValle, author of The Ballad of Black Tom

THE NIGHT MARCHERS AND OTHER STRANGE TALES
BY DANIEL BRAUM

Take a journey to the edge of civilization and go one step beyond to enter mind-blowing worlds of magical wonder and personal revelation that defy conventional reality. Travel the darkly strange passageways of *The Night Marchers*.

Daniel Braum's unique brand of speculative fiction effortlessly blends fantasy, science fiction, mysticism and horror in every verse. Weaving a tapestry of quantum intelligence, multi-dimensional vistas and dark spiritualism, the tales in *The Night Marchers* explore concepts of advanced science as they collide with magical realism in an effort to explain the unexplainable.

Listen to the chords of a psychedelic jazz tune that threatens to herald the end of the world. Travel the sun-soaked beaches of the Caribbean with a young girl possessed by an inexorable power. Play a game of cat and mouse with demons in the lush Central American jungle. Experience a dance of redemption led by the reincarnated soul of an enigmatic Native American warrior. Spend an erotically charged evening in the desert that may end in redemption or embraced by the arms of evil. Learn the future from a treacherous Egyptian beast with its sites set not on Bethlehem but Brooklyn.

Partake in all this and so much more with the dangerous and delightfully weird stories of *The Night Marchers*.

"A stunning debut from an author who's been adding to the field of darkly weird literature for years." – LEE THOMAS, author of *The Butcher's Road*

"I give very few quotes. I only make exceptions when a novel or collection knocks me out. So...short and sweet: buy Daniel Braum's The Night Marchers. It's good, damn good. This man has one hell of a career ahead of him." – JACK DANN, editor of the *Wandering Stars* anthologies and author of *The Economy of Light*

GREY MATTER
PRESS

greymatterpress.com

DREAD
a head full of bad dreams
JONATHAN MABERRY
BRACKEN MACLEOD
WILLIAM MEIKLE
JOHN C. FOSTER
JOHN F.D. TAFF
MICHAEL LAIMO
TIM WAGGONER
RAY GARTON
JG FAHERTY
JOHN EVERSON
TRENT ZELAZNY
AND MANY MORE
from editors
ANTHONY RIVERA
SHARON LAWSON
THE BEST OF GREY MATTER PRESS VOLUME ONE

DREAD
A HEAD FULL OF BAD DREAMS

There are some nightmares from which you can never wake.

Dread: A Head Full of Bad Dreams is a terrifying volume of the darkest hallucinatory revelations from the minds of some of the most accomplished award-winning authors of our time. Travel dark passageways and experience the alarming visions of twenty masters from the horror, fantasy, science fiction, thriller, transgressive and speculative fiction genres as they bare their souls and fill your head with a lifetime of bad dreams.

Dread is the first-ever reader curated volume of horror from Grey Matter Press. The twenty short stories in this book were chosen solely by fans of dark fiction. *Dread* includes a special Introduction from Bram Stoker Award-nominated editor Anthony Rivera who says:

> "Readers who embrace darkness are souls of conscience with hearts of passion and voices that deserve to be heard. It's from this group of passionate voices that the nightmares in *Dread: A Head Full of Bad Dreams* were born.
>
> "Turning over the reins of editorial curation for this volume to the readers who matter most may well have been the best decision I've ever made. This book that you've created embodies your passion for dark fiction and serves as your own head of bad dreams come to life."

FEATURING:

Ray Garton	Jonathan Maberry
John F.D. Taff	JG Faherty
William Meikle	John Everson
Rose Blackthorn	Michael Laimo
Bracken MacLeod	John C. Foster
Tim Waggoner	Jane Brooks
Chad McKee	Peter Whitley
T. Fox Dunham	J. Daniel Stone
Edward Morris	Jonathan Balog
Trent Zelazny	Martin Rose

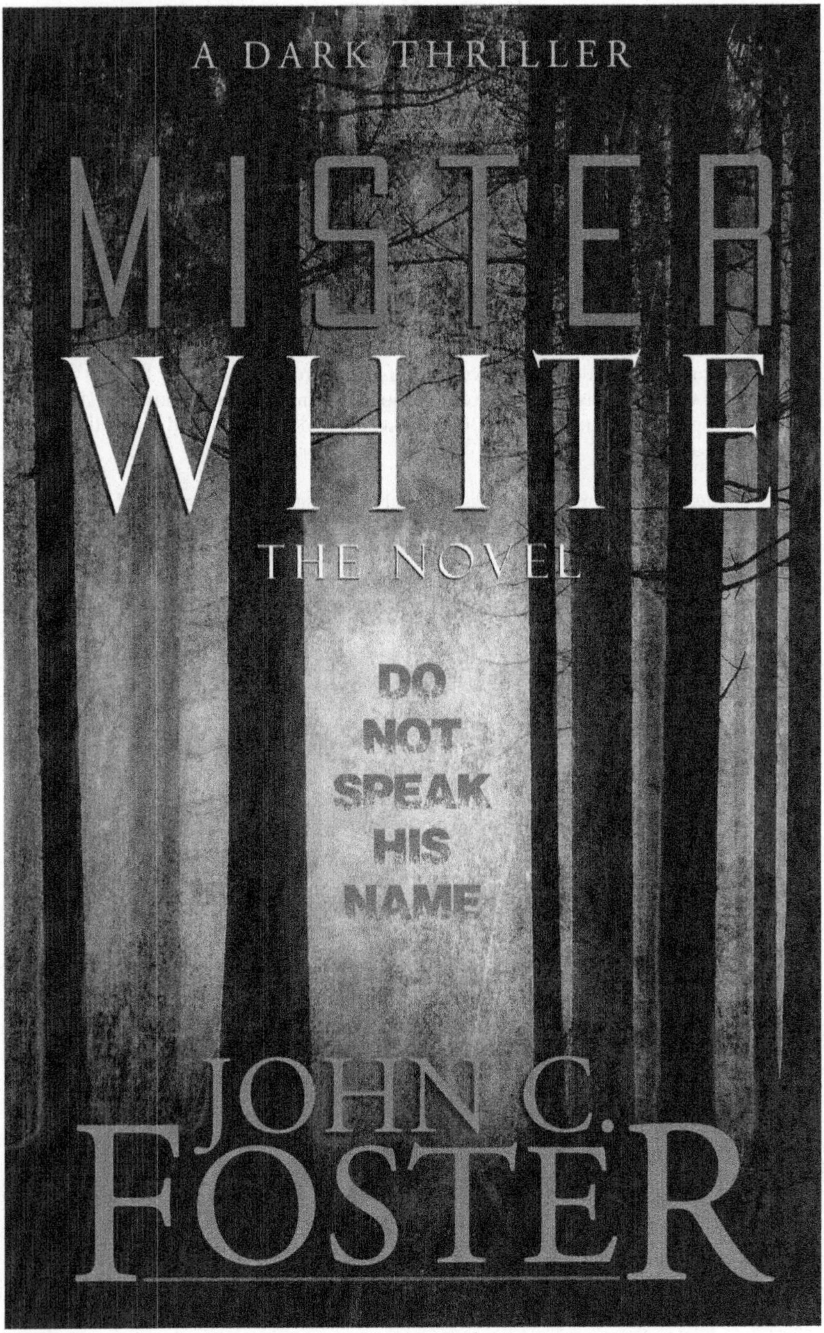
A DARK THRILLER
MISTER
WHITE
THE NOVEL
DO
NOT
SPEAK
HIS
NAME
JOHN C.
FOSTER

MISTER WHITE
BY JOHN C. FOSTER

In the shadowy world of international espionage and governmental black ops, when a group of American spies go bad and inadvertently unleash an ancient malevolent force that feeds on the fears of mankind, a young family finds themselves in the crosshairs of a frantic supernatural mystery of global proportions with only one man to turn to for their salvation.

Combine the intricate, plot-driven stylings of suspense masters Tom Clancy and Robert Ludlum, add a healthy dose of Clive Barker's dark and brooding occult horror themes, and you get a glimpse into the supernatural world of international espionage that the chilling new horror novel *Mister White* is about to reveal.

John C. Foster's *Mister White* is a terrifying genre-busting suspense shocker that, once and for all, answer the question you dare not ask: "Who is Mister White?"

"*Mister White* is a potent and hypnotic brew that blends horror, espionage and mystery. Foster has written the kind of book that keeps the genre fresh and alive and will make fans cheer. Books like this are the reason I love horror fiction." - RAY GARTON, Grand Master of Horror and Bram Stoker Award®-nominated author of *Live Girls* and *Scissors*.

"*Mister White* is like Stephen King's *The Stand* meets Ian Fleming's James Bond with Graham Masterton's *The Manitou* thrown in for good measure. It's frenetically paced, spectacularly gory and eerie as hell. Highly recommended!" - JOHN F.D. TAFF, Bram Stoker Award®-nominated author of *The End in All Beginnings*

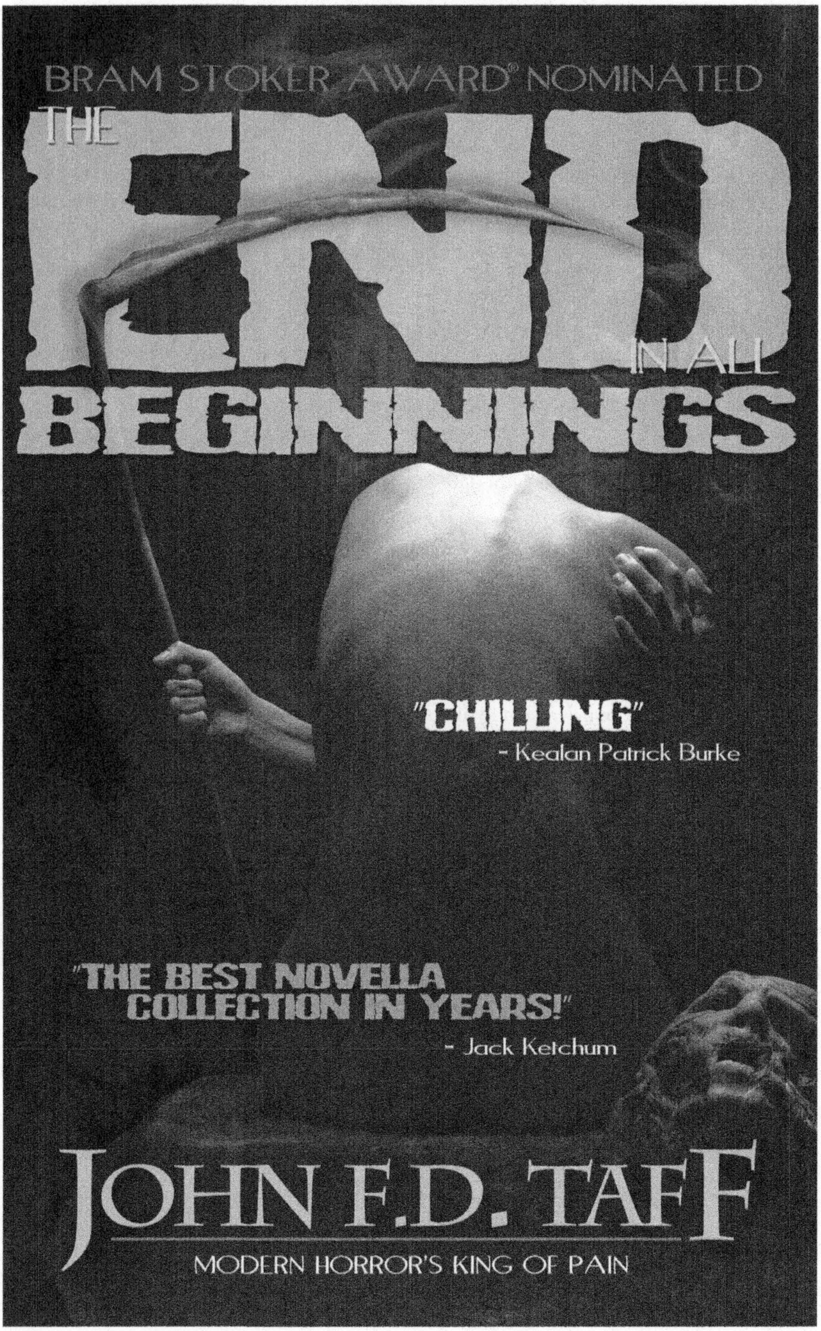
BRAM STOKER AWARD® NOMINATED
THE END IN ALL BEGINNINGS
"CHILLING"
- Kealan Patrick Burke
"THE BEST NOVELLA COLLECTION IN YEARS!"
- Jack Ketchum
JOHN F.D. TAFF
MODERN HORROR'S KING OF PAIN

THE END IN ALL BEGINNINGS
BY JOHN F.D. TAFF

The Bram Stoker Award-nominated *The End in All Beginnings* is a tour de force through the emotional pain and anguish of the human condition. Hailed as one of the best volumes of heartfelt and gut-wrenching horror in recent history, *The End in All Beginnings* is a disturbing trip through the ages exploring the painful tragedies of life, love and loss.

Exploring complex themes that run the gamut from loss of childhood innocence, to the dreadful reality of survival after everything we hold dear is gone, to some of the most profound aspects of human tragedy, author John F.D. Taff takes readers on a skillfully balanced emotional journey through everyday terrors that are uncomfortably real over the course of the human lifetime. Taff's highly nuanced writing style is at times darkly comedic, often deeply poetic and always devastatingly accurate in the most terrifying of ways.

Evoking the literary styles of horror legends Mary Shelley, Edgar Allen Poe and Bram Stoker, *The End in All Beginnings* pays homage to modern masters Stephen King, Ramsey Campbell, Ray Bradbury and Clive Barker.

"*The End in All Beginnings* is accomplished stuff, complex and heartfelt. It's one of the best novella collections I've read in years!" - JACK KETCHUM, Bram Stoker Award®-winning author of *The Box, Closing Time* and *Peaceable Kingdom*

"Taff brings the pain in five damaged and disturbing tales of love gone horribly wrong. This collection is like a knife in the heart. Highly recommended!" - JONATHAN MABERRY, *New York Times* bestselling author of *Code Zero* and *Fall of Night*

A NIGHTMARE OF SUPERNATURAL, SCIENCE & SOUND
DARK FICTION
INSPIRED BY MUSICAL ICONS
HARD ROCK
HEAVY METAL
ALTERNATIVE
PROGRESSIVE
CONTEMPORARY
ELECTRONIC
CLASSICAL
BLUES
AND MORE
SAVAGE
BEASTS
FROM BRAM STOKER AWARD-NOMINATED EDITORS
ANTHONY RIVERA AND SHARON LAWSON

SAVAGE BEASTS
A NIGHTMARE OF SUPERNATURAL, SCIENCE AND SOUND

SAVAGE BEASTS is a volume of contemporary dark fiction inspired by some of the greatest artists in musical history. A thrilling and thought-provoking nightmare of devastating supernatural experiences exploring darkly introspective science fiction and fantastical alternative realities, each accompanied by the sound of the music that defines your life.

The short stories in *SAVAGE BEASTS* shine a light on eleven dark worlds with fictional work inspired by Nine Inch Nails, Pink Floyd, The Cranberries, Genesis, Tom Petty and The Heartbreakers, Pestilence, Grace Jones, Underground Sound of Lisbon, School of Seven Bells, Wolfgang Amadeus Mozart and Johann Sebastian Bach and more.

FEATURING:

Edward Morris
Daniel Braum
Karen Runge
Maxwell Price
John F.D. Taff
E. Michael Lewis
Shawn Macomber
T. Fox Dunham
Konstantine Paradias
J.C. Michael
Paul Michael Anderson

"The tales in *SAVAGE BEASTS* are as varied as their inspirations. Many of the contributors don't just use music as their muse, they place it front and centre in their narratives. Here, music has the power to save and to kill, and nothing buried in the past stays buried forever, regardless of how frightening it is."
- *RUE MORGUE*

A COLLECTION OF MODERN HORROR
DARK VISIONS 1
VOLUME ONE
EDITED BY
ANTHONY RIVERA AND SHARON LAWSON

DARK VISIONS ONE
A COLLECTION OF MODERN HORROR

Somewhere just beyond the veil of human perception lies a darkened plane where very evil things reside. Weaving their horrifying visions, they pull the strings on our lives and lure us into a comfortable reality. But it's all just a web of lies. And this book is their instruction manual.

The Bram Stoker Award®-nominated *Dark Visions: A Collection of Modern Horror - Volume One* includes thirteen disturbing tales of dread from some of the most visionary minds writing horror, sci-fi and speculative fiction today.

Dark Visions: A Collection of Modern Horror - Volume One uncovers the truth behind our own misguided concepts of reality.

FEATURING:

Jonathan Maberry
Jay Caselberg
Jeff Hemenway
Sarah L. Johnson
Ray Garton
Jason S. Ridler
Milo James Fowler
Jonathan Balog
Brian Fatah Steele
Sean Logan
John F.D. Taff
Charles Austin Muir
David A. Riley

"This compilation of stories acts as a guide book for the evil minions that lurk within humankind and try to destroy it. Think of *The Twilight Zone* introduction from the popular TV series, and you will get the idea that this compilation is more than just a series of short fictional works." – *HELLNOTES*

A COLLECTION OF MODERN HORROR
DARK
VISIONS 2
VOLUME TWO
EDITED BY
ANTHONY RIVERA AND SHARON LAWSON

DARK VISIONS TWO
A COLLECTION OF MODERN HORROR

Dark Visions: A Collection of Modern Horror - Volume Two continues the terrifying psychological journey with an all-new selection of exceptional tales of darkness written by some of the most talented authors working in the fields of horror, speculative fiction and fantasy today.

Unable to contain all the visions of dread and mayhem to a single volume, *Dark Visions: A Collection of Modern Horror - Volume Two* is now available from your favorite booksellers in both paperback and digital formats.

FEATURING:

David Blixt
John C. Foster
JC Hemphill
Jane Brooks
Peter Whitley
Edward Morris
Trent Zelazny
Carol Holland March
David Murphy
Chad McKee
C.M. Saunders
J. Daniel Stone
David Siddall
Rhesa Sealy
Kenneth Whitfield
A.A. Garrison

"There is something for every horror/sci-fi aficionado in this collection of modern and speculative horror. Fourteen incredibly terrifying stories varying in degrees of horror." – *HELLNOTES*

SPLATTER
REAWAKENING THE SPLATTERPUNK REVOLUTION
LANDS
COLLECTED AND EDITED BY
ANTHONY RIVERA AND SHARON LAWSON

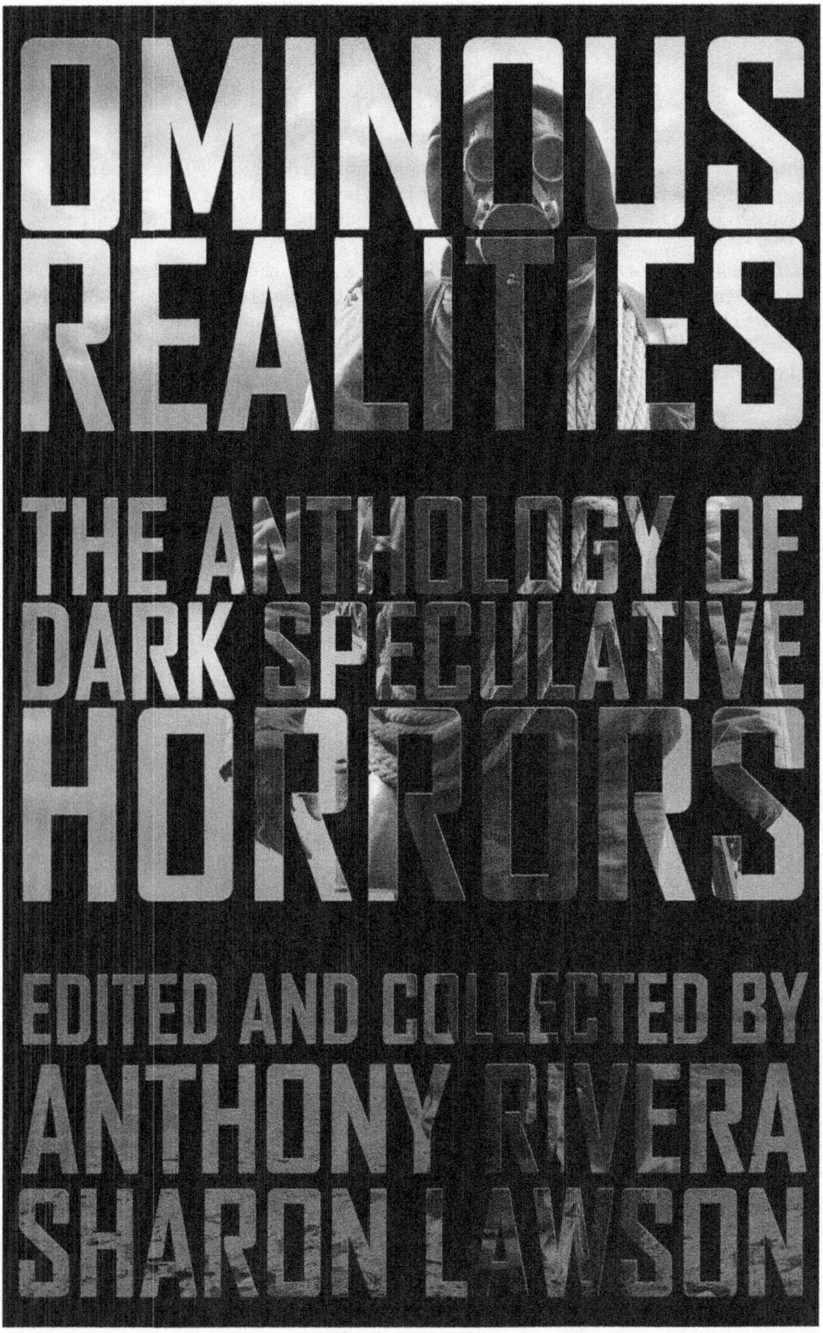
OMINOUS REALITIES
THE ANTHOLOGY OF DARK SPECULATIVE HORRORS
EDITED AND COLLECTED BY
ANTHONY RIVERA
SHARON LAWSON

OMINOUS REALITIES
THE ANTHOLOGY OF DARK SPECULATIVE HORRORS

Ominous Realities: The Anthology of Dark Speculative Horrors is a collection of sixteen terrifying tales of chilling science fiction, dark fantasy and speculative horror.

Prepare to travel through an ever-darkening procession of horrifying alternate realities where you'll explore shocking post-apocalyptic worlds, become enslaved by greedy multinational corporations that control every aspect of life, participate in societies where humanity is forced to consider perilous decisions about its own survival, experience the effects of an actual Hell on Earth and discover the many other disturbing possibilities that may be in our future.

FEATURING:

John. F.D. Taff
William Meikle
Ken Altabef
Hugh A.D. Spencer
Martin Rose
Edward Morris
Paul Williams
J. Daniel Stone
Bracken MacLeod
Gregory L. Norris
Alice Goldfuss
T. Fox Dunham
Eric Del Carlo
Jonathan Balog
Ewan C. Forbes
Allen Griffin

"This is what happens if the works of Ray Bradbury, Isaac Asimov, H.P. Lovecraft, and Stephen King consummated and had a baby. Excellent anthology!" – *HORROR NEWS NETWORK*

I CAN TASTE THE BLOOD

EDITED BY JOHN F.D. TAFF AND ANTHONY RIVERA

GREY MATTER
PRESS

CPSIA information can be obtained
at www.ICGtesting.com
Printed in the USA
LVOW03s2239270617
539565LV00001B/60/P

9 781940 658728